Embrace

Embrace

Evolve Series, Book 2

A novel by
S.E.Hall

Table of Contents

Dedicated to everyone who ever had their prayer of true love go unanswered...only to say "Thank You" when it actually was.

Chapter 1

Dear Laney
Evan

My phone is burning a hole in my pocket. Ninety percent of me wants to respond to the text Laney had sent about an hour ago, but the other ten percent, the shred that still has some dignity, is winning. As much as I want an exact explanation, I simply can't bear to hear it right now.

Sawyer's a godsend, shoving beers in my hand and attracting every girl in the bar over to our table. He's doing a better job than anyone else could at distracting me, including the brunette currently perched on my right leg… Manda? Mandy? She's hot with long dark hair, full lips and huge tits that she's not afraid to let play peek-a-boo. She even smells decent and her hands know no boundaries, but all I can think about is the one who got away; a beautiful blonde with a quick wit, smart mouth and devastating smile.

"Dude, you need another one?" Sawyer's question drags me from my mental misery, and I'm almost sure he's asking about another beer, not another girl.

"Sure," I respond with no feeling whatsoever. It's sadly the correct answer no matter what he was asking.

"Want me to get it, sugar?" Man—whatever asks with a syrup to her voice that I just noticed and don't particularly like.

"Two, Amy," Sawyer directs her and hands her some money.

Amy? Shit, I wasn't even close. Good thing I hadn't spoken to her even once.

"She's hot, bro." Sawyer raises his brows and motions to Amy with his head, to which I shrug noncommittally. "What is it, you need a blonde? I figured that'd be too much, but I can—"

My hand shoots up, cutting him off. "I appreciate it, man, I do," I stop and take a swig of beer, "but a parade of girls isn't gonna help me tonight. I just need to crash; wake up to a new day. You think you can take me to my truck?"

"Nah, but you can bunk with me." He throws some bills on the table and stands. "Let's go."

We leave the bar, not collecting the beers he'd already shelled out money for and not saying goodbye to Amy. I appreciate the hasty retreat.

"Why are you going out of your way for me?" I ask him as we drive back to his dorm—*her dorm.*

"Real talk?"

"Please."

"I'm not just helping you. I mean, I feel for you; damn, do I feel for ya." He chuckles and reaches over to punch me in the arm, offering a grin covertly lined with sympathy. "It's more than that though, Laney's my girl, and I know she's probably worried as shit about you right now, so I'm partly looking out for ya 'cause she'd want me to. She'd feel better knowing you're not off crying in your beer alone." He laughs again. "But mostly, Dane's my boy. Not only is he my employer, but he's one of my best friends. And he *loves* Laney, so I'd be lying if I pretended this wasn't a little about distracting his competition." He parks his car and turns to me, waiting for my reaction to his honesty.

"She texted me." I have no idea why this is what I'd chosen to respond with.

"Oh yeah?"

Yeah." I rub my eyes with the heels of my hands, fighting off the beginnings of a headache. "I didn't answer her. I have no idea what to say."

"Don't ask me," he says as he gets out of the car. "I'm terrible with women. Well… I'm terrible at talking to women about important shit." He opens the door to the dorm, letting me walk in first. "Never saw the need."

I crash on Sawyer's couch, resting another beer nightcap on my bare chest, thoughts of how differently I saw things panning out swirling in my head. She *had* warned me. I knew this Dane kid was creeping in; I'd gotten here as soon as I could. Just not soon enough.

How naïve I'd been, thinking Laney and I were forever, that distance wouldn't affect our closeness. The thought of Laney coming out of the box she keeps herself in long enough to *meet* someone, to actually fall for them, shutting me out—I'd have bet you all the money in the world it would never happen. Well, there goes that safety net. You know what they say—take care of your woman or another man will.

I don't even know how to proceed with this—I certainly don't know how (or if) to respond to her messages. I'm definitely not qualified to write the manual on Plan B, since Plan A, plunge head over ass into a year of ineligibility for the girl who is now with another guy, blew up in my face.

Delirious with grief, jealousy, and a million other things, I rudely dig around Sawyer's living area until I find a pen and paper. Who writes letters anymore? This guy, apparently. It just feels more personal than a text, and if Laney and I are even one single thing anymore, we're personal. No matter what Dane has with her now, he can't undo ten years of us.

I can imagine what she demands of him, what she expects. I helped set those precedents. I proved to her there are guys that will listen and treat her like a queen. Since she was a little girl, I showed her how a man should treat a woman as special as her. So he's getting a real lady…

You're welcome, asshole.

I want to know *why*. What had he done, so well, so quickly, that I'd been forgotten; replaced? Is there anything I can do to get her back? Do I want her back?

It's around 4 am when I finally finish my letter to her, calmer now that I've gotten some of it out on paper, the racing questions in my mind slowed down enough that I can finally fall asleep.

No sooner than I finally fall asleep, I'm awake, sun streaming obnoxiously through the curtains and straight into my eye. The microwave clock says it's 9:12. Ugh. I wanted to sleep so much longer than five hours.

The least I can do is run out and grab breakfast. Sawyer's been pretty cool, and since I'm starving and he's got twenty pounds on me, he's got to wake up ravenous. I get up and dressed, checking my phone out of habit. There's six texts waiting, all from Laney, the last one from around midnight. I didn't answer her then and I don't answer now, heading out with my letter and appetite.

I hit the nearest drive thru and curse myself for not grabbing Sawyer's keys. I wait about fifteen minutes in front of the dorm, holding bags of breakfast in my hands, before a cute co-ed lets me back in the door. I thank her and walk slowly down the hall, giving her a chance to gain some ground. I don't want her, or anyone, to see my pathetic next move.

I'm not sure how I remember, but I find Laney's door easily. Pulling the letter from my back pocket, I bend to slip it under her door, shocked when I hear her sweet laugh from the other side. She's here? She's not with him anymore? My heart suddenly lifts, as does my hand, ready to knock, when his voice reaches out and rips my heart out of my chest.

I should walk away. Definitely the right thing to do.

Fine, open a spot in hell for me, like it's so much different than where I'm at right now anyway—I'm not moving. Their voices are muffled and I'm straining to listen, but I hear it.

"So you forgive me?"

"Yes, caveman, I forgive you, but I'm still not ready to forgive myself. I mean it, though, don't ever do anything like that, ever again."

"I promise, baby. I love you."

"Me too."

Ah fuck. *Me too?* Whatever does or doesn't happen now, no matter what words she says to me, it's those words, those last ones to *him,* which will ring in my ears.

How could she *love* him? I've had ten years with the little girl, the young lady, and apparently the "I love you as a best friend," but in the span of only months, he'd taken the woman. This realization sends a wave of nausea and loneliness through me, but I muster the energy to move my feet, not wanting them to open the door and catch me standing here like the loser I've become.

I make my way to Sawyer's room and a new fervor flames inside me with every step I take. *Yes,* my face grazed tits and she'd gotten a picture of it. *Sure,* her best friend woke up in my room, her only clothing mine…but I never told anyone I loved them! I never gave my heart! I transferred schools for her, gave up a scholarship, fought like hell with my parents about it…damn right she shouldn't forgive herself. I flex my hands in and out of fists, rolling my neck, fighting the urge to punch a hole in the wall. Nostrils flared, chest heaving rapidly, I take a few deep breaths before finally knocking.

When Sawyer opens the door, I have only one thing to say. "Last night was a bust. Think we can do better tonight?"

He smiles and fist bumps me, which I take as a yes.

Fuck this. Disney movies suck anyway—bring on a porno!

Chapter 2

Georgia Heat
Dane

After such a big argument with Laney, I want to give her some fun tonight, so we're headed to The K. I've invited The Crew, on me, for a night of light-hearted hanging out. Tate isn't quite up for it yet, but everyone else is back from their holidays and agreed to join us.

I glance from the road to her, so quiet in her seat. "You ready to have some fun tonight?"

"Sure," she answers softly, offering me a weak smile.

She said she forgave me, but clearly she's still beating herself up. She'd left me, furious about the scene with Evan at my door, and I never want to feel so empty and helpless again. I'm no stranger to loss, but now that I've let Laney in and handed her my whole life and heart, being without her simply isn't an option. So I have to learn to deal with the Evan thing a little more tactfully—I can handle that.

"You still mad at me, baby?" I reach for her hand and feel a twinge of pain when she flinches at my touch.

"No, I said I forgive you, and I do." She sighs heavily. "I just feel bad, going out and having fun, when I know he's hurting."

I knew from day one that Evan was important to her, so I'd be a fool to think she'd just turn it off *like that*, but it was much easier to accept when he was hours away. Now he's here and I don't know what the hell to do—do I talk about it? Ignore it? Whisk her away on a relaxing trip in hopes she'll suddenly tell me what she's really thinking? I lift her hand to my lips, kissing it softly, choosing my next words carefully. I hadn't handled Evan at my door with class, she was right, and disappointing her cut deep. Usually when she looks at me, I see love and acceptance; when she'd walked away, her eyes had been full of disgust. I don't want to ever see that look from her again, so I'm walking a tightrope, trying to balance her peace of mind and our future simultaneously.

"Give it some time, Laney. Let him calm down, then maybe you two can talk."

It takes everything in me not to snarl my teeth at the thought of them together, talking, but she's my one true love, my air, and I hate the idea of her being unhappy more. Getting to know her and letting her get to know me has been the best thing that's ever happened to me. I love to make her laugh, the sound is my Zen, and she's the funniest person I've ever met. I've numbly gone through the motions of life for years, and now that I've found a reason to smile, anticipate, imagine… I have to make sure I do everything I can to make her feel the same, even if that means giving her some room with Evan. She needs to find the place with him where she can forgive herself, but nothing more—the only way I'll be without Laney is if I die in the fight.

Her eyes are watery, the tip of her nose pinking with the threat of tears. "Do you really think so? That he'll actually forgive me?"

I can't stand to see her like this. I can't park the car quickly enough, and within moments I'm pulling her into my arms, rubbing her back. "Yes, Laney. I think one day you'll be friends again, and eventually, he'll see that you're happy."

She smiles at me, reaching up to cup my cheek in her hand. "I am very happy," she says. Her voice is sincere but her eyes betray her guilt. "I love you, Dane. You make me more than happy. I just hate that I had to hurt him to love you. But that's not your fault." She presses her soft lips to mine and when she looks back up at me, her eyes are dry and her smile is bigger. She's put on a mask, hiding her sadness to ensure my happiness. "Let's go inside and have fun, okay?"

"Are you sure? We can go home right now." I rub a finger along her lips, wanting to feel them against mine again.

She kisses my finger, sending a longing through me, and giggles at the loud breath I suck in. "We're already here. Come on."

"For you," I concede, lacing my fingers through hers.

She looks amazing. My jaw clenches and temper flares with every devouring look I see cast her way, but Laney doesn't even notice. That's one of my favorite things about her—she has no idea her effect on any man with a heartbeat. She's wrapped up in conversation with Kirby, but her sweet little hand never leaves my thigh. I try my best to stay engaged with Zach, who's talking to me from across the table, but one eye never leaves Laney.

When Zach leads Kirby to the dance floor, my love bends to grumble lowly in my ear, "freakin' Sawyer! We owe Tate twenty bucks!"

Tate, Bennett, Laney and I had all laid secret bets with one another in the beginning of the confusing, yet very intriguing, *ménage á quatre* between Sawyer, Zach and the Andrews twins. It seems now that Sawyer has dropped totally out the race, costing Laney and I each twenty dollars. I thought we'd break even if Zach ended up with Avery, but since he's currently tangled up with Kirby on the dance floor, it looks like we're gonna owe double.

I chuckle, relieved that her mood has lifted and she seems more her spunky self, and kiss her sweet lips. "I'll pay your debt, baby," I assure her.

She shakes her head, rolling her eyes. "Sawyer isn't allowed to work his way through my softball team, Dane. I will have his ass."

"I'll tell him," I laugh again, loving how cute she looks with her little brow scrunched in anger, "or feel free to line him out yourself." I wink at her and raise my arm to get Sawyer's attention. He's working tonight, but knows his priorities; come out from behind that bar and help with my plan. He comes over to our table and, of course, scoops my woman up in a big hug. I'm glad they seem to be good buddies again. She'd been furious at Sawyer when he showed up at my door, unannounced, with Evan, but he *had* told me and I'd foolishly chosen not to relay that information, which was my bad—not his. I made sure she forgave Sawyer of any fault while groveling for my own forgiveness.

"Watch her," I mouth to Sawyer, waiting for him to acknowledge me with a nod before sneaking away.

I pull the guitar strap over my head and watch her looking around, eyes darting, neck craning; poor Sawyer is about to get slapped if he doesn't tell her where I went. Two chords in, her shoulders relax and she turns, her face now serene as she locks eyes with me. I sing for her, to her; it's the one way I can reach her soul immediately. Music is one of our deepest connections and tonight I've chosen "Endlessly" by Green River Ordinance, with some of my own styling strummed on my guitar. The words couldn't be more fitting for us.

Oh, my tough girl. I watch as her little pink lip quivers, so she bites it, refusing to let the pools I can see shimmering in her eyes from here, escape. She smiles and mouths an "I love you," sending my heart to new spheres. I'm so tempted to stop the song right now, but I manage to power through and finish to surprisingly raucous applause.

I weave frantically through people clapping me on the back to get to her. She throws her arms around my neck, a glowing smile making her face even more beautiful, and I know it was the perfect way to get both of our minds off of everything wrong and shift our focus to everything right.

"That was unbelievable, Dane. I love it when you sing to me."

"I love you." I blow in her ear, caressing it with my mouth.

"Take me home," she coos.

I thought you'd never ask. Linking our fingers, I pull her towards the exit, giving quick goodbyes to our group.

He's already glaring at us when I notice him standing directly between us and the door. I know the second Laney spots him because her hand tenses in mine and a shiver runs through her. I pull her tighter to me; no matter what happens, she's not leaving my side. I'm not gonna be a dick; I promised her I wouldn't do that ever again, but I'm also not going to roll over. He stands his ground as we come closer, his eyes hard, moving to Laney. She trembles, but quickly gathers herself, pushing her shoulders back and standing tall.

"Hey, Evan," she says stoically.

He gives her only an obligatory brow raise.

"I called and texted," she offers weakly. "I thought we could talk."

"I got them," he sneers.

I remain silent, letting her get out what she needs to, biting my tongue to refrain from telling him to watch his tone.

"Oh, okay then. I just thought—"

He holds up a hand to cut her off. "Let's not do this," his eyes cut to me and back, "here."

She nods curtly and tugs on my hand, ready to leave.

Well, this night just went to hell in a hurry. The car ride home is hauntingly silent, her anguish palpable. I *almost* let her stew…

"Talk to me baby," I finally say, rubbing her thigh. "Tell me what you're thinking."

Her exhale is shaky. "I hurt him, worse than I even thought. Evan is never unkind, and the way he acted tonight… Well, now I know it's really bad."

I reach for her hand, rubbing my thumb over hers.

"I think you're wrong, Dane," she says with a sad sigh. "I don't think he'll ever forgive me."

What do I say to that? I can't express my real thoughts—how long is this going to go on? When can we quit talking about this? I remain silent and stare out at the road in front of me.

She turns her sweet face, resting a cheek against the seat. "Don't do that, Dane."

"Do what?" I wish I wasn't driving right now so I could stay focused on her expression. That would answer all my questions for me, without a doubt.

"You're not the only one with ESP. I know what you're doing."

I can't help my grin, pleased that she does, in fact, know me as well I do her. "What am I doing, baby?"

"You're doubting us. Again. We can't do this every time we see him, Dane. It's going to bug me, every single time, to see the pain in his eyes. But it doesn't mean anything changes for us. I won't change my mind." She lifts our joined hands, kissing mine tenderly then resting them against her chest. "He was my first love, and I'd like to keep him in my life, but *you* are my forever. You're the key to unlocking parts of me I didn't even know existed."

Thankfully, I pull into my garage as she finishes speaking, because I can't wait another second to hold her. "Laney…" I grab her face in both my hands, sealing my lips with hers in hunger. Her mouth molds with mine, tasting like her fruity drink and Laney, and her moan tells me to take more, roughly, so I gladly do. Both our chests are heaving when we break apart but I manage out breathily, "You are my all day, every day. I will love you, hard, every day for the rest of my life. I swear it."

"I know," she hums, kissing me once, quickly, before opening her door. I follow her into the house, stopping to turn out the lights and lock up.

She walks right in like she belongs here, and it makes me damn happy she feels that way.

⸜∽⸝

After her nightly routine, she crawls into bed with me, throwing one long, toned leg over mine and resting her head on my chest. She smells of her favorite lavender lotion, her skin even silkier than usual as my fingertips trace just above her knee, exposed as her silky nightgown rides up. Having never been in love before, or in a real relationship with a woman, I'm not positive what I'm supposed to do right now. Something tells me I need to be sensitive to her difficult night and just hold her, but the man in me is screaming to mark her, claim her, and give her all she'll ever need from me and only me.

I've almost convinced my dick he's not running the show when she snuggles up closer against me, shifting so the warm, barely-there crotch of her thong slides along my thigh. My arm instinctively tightens around her, a grumble sounding from me. "Laney?" I know she's not asleep. *Tempting little faker.*

"Hmmm?"

"Trying to be the sensitive, caring gentleman here."

"Whatever you think is best," she mumbles in mock sleepiness, rolling her hips slightly.

Ah fuck.

She's on her back, hands pinned above her head with my body covering hers, before I know what hit me. I lower my head, breathing in her sweet scent, sucking on the spot where her neck meets her shoulder. Helpless without her hands, she writhes beneath me, groaning. I drag my tongue from the base of her throat all the way to her ear where I groan, "Whose baby are you?"

The stubborn, sexy girl holds out, refusing to answer me, so I use my one free hand to push her nightgown up her body. Her muscles quiver beneath my mouth as I bite and lick her stomach, kissing her navel as I would her mouth. Her legs come up, gripping

11

around me as she raises her lower body from the bed, seeking contact.

"Say it, Laney. Whose girl are you?"

She bites her bottom lip, fighting against her words, coaxing me to torture her more. I'm on to her game and more than willing to play. My cock is achingly hard enough to do some serious damage, and I press between her thighs. "Who do you want there, baby?"

Those doe eyes of hers narrow in lustful challenge as she teasingly drags her tongue across her bottom lip. God. That move drives me crazy and she knows it. In one tug, I rip her thong in the middle, leaving the band around her waist, and inch a single finger down, tracing, teasing her right back.

"Dane…" My name is a drawn out moan as her head thrashes back and forth, her cheeks flushed.

There we go—my name. I'll support her in all the ways she needs me to, always be the sensitive, caring partner, but at the end of the day, *my* name will be the one she moans. My arms will be the ones that hold her. Laney is mine. I really hope no one mistakes my kindness for weakness; that'd be a *big* oversight.

"I'm right here, gorgeous." Releasing her hands, I take her clothes all the way off and she wriggles to help. "Feed me one," I say, my demand a growl, at the sight of her glorious chest.

With a look of shock, then a smirk of wanton comprehension, she cups one breast and lifts it to my mouth. I latch on to a rosy nipple as soft and pink as her lips, sucking as I firmly grip the other. Soon I switch, showing both mounds equal appreciation while Laney's hands fist tightly in my hair and smash my face into her. She's so reactive to foreplay, her nipples a sensitive hot spot, and I show her how much I love them.

Unable to take it much longer, but mindful that I have to get her plenty ready to take me inside her, I release a breast from my mouth with a pop. She whimpers at the loss and tries to pull my head back to her. I snicker at how adorable she is and run my nose along hers, another of her favorite moves.

"I wanna taste you," I say against her lips.

This will be another first for us, and I'm almost positive her first at all, but the possessive animal in me has to know. "Will I be the first to lick you there, Laney? Hmmm?"

I don't miss her little gasp. "Yes, just you," she answers huskily, actually pushing my head down there.

Greedy little thing! I love it; love how bad she wants me, how she forgets she's a novice when it's just her and I together like this. Oh, how it fucks with my head, my heart, to know I'm her first at this too. The first taste of her is heaven. She's smooth and sweet, her scent of innocence and want flaring my nostrils and sending my primal instincts into overdrive. I could feast on her forever, just like this. I push my tongue in and out of her, then lick the edges slowly, finally placing a gentle bite on her clit. She yelps and arches off the bed, so I grab her hips to hold her in place, repeating the pattern. Her thighs begin to tremble and her wail is one long, non-stop noise, so I abruptly add two fingers, sending her completely over the edge.

"Oh my God, Dane!" she screams as I lick slowly, my tongue wide and flat, humming against her, drawing out her orgasm as long as I can, until she relaxes with her finish.

I lift my head and meet her lazy, satisfied gaze. "You want me, Laney?"

"Mhmmm," she purrs, reaching up to twine her arms around my shoulders, pulling me up her body. "Now," she mumbles, still a little out of it.

"Now what?" My fingertips skim her inner thigh, earning a shudder from her. I rise to my knees, between hers, and pull off my shirt, grinning as I watch her eyes roam over me.

"Make love to me," she whispers, licking her lips and staring into my eyes.

"Well, okay, baby." I laugh lightly as I shift and lose my pants and boxers. "You should have said something sooner." I wink and she giggles.

I love how harmonious we are in the bedroom. While I need control, I also thrive on her interaction, the taunting wit and sexy playfulness that only I get to see. She matches me, and often exceeds me, on many levels, and in the bedroom—phenomenal. If I'd filled out a questionnaire and mail-ordered for my perfect fantasy, they would've shipped me Laney Jo Walker.

Unhurriedly, I ease into her warmth and just like the first time she welcomed me there, it feels like home; the single most perfect place I'm supposed to be. The place I'm meant to be.

"Fuckkk," I drag out the growled words as long as it takes me to work myself in. Her arms reach around, grabbing my ass to push me in her deeper. "Easy, I don't want to hurt you." She's still very new to this and she'll feel it tomorrow, so I hold myself back despite her urgings. "I wanna go slow and feel every minute of it," I pant. Being inside her, her body a scorching vice around me, feels incredible, like nothing before. "You feel so good, Laney, so soft and tight for me."

Honestly, it's never even been close to thi—*shit! Condom!*

She must feel my body tense. "Dane?" Her scared eyes look up at me and she clutches my shoulders. "Did I do something wrong?"

I'd rather do anything than pull out of her right now, but that'd be way too selfish, and Laney comes first, literally. Grimacing, I withdraw, swiping a hand down my face. "Laney, I'm so sorry, baby. I forgot a condom."

She giggles—*giggles!* I'm waiting for her to cry, or slap me, and she's laughing! She sits up and wraps her arms around my waist. "I trust you, Dane. You'd never intentionally hurt me. If there was anything you needed to tell me, for my health, you would."

Whoa, wait! "Laney, I'm clean. I have physicals every year, the insurance on my companies demands it. And I haven't been with anyone else since, well, awhile... before the last physical by a long shot."

"Then why are you so worried?" She kisses my chest, moving one hand to rub my back. "I think it's safe to say I'm clean."

Do I really have to map this out for her? Nope, it takes a few more seconds before she simpers again, peering up at me.

"You ever been in the middle of a softball tournament, away from home, in the Georgia heat and white pants, when all of a sudden you start your period?"

I wait for her to continue, pretty sure I don't actually have to answer her.

"Well, I have, and it sucked. On the pill, you know exactly when it's coming. I've been on it ever since; it's the best advice Kaitlyn ever gave me." She kisses the end of my nose and smiles reassuringly. "We're good, babe."

Holding in a gasp of relief, I try to return a positive smile, still a little shaky. Laney's 19 years old, with a sex life still in its infancy, and I'd been careless with her. I wince a bit at the thought, 'cause it really had felt fucking incredible.

Focus, man!

"Now. Where were we?" She nibbles along my jaw, trailing up to suck on my earlobe. "You're not a quitter are you?"

"Not. Even. A. Little. Bit," I warn her as I lay her back, reaching to the nightstand to do things right this time. Moving over her again, the teasing mood is gone and her eyes are sultry, breathing choppy.

"Love me, Dane," she says and her back bows, her knees falling open as I bury myself in one smooth thrust.

"I do, baby, I do."

Chapter 3

Stomping Grounds
Evan

Seeing them together, again, really knocked the wind out of me. I'd better get used to it, since Southern is my new stomping grounds and not that big. I've been sitting on this barstool, replaying the scene in my head over and over way too many times, for what feels like hours. I must look as helpless as I feel since Sawyer cracks a beer open and slides it my way.

"Thanks."

"Not a problem. I didn't ask the other night, but you've got an ID just in case, right?"

I nod in affirmation.

"Just making sure. Dane's place and all, wouldn't want to jeopardize it for him."

Dane owns this bar? Of course Dane owns this bar. And a mansion. And now he's got Laney too. *For the love of crap—could he be more impressive? More lucky?* There's nothing wrong with hating the guy, and boy, do I. So yes, I will gladly sit here and drink all of his free fucking beer I can stomach.

Yeah, you really got him there, Evan.

The faint smell of sweet musk drags my attention away from Sawyer's bottle-flipping skills, and out of the corner of my eye, I see the blonde who's scooted up to the bar. Oh what the hell—I lean back, running my eyes up and down her body. *Not bad at all.*

"Hey, Sawyer," she says loudly over the music. "Can I get a couple of lemon drops?"

Sawyer gives her a look, not sure what kind exactly, and starts to make her drinks. As though she can feel my curious gaze, she turns to me, big blue eyes assessing quickly before turning back to Sawyer, brows raised in question.

"Whitley, this is Evan. Evan, Whitley," he introduces us. Behind her back, he runs his finger across his throat, vigorously shaking his head.

I bite back a laugh, extending my hand to her. "Nice to meet you, Whitley."

"You too, Evan," she responds coquettishly, not releasing my hand. "How do you know Sawyer?"

I shrug a shoulder. "By default. I met him through a girl I know here."

Her brows crease at this, her bottom lip pouting out just a bit. She looks back to Sawyer, again silently asking him to fill in the gaps.

He waves her off. "Go dance, Whit. We'll catch up with ya later."

Not happy about being dismissed, she grabs her drinks with a "hmmpf" and walks away.

"Don't go there man, trust me."

I'm not "going" anywhere, but now he's piqued my curiosity, so I engage. "Why's that?"

"First of all, she's a bat-shit crazy clinger. Second of all, Laney hates her."

I try not to show any signs of reaction, but he's got me full-blown intrigued now. "Why does Laney hate her?" I ask entirely too eagerly.

He waits on another customer, letting me simmer. He knows damn well that his silence is killing me. *Bastard.*

"I'll tell ya," he throws over his shoulder as he reaches down in a cooler for a new order, "but it'll cost ya."

"How much?"

"A trifecta."

A trixhatta? I think Sawyer's been nipping a little from the well back there. "Come again?" I glare at the shot he just passed me, knowing it's a terrible idea after starting with beer. How many times have I heard the "beer before liquor, never been sicker" adage?

17

Against my better judgment, I down it, highly suspecting I'm gonna need it if I continue to patronize this crazy place.

"Trifecta. Dance with a brunette, a blonde that's *not* Whitley, and a redhead. When you're done, I'll tell ya why Laney hates her. Get one of their numbers and I'll throw in the story about Laney threatening to beat her ass the first time they met."

I see what you're doing here, Sawyer. Single and ready to mingle? Not really, but any Laney stories I can get out of him are worth it—maybe the information will help me. And if it doesn't, it will at least give me an idea of what she'd been doing all those long months we were apart; how she went from my sweet, innocent Laney to...not my Laney. His Laney. Sawyer's info may be all I ever get.

"I'm not much of a dancer," I mutter, flabbergasted that I'm even considering this dumbass plan.

"Katie!" Sawyer screams and immediately a knockout redhead slinks saucily up to the bar, lifting her torso across it to jab her tongue down Sawyer's throat. "Teach my boy how to dance, sexy?" he fake asks her when he comes up for air.

She turns her attention to me as though Sawyer is running her with a remote control and grabs my hand, pulling me from my stool. "Come on handsome. Mama'll teach ya a few tricks."

Two songs later, I've decided Katie deserves a certificate, because she taught me *plenty*. I didn't have the heart to tell her I knew how to dance, that I'd just been making an excuse to Sawyer, though once she got started, I didn't *want* to tell her. That girl's got no shame and she dances with her entire body—tongue, hands, you name it. It was fun, my mind welcomingly distracted for a while, but I was about over it now. Girls like Katie are a dime a dozen; she'd shoved her tongue down Sawyer's throat five minutes before grinding her ass into my crotch—that kind of looseness just doesn't do it for me.

Redhead, though—check!

Whitley walks into my line of vision and I glace around, trying to seek out the most harmless looking brunette or blonde in the place so I can complete Sawyer's asinine scheme and get my Laney info.

"You look miserable," Whitley surmises.

Observant girl. I can't help my slight smirk. "That obvious, huh?"

"Yeah." She nods. "Katie not your type?"

Shaking my head, I give her an attempt at a smile. "Not at all. Sawyer's idea."

"Come on." She takes my hand and leads me to her now empty table. "Have a seat."

I comply immediately. I'd just go home, but I'm kinda in limbo. The new semester hasn't started yet, so my room here isn't officially mine for a few more days and I'm in no condition to drive back to my parents' house. Quite simply, I have absolutely nothing to lose or better to do than sit here and talk to Whitley.

"So, why does a guy who looks like you need Sawyer to find him dance partners? If you wanna call that dancing." She's blunt. And right—that wasn't dancing.

I shrug. "He's trying to cheer me up; get me to meet girls, I guess."

She snickers. "I doubt you need help meeting girls either."

It just popped out; when she realizes she spoke it out loud, her face flushes and her eyes dart down. It's a pretty look on her, softening her somehow. Whitley's very attractive; too perfect though. When I look at her, I see money; she's very much a practiced, methodically-planned, well-put-together girl, who, if I'm not mistaken, wants to be anything but. Her shoulders don't ever slump, her back is pin straight, her posture nothing short of perfect. Not one shiny, blonde hair dares to fall out of place. But her eyes… Her eyes are a blinding blue and the genuine sadness in them is one of the few things about her that isn't deliberate.

"Thanks." I look away, more embarrassed at her compliment than Katie's dry-humping. "I just don't know anyone here yet, so he's actually trying to be a good guy and help me out."

"Sawyer's a really good guy. He just doesn't know it." Her expression is sincere; she's not being snarky.

I feel bad for her, complimenting Sawyer when he was just so rude to her and badmouthed her to me. I barely know either of them, though, so maybe there's more to it.

"But I know enough about Sawyer. Tell me something about you." She smiles, encouraging me.

"What do you want to know?"

Before she can answer, Sawyer joins us, abruptly pulling up a chair. "Bro, you got two to go. Why are you just sitting here?"

What Whitley must think right now? Certainly I don't want her to get the impression I number and categorize women on a regular basis—all Sawyer on that one.

19

"Eh," I shoot Whitley an apologetic smile, "I wasn't feeling it. This pretty lady is great company, however."

She blushes again and it's even prettier than the last time.

"Fuck," Sawyer grumbles, turning to Whitley. "Way too sticky, Whit. Walk away. He doesn't know better, yet, but you…"

Her shoulders tense and her eyes narrow, trying not to mist up. "What are you talking about, Sawyer? We're just talking, and what is so wrong with *me*?"

"Shit, Whitley," he motions to his replacement bartender for drinks, "where do I start?"

Damn. That's the first really not right thing I've seen or heard from him and it doesn't sit well with me.

"People are always pissed off around you, woman," he points out. "Things can be going great, and then you show up, boom—it goes to shit."

"Now back up," I interject, no longer able to sit idly while he insults a female. Man, how I'd love to set him loose on Kaitlyn, but not Whitley. "What'd she do that's so wrong?"

Sawyer smirks. "I told ya, your girl hates her fucking guts."

Whitley eyes me warily. "Who's your girl?"

"She's not my girl, and he knows it." I give Sawyer a pointed glare. Hadn't he told me straight up that Dane's his friend and he's basically running interference for him by hanging with me? He's more than aware Laney is no longer "my girl," so why is he antagonizing Whitley? I run a hand down my face, becoming increasingly frustrated and completely opposed to continuing this conversation. I certainly don't want my own misery broadcast to the bar, so I'm willing to forego my interest in why Laney hates Whitley.

"Who are you talking about?" She tries her luck with Sawyer just as our drinks arrive.

I sip mine slowly, watching their showdown back and forth over the end of my bottle.

"Evan?" Sawyer looks at me questioningly.

Oh, now I'm allowed input into the public dissection of my agony? I shrug, giving him a "take it away" hand wave. What do I really care? Might as well let them talk about it in front of me rather than after I walk away. I've got a good buzz and no bed in close proximity to call my own…fuck it.

"Evan starts here this semester. He gave up his scholarship in

Athens to follow a girl here."

Yes, I'd told Sawyer my woes, shedding some light on the seriousness of my love-induced fuck-up. Somehow I'd hoped he'd forgotten most of what I said. Alas...

"But when he got here, he found that said girl is otherwise occupied. *So...* I was trying to get his dick wet. Until you interrupted, that is."

Sawyer: good guy, terrible mouth. Kinda funny, though. He goes from the eloquence of "found that said girl" to "dick wet" in the same breath.

Whitley gasps, so I quickly jump in. "I wasn't trying to, well, what he said. Like I told you, his idea. I swear."

Her lips tighten in a line, but her slight nod says she believes me. I don't care that I've only just met her, I need her to know my mama didn't raise me like that.

"And who'd you say the girl was?" she digs again.

"He didn't," I answer, "but it's Laney Walker. You know her?"

"Really?" she sneers, her face literally that of someone who just got force fed a lemon wrapped inside a lime.

It's the only cattiness she's shown all night, even when Sawyer was being a dick, and is it ever catty. One thing's for sure—Laney's feelings about her are reciprocated.

"Really." *I wish it wasn't all true, either, trust me.*

"Yes, I've run into her a few times," Whitley admits, awkwardly clinking the ice in her glass, seemingly fascinated by it. "None of them were pleasant."

"And why is that?" I ask, wondering if I'm going to get the real story here. Maybe Laney took her spot on the softball team, though Whitley doesn't look like much of a baller...

Sawyer scoffs loudly at my question and rudely answers for her. "Whitley here's been stuck up Dane's ass for years, ever since they were kids. Laney was here five minutes and had that boy whipped. Isn't that right, Whitley?"

Her eyes are blatantly watery now, and not only do I feel bad for her, but I know exactly how she feels.

Smiling at her, I stand, offering her my hand. "Hungry? You drive, I'll buy."

"Yes!" She practically leaps out of her chair, latching on to my hand. For comfort, I'm guessing, and strangely, I get the sense of the same as soon as she touches me.

"Sawyer, I'm gonna feed the lady. I'll text ya." And with that, I lead her out, soon becoming the follower as she heads to her car.

———————⌒⌒———————

We've been sitting at a late night diner for a while, bellies full of greasy goodness and every topic from Shakespeare to rollerblading (which neither of us are good at) discussed, when it occurs to me that I have nowhere to sleep. I could drive back home to my parents, completely sober now, but that sounds excruciating. I texted Sawyer and begged for his couch, but he has yet to answer, and it's been so long now, he's probably not going to. I guess I'll just have Whitley drop me off at my truck; maybe I'll sleep in it and head back in the morning. I can't wander around like a vagabond until school starts, but I have time to think about that later. All I have to solve right now is tonight's arrangements

"Penny for your thoughts." Her gentle voice intrudes on my woes.

"Why are you dipping your French fries in your milkshake?" I ask, cringing but thankful for the lighthearted conversation starter rather than what I'd really been pondering.

"Because it's good and my mother isn't looking." She bounces her eyebrows and snickers, like she's really gotten away with something.

"I wish I wasn't looking, either," I joke with her, "it's disgusting."

"Have you ever tried it?" she challenges me with a smirk.

"No, and I'm not going to," I fiddle with my straw, slurping up the last of my drink

"Au contraire, mon frère. You *are* gonna try it, and you wanna know why?"

This I gotta hear. "Enlighten me, please."

"Because you need a place to sleep tonight, and I'm not letting you have my guest room until you try it. So grab a fry, you big wuss, and get to dippin'!"

"Now how did—"

"Evan, I'm gonna let you in on a big secret. You can *never* get your cell phone far enough away or hidden well enough from a girl if she really wants to see what you're typing." She winks this time and giggles. "Annndd, I think you owe me eating another icy fry for that little pearl of wisdom."

That's good shit to know, so I happily dip a fry in her shake and pop it in my mouth. *Not bad.* Not good, per say, but not bad.

"One more," she teases, waggling a fry at me.

"No, no," I protest, shaking my head, "I can't stay at your place. I barely know you. In fact, please tell me you don't usually let guys you hardly know stay with you."

That pissed her off. Her eyes have narrowed to slits. "I will have you know," her perfect fingernails drum against the table, "that I have lived in my home for almost two whole years and not one man has ever slept there. In fact, I've never even brought a date back there!"

"I didn't mean to make you mad, Whitley. I'm sorry. It just worried me because it sounded kinda unsafe. I wasn't alluding to anything *else*."

"It would be unsafe if I did that, but I don't. And I may barely know you, but I already know enough to be absolutely sure I'll be safe and sound with you in my home. You, Evan Allen, are a true gentleman. You couldn't hide it if you tried."

I grin coyly. "Oh yeah, how do you know that?"

"Because you didn't like Sawyer talking down to a girl. You hold open all doors for me. You led me to this booth with your hand gently on my back," she blushes, "and you're arguing *not* to stay the night with me."

"Sounds like you've got me all figured out. So what about you?"

"What about me?" She tucks her shiny, golden hair behind her ears. The tops of them are pink; she's nervous to be the one under the magnifying glass.

"I don't know. Pick something you want to tell me. How about... What's something you're passionate about?"

"Singing," she answers instantly, a glow taking over her face. "I'm this year's captain of the Lovely Larks, the school a cappella group."

"Very nice." I nod with a grin. I can totally see her as a singer. "You'll have to sing for me sometime."

"Someday."

"Someday like tomorrow, or someday like it's never gonna happen?" I laugh, just kidding her.

"The day I figure out the perfect song to sing to you," she whispers, looking down.

I try desperately not to think of how that single statement reminds me so much of someone else I know. Or at least, someone I used to know. Someone I *thought* I knew.

"Okay, one more fun fact and I'll feel safe sleeping under the same roof as you," I request, giving her a playful kick under the table.

"My major is Music Education. I want to be a music teacher in an elementary school, where the kids are still young enough to just love the music."

"You'll be great at it." I shoot her a wink.

"How can you be so sure of that?"

"The passion in your eyes when you talk about it." I shrug, the explanation self-explanatory to me. "You could never be bad at something you feel so strongly about."

I don't know her well enough yet to pinpoint the exact emotion that passes through her eyes before she centers her shoulders and lifts her head just a little higher. "Thank you, Evan."

"Thank you," I give her a grateful smile and pop the second dipped fry in my mouth, "for giving my sorry butt a bed. You ready?"

She nods and I stand up, offering my hand to hold as she slides out of the booth. I settle the bill and hold the door open for her, thinking how easy she is to talk to.

"Here you go," she says cheerfully, walking into the room ahead of me, turning down the bedspread and sheet. Then she fluffs my pillow and turns to me with a smile. "Do you need anything else?"

"No, this is more than enough. Thank you so much, Whitley, for taking in this gypsy. Are you sure you're comfortable with this?"

She bobs her head, smiling. "It feels nice to have someone else here. I don't know," she pops her shoulders, "maybe we could make popcorn and watch a movie, or sit up and talk, or something," she bites her little lip again, "if you're not too tired."

I try not to let the wonderment show on my face. How is this beautiful, kind, trusting girl lonely?

"What movie ya thinking?" If she says anything Disney, I'm jumping out the fucking window and sleeping on the sidewalk.

"I don't care," she says, the happiness in her voice at the prospect of a movie buddy almost sad. "You can pick." She grabs my hand and pulls me to the living room like a kid at Christmas. "Come

24

on."

We get settled in on the couch, *The Avengers* about to start when she says softly, never breaking her fixed gaze at the TV, "Evan?"

"Yeah?"

"It was really nice meeting you."

"You too, Whitley."

Chapter 4

Wingman
Laney

When I walk into my Algebra class on Thursday morning, he's the first person I see. It's the first time I've seen him since that night leaving The K. I'd given up texting and calling; he wasn't going to answer. I heard from Sawyer that he's living in Morgan Hall, one building down and across the street from me, but that's all the information I have. Honestly, I don't know why I let it bother me. This distance between Evan and me started the minute we both left for college, but knowing that even though he's here now, close enough I could reach out and hug him, and we're still apart has an extra bite. I know he doesn't want a hug from me right now, but someday we'll be on speaking terms… Someday we'll hug again, right?

How I wish I hadn't hurt him. It'd be so nice to talk with him, to tell him about my mom, my life… I miss my friend. Evan will always be the best part of my past and the minute he's ready, *if* he's ever ready, I will welcome him back into my life with open arms. But I love Dane. I've spent a lot of time lately thinking how I would feel if the roles with reversed. What would I have done if Evan found someone new at UGA? I'd like to think I'd understand and still be his friend, but maybe I'm wrong. And if I'd have given up my team and went there for him… Well, when I throw that in, I'm right back to knowing his reaction is valid.

I heave a sigh. I'm beginning to think there's no win to this situation. Even now, staring across the room at Evan's downcast eyes and stiff posture, the image of Dane's heated gaze and sexy smirk fight for headspace. I'm way too far gone to backtrack with guilt now, so I plaster on a confident smile and head over to say hello.

"Hi, Evan." I fold into the chair next to him and get my stuff for class out of my bag.

He doesn't look up but mumbles, "Laney. How are you?"

"Good. You?"

"Oh, just dandy," he snorts sarcastically.

I sigh, not knowing what to say. Maybe the more I try the worse I make things? All I want to do is hug this wonderful guy and make it better, but I know it wouldn't. A hug is much less than he wants, what he thinks he needs, and I can't give him anything more. My heart's no longer mine to give anyway; Dane took it, he owns it. I wish Evan and I had just stayed friends now. The few months we spent as a couple flew by, hardly a blip on the radar, but ended with major, maybe irreparable, collateral damage.

Luckily, the professor walks in and begins as we sit there, worlds apart, the silence screaming. Class seems to take forever, and when it's over, Evan's out of his seat and through the door before I even have my bag over my shoulder. No "goodbye," no "catch ya later." I try, God, do I try, to hold them in, but I think it actually makes it worse… The silent teardrops start to fall. Evan's back turned on me just isn't a view I'm used to and I'm glad I'm not practiced at it; once is more than shattering enough.

When I need to talk something through, I talk to Dane. When I need to cry, he holds me and tells me he'll make everything better. When I laugh, it's usually because of something he said. But now, can I really call him to boohoo that the hurt I caused is coming around to bite me in the ass? Nah—I better not. A small snicker actually leaves me as I hear my dad in my head. "You found your way in this mess; find your way out. It's called 'taking your licks,' Slugger."

With Dad's words in mind, I suck it up, wiping my face with the sleeve of my shirt and snorting my runny nose in the most ladylike way I can manage. Putting the problem with Evan out of my mind is all I can do right now—I can focus on lots of other things, like school and ball and Dane. Evan can wait until we're both ready to talk face to face, right? Maybe the guys will have some advice for me…or at least take my mind off everything. A girl can hope, right?

Trudging to lunch is a chore; if I was walking any slower, I'd be headed backwards. Why I even bother with food I'm not sure. My stomach is in knots and I glance around for my boys, *almost* perking up when their friendly eyes meet mine.

"Hey," I manage, slouching into the seat beside them, not capable of fighting Sawyer off his immediate attack of my tray like I usually do. No, today I peacefully concede my whole plate over to him; this should be their first clue as to my mood. *Boys.*

Zach's mesmerized by his phone, as usual, so I kick him under the table. "Ow!" He rubs his leg. "What the hell was that for?"

"I don't know." I shrug. "Tell me something interesting."

"Avery says hey," he says, staring at his phone again.

"Oh my God, if that's the best you've got, I'm screwed." I bang my head on the table.

Sawyer stops inhaling his, make that *my,* food just long enough to interrupt. "Avery, huh? Kirby get on your nerves too?"

Okay, this is a conversation that may actually keep me entertained. I could use a diversion.

"Kirby's cool. She doesn't get on my nerves, but I'm definitely more into Avery," he says, smiling shyly.

Yes! I lost twenty bucks on Sawyer, but just won the same with Zach's confirmation, so I break even!

"Well, no wonder Kirby's gone if you're getting *into* Avery more."

"Sawyer!" I smack the back of his head. "Say nothing, Zach, I mean it." This conversation is going downhill fast but actually gets worse when Sawyer speaks again.

"Sig party tomorrow night, man, you in? We're heading over when I get off, 'bout eleven."

"Who's we?" Zach asks.

"Me and Evan." Sawyer darts one eye at me, shifting a bit in his seat.

"Nah, man, y'all go. I'm gonna hang with Avery. What are you gonna do, Laney?"

"Um, not go to a party with Sawyer and Evan." I laugh halfheartedly. "I'll be doing whatever Dane has planned, I'm sure. And Sawyer?" I stare at him until he reluctantly meets my eyes. "I appreciate you taking Evan under your wing, honestly. Just make sure you and I stay close too, all right?" I give him a smile and wink. I'd really miss Sawyer if we grew apart.

"You got it, Gidge." He pulls me into his lap for a big Sawyer hug. "I promise."

"We're *all* very lucky to have you, big guy." I kiss the top of his head and bend mine to his ear. "Please tell him I'm sorry I hurt him," I whisper, "and I hope he finds someone to love him like he deserves."

He nods, kissing my cheek. "So how's my boy? He treating you good?"

"Dane is wonderful; amazing in fact." I climb out of his lap, grabbing my bag and hugging Zach goodbye so I can leave on a high note. It's not like I was eating anyway… "Evan'll be on the football team with you, Zach. You should hang out and get to know him. He's a great guy."

His green eyes meet mine, a sweet sympathy in them. "Sounds good, Laney. I'll holler at him."

I give him a curt nod that his smile tells me he knows means "thank you."

"Walk me to class, Sawyer?"

He stands and offers me his arm and a smirk. "That's a real good look on you."

"What look?" I look down at my outfit, which is nothing special.

"Happy."

I blush, embarrassed he can see it written all over my face. "Yeah? Feels pretty good too." I clear my throat after a few minutes of quiet walking. "So…his birthday is coming up and I don't know what to do. After the birthday he gave me, anything I do will seem lame in comparison. I just want to make him as happy as he makes me."

"Wrap your naked self in a bow and blow his candle out."

Oh dear God.

"You should see your face right now." He bends over laughing, clutching his sides, and I whack him…for the second time today. He's on a roll. "Okay, seriously…if I know Dane, the best thing to give him is alone time with you. No outside world or bullshit."

"How do I pull that off? I live in a dorm and Tate lives with him right now. Alone time is scarce these days."

"Hmmm." Lines crease his forehead with deep thought,

suddenly replaced with a huge, beaming smile and a snap of his fingers. "I got it! Dane has a cabin in Rockhurst, like 40 miles from here. Take him there for the weekend. I'll get you directions. You could cook for him, strut around naked, whatever."

"Really? Ya think? I was thinking maybe a puppy, for when Tate leaves and he's all alone in that big house again."

Sawyer laughs and wraps a ginormous arm around my shoulder. "Gidge, dogs are all well and good, and it's true that men like them, but he'd rather have a kitty. Your kitty."

I can feel how red my face is and I'm not sure why I ever let his words shock me. "Why do we let you speak again?"

"Cause you love me and I have great ideas, of course! Go with the cabin, I'm tellin' ya."

We're at the door to my class now so I give him a quick squeeze and peck on the cheek. "Thanks, Sawyer! You're the best!"

Chapter 5

Lead the Way

Evan

The Sig house is hoppin'. Trash, toilet paper and a few smokers huddled together for warmth decorate the front lawn. A loud bass line thumps from inside and Sawyer's head is bobbing to the music like a dashboard doll as we make our way up the walk. Neither one of us is a Sig, but I'm thinking nobody tells Sawyer he can't join the party, so I figure I'm golden.

All I want to do tonight is forget; I want erase from my mind all that is my new school, my forfeited jersey and my lost girl. Maybe I can just pretend to be somebody else.

Seeing Laney in Algebra every week is gonna suck, and I'm not sure how long I'll be able to treat her with cold indifference; it just doesn't feel right. We were friends for so long before we were anything else, but I'm not sure yet if we can get it back there. Not having her in my life at all is foreign and hurts like hell, but I don't know if I can pull off anything more than cordial distance right now, and the cordiality is sometimes a stretch.

Not wanting to do the mental debate thing for the hundredth time, I follow Sawyer into the party, vowing internally not to think of it, her, us, them, again tonight. We hit the keg straight away, then head over to a group of people Sawyer knows. Introductions are made and the only one I register is Josie, a short, really pretty brunette across from me. Yes—I still have eyes.

I give her a smile and hold her hand in mine longer than a normal "nice to meet you" shake, rubbing my thumb across her wrist on the release. I just want to connect with someone, anyone, even for a moment. I've always been half of a whole, always known the girl in the room who was "mine," and now I'm lost.

Sawyer picks up on my interest in her and gives me a nod, turning his attention to her friend, guiding her away to dance.

Very nice. I've got one foot in the stirrup, ready to fling my leg over and get back on the horse when a pair of small hands covers my eyes from behind.

"Guess who?" a sweet voice says in my ear.

The hands lift and Whitley pops in front of me, totally disregarding Josie, who's now standing behind her. I have to grin at her boldness.

"Hey, Whitley, how are you? Do you know Josie?" I awkwardly indicate to the girl throwing daggers into her back.

Whitley swiftly turns her head, giving Josie a once over, then looks back to me. "Nope," she says nonchalantly with a shrug. "Who are you here with?"

"Sawyer. He's around here somewhere." I cast my eyes around as though looking for him, not daring to make eye contact with Josie. I don't think I've ever been the ball of nip in a catfight before, and the thought is making me sweat in a nervous, "I'm not breaking this shit up" kind of way. Don't get me wrong—I love a good catfight as much as any other guy, but I don't want to be in the middle of one.

"I don't care where Sawyer is." She giggles. "Come on, let's dance." She drags me into the middle of the room, furniture moved to provide a makeshift dance floor, before I can decline.

I look back over my shoulder to try and apologize to Josie, but she's already rubbing the arm of some blonde guy. That's all right—I prefer blondes too.

Whitley's a great dancer; not too provocative, not too shy. She's fun and flirty and helps take my mind off everything else. When the room starts feeling like a sauna, I pull her outside to cool off. The deck, like the front yard, is trashed, so surely no one will care that I swipe part of a Poinsettia out of the pot to my right, the only other thing of beauty out here.

"I got you a flower." I wink, handing it to her.

She blushes and giggles at me. "Thank you for the *plant*."

Plant, flower…she likes it.

"Who are you here with?" I ask.

"Some of the Larks. I had nothing better to do." She shrugs and then smiles, smelling her flower. "What's your excuse?"

Before I can ramble off some bullshit reason, we're coerced into a game of Baggo by the group playing in the yard. Now, where I come from, Baggo (or some call it Cornhole) is a time-honored tradition, but it's doubtful Whitley plays much.

"Do you know how to play?" I ask her, leading her over to the game by the elbow. The patio lights don't help much where the game's set up in the yard and I don't want her to fall.

"You throw the bag in the hole, right? How hard can it be?" she teases.

"Okay, smarty pants, we'll see," I say as I size up our competition.

I already see a problem. Whitley has to stand on the opposite end of the yard as me, and I already feel bad about leaving her alone with either one of our opponents. I don't know their names; they're definitely frat guys, so they probably have nicknames of which they're very proud, but I've renamed them. The one closest to us shall be called "Teetering Beer Burps" and his friend down there is now "I Smell as Bad as You Expect." They aren't quite as "cool" as the traditional fraternity nicknames, but I'm working on the fly here.

"We stand on opposite ends since we're a team," I explain. "Which end do you want? Or we don't have to play at all."

"I'll stay here," she says and pushes on me to go. "I want to be with the brighter light." She waits until I've walked away to add, "So you'll be able to see how it's done."

Part of me wants to really appreciate her and all the cool things about her. If I'd met her *before,* I would have instantly liked her—a lot. But it's not before and she deserves more than I have to give.

Ain't that just a kick?

Turns out Whitley is all talk and actually sucks at Baggo. We got royally skunked and commiserated in our defeat by getting back on the dance floor. She's in the middle of perfecting my sprinkler, one hand braced on my shoulder to hold her up in her laughter, when Sawyer slaps me on the shoulder.

"I'm out, man, can you get a ride home?"

I give Whitley a helpless look.

"Yes, I'll take you home," she agrees with a smile. "You do have a home now, right?"

"Yeah," I chuckle lightly.

Satisfied, Sawyer and his "date" walk away and I turn back to her. "Can I feed you first?"

She nods and holds up a finger, walking away as I wait right there. I watch as she navigates her way through the masses, finally spotting what must be her friend and speaks in her ear. The friend's eyes move over me, a curious smile on her face, before she hands Whitley some keys she pulled out of her pocket.

"All set, let's go!" she says once she's back to me.

I settle a hand on her back and guide her to the door, helping her into her coat before stepping outside. She pulls her hair out from under the collar, tossing the locks over one shoulder. I'm not even sure why I notice such an insignificant move, but I'm quickly discovering that Whitley has an unmistakable grace about her, an elegance really, that I can't help but appreciate.

"So, what's open this late around here?" I ask as we walk to the car, which I see is hers, not the friend's, once we get to it.

"Taco Shack or... Taco Shack. Your choice." She snickers, climbing in as I hold open the door for her.

I let her pick, and we end up standing at a window cut into the side of a small van in a random parking lot. How in the hell a girl like Whitley even knows of such a mobile eatery, or that the friendly guy inside the window clearly knows her, is beyond me.

"Ah, Sunshine Girl, what can I get for you?"

Normally I'd think it rude for him to hit on her with me standing right here, but I can't even force myself to be bothered by this kid, despite how attractive she must find his wannabe porn moustache.

"Happy Man!" She beams, giving him a side-five, front and back. "I'll have my usual, and," she turns to me, "Evan, what do you want?"

A Hepatitis C shot.

"Same as you will be fine. And a Coke."

"Make that two of my usual, and two cokes, please."

"You better not be digging in that purse for money, woman," I growl at her, easing her to the side. I take out my wallet to pay

34

"Happy."

"Nice girl," he mumbles while he hands me one of our drinks, "deserves some happiness, you know?"

Just how well does she know the taco guy?

"Yeah, man, I got it," I grumble as nicely as possible.

Meals on wheels is speedy, and not even five minutes later, we're digging into our grub, strolling down the street.

"Will you hand me a napkin?"

"Sure," she replies in a sweet voice, looking down into the bag. She gasps loudly, whipping her head at me, eyes wide and wild.

"What?" I ask her anxiously.

She flicks her head this way and that, tugging my arm and pulling me behind the nearest building. I kinda hear the "dun dun dun" crime scene music in my head.

"Whitley, what?"

"Shhh!" she spits at me. We're now crouched behind a building, on I have no idea what street. "Are these not the best tacos you've ever eaten?"

Come again? Why this is an undercover question I'm not sure...but yes, damn good tacos.

"Actually, yeah, really good. Why? What the hell is wrong with you?"

"I want to remember you said that, okay? That's the only reason I go there, I swear. I love their tacos, and that is the *only* thing I've ever ordered."

I can feel my brows dip as I look at her suspiciously, watching as she slowly lifts a joint out of the bag. Man, taco guy wasn't kidding, he really does want her to have some happiness.

Two thoughts wage war in my head—I just tested with the transfer and we're in off-season, and we need a lighter. "Put it back in the bag and come on, *Miss I Only like Their Tacos*," I direct her teasingly, dragging her back down the road toward the store we had passed.

"Evan, I swear. I had no idea, and I've never... I think he was just being nice. I'm an excellent patron, I always tip well—"

Laughter busts out of me. Whitley just went from nice to be around to fucking cute as hell. Who innocently justifies the taco vendor slipping you a joint because you're a good patron? Too funny.

"I believe you, Whitley, really. Now walk, woman, we need a

lighting apparatus mucho pronto."

I can't believe how excited I am. One quick trip into the convenient store, a covert smoking stint behind a dilapidated building and a frantic jaunt back to her car later, and we're both pleasantly toasted, which is *my* excuse for just busting out the big guns.

"So why exactly does Sawyer not like you?" Through their curt words to each other, I got a hint of why Laney doesn't like her, apparently something about Douchebag Dane, but that really didn't clear up Sawyer's animosity.

"I don't know." She leans her head back against her headrest and sighs. "I guess because of Dane, although I've never done anything bad to Dane…or Sawyer. How do you even know Dane? From Laney?" she asks as she looks over at me.

I just nod, looking down and grinding my back teeth.

"So, are they together now?"

"Yes." It kills me to say it out loud, to admit it to another person. It makes it too real.

"Can't say I didn't see that coming a mile away," she says, wincing for me. "And you what, got here too late?"

"Looks like it. She was at his house when I hand delivered my transfer slip. *Surprise!*"

"Damn, I'm sorry, Evan. That had to hurt. But couldn't you fight for her? Do you guys have a long history?"

I run my hands through my hair, squeezing my eyes shut. "We do…" I grapple for my words, trying to keep my voice steady in front of her, "but mostly as friends. We'd only just begun anything more than that, and college pretty much ruined it. It was new and obviously not strong enough to last. Maybe even the wrong thing for us." I blow out a deep breath, finally opening my eyes and turning to face her. "I'm learning that now, the hard way."

She says nothing, just meekly smiling, her eyes filled with pity, which I hate. When it's clear she's remaining silent, waiting for more of my pitiful story, I switch it up.

"So what's the story with you and Dane?"

I'm guessing this is the "deep thoughts" part of a high, because normally I wouldn't want to discuss him at length and Whitley and I had been doing so well avoiding these topics. I still can't believe I slept at her place and am just now learning why my lifelong best friend hates her. Bass ackwards.

She smiles nervously, drawing in the side of her lip to nibble on it, her hands fiddling with the hem of her shirt. "Dane and I grew up together. Our parents were very close and threw us together for everything—music lessons, singing lessons, same private schools, dances—you name it."

I nod, giving her a comforting smile, urging her to go on. "It was always assumed, well, with the help of endless blatant comments from our parents, that Dane and I would simply end up together. At first, I was all for it." Her voice falters and her gaze drifts past me, far-off and disconnected. "I'm not sure now if that was because I actually liked him like that or it was just another one of the programs my parents installed that I mindlessly followed."

I can almost hear the self-analyzing going on in her head, but just as quickly as she'd gotten lost, she's back, looking at me once again. "Doesn't matter either way." She smirks facetiously. "Dane never wanted me."

Pain etches her eyes and she quickly recovers the frown she doesn't think I noticed. "Then when his parents died, and he came here to be near Tate, well… I followed him. I thought if nothing else, we'd be friends. I'd known him so long, and he was lost and alone. I just wanted to be the one constant, the one familiar comfort, in his life."

I can't even help it, I reach over and take her hand in mine. She looks down to our joined hands and a small, soft smile appears before she goes on. "I think maybe he appreciated it, until Laney came along."

And there you have it—two peas in a pod. No wonder we had formed an instant, unspoken-but-understood friendship. The finer details may be different, change a few names and exacts, but Whitley and I share the same story. I know exactly how she feels, which is why I remain silent. There's nothing really for me to say, anyway. She doesn't want me to tell her how bad it sucks—she knows that. She doesn't need me to tell her "I'm sorry," because pity doesn't solve anything, nor does she want me to make a joke and lighten things up; our pain is not to be trivialized.

"Do you have any of your Coke left?" she asks me out of nowhere, clearly done with the intellectual portion of our buzz. "I have," she smacks her lips, making the face of someone who just licked the bottom of a shoe, "like absolutely no moisture in my mouth right now."

I can barely pass her my drink I'm laughing so hard, when she again spurts out the random.

"Evan, look!" she squeals, latching onto my arm. "Look over there!"

My eyes follow the end of her pointed finger to a red balloon bouncing aimlessly along the ground.

"Go catch it for me, pleasssseeeee?!"

Um yeah, I can do that. No problem. I lumber out of the car, my head a bit foggy but the fresh air instantly helping that. Luckily, the balloon's lost most of its oomph, so I catch it easily, handing it to her when I notice she's now standing behind me.

"Going flat, but still hang on, just in case. We don't want it losing its way again."

"Thank you." She smiles, her voice low and tender. "I'll go put it in my car."

I watch her as she walks there, tucking the balloon in the backseat with great care, then makes her way back to stand in front of me.

"I don't want to be an underdog anymore. Do you?" I had no idea it was coming out of my mouth, but it just did.

Her face slowly lights up and she shakes her head back and forth. "Not at all. I'm too cute to be an underdog, right?"

I laugh, jealous of her resiliency. "Definitely too cute," I agree with a wink. "That settles it. We are now the opposite of underdogs. We are—"

I've almost made the connection when she shout-giggles it for me.

"We're overcats!"

"Hell yes we are! Over, badass, sexy, freaking cats! And I say we officially start our journey, with say…" Again I have to stop and think, but my partner in crime has it all figured out.

"Tattoos!" she squeals, giving me a vibrant smile. "I've always wanted a tattoo! Something my mother would think is ghastly!"

"Did you just say ghastly?" I fail at containing my laughter.

Whitley is exactly the prim Ms. Proper who says things like ghastly, and ten bucks says she gets a tiny butterfly or heart on her ankle.

"Okay, so maybe tomorrow we can—" I start.

"There's a tattoo shop one street over! I *so* bet they're open, come on!" She's dragging me by the hand as she says it.

"Whitley, we're gonna get busted. We're messed up, wandering the streets, leaving your car…" I can't even articulate all the things wrong with this plan.

She turns back to look at me, puckering out her bottom lip. "Evan, this is downtown. We aren't the only stoned college kids out right now. Relax."

If the debutante thinks I need to relax, I must be acting like a phenomenal pussy, and we certainly can't have that. "Hop on," I turn and bend, letting her jump on for a piggyback ride.

Whitley is trying so hard not to turn up her nose right now it's hilarious. Her big blue eyes are about three times their normal size, taking in every nuance of the shop. There's indents in her lower lip from her teeth that just loosened their grip, and her once creamy complexion is now simply pale. I'm tempted to tease her, but don't really want to draw attention to our current "condition," because I know they'll turn us away.

"Y-you'll go first, right?" she asks with a shaking stutter to her voice.

I lay one hand on her shoulder, squeezing reassuringly. "I seem to remember this being your plan," I remind her, quirking a brow, "but yes, I will go first."

She lets out a deep breath, her face and shoulders relaxing with it, and gives me a grin. "What are you going to get?"

I have no idea. A tattoo should mean something, right? I wrack my brain, but nothing stands out. Can't get my school or ball team symbol; I've hardly built a deep-rooted love for Southern yet. Can't get anything to do with you-know-who; enough said there. Realizing it really doesn't matter what I get, just that I do it with this kind, accepting girl beside me, I smile devilishly. "You pick."

The look on her face is even more sinister than my own. "And you pick mine?!" she says excitedly. "No peeking, no rules on what or where?"

"Deal."

"Okay then, we'll go at the same time."

So when the artist comes up and ask which one of us wants to go first, we explain we'd like to be done at the same time, away from each other. He looks at us like we're crazy when we ask about blindfolding each other and tells us to work that part out on our own, before yelling to a girl called Jess, who saunters from the back.

"You take the guy, I'll take the girl. They want to be apart and tell us what the other one is getting."

Jess rolls her eyes, but the side of her lip deceives her…she thinks it's a fun plan. "So tell me what to do to him," she conspires with Whitley, as they move away to conspire.

Guy looks at me, arms crossed over his massive chest, eyebrow raised and viper bites shining in his face. "So what's the plan for her?"

Luckily the girls are across the room, so I don't have to get too close for him to hear me and can still keep my voice a bit low as I tell him my plan. He doesn't need to draw it up and we're set.

Jess comes back over and motions to me. "Come on, hunky, you're with me."

I walk down a hall with her and she opens the door to a small room, walls covered in artwork and pictures of various people and their tats, asking me to have a seat in the chair. "Shirt off, which your girl said to wrap around your eyes. And no peeking," she reminds me. "Her words, not mine."

After a few minutes of listening her prep from behind my makeshift blindfold, aka my shirt, I feel her hand move to my right pec, pressing down a piece of paper, I assume to transfer her drawing.

"Ready?" she asks me.

"Yup," I say with as much assertion as one can provide seconds from their first (surprise) tattoo. I'm not nervous *exactly*, but the thought of getting a permanent picture of whatever the hell Whitley, a girl I hardly know, has chosen does sober me just a bit. What if she picked a big ass dragon? I'll be in this chair for hours. Worse yet, what if she picked something humiliating, like a unicorn or some shit? I'll have to carry it on my body for the rest of my life.

I am giving Whitley an obscene amount of trust right now. Crazy.

And what I'd picked for her—what if she hates it? Regrets it in the morning?

Jess's words break the paranoid cluster whirling in my head. "It hurts less if you're not all tensed up."

"Right," I mumble, rolling my neck and taking a deep breath. "I'm ready."

You know the sound of the drill at the dentist? You know you won't really feel it, since the doc's loaded you up with excruciating shots of Novocain and you're sucking in the gas like a fiend, but you still know there's a fucking drill heading into the core of your tooth, where there's a bundle of trigger happy nerves?

That is exactly what Jess's drill o' art reminds me of at this moment.

―――――― ∽ ――――――

"Did you peek?" I ask her as we walk back to her car, my voice laced with suspicion.

"No, did you?"

"Absolutely not," I reply confidently and bump her shoulder with mine. "Though now that I'm completely in my right mind, I'm hoping you didn't brand me with a rainbow." I give her a wide smile, part of me knowing she'd never do that. "You regret it?" I ask pointedly.

"No matter what you gave me, I don't regret it. Yolo!"

"Yeah, me either," I laugh; I can't believe she just said yolo…that word fad needs to die out. I open the door for her and once again climb into her car. "So, we gonna do the big reveal now?"

"Sure." Her small hands tremble as she unbuttons her pants, lifting her hips slightly to scooch the waist down just a bit. I'd instructed her tattoo be placed in the crook of her hip, that sweet little dip women have that can be their secret, unless they choose to show you, and low enough to still be covered in a bikini. Yes—I thought of everything, even inebriated.

She pulls the covering off and gasps softly as she sees it. "A red balloon. I can't believe that's what you picked." Her eyes water a bit as she looks at me thoughtfully and I smile.

"You like it?" I ask nervously.

"I love it."

"I wanted you to remember the night we decided our worth. You're awesome, Whitley, and I have a ton of fun with you. Everything does not go to shit when you show up, so don't believe that. You're beautiful and kind and I'll hang with you anytime you want. So every time you look at that balloon, you block out their words and hear mine instead. Okay?"

"Oh, okay," she says softly, sniffling back her tears. "Look at yours now before I make a scene."

I reach behind my neck and pull my shirt off, anticipation eating away at me. I go without a shirt a lot, so I'm silently praying she wasn't too blasted to make a good choice.

I pull off the covering, revealing an intricate and really quite stunning compass rose. The lines are black and bold, shadowed with red. The N, S, E and W letters are scripted and also shadowed. I'm relieved and amazed simultaneously. It's awesome and I love it. But I don't understand why she chose it.

When I look from my chest to her, she's biting her bottom lip, question in her eyes. "You like yours?"

"Yeah." I nod and beam. "I actually like it a lot; it's kickass."

"It's so you never lose your way again."

My eyes bore into hers, never straying, as I let the gravity of it all sink in. Practically strangers, stoned, and yet we connected profoundly over the same moment in time—a random act of chasing a deflated balloon around a parking lot.

Words like "kindred spirits" are bouncing around my head and quite frankly tripping me out, so I clear my throat and quickly put my shirt back on. "We better get going; it's late."

She says nothing as she starts the car and drives me to my dorm. When I hop out, I thank her for the ride and she thanks me for paying for her tattoo. We make no specific plans to hang out again, but something tells me we will. I have no idea what she's thinking. I'm not even sure what I'm thinking, but I do fall asleep with a smile.

Chapter 6

Torment

Evan

"You gotta bring in some ringers or you're screwed." I bend over, holding my side and laughing so hard I snort.

"What do you mean?" she puffs out as she, too, is bent over, bracing her hands on her knees, her face flushed.

"Whitley," I gulp in a deep breath, composing myself, "when you asked me to coach your Larks for the flag football game, I assumed at least some of you had played before. Or at least watched a game on TV? Googled it maybe?"

"Are you saying we suck?"

Suck isn't even close to a strong enough word for it. Not one of her songbirds can catch...or throw...or even run fast. And once the girls' athletic clubs get ahold of them, it won't be pretty.

"You need to go out and find a couple of the fastest, then a couple of the biggest, burliest girls on this campus and make them a Lark. I'm talking midnight initiation tonight, Whit, even if their singing sounds like a cat's tail's stuck in the door, or you guys will be a laughingstock."

Too harsh? I feel guilty for a split second and quickly shake it off. I'm guessing it's not as harsh as making fools of yourselves in front of the whole campus, so my intentions are on point.

Aggravated now, she tosses down the water bottle in her hand and steps into me, one perfectly pink-tipped nail poking me in the chest. "We are smart girls, and *you* are supposedly a football stud, right? So teach us some tricky moves or sneaky plays like you're supposed to, and we'll be fine."

"While that sounds like a helluva plan," I tilt my head and give her a patronizing grin, "it won't work. Even if I teach you to throw, who will catch it? If I teach you to hand-off, who will run it? The volleyball team, soccer team, and the soft—" *Oh, God, no!* The words hang in my throat and I have to force them out. "And the softball team will all be entered, right? Finely tuned, athletic machines running straight at you…this is a bad idea, Whitley."

"Oh please," she scoffs, lightheartedly slapping my arm, "this is *flag* football, Evan. We don't want the trophy, we just want to participate for the camaraderie."

That sounds right and reasonable. I'm taking this too seriously. I just see a field, a ball and a hint of competition and go crazy. This is girls' flag football for Christ's sake, how bad can it be?

"Okay, you're right," I concede. "Come on, I'll show you some plays."

"Yay!" Whitley bounces up on her tiptoes and plants an exaggerated kiss on my cheek with a loud "MWAH!"

I think her exuberance surprised even her, because her cheeks pink a bit as she bounces along beside me back toward the group of girls waiting for us. We've taken about ten steps when we hear a bellow.

"Should I make a path, Coach McGrath?"

Okay, good one. Great movie too. I turn my head with a chuckle, seeing Sawyer amble over to us, his smartass smile on full display as he glances at the group I'm working with.

"Hey, man, you come to help me out?" I ask, the desperation pathetically evident in my voice.

"No can do," he retorts all too happily, "I already bet fifty bucks on the softball team."

Smart bet. Those girls will be in it to win it if they're anything like L—

Speak of the devil. There she is.

As soon as I see her headed across the field, I panic. *Had she seen Whitley kiss me? Will she react if she did?* I forget Sawyer and turn quickly to Whitley. "What time did you say we had the field until?"

"I guess now." She shrugs casually. "Surely we were about done, right?"

44

Um, not even. We had practiced maybe forty minutes, tops. We learned one play. Well, I showed them one play…not sure the term *learned* is applicable in this situation. Whitley is by far the one with the most potential, so she'll definitely be playing QB. I guess I'll practice with her some more, one on one, but right now I've got bigger problems…and she's walking right towards me.

"Hey, man, y'all bout done?" Zach calls as he approaches with the team. "I gotta show these diamond dolls some moves." He smiles and gives me a fist bump.

We'll be playing football together, so we're working, slowly but surely, on a "broship." It's just so damn awkward because they're all close with Laney. But what decent guy worth knowing wouldn't be Laney's bud? It's always been that way, I don't ever have to waste time "feeling somebody out," because I've always had the inside track to Laneydar. If she likes you, you're all right. Her record is so far flawless in gauging guys.

Girls? Well…the only time she's ever been wrong is Kaitlyn, and even Psychic Friends Network didn't see that coming. Oh, and Whitley. She's way off hating her.

I shake myself out of my thoughts and realize that the whole time I was off in my own world, which was way too long for my taste, I was staring at Laney. *Just great.* She's standing a little ways behind Zach, pretending not to notice me, but she does. Her whole body is tense and she's sliding the tip of one cleat back and forth on the turf, watching it like it's the most fascinating activity on Earth…she's well aware of exactly where I am.

"Yeah, we're good for today," I finally answer Zach, then ask Whitley to let the other girls know we're done. I wait until she's walked away to half-mumble my next question. "So you're coaching the softball team, huh?"

"Looks like it. Avery's on the team, ya know, so…" He waggles his eyebrows at me. "Coaching gets me brownie points."

"Well, I know you're off to a better start than me. At least yours are athletes." I hang my head in a combination of mocking and honest shame. "Mine are *singers.*"

"Hey! I heard that!" Whitley's back and just used her very tiny fist to inflict some very large pain in my chest…right over my fresh tattoo.

I wince despite my best effort not to, rubbing my chest, so she feels bad and starts coddling me, going all out with her apology.

"Shoot, Evan I'm sorry, I forgot." She covers my hands with hers, essentially helping me rub.

It wouldn't have been that big of a deal, just a little sting at first, but now...well, we've officially caused a scene.

"It's okay, Whit," I mumble, "forget about it, *please.*"

Wishing the ground would open and swallow me whole, I can *feel* her staring at me, and then...

"What's wrong?" Laney rushes to me, her voice edged with concern, her eyes worried. "Evan, are you actually hurt?" She went from ignoring indifference to Florence Nightingale in milliseconds.

"I'm fine," I bark, looking at the ground. *Except I'm not fine since you're in my air space and now I can't breathe. And I can smell you from here; I can smell that lavender lotion and the shampoo you love that comes in the green and white bottle.*

"Bullshit, I saw you flinch. What is it?" Her face wears a mask of anger, so focused on me I don't know that she realizes she just hedged Whitley out of the way with her shoulder and hip, grabbing at me now, pushing my hands out of her way and pulling on my shirt, trying to get a peek.

The most interaction we've had in eons and this is it? Her mauling me in front of everyone, thinking I'm hurt and need her to save me? My body is happy she's near, my heart so ready to soak up any attention she offers and quit aching, but my mind...my mind is still pissed.

"I'm not hurt, all right?" I speak too loudly, too gruffly, and even Whitley twitches at my tone.

But Laney? Laney holds strong, her mocha eyes challenging me like they always have.

"It's a tattoo, geez," I grumble, pulling up my shirt to show her.

Now it's Laney's turn to gasp. "What the hell is *that?*" She shakes her head, squeezing her eyes shut and opening them again quickly, as though she was hallucinating and just needed to refresh her vision. She's gonna be disappointed, cause it's still there. "Since when are you into tattoos?" she bites out, one hand on a very angry cocked hip.

"Since now, I guess," I offer with a gratifying simper on my face. "Guess we're both into new things these days, huh?"

The torment that flashes in her eyes is unmistakable, even if fleeting, and like always, I feel bad. All I was trying to do was stand up for myself, but I feel like shit. This isn't how I wanted to do things.

"Isn't it cool?"

Oh Lord, here we go, is all I can think as Whitley taunts Laney with her purring question, her hand now on my shoulder.

"Well, since I'm pretty sure you're not all of a sudden a sailor, or wilderness guide, *Evan*," she starts, her tone scathing, "why'd you put a compass on your chest? Do your parents know?"

The inflection and glare she wears is probably the only warning Whitley's gonna get to butt the fuck out or get cold cocked, and I'm nervous for a second that Laney's gonna hit her.

"Whitley picked it, and no, they don't know…yet."

She no more heard the last six words of that sentence than the man in the moon. Laney checked out, and Maleficent, her favorite Disney witch, checked in right when I announced Whitley's involvement. I am a bad, bad man and my mama would test my ass if she knew my thoughts right now, because while I am seriously concerned for Whitley's safety at this moment, the bigger part of me is tickled shitless that Ms. Laney Jo Walker is pissed as hell.

"Why would you pick a compass?" she now asks Whitley, advancing a step toward her, seething.

I slide over just a tad, cutting her off at the pass. It isn't looking good. She must have seen the kiss; this reaction is about more than just the tattoo.

"Why would you care?" Whitley challenges.

Not good! Abort mission!!

Laney shifts her fiery eyes at me, and I know what she's waiting for. She's expecting good ol' Evan to jump in and defend her. Yes, my every instinct, and my heart, tell me to do it…but my mind wins, and I simply give her a sheepish shrug.

"Why *would* you care, prince—" I stop myself and clear my throat. "Laney?"

Her sweet little mouth drops open and her face heats scarlet as the flush sweeps up her neck. She's ready to spew venom, but then clamps her mouth shut in an attempt at self-preservation. She looks like a guppy. I don't get an answer. She spins abruptly on one heel, away from us, calling to Zach, who raises his head from where he's bent over, helping Avery with something, and looks at her. "I'll catch up with you guys next practice. I'm good anyway," she flips her head back around and cooks Whitley with her blazing eyes, "Evan taught me how to play my whole life."

"Show's over then? Cool!" Whitley happily places both hands on my shoulders and grips down. "Catch me, Ev!" She jumps on for a piggyback ride and giggles. "Let's go!"

I walk away as fast as I can, toting Whitley, just wanting to get us out of everyone's scope.

Chapter 7

Don't Ask, Don't Tell
Laney

"Hello?"

"Zach, don't say my name," I choke out, storming across the lot as fast as my shaking legs will carry me.

"What's wrong? Where'd you—" his voice comes loud and worried through the phone.

"Don't say that!" I interrupt. *God, how embarrassing.* "Can you walk away from everyone and talk to me for a minute? Where no one can hear you." My voice is nasally and obnoxious, getting on my own nerves.

"Yeah, Mom, hang on."

Note to self: Zach—not a great actor.

"Okay, Laney, I'm by myself now," he whispers.

"I'm sorry I bailed on practice, and I'm sorry to bug you now, but I need a Zach of Infinite Wisdom fix real bad right about now."

"Let's pretend I don't already know what's up your ass and you go ahead. It'll give you a chance to vent."

All right, so that *almost* makes me grin.

"He just hung all over that bitch right in front of me just to piss me off, and it worked! Seriously, she's picking out his tattoos? Nothing I did was to purposely hurt him. How long did I absolutely torture myself NOT to hurt him Zach, huh? A long ass time!" I come up for air, waiting for him to tell me how right I am while I climb in my truck.

"Laney, you know I love you, right?"

This can't be good.

"Yes…"

"Then you know it's with love when I say this."

His dramatic pause that makes my skin crawl.

"Get over yourself! I don't care if he fucked her on the field and asked you to film it. You may not have meant to, but you *destroyed* that kid. He's here with no friends, no girl and a new team. Sound familiar? He's just trying to put one foot in front of the other every day, just like you did. You got your happily ever after, so back the fuck off and let him *try* to find his."

Well then. Zach-1. Laney-0.

It hurts; I'm not even gonna pretend it doesn't, but his words are honest…and absolutely dead on. It makes me angry at myself for being the cause of such sad, but true, words describing the crushing of my Evan. It's a lot to think on and I have to do that now before I cruise right out of control.

"You're right, Zach," I whisper. "That's why I call you. I'll always get what I need to hear straight up. Thanks."

"I love ya, Laney. Don't be mad at me, but don't ask for my advice if you don't want it."

"God, if that isn't the truth," I scoff loudly. "You're harsh, but right. That's why you're my number one advisor. I'm not mad, I swear. Now go coach! I'll talk to ya later."

"Later, Laney."

I hang up and stare out my windshield, pondering. Zach is right, I'm being a selfish bitch. Sure, I hate Whitley and would rather Evan engaged in orgies than in her, but he's absolutely justified in doing whatever he wants. I start my truck, headed nowhere on gas I can't afford to waste, and drive until I make about a two mile circle twice, finally pulling into the very back of my dorm parking lot, hiding my truck as well as possible between a big dually and the dumpsters.

I lay down across my seat so no one will see me just sitting alone in a parking lot and pull my phone out of my pocket, because no pity party is complete without music, right? I let the music take over, my thoughts drifting aimlessly, to nowhere in particular, on a whim. Wouldn't it be nice if life was like that? But it's not. Every action has a reaction, a consequence, for which the collector will one day come to get your toll. I made a choice, one I don't regret on every single level, yet feel remorse for in my every pore. Like a fool, I thought it'd all be fine, that I could hide behind the miles between us, in my Dane bliss, like a heartless wench. But the toll collector came a callin'.

Evan is here, and yet, I miss him more than ever. Yes, this is the part where everyone around me screams, "If that whiny bitch double dips or flip-flops again, I'm gonna kick her ass myself!" Not what I'm doing. I love Dane, completely and unashamedly, and I'm not walking away from him, no matter what...but I have to fix my core, the basis of a lifetime of events that made me *me*, and that core is Evan and Laney, the best kind of friends.

When "I Never Told You" by Colbie Caillat starts playing, I decide it's a sickly, ironic sign that I've wallowed in a pool of self-pity long enough and get up. I climb out and wrap my arms around myself, shuffling slowly to my room.

------&------

"Where you been, baby?"

Dane, of course, is looking perfectly beautiful, a crisp white dress shirt untucked over dark wash jeans and "I dare ya to mess it up more" hair, and waiting in my dorm room when I slug inside.

"Flag football practice," I mutter, sitting on the edge of the bed to pull off my cleats and socks, shrugging off my jacket as well. When he doesn't answer, I look up at him to find a scowl. "What?"

His arms cross over his chest and he widens his stance, though I don't think he knows he did it. "Oh yeah? How'd it go?"

He knows I'm hiding something. Decision time—fess up or roll with it? The latter is a horrible idea considering I suspect Dane really does have a Laney crystal ball tucked away somewhere, but you know me....daredevil. "It went good; I think we'll win." Of course we'll win, we're the freaking softball team for crying out loud! The intimidation factor alone is worth a touchdown.

His arms drop and he stalks my way, bending over me, forcing me to lay back on the bed. "That your final answer?" he growls.

Speaking of holy hotness intimidation factor... I swallow hard and mentally chastise my libido before looking up at his gorgeous face and answering him in a quivering voice. "What do you mean?"

"I mean," he runs his nose the length of mine, blanketing our bodies together, "that I don't like it when you lie to me."

That bossy mouth of his skims my jaw, his teeth taking little nips along the way until he's sucking right below my ear. Oh yeah, he knows all the weak spots to elicit a confession and he's hitting them all just right.

"You don't play fair," I moan, pulling my legs up to rest my feet on the mattress, tightening my knees around him, my deceitful hands running up his back.

"And you don't lie," he breathes against me, "so tell me what's going on before I flip you over and spank that tight ass red." Is he trying to help or hurt his cause? 'Cause I gotta say...my jury is still out and my heart is actually sweating right now.

"I went to—" *Oh God, never stop doing that.*

He grinds against me, curving his body down and in then back up, sending my mind to meltdown. "Go on," he orders me in a deep grumble.

"I drove in big circles, then sat undercover in the parking lot to think. Today was awful."

There. You win...you sexy, playing dirty God.

He moves off me, dragging his fingertips down me as he goes, and sits up beside me on the bed. "Come here," he says faintly, holding out his hand to pull me up. When I'm sitting up with him, he cups one of my cheeks with his long, brilliant fingers, running his thumb along my bottom lip. "Tell me what's wrong, baby." He drops a sweet kiss on the end of my nose. "Talk to me."

"It's nothing; all better now." I attempt to climb into his lap, wanting nothing more than for him to heal me, love me, make everything better, but he laughs lightly and holds me back with his hands on my shoulders.

"No way, not until you talk. I want your all, Laney. That means when something's not right with you, then nothing's right with me." He ducks his head and tilts it, forcing me to meet his deep brown gaze. "Tell me what's wrong and I'll fix it."

"I-I saw Evan," I stammer lowly. "He's coaching *Whitley's* team. She picked out his new tattoo."

If he'd have just said it to me, I know exactly what I'd say, so his response...I could have quoted it verbatim for him.

"And you care why?"

Yep, I'd say that's about right, word for word. His glower is angry, his eyes questioning. I don't blame him a bit, but he asked. In fact, he lusciously coerced me.

This time I don't let him stop me, I successfully curl myself into his lap and bury my face in his neck. He smells so freaking good and I can feel his displeased heartbeat against my chin.

"I don't know the right answer, and I don't want to make you mad," I admit.

The deep breath he lets out ruffles my hair. "There's no right or wrong answer, Laney. Just tell me exactly what you're feeling, what you're thinking. I'm so sick of talking about him I could rage, but I know it's a whole new level of difficult since he's here now. So let's do this one more time; let's talk." He kisses my forehead, gliding his hand along the back of my hair, telling me it's okay, that he wants to hear what's inside me because he wants to live there too.

"I love you. You are my fire, my intensity, my must have, my awakening," I say sincerely. "You're the lap I always want to cuddle in, the lips I want to kiss, the mind I want to challenge, the laugh I want to draw out. Okay?"

The smile that lights up his face and the secure calmness that takes over those deep brown eyes is breathtaking. "I know, baby. I love you, too, so much. And later, I want you to moan all of that in my ear, over and over, while I make love to your sweet body all night long. But right now, I want to figure this shit out so we can move on."

Well who the hell can think when he says things like that? I clench my thighs together, tightening my grip around his neck.

"Fine," I huff out, "I'm jealous that he's doing shit with her and he's not even my friend anymore. It pisses me off that my best friend inked up his fucking chest and I didn't even know. But most of all, I hate that one of the most wonderful people in the whole world hates me." One lone tear dares to drop out of my eye and I feel him startle when the moisture hits his skin. "Usually I don't care what people think of me, but someone like Evan, well, you give a shit if he thinks badly of you. It means you really are a crap person."

"Baby, I'm gonna say this once, then I'm going to get up and walk out so that I don't change my mind. I love you and I trust you, so go find him, text him, whatever… Fix it. I'll give you until ten to come to me, and when you do, it's just me and you. No one or nothing else gets in. Deal?"

I lift my head in shock. What guy sends their girlfriend to find their ex? Dane Kendrick, in all his domineering, secure, sexy fucking excellence, that's who. He even bosses me when he's sending me to find Evan… It's the sexiest thing ever.

I nod and then I grab his face and kiss him like I'll never get to again. His hands slide around my waist, pulling me against him, our bodies molding like our mouths. He breaks away first, setting me off him and onto the bed, standing and moving swiftly to the door.

"Ten o'clock," he repeats, turning back to look at me, my hair mussed and my lips swollen, "or anytime really. Call me if you need me and know I love you."

With a wink, he leaves and I grab my phone to text Evan. That is, once I regain full use of my senses.

Chapter 8

Unfair Comparison
Evan

Laney: We're long overdue for a Come 2 Jesus. Tell me where 2 meet u in next few mins or I'll hunt u down.

Her text doesn't surprise me at all. Today had been disastrous; I know Laney—too much and she's done. Really, so am I. Now is fine with me.

Evan: U at your dorm?
Laney: Yes.
Evan: I'll pick u up in 10. Be outside.
Laney: K.

She's already outside when I pull up. I don't get out and open her door, but rather just pop the lock and stare in front of me as she climbs in. Instantly, the whole cab smells like lavender and I run a hand down my face, hating myself for sniffing extra hard.

"Hey," she says so quietly I barely hear her.

"Hey."

Well thank God this isn't awkward.

"Where to?" I ask, still not looking anywhere near her direction.

"I don't really know. You hungry?"

"No, I just ate."

"I don't care where we go; surprise me."

"So…" I mutter as we pull out of the lot. "What'd you want to talk about?"

Smooth.

I don't get an answer right away and can see her lay her head against the window out of the corner of my eye. As I make the turn, she finds her voice.

"I miss you, Evan. I can't deal with you hating me. Remember how good we were as friends, before all the other stuff got in the way?"

I didn't think it was stuff and I didn't think it was in the way. I thought it was love and I thought it was great. But clearly, I'm not all that omnipotent.

"I miss you too, Laney," I reply quietly. "I've missed you since the day I left for college."

"Me too," she whispers.

This is the best spot I know, the middle of our campus. It has flowers and benches and no one will be here this time of evening, except maybe a random or two walking through. When we're parked, she gets out first, reaching behind my seat to pull out her blanket. Yes, it's still there. I amble out and follow her, failing miserably to not notice the way the breeze lifts her hair and carries its scent on it.

"Sit down," she says, patting the spot beside her on one of the benches farthest in the back, the blanket wrapped around her shoulders. The girl is always cold.

Knowing better, I sit down but leave optimal space between us.

She remains facing front but slides one of her little hands over to embrace mine. "Evan," she starts. "I'm sorry I hurt you. I didn't mean to; I tried to fight it."

"Fight what exactly? Explain it to me, Laney, 'cause I just can't swallow how I was so easily replaced."

She pulls her hand out of mine and I know it's because of how abrasively I spoke. I'm not sure if I'm relieved or sorry that she did. Touching her now confuses me, not feeling wrong, but no longer feeling completely right.

"You weren't replaced. You and Dane are totally different. One doesn't replace the other." She sighs, angling her body towards me and looking me in the eye. "Evan, when I got here, I missed you so much I physically hurt. I thought about leaving, quitting, and every other emotion across the gamut. Then I met Dane," her eyes flit away now and her voice drops, "and I tried to quit that, too. I swear I did, Evan, but it's not quittable. I'm so sorry."

"What do you want me to say?" My voice cracks and I hate myself for it. I stand and scoop up some rocks, tossing a few here and there, my back to her. "Did you ever love me? Did you ever mean it?"

"Yes," she answers and I know as sure as I know my own name, still facing away from her, that she's crying…and that there's more she didn't say.

"But?"

"Evan, don't—"

"Tell me!" It's the loudest I've ever spoken to her in my life.

"I love him differently."

I turn around now and move to her, squatting down in front of her. If I have to hear it, she's gonna woman up and say it to my face. "Differently how?" My fingers itch to wipe the tears streaming down her face, but I just can't do it. I give her a "go on" look; enough stalling already.

"I don't know…"

"Bullshit! You do know. Tell me. Does he treat you better than I did?"

She gasps and shakes her head rapidly. "God no! You've always treated me like a queen. Don't do that, Evan, you're comparing and that's not fair. You're Evan and Dane is Dane. He doesn't treat me *better*, no one could treat me *better* than you. He treats me differently. I don't love him *more*, I love him differently. There's no easy way to explain it, and I didn't ask to talk to you to explain it. I just wanted to tell you that I'm so, so sorry, I miss you, I love you dearly and I will always be waiting to be your friend again, when you're ready."

Best friends for years, a "couple" for a flash, separated and technically broken up, finally back together in the same place, barely speaking. A crazy ride. I miss the hell out of her and she really is my very best friend. Was, rather. Can I really live the rest of my life without her in it, in some capacity? Probably not, and that would suck, but tonight isn't the night I give in and become the bigger person.

I nod noncommittally, not knowing how to answer her. Do I hate her? Absolutely not, I could never *hate* Laney. And yes, one day I will be okay. One day, I'll be able to look at her and not wish like hell someone would just stab me so the pain would radiate somewhere other than my chest, my heart… But I'm just not ready to air those out loud yet. Instead, I stand, offering a hand and pulling her up.

"Come on."

Once she's standing, I release her hand and let her walk ahead of me to the truck, dead air between us. We're loaded and in gear before one of us dares to speak again.

"Have you heard any more from Kaitlyn?" I ask. This, this is conversation I can commit to right now. It's been bugging me, thinking that crazy bitch might mess with her again. Even if she marries Dane tomorrow, I'll never turn a blind eye to someone purposely hurting her.

"No." She runs a hand through her hair, her voice almost sad, but still holding a bit of relief. I'm sure she's still confused exactly how she feels about Kaitlyn and her deviousness. "She doesn't care about me, it was always about you. I'm sure you'll hear from her long before I ever do."

"I won't ever talk to her again."

"I know." She turns her sullen eyes from their gaze out the window back to me and smiles. "You're pretty great like that."

She's pretty great too. Despite it all, she's my favorite person. I doubt I'll be able to deny it much longer, but I don't air it right now, just let another curtain of quietness fall over us.

"I don't have a stalker," she blurts out.

I think she was going for nonchalance, but the shrill pitch in her voice and bend in her brows give her away. As if this wouldn't be big news to me, or her…it is. Very big news.

"What?" I ask, completely surprised. I had lots of theories about her stalker and it was on my list of questions to ask her when we were back on speaking terms, but her mom wasn't a suspect on my radar.

"It was my mom. Da— Um, I know where she is and it was her with all the notes and stuff."

Something inside me shifts right then, a flash in my mind of the part Laney and I always knew for sure; the friendship. This is a *huge* deal, one that I will support her through, no questions asked. I can't help but soften. I don't know how long she's known, but I do know the minute she found out, she needed and wanted to talk to me and I wasn't there.

But I am now, and when we're back in the parking lot of her dorm, that's what we do. We both turn in, facing each other, her with one leg bent on the seat and me with one elbow propped up against the back, and we dissect all that is my best friend's life-changing

58

development.

Chapter 9

Wonderment
Evan

"So you're gonna tag team with me for Valentine's Day, right?"

When Sawyer says "tag team," you ask for clarification. We could be talking about anything at this point.

"What do you mean?" I ask with baited breath. Please don't let him have entered us in coed mud wrestling or some other "great" idea.

"Well, you don't have a girlfriend, and because Jesus loves me, neither do I, so I figure we'll hit The K together. Pick up a few honeys for the night, whatever."

"Sawyer," I laugh, "are you asking me to be by your side on Valentine's Day?"

"Fuck you." He slugs me in the shoulder, which I'll feel tomorrow since he's the size of a Gladiator. "This ain't no bromance. We walk in together, but we're leaving with women. Valentine's Day, dude, every chick in there will reek of menthols and desperation, all alone on the big day."

Well when he makes it sound so appealing...

"I can't," I say, stifling a chuckle, "I promised Whitley I'd go watch her group sing. A frat hired them to sing at their V-Day party. It's a paying gig, so she's really excited."

"You're gonna leave me hangin' for *Whitley*?"

"Don't say it like that, man. Whitley's actually a very cool girl, and I like her. She's never done a damn thing to any of you. So what if she was a little clingy with Dane? She was trying to be a good friend. You need to lay off."

He's staring at me with a weird look on his face. I'm really hoping it's not the look he gets right before he kicks someone's ass for talking to him like that. I'm no slouch, but I'm also no Sawyer. I don't know how many times my dad has told me, "you go looking for a fight knowing you're gonna lose, your dumbass deserves to get kicked." I'm not looking to even have cross words with Sawyer. He's a cool guy, but the Whitley shit is false, undeserved and enough.

"Hmmm."

"Hmmm, what?"

"Nothing," he says with a shrug.

"Surely there'll be single girls at the party she's singing at, right? So why don't you come with me?"

He considers it for a minute then smiles. "Yeah, I can do that."

"Well, there ya go, problem solved. And will you please try not to be so mean to her?"

"I can do that too. Now that you mention it, Dane never really said anything bad about her. I guess it was mostly her getting on my nerves *for* him. I'll let up, I swear."

"Thanks."

"So what's going on with you two anyway?"

"Not what you're thinking," I laugh. "But she's cool. I like my time with her."

This year Valentine's falls on a weekend and the party is packed. I'm glad for the turnout; I know it will make Whitley's day. She's talked about nothing but tonight's performance for days and I'm actually kinda nervous for her. I still haven't heard her sing, but surely she's good if she's the captain, right?

"Sawyer!" An inebriated Kirby falls onto him.

"Hey, Kirb," he responds stiffly, giving me an exasperated look.

I have to look away to hide my grin at his fate. I've heard all about Sawyer's former interest in Kirby and her twin, Avery, and how it haunts him even now, obviously, as one of them is draped over him like a cheap shirt. Apparently Avery and Zach paired off, leaving "poor Sawyer" with one very clingy Kirby. And Sawyer does NOT do clingy. I'm pretty sure it's in the Welcome to Southern handbook, so how Kirby missed that lil' tidbit is beyond me.

"Are Zach and Avery here?" he asks, gently removing her hands from his chest, desperately looking around the room for someone to pawn her off on.

"Nooo," she slurs, "they're on a romantic date. Just like Tate and Bennett and Dane and Laney. Lucky bitches," she pouts.

And I've officially heard enough.

"I'm gonna go find Whitley and wish her luck!" I yell to Sawyer as I make my getaway, leaving him stranded and not giving him a chance to try and stop me.

I spot her in the main room, pointing and bossing all the other girls around. I slip up behind her and speak softly in her ear. "Nervous?"

"You came!" She turns around and gives me a vibrant smile.

"Of course I did." I tap the end of her nose. "I told you I would. Now where should I stand for the best view? Is this a dance around or stand in one spot thing?"

"Go stand right over there." She points to a spot in the front. "We're about to start."

They're really good, incredible even, and the sparkle in Whitley's eyes is mesmerizing. Her voice is smooth and sensual, much deeper when she sings than when she talks. And the things they do with these songs? It's the coolest thing. They're singing a bunch of love songs, of course, but the way they change up the rhythms and stuff makes it enjoyable even for a guy.

The crowd loves them, and I'm pretty sure I saw a couple of girls in the masses crying when they sang "The First Time Ever I Saw Your Face." It was moving. Whitley really commands a room when she sings, and if she had the same confidence in everyday life, she'd be unstoppable.

For the boys, they perform "Red Light Special." My eyes bug out and Whitley smirks, winking at my shocked expression. DAMNNNNN. These Larks got a lil' sexy in em'. One Lark in particular is a whole head of seduction above the rest. At least in my book.

Interesting indeed.

Sawyer comes up behind me and slaps me on the shoulder. "Well I'll be dipped," he booms. "Whitley's got a fucking hot side."

Did I just growl? *Nah, surely not.*

Speak of the siren, Whitley steps up front and center now to close the show. "Thank you all so much. We're your Southern Lovely Larks and we'd love your support at our performances this year." She pauses for the clapping and whistling from the boisterous onlookers, me joining right in with them. "This will be our last song of the night. I chose it because," she ducks her head shyly, looking up and at me through her lashes, "well, because I finally figured out what to sing."

It's only her voice, soft and slow, singing "Wonderwall," the old Oasis song. My eyes never leave hers, we're locked on one another's gaze every last note. And as sappy chick shit as this may sound, I feel a little crack in my heart seal back together. There's nothing else in this divot of time, no one else in the room but Whitley and I, her message ringing loud and true, straight to me.

When the last note eases from her mouth, the crowd explodes around us. It was a moving performance, words unable to describe what it meant to know that it was for me. I step to the stage and offer her my hand, which she takes with a timid smile. Her small hand in mine, I help her down and wrap her in a hug.

"You're really good Whitley, that was amazing," I exhale in her ear.

"I'm glad you liked it. I sang it for you."

"It was perfect." My cheek rubs against hers as I nod my head; I knew who she was singing to.

Who knows, maybe she's gonna be the one who saves me.

Chapter 10

Flag on the Play
Laney

It's been a long few weeks.

I took Dane to his cabin for his birthday weekend (with Valentine's Day mixed in) and it was heavenly. I'd ended up getting him a book of vouchers that I made myself, being broke and all, but he seemed to love it. So far he's cashed in the ones for "pick the movie tonight" and "sit back and watch my striptease."

On my wrist is my Valentine's present, a beautiful silver cuff bracelet inscribed with "Love: friendship set to music."

That man.

It was *his* birthday, but I'd been pampered and tempted to the point of never coming back. Dane always makes me feel special, loved, but oh the other things he gives me. One whole day, he forbade me from wearing any clothes, hid them from me in fact, and we fell asleep that night in front of the fireplace, sticky with sweat.

I kinda have trouble even walking when I think back on it.

We're closing in quick on the start of softball season and the team looks great! That also means, however, that my 11 pm curfew is in effect most nights, much to Dane Kendrick's dismay. Coach is pretty lenient though, so Dane will live.

The best news? Evan and I talk every Thursday in Algebra class, not exactly like the old days, but much better than not so long ago. He's made fast friends with Sawyer, and even Zach now, and I couldn't be happier about that. One great guy deserves another two!

Tate is all healed up and back at the dorm, which means my breath of sunshine roommate is back. I don't think I realized just how much I'd missed Bennett until she came back.

All in all, the spring is shaping up nicely! Things are finally starting to feel normal again.

The only untouched left is my mom. I wrote her a long letter, but it has yet to even be stamped. Or sealed, for that matter. I don't know the rules. Can she even receive letters? Not that it matters, since I'm nowhere near ready to mail it, but writing it was therapeutic, and dammit, I'm proud just for that! My dad says I should send it, as does Dane, but it's not up to them.

So, it's with a pretty happy heart that I grab my gear and head out to the flag football game. We've been practicing our butts off and Zach, it turns out, is quite the drill sergeant, but I'm pretty confident me and my girls are about to bring home the banner!

Dane's waiting in his car when I head out the door but quickly scrambles out to grab all the stuff in my hands and load it up for me, treating me to a soft kiss first. "Hey, baby, you ready to score?"

It's like the tenth time he's used that line, he thinks it's so cute. It kinda is.

Rolling my eyes at him, I get in the car, immediately turning on my "pump me up" music, "Let Me Clear My Throat" by DJ Kool. I mean really, is there any other choice? He's chuckling as he takes the driver's seat and acts like he's gonna turn the music off, barely getting his hand pulled back when I move to slap it. The sun roof is open, as the air is, as usual, unseasonably warm, and I feel good.

———————— ༄ ————————

The rules of the flag football tournament are simple: you win, you keep playing. No round robin, no break, no pool play—your win, your field, until someone knocks you off of it. This could be grueling for lesser women, but three wins in and the Lady Eagles softball team isn't tired. If anything, we're hungrier with each win; pumped, primed and ready for the next battle!

Game four is against none other than the Lovely Larks. I see Whitley prancing to the middle of the field for the coin toss, so I matter-of-factly tell my team I'll Captain this game and make my way there.

I don't even try to hide my bitchy smirk as I stare her down.

"Winners' call," the ref, an upperclassman named Xander, and I only know that because he's felt the need to tell me four times throughout the day, says as he sends the quarter in the air.

"Tails," I say, my eyes never leaving hers.

"Tails," Xander confirms.

Statistics say you should always pick heads and my dad has given me that sermon more times than I care to count, but I always go with tails. I knew that's how it'd land just as sure as I know I'm about to school Whitley's ass. I have no idea where her and Evan stand. We don't broach the subject in our blossoming Algebra conversations, but I know what hasn't changed—I still hate her.

✌

Dane

I realize that taking over my father's business ventures at a young age had put me out of touch with playing any team sports since high school, but I'm almost positive the word "flag" in the title of "flag football" carries some literal meaning.

Which is why I'm puzzled watching my girlfriend tackle Whitley for the third time. The first time she did it, Sawyer, sitting beside me, laughed his ass off, muttering something about a "spitfire." So I thought, no big deal, it did kinda look like she just lost her grip on the flags and fell, taking Whitley down with her.

The second time, even Sawyer toned down his snickering and agreed with me it looked a bit suspect, especially when the official blew a whistle in Laney's ear and moved the Larks up several yards. Zach had benched her after that one, but with a lot of her pacing and arm-flailing in his face, which was quite a show for us spectators, he put Laney back in.

But now, a third time? Laney is still laying on top of Whitley, showing no signs of getting up, until the ref runs across the field and throws the flag (not that Laney acknowledges flags), giving Whitley a moment of reprieve to once again brush herself off and adjust her clothing and hair. Evan and Zach both call time loudly and quickly march simultaneously onto the field, toward my girl.

"Go get her," Sawyer groans as he bumps me with his shoulder. "I'll bring the car around."

So, ever the level-headed one in our relationship, I jog down the bleacher stairs in my quest to contain one very fired up Laney Jo Walker. If she wasn't so damn adorable, with her cute little football pants and black streaks under her eyes, I'd be upset right now, because I know why she's attacking Whitley. She feels powerless over the situation with Evan, so she's going for the easy, direct hit on the girl who's been sniffing him.

Laney's been great about things lately, slowly having friendly words with Evan in their class together, and I can see her mood lightening each week. It's giving her some sanity, some resolve and closure, so she's my happy, witty sparring partner again, not talking about the woe is me that is Laney and Evan all the time. Because of all this, I'm gonna take it easy on her. I'm not gonna berate her for her real intentions and what that means. But I am gonna drag her off this field and take her home where she can really take her frustrations out…on me. *Yes, please.*

Keep a straight face. Keep a straight freaking face. I chant the mantra in my head as I open the gate and jog over to gather Laney "Killer" Walker. Whitley looks like a hot mess—steam is rolling off her, there are bits of the ground in her hair and her clothes are covered in grass stains. Evan is on one knee in front of her, using a water bottle to wash the dirt and blood off her legs. Laney, however, is glowing, bouncing on the balls of her feet from side to side, literally begging not to be thrown out.

"You bout ready to go, badass?" I ask her, reminding myself again about the whole straight face thing.

"Oh, thank God," Zach huffs out, finally relaxing his shoulders, which have been pulled up to his ears since the first quarter.

"I don't see what the problem is," Laney says in a sugar-coated voice, which I'm sure hurts her throat. "She's the quarterback. Of course I'm gonna gun for her. I can't help it if the grass is slippery. And," she holds up one finger democratically, like the point she's about make will really bring it home for her, "it's hard to stop forward momentum."

"Which is why football players are able to do it every day, Laney?" Zach is trying so hard not to get mad at her, visibly struggling, with clenched fists at his sides, to restrain himself. "Anyone who pummeled the QB *after* the ball left his hand, *repeatedly*, would never see the field. We won't even talk about the flags you're simply supposed to pull!"

I have to turn my head and feign a cough to camouflage my laughter at Zach's reply. She really thought she had him.

"But—" She starts to whine and actually stomps her foot, but I'm way ahead of her. Before the next word leaves her mouth, she's over my shoulder, flailing and slapping my butt and back. "Put me down, Dane! The game isn't over and my team needs me!"

"Ha! You cost your team thirty yards in penalties, hothead. I'm surprised they're not clapping right now, thanking me! Now stay still," I swat her ass hard and she yelps, "or I'm gonna drop you."

Sawyer's pulled the car right up to the exit, and as soon as we come into his line of vision, I see him throw his head back and laugh hysterically.

"Open the door!" I yell, which thankfully he hears, jumping out to open the back door for me since my hands are full.

"There she is, ladies and gentlemen, the MVP!" he teases her.

"Shut it, Sawyer!" she hisses.

"I'm gonna throw her in here, then you stand in front of her door while I walk around. When I'm in, I'll lock the doors, with yours open, then you hop in and gas it. Got it?" Sadly, I know Laney, and it is completely necessary to have a covert op planned out if we don't want to chase her down again.

"All over it," he salutes me.

"Hear that, baby? We got it all figured out, so no escape attempts."

She grumbles something under her breath as I toss her in the back and slam the door, running hastily around to the passenger seat.

"Okay, Sawyer, go!" I yell, turning to look at Laney pouting in the backseat with her arms crossed at her chest, a scowl on her face and her eyes purposely looking anywhere but at me.

Stone silence fills the car as we make our way down the street. At the first stoplight, Sawyer plugs his phone into the radio. I'm grateful for the upcoming distraction, but only for a split second, when I see him adjust the rearview mirror with a smirk. Whatever he has planned, he wants to be able to see Laney's reaction—God help us. Seriously, being with the two of them together is like a bad Heckle & Jeckle cartoon. But right at the moment the music starts, he's reeled me in. I slap my leg and bust out laughing. "Mama Said Knock You Out" blares through the speakers, and when I shift to look at how pissed Laney is, she's air-punching, singing every word with a beautiful smile.

Leave it to Sawyer.

Chapter 11

Balls of Steel
Evan

Laney: Don't say no right away. The Crew is hanging out tonight at Dane's house. I know it's weird, but Sawyer and Zach, your friends, will be there so we'd all love 2 have u. Please.

Where do I start? There are so many things wrong with this, I don't even know where to start. If somehow Laney took my civility in Algebra to mean "may I please hang out with you and your boyfriend at *his house?*", then I really need to work on my delivery.

"What's wrong?" Whitley sits across from me, peeling away most of the bread from her sandwich.

I eat lunch with her almost every day, and except for the whole picking her food apart thing, she's great company. My favorite thing about her? She's always humming. She doesn't even know she's doing it, she's completely lost to the music in her head. I find it especially precious that the song she chooses always fits the mood or scene too—it's like she's scoring the soundtrack of our day moment by moment. One day we were walking together after class and a downpour came out of nowhere, soaking us to the bone. Whitley hummed "Umbrella" by Rihanna the whole time we were running to the car. I didn't comment on it out loud, mostly because I was busy running for cover, dragging her behind me, but I laughed inwardly at how cute it was.

"Evan? Hello?"

"Sorry." I shake my head and grin at her. "What'd you say?"

"I asked what was wrong. That text you got obviously didn't make you happy. Your face looked like you smelt a skunk."

Whitley's a very down-to-earth girl once you look past the fancy, never-chipped manicure and the bread picking, and a straight shooter. I'm more than used to that and like it, so I go ahead and hand her my phone. We'll see what she thinks, since I'm having trouble wrapping my brain around it.

"Hmm." She chews her lip and takes her time looking up from the phone at me.

Now I may not be the most perceptive guy on the planet. I'll never be able to name the artist when you show me a painting, I don't see meaning in brushstrokes and colors, and chances are I'll never be able to distinguish between all the different shades of pink, which Whitley swears are legitimate, distinct colors, but I damn well know one thing when I see it—piss and vinegar. And the girl sitting across from me is giving me a look right now that's full of just that.

She smirks and licks her lips. "We should go."

Told ya. Piss and vinegar.

"Why in God's name would we do that, Whitley? I don't exactly care for Dane and he hates me. Laney hates you, you hate her. Last time you two were together, she tackled you *three* times! Flag football is *NOT* a contact sport! So let's all hang out together on purpose? Why do I even need to explain what a bad idea that is?"

"I don't hate anyone and neither do you. And I know Dane; he doesn't hate you at all. I think we should go and see what happens. If you want to leave, we'll leave. But I think we should at least try, show we can handle it." She runs one finger in a circle around the rim of her drink. "Unless you don't want to be seen with me…"

I laugh out loud, knowing exactly what she's doing. "Nice try, woman. You really think that's gonna work?"

She peers up at me, blue eyes shining and treats me to a slow grin. "Did it?"

"Yeah, it worked," I grin, but in defeat, "we'll go."

Game. Set. Match.

"Wonderful!" she squeals, jumping up and coming around to hug me. "I'm proud of you," she says, running her fingers in the front of my hair and pushing it back off my forehead where she lays a soft kiss, "playing all nice."

"Uh huh," I mutter, leaning over to pluck the orange flower that just caught my eye. "Here you go, troublemaker."

———————⌘———————

The last time I was at this door, I got handed my heart—mangled, battered, and broken. This time, I'm carrying a bottle of wine and dressed all fancy-like because the little pixie with her hand laced through the crook of my arm said to.

She put me in khaki pants and a light blue button down shirt, tucked in of course, and some brown churchy shoes that she'd run out and bought for me. The pants are stiff, the collar on this fucking shirt is seriously inhibiting my breathing, and the shoes look like I ought to be walking up to the front of the pulpit to get baptized. I look like a fucking idiot until I stand next to her in her gray pants and light pink sweater, perfect blond hair straight down her back and pulled from her face in a ribbon. When I stand next to her, I look like the other half of the picture she wants to paint.

I'm already in a mood and the outfit isn't helping, but when Dane opens the door, dressed how he wants to be and Laney is behind him, comfortable in yoga pants and a jersey, I feel like a whole different kind of ass.

"Hey, guys, thanks for coming. Come on in," Dane politely greets us and steps back for us to enter.

Laney moves with him, and because I know her like my own skin, I know exactly what she's doing. Right now she's deciding if she's pissed that I brought Whitley without asking her or if she wants to bust a gut laughing at my clothes.

The latter is the obvious right decision, but I'm relieved she restrains herself.

"Thanks for having us," Whitley responds cheerily, taking the wine from me. "We brought you this." This she says to Laney, handing her the bottle with a sincere smile.

My ugly mood tapers a notch because that was a classy move.

"Th-Thank you," Laney manages to say in a shocked stutter. "That was sweet, Whitley. Would you, um, like to come with me and we can try a glass?"

"Yes, please." She lifts her face to me and pats my chest. "I'll be right back, Evan. You want some?"

"Are you gonna be okay?" I lean over and ask quietly in her ear.

She gives me a subtle nod that she is, so I straighten and answer loudly, "how about a beer instead?"

"I'll grab that for you," Dane offers, so I part ways with Whitley and awkwardly follow him.

"Hey, there he is!" Sawyer jumps up from the couch as we enter the room and comes over to give me a one armed hug/back slap. "Glad you came, man! Dane never lets us come here, so you picked the right night. This place is killer."

"Don't get used to it," Dane grumbles, returning to us and handing me a beer.

Not that I'm thirsty, or have to drink beer all the time, but I'm gonna chug this bitch because it's exactly the relaxant I need right now.

The doorbell rings, so Dane excuses himself, leaving Sawyer and I alone. The second he's gone, Sawyer starts in.

"So you gotta be feeling awkward as fuck right about now, huh? I'm glad you came, though. Shows me you got some balls. I feel even better about being your friend now," he says with a laugh. "I see you remembered how to get here okay."

"Even if I hadn't," I down half of my bottle, wanting it to kick in before Dane gets back, "Whitley knows."

He coughs and bangs his chest. "Whitley? As in, Whitley came with you?"

"Yeah," I respond casually with a one shoulder shrug, "why?"

"Fucking balls of steel!" He laughs loudly, slapping me on the back again. "Damn, dude. This is gonna be hella fun! Where is she?"

"In the kitchen with Laney."

It's the only, and probably the last, time I have ever seen Sawyer Beckett speechless.

"Guys," Zach says as he walks in, Avery on his arm, "what's up?"

"Hey, Zach." I shake his hand and turn to Avery. "Avery, nice to see you."

She smiles. "Hi Evan, how are you liking it here?"

"Not bad, I—" I stop because the look on Zach's face distracts me. "What is it?" I ask.

"Look at Sawyer. What the hell is he doing?"

I had totally forgotten about him, but follow Zach's stare to find Sawyer poking his head around the doorway to the kitchen, holding up his phone. I creep up behind him, Zach and Avery following, and tap him on the shoulder. "What are you doing?"

"Shhh," he spits out, turning back around to face us, "I'm filming. Any minute now…"

"Any minute what?" I ask in a hushed voice.

"They'll go at it, and this time I'll have it recorded. I'm gonna sell this shit to Girls Gone Wild and be rich. You ever watch those chick fights? High dollar stuff, man."

I poke him in the forehead a few times, just making sure he's real, while Zach starts hee-hawing and Avery slaps him on the back of the head.

"Sawyer, you are unbelievable. Come on, Evan," she grabs my hand and pulls me toward the kitchen, "this is not a good idea. We need to get in there."

Zach's done laughing, his eyes wide in realization. "Oh shit, you're right, babe." He actually passes us in his hustle to the kitchen.

Sawyer's gonna be disappointed, cause all we walk in on is an amicable conversation. Whitley's perched on a barstool, giggling, along with Laney, Dane, and Tate, at something Bennett just said.

"There you are!" She turns and smiles at me when I walk up beside her. "Where you been?"

"Don't ask," I mumble, bracing my forearms against the back of her stool to stand behind her.

"Evan, have you met my brother?" Dane asks.

"Not officially," I say, offering my hand to Tate. "Evan Allen, nice to meet you. Good to see you doing so well."

"Nice to meet you too," he says as he shakes my hand. "Thanks for getting my girl there that night." He wraps his arm around Bennett's waist, pulling her in to kiss her temple.

"Not a problem." I give Laney's pretty redheaded roommate a smile.

"So," Laney clears her throat, her eyes darting to each person before landing on mine, "what's everyone feel like doing? And P.S., I'm so glad we did this. I've missed you all." She's staring at me, her eyes begging me to return the sentiment.

"Oh, I know!" Bennett pipes in exuberantly, which is how I think she says everything. "How about charades?"

Collective groans.

"Well fine, nobody else suggested anything." She sticks her

tongue out at the group.

"Strip poker?"

Any guesses who said that?

"No, Sawyer!" Dane, Zach and Tate all yell simultaneously.

"You are never seeing our women naked. Ever. Give it up," Tate finishes.

Whitley very shyly and almost not at all, raises her hand.

"Whitley?" Tate points and calls on her with an amused look.

"I saw a lot of people play this game at a party once, and they seemed to be having fun. It's where you line up and drink your beer then flip your cup over on the table."

"Flip cup! Hell yeah!" Sawyer whoops and bends across the bar, giving her a high-five. "Atta girl; good plan!"

"Well the DDs can't play," Bennett wisely points out, "because that game gets you very drunk."

Tate gives her a curious look.

"Before I met you, honey," she assures him with a kiss. "High school."

"So the first time I let you fools in my house, and you're gonna flip cups of beer?" Dane's not kidding, I don't think. His face is pinched, and surprisingly, I see his point.

"Bro, let's play downstairs in the rec room. It's tile."

Dane nods at Tate's suggestion. "Bennett's right, though, no drivers play or you sleep here. Your call," Dane reaffirms.

"You play, I'll watch and drive us home," I say quietly to Whitley.

She turns to me, a conspiring grin. "Or, we can both play and I'll have the car service pick us up."

Or that.

"Okay." I tap the end of her nose. "But why do you have a service? You have a car."

"I don't know, ask my father." She waves me off like a car service is a completely normal part of life.

"Let's pick teams then," Laney announces loudly. "Whitley, you captain one since it was your idea. I'll take the other."

"Oh, this is gonna be so fun!" Bennett skips to what I'm guessing is the direction of the rec room and most everyone follows.

"You need help carrying beer?" I ask Dane.

"There's a full fridge down there, but thanks. Come on." He

74

leads the way.

The doorbell rings again, just as we're passing the front door ironically enough, so I naturally stop while Dane goes to answer it.

"Hey, Kirb, come on in. You're late."

"Sorry, I had stuff to do. Where is everyone?" she asks, glancing around.

"Downstairs, we're just headed that way."

"Oh, hey, Evan," she sees me and gives a finger roll wave, her voice full of creepy seduction.

Never gonna happen. Not enough beer on the planet. This girl gives me the creeps, and with all I've seen and heard from Sawyer…no thank you.

"Um, hey."

"How are you?" She's now beside me, one hand on my arm.

"Good, you?" I can't believe I'm doing this, but I actually give Dane a "help me" look and he grins.

"Come on, Kirb, down here." He puts a hand on her shoulder and encourages her downstairs. I follow, extremely thankful that Sawyer is down there, just waiting like a sitting duck for Kirby's attention.

"Good, they're here. Oh, hey, Kirby. You pick first, Whitley." Laney directs the group from her side of a long table, Solo cups all in a row down each side.

Laney and competition is priceless—her voice rises in volume and pitch, she gets real bossy, and there's legit fire in her eyes. As long as she doesn't tackle anyone this time, I fully support the game. I still can't even believe we're here right now, all trying to act as civil and non-uncomfortable as possible. I know there's something to be said about being the "bigger person" and all, but there's also a saying about whacking a bee's nest with a big stick. I must be the only one who got *that* memo.

"Sawyer," I hear Whitley say, interrupting my internal philosophizing.

WTF? Did she really just not pick me first?

"Smart girl." Sawyer slaps her on the butt.

Well at least he's being nice to her, right?

"Dane," Laney picks, like she should. Even I, of all people, know that should be her first pick.

"Evan."

Now she picks me. Everybody knows second place is first loser and I'm not happy. Why is that? I don't know and don't care, I just am. I must be talking with my face right now because she's chewing that bottom lip as I walk over.

"Not too smart, girl." I slap her on the butt, earning a laugh from Sawyer.

"Uh oh, Whitley. He's all butt hurt you picked me first."

"Are you really?" she asks me, all doe-eyed and innocent.

I lean down and brush her hair back, my lips low over her ear. "You're in big trouble, little lady."

I have no idea where that line came from, but her gasp and shiver tell me I needn't worry that I actually scared her with my playful threat—perhaps there's more intrigue there than I anticipated.

Laney must have been watching our little show, because she immediately and loudly chooses Bennett, and so it goes, back and forth, until we're ready to play. It's Whitley, me, Sawyer, Avery and Kirby versus Laney, Dane, Zach, Tate and Bennett. Whitley offered her driver to all the others, so everyone's playing, which is pretty awesome. Their team has three guys to our two, but I'm not too worried about whether or not we win…until Sawyer opens that damn mouth of his again.

"All right, Gidget, what's the wager?" He's talking to Laney, who loves to bet, so this could get scary.

"I don't know. Whatcha thinkin', big boy?" She's just toying with danger now.

"God help us." Dane rolls his eyes and walks over to turn on some music. "Baby!" he calls out.

Ouch! Could've gone forever without hearing that…

"Please don't egg Sawyer on. No females are getting naked, I mean it."

All eyes in the room are on these two, waiting on them to decide the fates of their team. Whitley is humming the theme to Jeopardy softly beside me, and I grin hearing it.

"How about this? Losing team has to make the winning team dinner?" It's a great, safe, couth suggestion from Bennett.

"Borrriiinnnggg." Sawyer feigns a yawn.

"How about if the girls wear bikinis while they serve it?" Whitley adds and I flip my head to look at her, surprised at her boldness.

"Game on!" Sawyer yells.

"Y'all are fucking cheating! Look at Whitley's shirt!" Zach points a wobbly, drunken finger at her chest. "She's not drinking her beer, she's wearing it!"

I giggle as I look at Whitley. She really has doused herself in the hurry of the game, and in light pink, wet…well, she's wearing a black bra, let's put it that way. "Come on, Whitley. I'll get you another shirt." I hold out my hand and lead her upstairs.

We stumble a bit, laughing as we climb, until we reach Dane's room. I keep one drawer in his dresser filled with my stuff, and dig her out a navy t-shirt. "You can change right there in the bathroom."

"Thanks, Laney."

When she's in there, and I have the barrier of the shut door between us, I unload. "Hey, Whitley?" I say, a hair above a whisper, with my forehead braced against the door.

"Yeah?"

"I'm, uh, I'm really sorry I tackled you the other day. It was mean and I shouldn't have done it." *Three times.* No, it's not just the alcohol talking. I really have felt bad about it for a while.

"It's okay." Her answer is as soft and hesitant as my apology.

"You seem so different tonight, Whitley. More… Maybe I've misjudged you. I'm sorry for that too."

"Me too." The door opens and she peeks around it, her eyes watery. "I didn't like you either, and I've antagonized you every chance I got. I shouldn't have drawn attention to the tattoo. And I…" she bows her head and reaches up to wipe the now falling tears, "I'm sorry."

"Come on," I walk over and sit on Dane's bed and pat the spot beside me, "let's talk."

She timidly walks over and sits as far away from me as possible.

"Okay, so we've both been mean for no real reason. How about if we start over—clean slate?"

A deep, dramatic breath escapes her. "I would really, really like that, Laney."

"Same." I nod and smile. "Nice to meet you, I'm Laney Walker," I say, holding out my hand. "I'm a standoffish, mouthy smartass, but once I have your back, I have it 200%."

She shakes my hand and giggles. "Whitley Thompson, nice to

meet you too. I'm not athletic, but I can take a hit, or three, like nobody else. And I'm a really good friend if you let me be."

I'm not drunk enough to cry, hug her, or any other huge jump past a good start, but I do wear a big smile and my soul feels lighter. I start to stand up and head back when she lays a hand on my arm.

"Laney?" I turn back, giving her a curious look. "Can I ask you something?"

"Sure," I concede, sitting back down.

"Are you gonna hate me again if I really try to go after something with Evan? I mean, we just made up, and I really want to be your friend, but I also really like him."

It is at this exact moment that I truly understand how Evan has felt. Another girl will get to love Evan, with her heart, her soul…her body. She'll get his visits to her window, his sweet "Good Morning" texts, and his movie snugglethons. Reality hits like a brick in the face, but only for a moment. And in perhaps the surest sign I'll ever have of exactly how my love for Dane consumes me and how deep my friendship with Evan goes, the little cloud that passed over my mind and heart now disappears and I realize all the bullshit I've been feeding myself to make me feel better is true. I really do only want Evan to be happy, *and* whoever he chooses to do that better make damn sure she deserves him.

I can't lie to myself, Whitley is a beautiful girl. She's obviously very forgiving and shy with some hidden funky, yet still proper, refined, articulate…all the things I'm not. Evan seems very comfortable with her, and if this girl thinks she's the one for him, who am I to stop her? I'll tell you who I am—I'm the lucky girl who has Dane Kendrick, and the non-hypocritical good friend who's about to put her money where her mouth is! That's me.

"Not only am I not gonna hate you," I square my shoulders and raise my chin, "I'm gonna help you. But Whitley, I'm warning you. It's kinda like, 'I can say whatever I want about my family, but you better not say a word?' I may have hurt him, but if you do, I'll come for you with a vengeance. Got it?"

"Y-Yes," she visibly shivers, "got it."

"Great! Now that we've got that settled, let me give you some pointers on Evan. Starting with that ridiculous outfit you put him in."

She falls against the bed, giggling. "He's gonna kill me! I thought it was going to be like a dinner party."

"Whitley, anything I invite you to will *never* be a stuffy dinner party. If I'm there, he's safe to wear his ball cap, got that too?"

"Got it." She nods happily, biting back another snicker. "I bet he's uncomfortable. I should call our driver and end his misery."

"Yeah, it's getting late," I agree, moving to the door. "Come on, let's go wrap it up."

Whitley follows me back down to the game, talking on her phone as we go. I'm trying not to eavesdrop, but I can't help hear the panic in her voice. "Cancelled, what do you mean cancelled? Check again, please, we've used your company for years."

Evan's eyes catch mine as we enter the room, and they tell me he's been panicking every second I was alone with Whitley.

"Come here," I mouth, beckoning him with a back tilt of my head, to which he rushes over. "Something's wrong, she's freaking out," I tell him under my breath.

He lays a hand on her shoulder. "Whit, what's wrong?" His voice is all things Evan, tender and concerned.

"Well, can I just pay you for this one time when you get here?" she begs into the phone. "All right, thank you anyway," her voice quivers back after a slight pause. She hangs up, turning her confused and pained face to Evan and I. "That was the car service company. They say our service is cancelled. How weird is that?"

"Not that weird, Whit," Evan scoffs with an easy smile, "lots of people don't have car services. Come on, we only played two rounds, and there was wasn't much in my cup. I'll drive us home in an hour or so, no biggie."

"Y'all just stay here," I offer, "there's more than enough room. Seriously," I plead with both my voice and eyes.

"I'm okay with that plan if you are." Whitley turns to him and I back away, feeling like an intruder in their personal, private conversation.

I see him nod his head and pull her by the hand back to the game.

Guess they're staying.

Chapter 12

Reubens and Fries
Evan

"So you're sure you don't want to come? Last chance…" I try to tempt Zach and Avery one more time to join us for Spring Break.

"You don't know how bad we wish we could, right, babe?" Zach frowns and gives Avery's ponytail a tug.

"Yes," she answers in a whiny drawl, "but the minute Coach announced Mrs. Coach got put on bedrest and we actually got a Spring Break, we made plans with Kirby. I can't trust her to go on Spring Break alone; God only knows what would happen to her. You guys have fun, though. And just think," she smiles now, her voice more cheery, "when you get back, you'll be Zach's roommate!"

I can't even begin to tell you how happy that makes me. My roommate is a douche, and the few times I've actually been in the room at the same time as him were too many. Did I mention he's a "naturalist"? Whatever the fuck that actually means I'm not sure, but I define it as "dude who doesn't wear deodorant and whatever he eats makes his ass smell like…well, ass." Zach's roommate, apparently also a douche, had gotten himself suspended, and voila! After a little sweet talking from Whitley to Student Housing and I'm coming back from Spring Break as Zach's new roomie!

"Yeah, that'll be great. Okay then, if you're sure you can't—"

"Hold up!" Sawyer's yell interrupts me as he comes jogging towards us. "I'm in," he announces, throwing his bag in the back of my truck.

"How'd you get off work?"

He'd originally declined the invitation because of his shifts at The K, so I was curious how he pulled it off.

"Dane's in Hawaii, meaning Tate's in charge. And since he's my man, he made some new guy pick up my shifts! Sucka! So here I am! Now drive me to drunken co-ed paradise!"

I just shake my head and chuckle at him.

"Why are you shaking your head? Whitley said there was hot ass and parties everywhere, *right*?"

"Yes, Sawyer."

"Good, 'cause I'm not down to be a third wheel unless I'm getting laid."

"It's not like that. No third wheel to it."

"Uh huh, whatever."

Sometimes he exhausts me. "Just get in the truck."

We wave goodbye to Zach and Avery, climb in my truck, and head to Whitley's to pick her up. She's invited us to stay at her family's beach house on Hilton Head, about an hour and a half from school, for the whole week and damn if I'm not excited. Yes, Laney's in *Hawaii* with Dane. I did a shot of the hard stuff the first time I heard. I slammed the door the second time it was mentioned. But now…now all I want to do is get to MY Spring Break, lay back in the sun, take in the salty smell of the ocean and relax.

Whitley's not ready when we get there—shocker. She's ticking things off on her fingers and talking to herself. I sure as hell can't understand the muffled feline rumblings, so I hope her list has nothing to do with me.

"Whit? What can I help you with?" I ask for the third time, and when she still doesn't stop buzzing around to answer me, I dust her face with the flower I'd snagged her on the way in, finally getting her attention. "Chill out, woman. It's all gonna be fine. Anything we forget, we obviously don't really need or we can run to the store to pick up. Now hand me and Sawyer the stuff to load and let's go."

"Okay, okay, you're right. Get the pile by the door and I'll grab the stuff in my room, then I think we're ready. And thank you for the flower." She sniffs it again. "This is the first yellow one."

"She's a busy lil thing, ain't she?" Sawyer shakes his head with a smirk when she leaves. "She's gonna spin herself in the ground."

"Let's not let her. We gotta make sure she has fun."

"Oh, I think that's your department, stud."

I roll my eyes at him and throw him some bags. "Shut up and help me load this stuff."

Ten minutes later, all the gear is packed and Whitley's in the truck after she'd jumped out once to double-check that she locked her door. I let out a chuckle when I think of my current situation. Could you pack three more different people into the cab of a truck and send them on vacation together? No, no, you couldn't, and yet, I'm as at peace as I remember being in quite a while.

My contentment turns into full-blown happiness when I pick it up over the sound of the wind rushing in through my open window. Whitley's humming "On the Road Again," the old Willie Nelson song. And before I know I did it, I lean over and kiss the top of her head. She's just so cute sometimes, I can't help it. I recover quickly and stare out in front of me, nothing more fascinating now than the two yellow lines on the road. But I see her, out of the corner of my eye, blush and smile. And about that blush...now I wanna do it again.

Her hair was soft and smelt like clean and strawberries, clean strawberries. And I noticed because...

"How long 'til we're there?" Sawyer asks.

"About thirty more minutes or so," Whitley answers him sweetly. "I'm so glad you came, Sawyer." She pats his leg companionably. "I brought the stuff to make your favorite—Reubens and fries. Maybe I'll make it tonight."

Sawyer's mouth drops open and his lip curls, his brows completely vanishing into his hairline. I watch him out of one eye, hating that I have to keep the other on the road and may miss what comes next. "How'd you know that was my favorite?" he asks in a shocked, but tender, voice.

"You said it one time. You and I were sitting around with Dane and Tate, eating pizza one night, and you said, 'I'm so sick of pizza all the time. I'd kiss you boys square on the ass for a Reuben and some homemade fries.'"

I'm about to wreck I'm laughing so hard, because when she quoted him in that story, she did it in her best deep Sawyer voice. Classic.

And big ol' Sawyer, crude, rude and socially unacceptable, takes a minute to respond. When he does, it's in a voice I've never heard him use, and it's so quiet, I hardly hear it now. "I remember that, and you remembering it... Well," hear his gulp vibrates off the inside of the cab, "ah, come 'ere, you sweet lil' thing." He pulls her in and bear hugs her, kissing the top of her head.

Hey! That's my move.

"Sound good?" she asks him, pulling subtly away from him and shifting back to me, a little closer this time it seems.

"Hell yeah it does! You hear that, Evan? Whitley's gonna make us a feast tonight!"

Of course I heard it, I'm sitting two feet from you and not paying near enough attention to the road because I'm watching your interactions like a hawk.

"Yeah," I laugh, "I heard." I dip my head to her and take one last, quick sniff of her hair. "I'll peel the potatoes for ya," I whisper.

———— ❧ ————

The three of us are laughing when we pull up to the beach house, Whitley having treated us to a game of Name That Tune the rest of the ride. She may be better at it than anyone else I know, and yes I mean Laney. And Sawyer? Well he doesn't know the right words to a single song, no matter the year, the genre...the tune even, which is why we're laughing so hard. Seriously? Who doesn't know the words to "Rockstar" by Nickelback? Sawyer Beckett, that's who. In Sawyer's world, they play dirty Pictionary and drive filthy cars.

This place is amazing—at least three stories with white pillars and a balcony at the highest window. You can see the ocean right behind it from the driveway and the tropical plants and trees planted around the front certainly give it the "beach" look. It's magnificent, marred only by the sign in the yard. I look to Whitley, whose face is pale. Her eyes are filled with pain, telling me she, too, has spotted it.

Sawyer gets out and comes up behind us, first following Whitley's stare to the glaring red word, "Foreclosure," then looking over her head to me with "shit, what do we do?" eyes.

"Whitley, it's okay. We can go somewhere else." I put my arm around her shoulder and pull her to me. I have no idea where else we can go, but it's all I can come up with, since asking if she's sure we're at the right house seems as dumb as it was the minute it crossed my mind.

I lean my head down to look at her when she remains silent and see the tears trickling down her cheeks. "Hey, shh..." I murmur, tucking her head into my chest as she wraps her arms around my waist. "Sawyer, we'll be back in a bit. We're gonna take a walk."

He just nods and I take Whitley's hand, leading her around the side of the house, down to the beach. There's a low rock wall that starts off the sides of the patio, leading down to the water, creating a barrier between their beach backyard and the neighbor's, which appears to be about a mile away. Pretentious? Probably, but handy now as I guide her to sit down on it and take a seat beside her, rubbing her back.

We sit in silence for a long while just listening to the waves crashing on the shore. I give her time, walking down a few steps to break off a stalk of the eye-catching orange and purple plant I spotted as we sat and hand it to her with a sympathetic smile. Her tears finally start slowing, and as I look at her in concern, I force my lip not to curl at my thoughts—she even cries with class and elegance. No snorting, no snot sucking…just beautiful agony.

"I'm sorry you drove all this way for nothing. I didn't know," she says sweetly, her shoulders shaking with a sarcastic chortle. "They don't tell me the important stuff, you know. Just how to eat, walk, dress and keep up the *act* that we're perfect. The fact that they're obviously in financial trouble and losing my favorite place in the whole world? Well, that slipped their mind."

"It's not your fault, Whit, don't even apologize. I'm just sorry this happened to you. Do you wanna call your parents or something?"

"No," she shakes her head adamantly, "they'd be angry I came without telling them and found out. They'll tell me when they want me to know, I guess."

"I can tell you really love this place." I put my arm around her shoulder. "I can see why; it's great."

Well shit, that probably wasn't smart. No sense rubbing it in her face. I see now why my dad is so quiet and rarely in trouble with my mother. Noted.

"We'd come here every summer for two whole weeks. Most of the time with Dane and his parents, and in the beginning, when we were real young, Tate, too. Our dads wouldn't work while we were here, and no meetings meant they'd play in the water with us all day. My mom would always make red, white, and blue cake for the fourth and all the boys would set off fireworks for hours." She sighs deeply and turns her head into my shirt, her voice muffled and pained. "It was the only time of year when nothing came before being a family. I was allowed to be a little kid and play outside with other kids. My mother never noticed or yelled if I got dirty." She sighs. "This place represents everything I loved about my childhood."

I sneak a finger under her chin and lift her face, searching her eyes, as blue as the ocean beside us, for acceptance. "Whitley, I—"

"Y'all get lost?" Sawyer's voice startles us both and I drop my hand, standing quickly.

"Nah, we were just heading back."

"Yeah, whatever," he sniggers. "So, Whitley, I took the dark blue room. That cool?"

Whitley has now walked over to us and stands beside me, every bit as dumbfounded as I am. It's like one half of my brain knows exactly what he's saying, and why, but the other half is screaming "oh surely not!" She's thinking the same thing, one hand raised to her mouth, her eyes wide.

"So, my key still worked?" Her big grin is forced, as though begging him to answer correctly. She and I both know the dreaded response coming, though.

"Fuck no," he replies with a shrug, "guess they already changed the locks. No worries, though, the side door to the garage had a window and the interior door was flimsy as shit. Presto! Minimal damage, maximum entrance."

My head drops on its own, shaking, and I reach up to rub my eyes. I hear Whitley's sharp intake of breath right before she speaks.

"Sawyer...are you telling me you broke into my parents' foreclosed beach house?" She laughs, or chokes, it could go either way. "That's not what you're saying, is it?"

"Relax, sugar, no one will know. I yanked the sign out of the yard too."

Oh, well then. Problem solved! Why didn't I think of that? Cause everybody knows if you yank up the sign that cancels out the actual B&E.

I raise my head and block Whitley's chest with my extended arm, just in case she actually tries to give him the eye-clawing he's earned, and attempt to be the voice of reason. "Sawyer, you can't just break in, that's illegal, dude. The cops are probably on their way. We could go to jail!"

"Nobody's gonna go to jail, pussbag. Listen, I hid the sign. *If,* and it's a big if, the cops come, we'll say we didn't know and agree to leave. Whitley's parents didn't tell her, which they'd vouch for, so she thought it was her house and forgot her key. I mean, it's still filled with all her furniture and pictures of her, what would have tipped us off?" He throws up a hand, cutting me off open-mouthed. "Especially since there *was. NO. SIGN.*"

"Sounds good to me!" Whitley agrees cheerfully, reaching up to pat Sawyer on the cheek. "You boys run and get ice; I need to unpack and start Sawyer's special dinner." She starts walking to the house, a bounce in her step and not a care in the world.

I jog to catch up with her, reaching out to snag her elbow. "Whitley, this isn't a good idea. You're upset and not thinking clearly, but you know I'm right. We can't stay here."

"We *can* stay," she says forcefully, jerking around to face me, "and we will. This is my place and I'm not leaving. Now run to the store and I'll make us a nice dinner."

Oh great, she's shock-induced delusional, if that's such a thing. If not, she's whatever the right name for it is, because under normal circumstances, I'd like to think she'd see my reason versus Sawyer's, well, Sawyerisms. I should jump ship and save myself, but I just can't; Whitley has been my life preserver and she needs me. So I go to the store, hoping she's rational when I get back.

Her back is to us, "Down on Me" playing loudly as she swirls her hips, dropping slowly all the way down to the floor and gyrating back up again in the sexiest move I have ever seen. My right hand is up in a flash, subconsciously even, covering Sawyer's eyes. I, however, enjoy the show, no regrets...and no blinking. I have to use my left hand to quickly adjust, not wanting her to turn around and see evidence of the fact that I am a guy, shamelessly watching her little ass wiggle and pop in rhythm with the beating in my chest.

"Honey, we're home!" Sawyer spouts off, interrupting, so I drop my hand from his eyes, using it to pop him in the forehead.

She spins around with a squeal, hand clutching her chest. "Oh my God, you scared me!" She walks over and turns down the music. "No sneaking up on me while we're squatting, Sawyer. My nerves can't take it."

"Sorry," he snorts, "I forgot about that. So, what were you doing?"

"Nothing," her face blazes pink instantly, "just cooking."

I cock an eyebrow at her. "You need your own cooking show then, because people would *definitely* watch."

"Like you did?" Sawyer cocks off, slapping my chest.

"Anyway," I clear my throat, avoiding Whitley's eyes, and her now answering raised eyebrow, "you need help with anything, Whit? Want me to peel or chop or—"

"Help choreograph?" Sawyer suggests.

"Fuck off," I mumble, flipping a barstool around and sitting, ducking my head in embarrassment. I'm not shy about looking, anybody whose eyes weren't covered for them would have, but I don't think we need to keep announcing it.

"Here." Whitley's eyes are smiling, her voice patronizing as she hands me a short glass of amber liquid and ice. "Have a drink and relax."

"So, Whit, what gives? I thought your family was loaded?" Sawyer asks her with the subtlety of a head-on collision.

"I thought so too. I really have no idea what's going on and can't just ask them. How do you even bring that up?" She's cooking, busy as she holds the conversation, but I can see the signs…a slump to her shoulders that is *never* there, a crease between her eyes, and a borderline fake smile.

They continue to talk back and forth, but I sit in silent observation, no longer hearing the distinct words. The sun outside is starting to set, sending a ray of purple light in and casting a sultry glow around Whitley. Every time she turns, this way and that, preparing everything like a little hummingbird, her shiny blonde tendrils swish along her shoulders. When she measures something out, she purses her lips, transforming them into a rosebud.

For the briefest of seconds earlier, when I'd tipped her chin and she looked up at me with hopeful, vulnerable eyes, like I could fix anything for her, I'd thought about kissing her. Not so long ago, I'd have laughed if you told me I'd ever have the desire to kiss anyone other than Laney, but sure enough, the want was there, however short-lived.

Watching her now, I think of it again. I hate the way she wants me to dress. She'll never be able to play a sport. Her uppity family will probably dismiss me as an ignorant hick. She picks at her food and would mostly likely faint if I left the toilet seat up. But…the last rays of the day show her in her true light; radiant and thoughtful, taking care of others, rolling with the punches, making the best of a situation.

"Evan?"

"Huh?" Her voice brings me back to the present.

"Do you want another drink?" She's standing by me, having set my plate in front of me.

"No, water's fine," I mumble. That must be it—the drink she made me. That's why I'm having such crazy thoughts. One thing is niggling at me though; am I just finding myself drawn to Whitley because she's there? A convenient attraction? I mean, what are the odds that the first post-breakup girl you meet is captivating, different and alluring in a way that's all her? I have to be careful. I don't want to mistake rebound for interest and end up hurting Whitley or myself. I absolutely, positively cannot do that again.

I file all the confusion in the back of my mind and dig in; the meal she made is delicious and we all eat in semi-comfortable silence. And by that I mean they both seem fine and I'm squirming inside.

Just when I think I've got the questions riddling my head beaten, she fires the kill shot.

"Who wants dessert?"

"Is that a real question?" Sawyer pats his belly.

Back to the table she strides, bearing two heaping plates of…strawberry shortcake. My favorite.

She winks when she sets mine in front of me. "You didn't think I would make his favorite and not yours, did you?"

How did she know? I can't remember ever mentioning it. But with the first bite, I cease to care about the how.

Chapter 13

Drunken Words, Sober Thoughts
Evan

Saturday is a gorgeous day, perfect Spring Break weather. The water has a little nip to it, but it's warm and very refreshing. It's the first time I've ever been to the ocean, and the endlessness is quite a sight. And the atmosphere? Well, it's one big party. I'm trying to take it easy with the drinking, really wanting to actually remember the experience, whereas Sawyer found a vendor stand that serves your drink in a white bucket with a handle. No really, they stick a straw in a mini sand pail and turn you loose on society. This is Spring Break, after all…

Whitley hasn't made it down yet, and I should probably go back up to the house and check on her, but two things are stopping me. One, I don't think leaving Sawyer alone down here is a good idea and there's no way I'm getting him to go with me. Two, I think a little time away from her might be a good thing. Sending Whitley mixed signals isn't respectful, and I do try to be at least that. Using her as a rebound crush is out of the question, though wanting her a little more every time I'm around her is fucking with my head.

I sense the shadow over me, along with a shower of sand pellets he's kicked up, before I actually open my eyes.

"Hey man," he kicks me, "look alive. I want you to meet some people."

I shield my eyes from the sun and look at Sawyer, sitting up immediately. He's standing there, nursing his sippy bucket, with three very hot, very bikini-clad, women.

"Hi." I stand, running my hands down my shorts before offering it to one of them. "Evan."

"Amber," she answers giddily, raking her eyes up and down my body. I force my own to stay on her face, despite the fact that I have already stealthily assessed her stats—bout 5'4", dark tan, black short hair and those definitely aren't the boobs she was born with.

The little blonde next to her moves in, vying for my attention. "I'm Nikki." She's a little bitty one, maybe 5'1", tops, all natural except for the sparkly belly button ring winking at me. Her eyes are a shocking green, her smile big, and she has a dimple. A really cute dimple, actually, in her left cheek right above her lip.

"Nice to meet you. Evan," I manage despite my gawking.

"And this beauty," Sawyer slides his arm around her bare waist, his finger sliding along the fabric of her barely-there bottoms, "is Sasha."

"Hey, Sasha." I grin; clearly Sawyer has made his selection with the exotic brunette.

"Sawyer said you guys would come to our party tonight," Nikki's flirty voice trickles, her tongue teasing the corner of her mouth.

"We can do that," I answer with a wink, earning her giggle.

Wink=100% success rate.

Whitley finally decides to appear while we're still flirting with the trio. One would think, while on Spring Break, you'd see so many girls in bikinis that at some point they all start to look the same. There's only so many different colors of hair, most girls fall in a certain height range, and boobs…well, okay, those vary, but still. And Nikki, well Nikki definitely adds to her ambience with the belly button ring and dimple, but my thoughts are scarily close to the script of a chick flick when I soak in the sight of Whitley.

Her bikini isn't "look at me" string and scraps, it's modest, for a bikini anyway. Her breasts aren't fake or about to fall out, but natural, and, well, *big* for the rest of her dainty little body, and hidden just enough to make me wonder. And *I* know there's a little red balloon tattoo just underneath the pink fabric, tucked away nicely where that pale, lovely leg meets that perfect hip.

Too much sun. Gotta be it.

"Whitley?!" Amber yelps in a voice that surely only dogs were meant to hear. "Whitley, it *is* you!"

She runs over and throws her arms around Whitley in an exuberant hug, which Whitley politely, but much more calmly, returns.

"Hi, Amber," she pulls back, not even close to usually friendly Whitley, "how are you?"

"Soooo good! I can't believe you're here. Wait, where are you staying? I heard—"

"So, Whitley, you know Amber?" I hastily interrupt, compensating with the most obviously already established question I can think of for Amber's lack of tact. I'm sure she was about to announce to the beach about the foreclosure. "They invited us to a party tonight."

"Yeah," Nikki slides over and runs a hand up my arm, but speaks to Whitley, "you guys should all totally come. It's gonna be so much fun."

"Sounds good." Whitley gives her a smile that's as fake as the day is long, but perhaps only I noticed.

"Oh, Whitley!" Amber gasps. "Tyler will be there! You know he always had a thing for you."

Whitley's eyes dart to where Nikki's hand is still latched to my arm, then back to Amber with a friendly smile. "I'd love to see Tyler. We'll be there. Right?"

She looks up at me now when she asks. Now usually this is where a guy screws up and just says "right" or "sure," but I'm not most guys. Growing up with a sassy female as your best friend, you learn a lot. Therefore, I know that while Whitley and I are nothing more than friends, she's still jealous right now.

Female jealousy is a very tricky, very volatile matter, and one that should *never* be taken lightly. Though this is where I'm still a little fuzzy. Is she jealous because she likes me or she just doesn't like to be challenged by another female? Does she feels some kind of proprietorship because I came here with her or is she insecure over whether I think Nikki is prettier? The exact origin of the jealousy will probably forever remain a mystery, maybe even to Whitley herself, but that's not the point. Whitley's waiting for the typical male reaction here, to reassure her I am just that; another typical guy.

Brace yourself, Whitley, I'm all over this one.

I remove Nikki's hand from my arm and step to Whitley,

ducking my head to look in her eyes. "It's up to you, Whit. Whatever you want to do is fine by me."

Her pinking cheeks and sweet, small grin tell me I got it right.

"K," she nods, "we may see you there. We'll see," she says to Nikki cheekily. "I gotta feed my boys right now, though." She locks my hand in hers and starts toward the house. "Come on, Sawyer!"

Add public indecency to Sawyer's Spring Break rap sheet, because he and Sasha are laying on the beach making out like they have no audience…or modesty. It's a bit much, even for Sawyer.

"Sawyer, let's go, lunch!" I bark, embarrassed for him.

He makes no move to indicate he's heard me, and Whitley just snickers.

"Come on, just leave him," she says.

Fine by me.

"You wanna go get something for lunch?" I ask as we walk back up to the house. "I don't want you waiting on us the whole week."

"It's no bother, Evan, really. It's nice to have somebody, or two, to take care of."

I open the door for her. "Where'd you learn to cook?"

"My nanny, Mary. She was an amazing cook and always let me help. I had to write down all the recipes as I watched, though; she didn't use them," she recalls wistfully.

"So you sing, you cook," I pull up a stool, "what else do you do?"

"I don't know, this and that."

"Like?" I urge her, taking a bite of the sandwich she just put in front of me.

"I like to read. I like to mess around with crafts, scrapbooks, I don't know. Now that I say it out loud, I kinda sound like a grandma." She hangs her head. "God, I'm boring."

I bust out laughing, quickly reigning it in when she drops her forehead into her hand and groans. "You don't sound like a grandma. Well, okay, maybe a lot of grandmas cook and scrapbook, but my grandma's one of the best women I know. I'm not really that exciting either, Whitley."

Few people ever shock me, but Whitley continually throws me for a loop. On the outside, Paris Hilton. On the inside, Martha Stewart. Which is the real her? Or can those two really cohabitate in one body?

"And I'm pretty sure my grandma never got a tattoo, while high, or played Flip Cup, or performed "Red Light Special" for a frat house." I nudge her, now sitting beside me. "I'd say you're safe from grandma territory."

"I forgot all that," she admits, perking up. "You're right. I *am* cool as hell!"

"Right," I chuckle at her, "now speaking of grandparents…I'm gonna go take a nap." I yawn and stand, heading to my room. "What are you gonna do?"

"Maybe I'll head back down to the beach, check on Sawyer."

Do I offer to stay up and do something? Do I lay on the couch and ask her to—no, probably shouldn't do that.

"Take your nap, Evan," she laughs, her face hinting she may have guessed what I was just contemplating. "I'll be fine."

"Oh, ok," I stammer. "I'll see ya later."

I lay awake for a while, thinking things over and making a few decisions. Whitley is a beautiful girl, a wonderful friend, talented and giving, and she deserves a guy who's sure he wants *her* for *her*, with no inklings of doubt that his interest may be circumstantial; something more than I can give her.

Sawyer is a lot of fun, and his mojo seems to work for him, but it's a little much for me. So, it's time. Time for Evan to get back to being Evan. Not Laney's Evan, not miserable Evan, not wild and crazy Evan…just Evan. I've got some soul searching to do, all by myself. I'm gonna do what I've never done before—I'm gonna date.

───────── ❧ ─────────

I wake up a few hours later to a quiet, empty house. Once I've taken a shower and gotten dressed, Whitley and Sawyer still aren't back. I walk down to the water, their last known whereabouts, but they're not there, either. I spot a fire down the shoreline and I can hear faint music, so I take my chances that they went ahead to the party and head that way.

It takes me a bit to find either of them amongst the bodies, loud music and shroud of night, but just when I'm about to give up and turn back, Sawyer comes out onto the deck and yells my name. I meet him up there and can smell the liquor oozing out of his pores, noticing the girl curled around him isn't Sasha from this morning. How long had I napped exactly?

"Hey, where's Whitley?" I ask him.

"In there somewhere." He jerks his thumb towards the house. "Where you been?"

"Nowhere; I gotta go find Whitley," I brush him off, kinda pissed he's slammed and not watching Whitley better at a party full of drunken strangers.

She's not anywhere; I search the whole fucking house to no avail. I'm starting to get worried when Nikki spots me, waving her arms from across the room, dancing her way through the crowd to get to me.

"Hey, sexy," she growls in my ear, rubbing both hands up my chest.

"Hey." I want to find Whitley, just make sure she's okay. "Have you seen the blonde girl we're staying with, Whitley?"

"Why?" She scowls.

Gotta play this right, I need information. *Freaking girls.*

"Don't worry, gorgeous, she's just a friend. What kind of man would I be if I didn't watch over her? Hmm? Now will you help me find her?" I run a finger down her jawline and wink.

"She's out front with Tyler," she tells me, her smile showing she's happy at the thought of pleasing me; not at all about willingly helping another female at a party.

"You wait right here, and I'll go check on her and be right back, okay?"

She nods eagerly and I almost feel like I should pat her head like a puppy. I should probably tell her there's no chance in hell I'm coming back. Surely I'm not the only man who still thinks scruples are attractive?

Whitley's laughter fills the air before I can make her out in the dark, but I instantly breathe easier hearing that she's okay, laughing even, and I follow the sound. She's still in her bikini top but with short gray shorts covering the bottom, her hair down and wild. She's sitting on a bench in the yard beside some guy dressed pretty much in the same outfit she put me in the night at Dane's. Oh shit—what a goon I'd been in the same outfit; worse than I thought. He stands as I walk up to them, his face and stance defensive. *Please.* Don't scuff your loafers or wrinkle your slacks, bro.

"Whitley, I've been looking everywhere for you," I say, not even acknowledging Toolbag standing there.

"Evan!" She jumps up and falls forward, but I reach out and

catch her.

"Easy, easy." I hold her up, shooting the dude a menacing look. "You get her this drunk?"

"She's a big girl, she got herself drunk. Who the fuck are you?"

"This is Evan. He's my new friend. In love with Laney, who doesn't hate me anymore. She's sporty," Whitley rattles off drunkenly.

"What she said, sorta," I agree. "Who are you? And why do you have her out here all alone, drunk, in the dark?" If I didn't have to hold up Whitley right now, I'd gladly wrinkle that shirt of his.

"That's Tyler," Whitley supplies. "Family friend forever. He had the coolest fort in his backyard; I used to sneak over. He wants in my panties, and my dad's wallet, which is empty, I guess. Oops!" She giggles and covers her mouth.

"I'm taking her home." I scoop her up in my arms and make towards the house, not even caring to find Sawyer. Total bullshit he left her like this. Her arms snake around my neck and her head falls back, hanging over my arm.

"Evan?"

"What?"

"Why are you mad at me?" she asks, her head bouncing with each of my steps.

"I'm not mad at you. You just scared me. We'll talk in the morning." I stop, hitching her up and resetting my secure grip of her limp body.

"What if my dad's so broke he can't pay for school anymore? I'll have to leave. Who will take care of you?"

"Whitley, you're drunk. We'll talk in the morning."

"Not every girl will leave you. I don't want to."

I know better than to try and carry on a conversation with someone who's drunk, but drunken words are sober thoughts, and it seems as though she's got some pretty big ones plaguing her that she needs to get out.

"Whitley, I'm sure it'll be fine. You won't have to leave school. And don't worry about me, I'm fine. Okay?"

I look down when she doesn't respond, seeing she's passed out. Although difficult, I manage to get the door open and her tucked in bed, then lay a glass of water and some headache reliever I dug up in the kitchen on her nightstand.

Tomorrow, we'll have to talk. What she did tonight was

dangerous and she needn't try to drink away her fears. She also shouldn't be worrying about me. And I shouldn't be thinking about how good it feels to be someone's concern.

Chapter 14

Goin' Fishin'
Evan

"Dude, wake up."

I open my eyes, then squint against the sunlight, barely able to see Sawyer crouched by my bed, shaking me. "What?" The *one* time I'm not the first person awake and here comes this guy.

"I can't get this chick to leave. I need your help, bro. Get up and come run interference, say we gotta go somewhere or something."

I'm not too sleepy to grin ear to ear once I turn away from him; serves him right. I hope she's sniffing his clothes and doodling his initials when he walks back in there. "You're on your own, *bro*. You left Whitley alone, *drunk*, and you want help? You gotta be a friend to have a friend, Sawyer."

"I didn't leave Whitley drunk. I left her sober, with an old friend, who she said she trusted. I specifically asked her."

I roll over and look at him now, standing in the middle of the room, arms crossed and wearing a scowl. He can scowl all he wants, if he left Whitley like that, we're done. "She was blitzed when I found her, alone in the front yard, away from the crowd, with one guy." *Scowl right back at ya.*

"Yeah, Tyler or something, right? Listen, I pulled that girl aside and asked her, she said he was an old family friend and she trusted him. She was sober, on the sun porch thing with a lot of people when I walked away. I swear."

"You're sure?" I should have known he wouldn't just *leave her* like that. For all his obnoxiousness, he's a decent guy.

"You calling me a liar, Evan?"

"Nah, man, not a liar, I just wanted to make sure." I stand now and offer him a fist bump. "My bad."

"Yeah, well, I guess I could have gone back and checked on her."

"Just remember next time. Cool?"

"Cool." He nods, clapping me on the shoulder.

"Now what is it you need help with again?" I haven't forgotten, in the whole last five minutes, I just want him to have to squirm through telling me again.

"This girl, she won't leave."

There it is, the pained grimace on his face…so glad I asked again.

"Stop hooking up with randoms and you won't have this problem." I throw a shirt over my head and pull on some jeans; no sense risking the clinger taking a liking.

"Ah, small price to pay, my friend." He moves to the door and looks back. "You should try it; get your *heads* back in the game."

"Yeah, I'm gonna try to start dating, I think."

"I was kidding," he comments, turning fully to face me, "kinda. I thought maybe you and Whitley might start something up. Girl's gah gah over you."

"No, she's not. We're just friends. I can't do that to her, you know? What if I'm imagining something that isn't really there because of a rebound thing?"

"My hell, you are one complicated guy. We need to run to the store for some feminine products there, puss?"

"Fuck off," I mumble, brushing past him and opening the door. I instantly smell the coffee and hear two female voices cackling away.

"Good morning!" Whitley greets us with a huge smile and bright eyes.

Another fact learned about Whit—she is obviously immune to hangovers. Lucky.

"Evan, this is Portia," Whitley properly introduces us and I barely get out a hello or my hand outstretched before the stranger is draped around Sawyer's arm.

Sasha, Portia…maybe he needs to start trying girls named Jane, or Mary, or something he has a chance of spelling.

"Oh, and Nikki came by to invite you parasailing. Said to meet them in an hour at the dock if you want to go. You guys want some coffee?"

"Sure, thank you," I answer, but Sawyer… Yuck. That explains why Sawyer's silent…Portia is attached to his mouth.

Whitley hands me a mug of black coffee with a smile, her eyes not *quite* meeting mine. I don't know if that's because the display right beside us is making her uncomfortable or she's embarrassed about last night or what…but I can't delve into it with our spectators, even though I'm pretty sure I could scream "FIRE!" and those two wouldn't flinch. Which leaves me confused, 'cause now I'm not sure if I'm still supposed to help him get rid of her or slip him a condom behind her back.

"What do I do?" I mouth to Whitley with a shrug of one shoulder and a crook of my head to the "couple."

"I don't know," Whitley mouths back, suppressing a giggle.

"Do you have any creamer?" I ask her loudly, praying she says no, as this is my only idea.

"Sorry, no," she frowns.

Yes! Here's where my bro brilliance comes in.

"I can't drink coffee without creamer. I guess Sawyer and I will run to the store." I rise, feigning aggravation. "Portia, I can give you a lift home when we go."

No response.

"Portia?" I say even louder.

"Hmm? What?" She releases suction and turns to me, eyes glazed.

"Let us give you a ride home, we have to go to the store anyway."

"Oh, um, okay," she mutters, looking back at Sawyer with pleading eyes, just waiting for him to squash the take her home plan…which he doesn't. Once she realizes he isn't going to, she starts to shuffle slowly. "Let me just grab my stuff."

"Niceeeee," Sawyer praises when she's out of earshot, "I owe you one."

"Sawyer Beckett," Whitley chastises him in a low voice, "that is someone's daughter. You should be ashamed."

"Whitley, she came willingly…twice. I didn't make her any promises. How is it any more my fault than hers?" He shakes his head. "You women and your double standards."

I cough loudly when I see Portia walking back in. "You ready?"

"I guess so." She glances hopefully at Sawyer once more.

"We'll be back in a minute, Whitley," Sawyer says over his shoulder as he leads Portia out the front door with his hand…on her ass.

What a dog.

––––––––––⁕––––––––––

Evan: Don't worry about breakfast. I'll grab it while we're out. You want anything special?

Sawyer climbs back in the truck, having walked Portia to her door, which shocked the shit out of me really.

"I told Whit we'd pick up breakfast. What do you want?"

"Whatever you see first is fine with me."

Whitley: There's a place called JoJo's right on I-9. They have the best breakfast burritos.

"We're having breakfast burritos. We on I-9?" I ask.

"Hell if I know." He's looks around for signs. "Right there," he points, "get back over."

"Look for a place called JoJo's," I tell him as I navigate back across traffic, "Whitley says they're the best."

"So, no Whitley for you, huh? That surprises me."

"She's great, don't get me wrong. But I told ya, I think I'm reading things into it and will end up hurting her. Doesn't it seem a little too easy that Whitley, the first girl I meet here, ends up being the one? You know, when things seem too good to be true, it's usually because they are…"

"Whatever you say, man. I think maybe you think *too much*, but it's your call."

We pull through JoJo's, another random, grim-looking eatery (Whitley's specialty apparently), and Sawyer thankfully lets the subject drop, inhaling his burrito straight from the bag.

"Don't eat ours, Saw," I warn him with a laugh.

"I won't, crybaby," I *think* he says, his mouth full.

"So," he finally comes out of the bag for air minutes later, now speaking legibly, "we gonna go parasailing?"

"Don't know yet." I climb out of the truck, snagging the bag from Sawyer as I go, salvaging Whitley and I some breakfast. "Depends on what Whit wants to do."

He's still bugging me about it as we walk in. "Whitley, you wanna go parasailing?" he asks her.

"I don't think I was invited," she glances at me, "but you guys go ahead. I just downloaded a new book. I'll be more than happy laying out and reading."

Not happening.

"Cool," Sawyer shrugs, "oh and Whit? Don't get drunk alone with guys anymore, okay? Evan here about kicked my ass for leaving you alone, even though I assured him you weren't hammered when I left you. Not safe, sugar."

"It wasn't his fault," she says pointedly to me, "Tyler had a flask of whiskey I got carried away. Sawyer didn't know."

I nod briskly; I'd already settled it with Sawyer and he'd now issued the warning I wanted to, so no need to rehash it.

"I'm gonna hop in the shower, then we'll head out. Cool?"

"Nah," I answer him, "you go ahead. I'm gonna hang with Whit."

"Evan, you don't have—"

"Hanging with you," I cut her off sternly.

"You guys settle it," Sawyer laughs, "I'm going with or without ya."

He leaves to take his shower and I get up and gather the trash from breakfast, Whitley fixing an imaginary problem with the bottom of her shirt, a small smile hinting at the corners of her mouth

"So, what do you feel like doing?" I ask.

"Well, I know a really good spot to go fishing. We have poles in the garage I think."

My eyes pop and I look at her suspiciously, one brow raised. "You fish?"

She full-on smiles now. "I do if you teach me."

"You know where to get worms?"

"Um, the ground?"

I laugh at her innocent but correct answer. I was thinking of a Vendabait machine, but yes, the ground works too. "I don't know if we'll find enough that way, but we can sure try. Go get ready, I'll check the garage for poles."

"Okay!" She bounces all the way down the hall; I know this

because I watch with a grin plastered on my face.

It's gonna be damn hard to find people to date when I get home.

Whitley is the best accidental squirrel hunter I've ever met. Her hook has been up in the trees, which aren't exactly right on top of us, more times than not, so she must be trying to hook herself a squirrel. She apologizes profusely every time I have to put down my pole and help her, but I really don't mind. It's fun to watch her keep trying, her little tongue popping out in determination with every *attempted* cast.

Has she caught a fish? No.

Has she actually caught a squirrel? Still no.

Is being here, fishing, just what I needed? Yes.

Have I won the battle with myself to ignore the memories and comparisons? Damn near.

"I think I need an intermission," she says, propping her pole against a tree. "I'll just watch you for a while. Catch me a big one."

"We can go if you want."

"No way!" she gasps. "I'm having a great time, really. I'm just taking a break. Go on," she motions with her hands, "keep fishing."

"Don't worry, it won't be too much longer. I'm almost out of worms."

It's gorgeous here, the water calm and a bit clearer than back home, and no crowd; this back cove to a small lake Whitley's great little secret I guess . The air isn't as sticky as home, either, which is a blessing. Now I know everybody says there's nowhere as muggy as South Carolina, and maybe it's just me, but you sit by a body of water in a Georgia summer, your shirt's soaked in ten minutes. The breeze today may be helping, but this spot seems pretty close to perfect. It also doesn't hurt that sweet Whitley has been humming "Fishing in the Dark" by The Nitty Gritty Dirt Band quietly behind me since she started her intermission. It's a favorite of mine, and I'm shocked she knows it. It's all kinds of cute…another example of her "mood music."

I haven't gotten a single nibble the whole time I've been daydreaming, so I reel in, seeing I've been picked clean. When I reach down to grab another worm, the cup is gone. So is the humming.

"Whitley?" I lay down my pole, walking around to search for her. "Whitley?"

"Over here!" I hear her call from my right.

Pushing aside the tall grass and snipping off two flowers, I tromp over to find her crawling around on her hands and knees, dirt flying up around her.

"What are you doing?" I ask, dumbfounded yet amazed at what I've stumbled upon.

"Digging you some more worms, of course." She turns her head to answer me, pushing the hair out of her face and leaving a smear of mud across her forehead. "I've got eleven," she says proudly, offering the cup to me.

I take the cup and trade her the two flowers with a big smile. I look down—she really did find a whole pile of worms. That's true fishing dedication.

"Evan," she snickers as she smells the flowers, "I think these may be weeds."

"Even if they are, you pretty 'em up by holding 'em."

I gotta say—women look real nice in dresses, bikinis, or of course less, but when a little blonde is on her hands and knees, her tank top gaping down in the front, perky ass up in the air, her face smeared with mud, AND she's holding out a cup of worms she dug for you... This is the stuff country boys dream about. I'm so turned on right now, I want nothing more than to scoop her up and kiss the lips off her, but I just can't. It might ruin everything, and I can't lose another great friend because I misread things. One thing I've learned the gut-wrenching way—I'd rather keep the friend forever than have a month of two of "more."

I offer my hand to help her up. "This is a good look on you, Whit. You may have to trade in those pretty nails and fancy clothes for some cutoffs and boots."

"I have a pair of boots," she says proudly, "and cutoffs. But I like my nails. Even though there's dirt trapped under them right now." Her nose wrinkles just a smidge.

I can't resist playing with her just a little. "Well then, next outing, you're wearing them. You owe me since you dressed me like a preppy clown."

"Deal," she squeezes my hand, still holding hers for some reason, "and I won't do that again, I promise. I didn't know a gathering at Dane's house would be so informal. For what it's worth, I thought you looked very nice."

"I looked like Tyler."

Why did I just say that? Here I am, deciding to stay on the friend path with this girl, and then I go spouting off shit that makes me sound jealous.

"About that," she starts, dropping my hand and wrapping her arms around herself protectively. "I'm sorry about last night. I don't feel anything for Tyler, really. We were just talking and I drank too much. I know it's not a good excuse, but I just have a lot on my mind. Thanks for taking care of me, though," she lifts her head slightly from its bowed position and smiles apologetically, "and I'm sorry."

"Let's talk about that." I take her hand again, leading her through the brush and back to the clear spot where our poles rest. I sit down on the bank, pulling on her hand for her to so the same. "I know you're worried about your parents' stuff, but you said some other stuff, too."

"Like what?"

"Like you're worried about being able to afford school, having to leave."

"Oh!" she gasps and draws her knees up, wrapping her arms around them. "I don't want to leave Southern; I like it there."

"You need to call your parents, Whit. Ask them about it so you can stop worrying. Either way, it'll be fine. It may not even be a problem, and if it is, you could get student loans, a job; you'd have options. But you just need to make the call and figure it out, clear your mind."

She falls backs in the grass, laughing, her blond hair splaying out around her.

"What's so funny?"

"You," she answers simply. "You make everything so easy. That makes perfect sense and I've been driving myself crazy for nothing. From now on," she sits up again, tapping the end of my nose with her finger, just as I've done hers, "I'm just gonna run everything through the Evan Think Tank before I get all worked up."

"Brilliant plan," I agree with a wink.

It's dark when we finally leave, and that's only because Whitley can no longer see to dig more worms. I never brought up any of the other stuff she had said the night before—about me loving Laney, or her taking care of me... The line is dangerously close to blurry and doesn't need any help.

When we pull up to the house, it's immediately obvious Sawyer has company. I glance at Whitley, guessing she's going to be upset about it, but she just smiles brightly at me. I walk around and open her door for her, then unload all the gear, stalling for time, apprehensive of what we may be walking into; with Sawyer, you never really know.

Okay, so maybe not the worst possible case scenario, but damn close. Sawyer is currently hosting Amber, Nikki, Sasha, Tyler…and Portia. Awkward to have both "his girls" here? Not half as awkward as the fact that all the girls are half-dressed. Looks like Sawyer finally got some takers on his Strip Poker idea. And because *he* is completely naked, I'm thinking he should pick a game he's better at.

"Want me to make them leave?" I whisper to Whitley, who's grabbing my shirt and ducking her head behind my back.

"N-no, it's all right. It's Spring Break and all, and I'm not their mother."

"Oh, hey!" Sawyer finally notices us standing on the outskirts, and all the other heads turn to us. "Where y'all been? You want dealt in?"

"Fishing." I reach behind myself with one hand and find Whitley's, heading for the hallway. "We're beat. Gonna take showers and go to bed. Don't mind us, though. Carry on."

"Wait, Evan!" Nikki runs up, pink bra-clad breasts bouncing. "Come play with us. I've been waiting all day for you to get back."

"Really?" Whitley's sneer is hilarious, but I say nothing, curious as hell what *she's* going to say next. "He's tired, and *we* have to take a shower. Run along," she "shooes" Nikki with her hand, "Evan's too good for that."

Alrighty then. I follow Whitley's lead and turn, letting her pull me down the hall, leaving a gape-mouthed Nikki standing alone, staring after us I'm sure. Whitley's mumbling something about STDs, desperate, and I think lopsided as she drags me along, finally letting go of my hand at my door.

"Are you gonna go back out there, Evan?" she asks, fighting desperately not to tug her lower lip between her teeth and not meeting my eyes.

"Nah, I think I'll clean up and go to bed. All that fresh air, I'll sleep great. You?"

"Me too," her face lights up and she nods, "night."

"Night, Whit." And before I can help it, my lips are on her hair, kissing the top of her head.

———————— ✍ ————————

Last time I checked, I was still a red-blooded American male, and part of me is dying to go out there and look at naked chicks, but I remain in my bed, staring at the ceiling. The light knock at my door better not be any of them, 'cause I'm trying real hard to stay put here and be the man my mama raised. When I open the door, the visitor is indeed pleasant—dressed, for one thing, and looking subtle, classy…and sweet as sugar in a light pink pajama shorts set, hair damp from her shower.

"Were you asleep?" she asks nervously, her eyes locked on my bare chest.

I like that she's looking; just another mixed up feeling that I'll have to talk myself out of later. And dammit, I all of kinds of like the timid way she slowly lifts her gaze to mine, silently asking if her looking was okay, if I'm going to invite her in.

"No," I scoff. No way could anyone sleep with the racket coming from the living room.

The silence now is palpable, she's waiting for me to step back and open the door wider, to ask her in. I'm waiting for her to convince me that my doubts are okay and she wants to explore "us" anyway, see how it goes, and that she's positive it won't hurt her.

Neither happens, and eventually our locked gaze, blue on blue, becomes awkward.

She pulls her hands from behind her back, one holding a bag of cookies, the other a DVD. "Wanna watch a movie?"

"Yeah," I smile, moving back and opening the door wider, "sounds great."

I pull a t-shirt over my head quickly and fiddle with the TV and DVD player, getting things ready as Whitley grabs extra pillows out of the closet and situates them on the bed just right. I flip the lights back off and tentatively climb back in the bed, making sure to leave space in between our bodies. There's an uncomfortable stiffness to the air as we lay in the bed waiting for the movie to start, broken only when Whitley aims the open bag at me.

"Eat a cookie and relax, Evan."

It doesn't take very long into the movie for me to lose control. *What is this girly shit?!* I give it another ten minutes, and then I can't

106

hold my tongue any longer. "Whitley," I turn my head to her, the lights of the TV flickering over her profile, "what the hell is this movie called?"

"*Moulin Rouge*. Don't you love it?" her voice is breathy and wistful.

"This isn't even a movie, it's a musical."

"I know, aren't the songs wonderful?" She still hasn't looked at me, unable to break her attention from the catastrophe playing on the screen.

"No," I grumble, "it's driving me crazy, woman. One more song with guys dancing around and it's going off."

"Evan Allen." She pauses the movie and finally looks my way, giving me a quick poke in the ribs. "Broaden your horizons a little! This movie is artistic and wonderful."

"This movie is noisy crap."

"Fine," she crosses her arms, "what do you want to watch?"

"*Die Hard*."

"Oh, for heaven's sake," she rolls her big blue eyes at me, "I don't have Die Hard. I have…" She climbs over me and walks to the armoire, mumbling something about men not appreciating musical genius.

Maybe I'm spending too much time with Sawyer, or maybe the Laney haze really has lifted, because I have zoned in, while in almost complete darkness, and am positive she is *not* wearing panties under those shorts.

"How about *Shawshank Redemption*?" She turns back to me, and I jerk my eyes up to hers, praying I haven't been caught, but her smirk tells me that prayer was wasted. "That's a good compromise. Will that work?"

"Perfect," I clear my throat, "that's my favorite movie."

"I like it too." Her warm smile is glowing even in the darkened room.

"You sure about that? There's no fairy dudes in nightclothes jumping around singing."

I duck just in time to dodge the movie case aimed at my head.

———— ∽ ————

"Evan," I hear a voice through a fog and feel my body being shaken, "Evan, wake up."

"Mhm?" I open my eyes, slow to realize where I am. In bed.

And Whitley's snuggled up beside me. "What is it?"

"Your phone is going crazy," she says. Her voice is sleepy and raspy, her legs tangled with mine...and it's *morning*, so my body already has a head start on what my mind is registering. "I think you should check it; seems important."

I roll over, grabbing my phone off the nightstand, and see that I have five missed calls from my parents, all just minutes apart. Whatever it is, it can't be good, and my palms sweat as I push the button to call them back.

"Evan?"

"Hey, Dad, you called? What's going on?"

"Ah, son," he groans, "got some bad news."

I sit up, my stomach clenching, throat tightening. "What is it? Is Mom okay?"

"Your mom's fine. It's Dale. He's gone, son."

"Gone?" I croak out, feeling Whitley's small, warm hand move to my shoulder. "What's that mean, gone? What happened?"

"Angie found him out in the field. Looks like he had a heart attack. He passed, Evan. He's gone."

Dale Jones is, was, I guess, my best friend Parker's dad, and a helluva man. Parker, Laney and I were closer than close growing up, practically raised on the Jones' farm. Dale gave us each a calf every year as our own to raise there. We fished every pond a hundred times. We had cow patty fights. Dale taught us all how to drive a tractor. Parker and I put up hay every year and Dale always paid us in crisp, brand new hundred dollar bills. I know I'm crying, and Whitley can see it, but I don't care. I'm fucking sad. I loved Dale like a second father, an uncle, a mentor...and this sucks.

"How's Angie?" I manage.

Parker's mom will be all alone now. There's no way she can run that farm by herself and Parker's off at school, a great ball player.

"Not good, but your mama's been tending to her. Parker got home last night and funeral's day after tomorrow."

"I'm on my way, probably be late tonight."

"Sounds fine, just be careful driving, boy. And Evan?"

"Yeah?"

"Find Laney, let her know. Jeff can't reach her and doesn't need to be worrying. He's pretty tore up, him and Dale so close and all. Those two," he laughs passively, "one fishing tournament, they forgot to put the damn plug in the boat. Sank the damn thing right there at takeoff." He sighs sadly. "Anyway, get her home."

"I will, Dad, see you soon."

I hang up and say nothing, my head hanging as the tears keep coming. I can't look up. I don't want her to see me like this, crying like a little girl, but I know it's okay when I feel the small, comforting hand on the back of my neck. And when that same hand pulls me to her shoulder, the other arm wrapping completely around me, I sob shamelessly into her shirt, her shoulder, baring my soul.

I'm Evan Allen, and I cry when someone I love dies.

Butterfly kisses on my hair and wet cheek, accompanied with the occasional "I've got you" or "let it out" in the voice of an unjudging, compassionate angel tell me that soul is accepted.

It feels so good to lay my head in her lap and close my eyes, remembering all the good times I had with Dale, as she strokes my hair.

Chapter 15

We've Been Robbed
Laney

Evan: I need 2 talk 2 U ASAP. Please call me back.

He'd called three times right before sending the text, and I just hit ignore, not wanting anything to ruin our time here in Hawaii, even though I knew it had to be something if he's calling at all, let alone at this strange hour. I also knew he'd send a text right behind it if it *was* important, and I was kinda hoping I could just read it without Dane waking up.

"Who is it?" Dane asks against my neck from where he's snuggled behind me. "They obviously need something."

"It's Evan, says it's urgent."

"Call him back," he gets up now, moving to the bathroom, "sounds important."

This week in Hawaii has been so good for us. No schedules, no friends, no exes, no drama, no insecurities. I hope it's revamped "us" and we can stay this way once we're back, us against the world around us.

"Laney, hey," Evan answers, not jovially.

"Hey, Ev, what's up?"

"I've got some bad news, real bad. Are you sitting down? Is Dane there with you?"

"Yes and yes. Evan, you're scaring me. What's wrong?" Dane is right beside me now, his arms curled around me, his lips resting on my shoulder.

"Dale had a heart attack, Laney."

"Dale Jones? Well, is he gonna be okay?" Dane squeezes me tighter, placing kisses on my hair.

"No, Laney, he's not. He died. Angie found him out in the field, he'd been working. Dad just called, he said your dad couldn't reach you. He's pretty upset."

"Of course he is," I choke on the tears gushing out of me instantly, "that's his best friend. Why can't he reach me?" I look at my phone and see no calls from my dad, and he definitely didn't text. "He didn't call, Lord knows what he's dialing in his state. Anyway," I gulp down the sorrow making it difficult to talk, "how's Angie? Parker? Have you talked to him?"

My hand is shaking so hard I can barely hold the phone, and I can't see, and I may throw up. Why??? Dale Jones never met a stranger. His wife was his queen, his son his prince. He worked hard every day, he drove the Sunday school bus for the church, he gave all the teenagers summer jobs… He let me keep calves and baby sheep on his farm, for crying out loud. I jump up and run to the bathroom, losing all my dinner from the night before.

Dale was like my uncle, he and Angie loved me like their own. They rounded out my lack of adult family when my mother was gone and in some way, made me feel whole. The world will be less of a place without such a fine man in it, and I feel sorry for all of us that inhabit it, because we've been robbed of Dale Jones. I slowly gather myself and get up from the floor to clean up, my stomach now completely empty. I brush my teeth and splash my face with water, then pull my hair back. I'll call Evan back later, having just dropped the phone and ran. I'll call my dad later too. Right now, I'm just gonna sit back down on the floor and be.

"Come on, baby." Dane bends down and scoops me up I don't know how much later. "You're gonna wait in bed while I run you a hot bath. I got us almost packed; we fly out soon." He carries me to the bed and tucks me in with a kiss to the forehead. "Be right back."

"I need to call my dad, and Evan. I don't know when the funeral is," I moan, rolling over and sinking into the pillow, my body racking with sobs again.

His weight moves me as he sits down, rubbing my back. "All taken care of; I talked to them both. We fly back tonight and I'll drive you home when we land. We'll be there in time, baby, I promise, and we'll stay as long as you want. Now close your eyes and rest while I get your bath ready."

I don't close my eyes when he walks away, but rather, find my phone.

Laney: Thnx 4 calling. When r u heading home?

He answers almost immediately.

Evan: Packing up now, will be to Dad's late tonight. Dane said you guys would pull in Sun. You ok?

Laney: Not at all. You?

Evan: No, not really. Doesn't seem real. He was younger than my dad.

Laney: I know, I can't believe it. My heart aches. Will you plz check on my dad when u get there?

Evan: Of course.

Laney: Thnx Ev. Be careful driving.

Evan: Ok, take care of yourself. C U at home.

"Ready?"

I know he saw me texting, but he doesn't mention it, just gives me a warm smile. I nod, raising my arms for him to pick me up and carry me to the bathroom. I love it when he carries me; it makes me feel feminine, delicate…cherished. I bury my head in his neck and breathe in the comforting scent of the man who loves me, protects me, will never leave me.

"Will you get in with me?"

"Of course."

Laying back against his chest, in between his large, muscular legs, I close my eyes and go limp as a rag doll. He washes every inch of me with soft and tender strokes, kissing my hair the whole time. We don't speak, no words are needed; he simply tries to heal me with his loving care. When the tips of my fingers are wrinkly and the water is cool, he stands and wraps a towel around his waist before lifting me out and places me in front of him, drying me from head to toe. I brush my hair and give it a quick blow dry over it, pulling it back into a ponytail. I see him behind me in the mirror, holding my clothes.

"Turn around, baby," he instructs me in a gentle voice. I comply, like a robot, while he dresses me. Not long after, he calls down for bell service on our bags and leads me, his hand laced in mine, to our waiting car.

112

The drive to the airport is quick and I'm numb as we board. I'm going home to put another part of my past to rest. I'll never see Mr. Jones again. Parker will never get to hug his dad again. Angie will never again hold the hand of her love, her life partner. My dad will never swap fishing stories with his best friend. Life is really freaking unfair.

When you're young, all you can think about is how you can't wait to be old enough to drive, have no curfew, no parents telling you what to do, be old enough to drink, to vote, to get in clubs—all the exciting, glamorous things you think adulthood holds. I didn't have these exact thoughts, but I'm pretty sure it's the consensus, and I have now confirmed my original skepticism…growing up is not all it's cracked up to be. It's scary, it comes with a new set of drawbacks, and mostly, the more *you* change, grow up and move on…so does everyone around you. Your dad can't protect you from everything, he can't slap a Band-Aid on it or tell their parents and fix it. As you get older, the adults you love get older, the problems get bigger and less fixable, and the pain gets worse. And now I'm just letting my mind run crazy because I'm sad, confused, and overwhelmed…and he's there. He guides me to my seat, buckles my seatbelt, and covers me with a blanket.

"Take these, love. It's a long flight home." He hands me two pills and a cup of water.

I don't even ask what they are. One, I don't care, and two, I trust him impeccably. I know it sounds childish and trite, but one thing, above all, calms me and I need it so bad right now.

"Will you sing to me?" I whisper and lock onto his hand with mine, needing a physical connection as well. "Please? Just until I fall asleep?"

His answer is his smooth voice, telling me how he'll never let me fall, he'll stand up with me through it all. I know he will, and how he knows the exact things to say to me, melodic and healing; as he wraps his arms around me and rubs his cheek to mine, he too wraps me in love. I know it, "Your Guardian Angel" by The Red Jumpsuit Apparatus. It just might have been exactly what I'd requested, had he needed to ask.

When I wake, the inside of the plane is bright and small. We're obviously on a private flight that Dane had no doubt arranged at a moment's notice, for me. He's asleep in the seat beside me, head hanging my way, his hand on my leg. He looks beautiful with his brown hair mussed, his lashes long and dark. I place a soft kiss on his full lips, lingering until his eyes open, groggy and clouded with sleep, and he slowly smiles at me.

"Morning, baby."

"Morning. Where are we?"

He reaches above his head and presses a button, bringing to life a small screen. "About an hour left until landing. You hungry?" He turns and cups my cheek. "You haven't eaten in a long time."

"No, I'm not hungry. But I'd love to brush my teeth and get a juice or something."

"You and your teeth brushing." He chuckles lightly, releasing first his seatbelt, then my own. "Come on." He gives me his hand and leads me to the bathroom, handing me a wrapped toothbrush. "I'll grab you a drink. You sure you won't eat something?"

"Maybe later; just a juice for now."

"Okay." He gives me a disappointed look. "I'll be out here when you're done." He shuts the door, giving me some privacy.

When I'm feeling freshened, I come out and sit beside him, gulping down my apple juice in all but one swallow. "Do I remember you saying you talked to my dad?"

"Yes, I called him. He sounded all right, glad to get ahold of us. I told him we'd get there as soon as we could and stay a bit. This man who," he pauses, "died. You and your dad were pretty close to him?"

"Very," I reply, my voice cracking in my effort not to cry again.

His hands move to my hips and he pulls me in his lap, tucking my head into his hard chest. "Tell me all about him, please?"

So I do. I talk non-stop until we land about all my favorite memories of Mr. Jones, all the Jones'—their farm, their friendship, their love and acceptance. I cry the whole time, of course, Dane's rhythmic rubbing on my back never faltering. It feels really good to get it out—like I'm honoring Dale's memory by telling another exactly how wonderful he was.

Dane is sneakily insightful; he always knows just what I need just when I need it.

Chapter 16

Deflection
Evan

I arrive home, safe and sound, although I'm not quite sure how I drove. I felt a bit like a pansy for crying so much, until I got home and saw my dad's red-rimmed eyes; then I knew it was okay. Sometimes real men cry.

My parents are holding up pretty well. Dad's quiet, Mom's cooking up a storm. That's what my mom does—she puts her own feelings aside and takes care of everyone else around her. She makes sure everyone's fed, everyone gets enough hugs, and everyone has everything they need that she could possibly provide.

Well, what do you know? I've never compared anyone else to my mother, so selfless and giving, but a certain blue-eyed beauty, gentle and considerate, just crossed my mind.

Once I'm truly convinced my parents are all right, I head out to check on Mr. Walker. "Well, look who it is!" he greets me. "Evan, my boy, come on in."

"Hey, Mr. Walker. Thought I'd come by and see ya. Laney's on her way, bit behind me."

"Yeah, I talked to that fella of hers. Had her out in Hawaii," he grunts. "Guess you don't want to hear about that, though, sorry." He stumbles a bit to the couch, bumping into the coffee table which is lined with beers cans that fall over noisily.

Can't say I blame him, really.

"You had dinner, Mr. Walker?"

"Why so formal? You forget my name?" He laughs, but his eyes don't. "I'll eat when I'm hungry. Right now, I just wanna get drunk and try to get some sleep. Sure gonna miss my friend. Good man he was," he raises his beer can in the air, "the best."

"Jeff, can I use your restroom?"

"Why are you even asking? You know where it is."

I shut myself in, turning on the water to cover my voice. I don't want to trick anybody, but I'm a little out of my league here. I'm not about to tell a grown man to stop drinking, but I know Laney'd want something different to be happening right now.

"Hello?"

"Dad, hey, I need your help. Can you come keep Mr. Walker company? He's drunk and I need to go check on Parker."

"Ya, bud. Stay 'til I get there, I'm on my way."

When my dad arrives about ten minutes later, I leave them to it and head to Parker's. I haven't seen him in months, but he'll always be my brother and I know he's gotta be a mess. My phone rings on my way, and my chest feels a little less tight when I see her name on the screen.

"Hey, Whitley."

"Hey, how are you?"

I'd made her and Sawyer throw everything in the truck the minute I got the call, barely putting on the brakes when I dropped them back on campus. I'm not even sure what energy I'm running on right now.

"Hanging in there; 'bout to go check on Parker."

"Evan," she says, her voice gentle, "can I come help you? I hate that you're by yourself for all this."

Every part of me wants to say yes, I could sure use her here with me right now, a natural, easy comfort, but I've got to deter her from thinking she has to take care of me. I want to be her "cause" even less than I want to risk our friendship.

"I'm not by myself. I've got my parents. Besides, there's other people hurting worse than me. I've got to be there for them. But I appreciate it, Whit, I really do."

"Is Laney there yet?"

"No, probably late tonight, or morning even. Long way from Hawaii."

116

"Dane will come with her," she says matter-of-factly.

"I know, I talked to him. Laney was pretty out of it."

"Okay, I just thought—"

"Whitley, you don't have to stand beside me just because he's standing beside her. It's not a competition."

Shit. I'm tired and sad and talking out my ass, not only because of the obvious, but from this constant internal struggle I have about Whitley really starting to wear on me. I regret it the minute I say it and the hurt in her voice slices into me.

"I know that," she replies, calmer than I would be if she said the same thing to me. "That's not what I meant. I just want to help you if I can."

"I'm sorry, Whit. Ignore me. Just a shitty deal, shitty mood." Dammit! I slap the steering wheel; she didn't deserve that. "Listen, let's talk later, okay?"

"Okay, just call me if you need me."

A very beautiful girl, about my age I'd guess, answers the door.

"Is Parker here?"

"Yeah sure, come on in. You are?" she asks, holding the door open to me.

"Evan. Evan Allen." I take off my cap and offer my other hand.

"Oh, Evan! Nice to finally meet you. Parker talks about you all the time. Is Laney with you?" she asks, peeking past my shoulder.

Um, no, stranger, Laney and I don't travel in two anymore. Another jackass thought; God, I am in such a dick mood today. "No, she's on her way in from Hawaii. She'll be here soon. I'm sorry, I didn't catch your name?"

"Lord, my manners. I'm a little out of sorts. I'm Hayden, Parker's girlfriend."

"Nice to meet you, Hayden. So, where's our boy?"

"In the kitchen with his mama."

She turns to walk that way and I peek into the kitchen to see Parker at the table, his head in his hands, hair pushed back and sticking up through his fingers. Angie sits across from him, hands wrapped around a coffee mug, staring off into nowhere.

"Honey," Hayden says quietly, touching his shoulder, "Evan's here."

He lifts his head and his face explodes into a smile that drops just as quickly as it'd appeared; like he forgot for a second this wasn't just a happy reunion. "Hey, brother." He stands and wraps me in a hug. "How you been? Thanks for coming."

I hug him back, my eyes misting. "I'm so sorry, man. So damn sorry."

"I know, I know." He gives me another squeeze, then releases me. "Sure is good to see you, though."

"Mama Jones," I move over and bend down to hug her, "I'm so sorry for your loss. Your husband was one of the finest men I've ever known."

"Evan, my sweet boy," she grabs the back of my head and moves it to kiss my cheek, "you were always like a son to Dale. He thought the world of you." She pats my cheek. "You've gotten even more handsome since I saw you last. How are you?"

"Fine, ma'am." I sit down and clutch one of her hands in mine. "What can I do for you? How can I help?"

She cups her other hand over the top of our already joined ones and pats. "I think it'd be great if you would be a pallbearer with your daddy and Mr. Walker, and Parker, of course." She smiles up at her son. "That's who Dale would have picked."

"It'd be," I suppress a sob, "my honor. Thank you."

"What about Laney girl?" She almost laughs, sniffling. "You think she wants to help? You know her, I can just see insulting her by thinking she wouldn't want to carry with the men."

Parker and I both chuckle, despite the sadness, at the accuracy of Angie's words.

"It's okay, Mama, I think she'll be okay just knowing you thought of her. I'll tell her," Parker offers, moving to his mom's side.

That's all she could get out, her body now suddenly wrenching and the sounds escaping her positively blood-curdling. It's depressing and a little scary and I have no idea what I'm supposed to do.

"Come on," Parker says calmly as he helps her up, Hayden scurrying to the other side, "let's get you to bed now. Time for another pill."

I stay sitting right where I am, frozen to the spot. The house looks exactly the same... What a stupid thought, of course it does. It's looked this way as long as I can remember—why would it change just because he's gone?

"Evan, did you meet the love of my life?"

I startle at Parker's voice behind me and stand quickly, facing him and Hayden.

"Yes, I met Hayden." I give her a smile.

"Best girl in the whole world." He kisses her cheek and she leans into it. "Dad loved her first time he met her. Told me she was a keeper."

"Well, we all know he had a keen sense." I wink at her and she giggles softly.

"Y'all stop, you're embarrassing me. Can I get you a drink or anything, Evan? Babe?"

Parker looks at me and I shake my head no. "No, we're fine," he answers her. "You go rest, you been waiting on everybody."

"I'm gonna go sit with your mom, make sure she falls asleep all right."

"Thank you, angel," he says, squeezing her hand. "I love you."

"I love you, too, Parker." She gives him a quick kiss and he pats her butt as she leaves the room.

"Gonna marry her," he proclaims as sure as anything.

"She's wonderful. I'm happy for you, man."

"Come on, shitsack, let's have some beers. We can toast the old man. We gotta go in the barn though. If Hayden catches us, she'll think I'm *deflecting*. That's her favorite word." He laughs and grabs a six pack from the fridge.

I follow him into to the barn, the memories flooding me. "Hey, Sebastian." I pat the horse's head; Laney's favorite. Dale had let her name him, and of course, she'd done so after the crab in *The Little Mermaid*. There's a duck waddling around somewhere named Aladdin and the barn cat is Figaro.

"So," Parker interrupts my reminiscing, "let's deflect. Tell me about you, 'cause I can't think about my dad right now."

"Not much to tell, really. I transferred to Southern."

He nods, taking a drink. "I heard."

"Laney's in love."

"Heard that too."

"Kaitlyn turned out to be a two-faced snake."

"Already knew that."

Guess we're all caught up.

Parker takes the lead on our exhilarating conversation. "Laney coming?"

119

"Yeah." I go ahead and grab a beer out of the pack; if ya can't beat 'em and all. "Should be here soon."

"Bringing her new man?"

"Yeah."

He props his chair back, propping his feet against a stall. "I always thought the two of you would end up together."

"Me too." I pop one shoulder up. "Guess that's what we get for thinking."

"You all right?"

His father just died and he's worried about me? It makes me feel like a shallow ass that we're talking about my problems in the shadow of the much bigger picture, but if that's what makes him feel better, I'll take the heat. "Yeah, man, I'm fine. It sucked at first, but every day is a little easier."

I think of Whitley and almost feel guilty, in light of things, at the small grin that escapes. She's the reason it's a bit easier, plain and simple, no matter how I try to fight it. Then I think of how shitty I'd treated her earlier and my face falls; I could kick myself.

"Who is she?" Parker asks, a grin on his face.

"Who's who?" I ask, willing my face to look as blank as possible.

"The girl you're not telling me about."

"How'd you know that?" Damn, Parker's more aware of my life than even I am.

"I didn't." His grin widens. "You just told me."

"Dick!" I flick my beer tab at him. "She's just a friend. Can't go there with her, too risky."

"That's your problem, Allen, no risk. You've been wrapped up in Laney for so long, you've never opened yourself up to other possibilities. You ever think maybe Laney always seemed so perfect to you because you never dared let her have a little competition?"

"That's not true. I messed around with a few girls."

"Messed around," he scoffs. "Big deal. You ever date? Get to know anybody? Let 'em in?" He knows the answer, he just wants me to say it.

"Why are we talking about this anyway?" I turn now, engrossed once again in Sebastian. "Shouldn't we be figuring out what to do about your mom, or this farm?"

"Only thing that's gonna help Mama is time," he says. His voice holds a melancholy tone, but only for a moment. "Farm's simple; I'm coming home to run it. Gonna ask Hayden to marry me and come with. Give my mama some grandkids to love."

"Parker," I face him abruptly, trying to hide the condescension in my voice, "you're what, just turned twenty? Are you sure you're not rushing things? Your dad would want you to finish school, be sure. Your mom can hire somebody to run the place until you have summer breaks and graduate."

"I was always gonna come home and run this farm one day. Why do I need a college degree for that? Besides, I like farming. And I love Hayden, more than anything. I want her with me, always. I wish like hell my dad was still here," he takes a long drink of beer, "but he's not. I know what's right. This is what I'm meant to do. *Now.*"

"I just think you should—"

"Honey, you out here?" Hayden comes in the barn, her eyes seeking out Parker. "Oh Parker, are you out here deflecting?"

"*Told ya,*" Parker mouths to me, his shoulders shaking with suppressed laughter. "No, just out here having a beer with my oldest friend. Big difference."

"Come to bed," she wraps her arms around his waist, "you're tired. I'll give you a back rub," she croons persuasively.

I'm already walking to my truck, more than sure what his response will be. "I'll be back tomorrow, Jones. Try to get some rest."

———————⤴———————

Evan: You awake?

She's probably asleep. It's late and I'm a spineless heel for texting instead of calling in the first place, especially at this hour. But it dings.

Whitley: Yes. How are you?

Evan: Sorry.

Whitley: Nothing to be sorry for, Evan. It's a crazy time, I understand.

Evan: Can I call you?

Whitley: Anytime.

"Hi," she answers, her voice soft and kind like always, even after she's been undeservingly treated badly; not a doormat, never a martyr, just...*Whitley.* I feel sorry for every dumbass who didn't recognize her before, every fool who didn't appreciate the refreshing, beautiful traits this girl has to offer.

"Hi, Whit. Promise I didn't wake you up?"

"Promise."

"I just kinda need to talk. And," I take a deep breath, "I wanted it to be to you."

"I'm right here."

She always says the right thing. She always says it in the right voice. She confuses the hell out of me; I can only imagine what I'm doing to her.

I tell her about my night; my concerns about Parker's plans, my hurt for Angie, and even my greatest memories of Dale. She listens and offers little pieces of agreement, or advice, but argues with me freely when she feels the need. At this point in my life, I can honestly say, there's no one I'd rather talk to.

Already knowing it's a bad idea, I push away that thought, and force out the words. "I wish you were here, Whitley."

"I am."

"No, I mean *here* here, by my side."

"I'm at Bonnie's Bed and Breakfast. You know it?"

Of course I know it, Bonnie's been playing Bridge with my mom every Wednesday afternoon since I don't know when. "I know it." I pause and my heartbeat speeds up. "You're really there? I mean here?"

"I'm really here. I was hoping you'd want me, or need me, or whatever," she's whispering now, "so I came. I would have seen you at the service, but then...you called."

But then I called. And she's here. For me. Right down the road. Sleepy. Snuggly.

And I'm here for a funeral...thinking like this.

"What room are you in?" I ask as I jump up and pull on my jeans and boots. I pull a t-shirt over my head, not stopping to examine the excitement coursing through me; that doesn't seem right at this time and makes me feel guilty. But dammit if I haven't felt anticipation like this in a while.

"213," she rushes out, her breathlessness matching my own.

Does she feel the gravity of this moment like I do? Could I ever express to her in words what this means to me, how deeply and profoundly she has touched me?

She's here... I will never be the same.

"That's a bottom outside door, right?"

"Yes."

"Be there in ten."

Quietly, I pick up my keys and ease out the front door silently. My truck slips into gear and I roll it down the driveway like I'm not almost twenty and able to leave when I want to. When I'm a ways from the house, I start the engine, and in six more minutes, I'm standing in front of door 213.

Shit. She's wearing tiny shorts and a thin shirt, no bra, and her generous chest leaves no room for doubt. Her blonde hair falls around her shoulders and her blue eyes are sleepy, half-lidded. I force my eyes to stay on hers.

"Come in," she says quietly, and I step inside.

My pulse is hammering so hard I can feel each beat in my neck, my mouth suddenly dry as cotton. I run my sweaty palms down my jeans as I look around. There's one big bed and one chair in the room. She's got the TV on, but muted. That's the only light, the TV, which is plenty. I can make out the outline of her body through the worn material of her top. I can see her nipples, hard and wanting. I can tell her lips are shiny from being licked.

I shouldn't be here; this is a very bad idea. I could tell myself I just need a friend, for comfort, but that's a lie. I'm madly attracted to Whitley and I want so badly to throw away my worries about hurting her, or her hurting me, and selfishly take her in my arms.

Selfish it is.

When I move to her, she doesn't give an inch, but stays right where she is, her breath quickening and heavy, her eyes challenging. She wants me too. My hands move gradually, brushing up her neck to clutch in her hair, the moan escaping her making me twitch. Damn, but she's beautiful. Delicate. Fragile. She leaves her eyes open, drinking me in, telling me "yes, it's okay,'" without words. My lips are inches from hers, so close I can feel her warm puffs of breath against mine. I close my eyes, moving in for the taste of what I so desperately want.

And my phone trills loudly from my pocket, jerking me back in surprise.

Yeah, the phone rings at that exact moment…how convenient and unlikely, right?

It fucking happened.

Given the current crisis we're all dealing with, of course I'm gonna answer it. The moment now long gone, I rub the back of my neck roughly with one hand while I hold the phone with the other, staring at the faded brown carpet rather than Whitley.

"Hello?"

"Hey, Evan, it's Laney. Just wanted to let you know we're here, at Dad's. I sent yours home and got mine to bed. Thank you."

"Not a problem, glad you made it."

"So, I guess I'll see you tomorrow?"

"Yeah, I'll be there." I exhale, wishing it was anything but what we have to do the next day. "See ya tomorrow."

I hang up and take my time putting up my phone, examining everything in the room before I look back to Whitley. "I'm sorry, Whit. I shouldn't have come here. I'm an ass."

"Why do you say that?" She frowns. "I'm glad you came." She shifts, going to come to me, but I back up.

"I don't want to hurt you, Whit. You're such a great person, and I'm not sure what this is," I point from myself to her, "but I don't want to lose you."

"Why would you lose me?"

"If we became more than friends, and it didn't work out, we wouldn't be friends anymore. And," my hands move through my hair on their own and pull in frustration, "what if we're just, I don't know, convenient? Whitley, I'm just... I'm not sure what's real and I don't want to lose anybody else I care about. I've had all that fun I can stand."

She's on me in a flash, her arms hugged around my waist, hands rubbing my back. "Go home, Evan, and go to bed. You're tired and distraught. I don't want to be somebody's convenience, or second guess, but I will still be your friend. Okay?" She lifts her pretty face up to smile feebly at me.

"Okay," I agree, moving quickly to the door, feeling damn lucky she gave me an out. How can I do right by her, be honest with her, when I can't even make sense of things myself? The myriad of emotions lately, it's just all too much. Heartbreak to some relief to confusion to extreme grief; I just need to go numb for a while.

"I'll see you tomorrow. Night, Evan."

Chapter 17

Will The Real Slugger Please Stand Up?
Evan

Have you ever been to a sunny funeral? I know I've seen processions go by when it's nice outside, so it must happen, just not to me, and not now. Seems like it's always unseasonably cold, or a freak snow, or in this case…not really raining, but drizzling enough to remind you it's a shitty day.

We all look on as our friend, our mentor, is lowered into the ground. The pallbearers all wore a white rose on their lapel, and I unpin mine and toss it into the hole with Dale before finally turning to leave. I help Parker get his mom to the waiting limo, then walk with Whitley over to Laney, her dad, and Dane. Laney had spoken at the funeral and I want to tell her how beautiful it was. I know it was hard for her, but she held her head high and squelched her tears like a trooper.

"You did well, Laney," I say as we approach. "Dale would be real happy. You know besides Angie, you were always his favorite girl, right?"

"Yeah." She nods and grins sadly, looking at her feet. "He was one of my favorites too."

"Mr. Walker," Whitley offers her hand, "I'm Whitley Thompson, Laney's friend. Nice to meet you."

What an ass I am, not introducing her. I don't even remember if I'd officially done so with Parker or Angie; this whole day is a bit of a fog.

"It's nice to meet you, young lady. Thank you for coming today."

"Yes, sir."

"Well, I'll see you kids later. I'm gonna head over to sit with Angie a bit."

"Bye, Daddy." Laney gives him a hug. "I love you, so much."

"Love you, Slugger. See ya at home." He turns. "Dane," he nods, "Evan," he pats my shoulder.

Whitley's gasp turns all our heads. "Laney, you don't really hit people, do you?! And your father encourages it?"

Dane starts chuckling under his breath; he must get something Laney and I don't because her face looks as puzzled as I feel.

"What are you talking about?" Laney asks.

"Slugger?" Whitley answers, like *duh.*

Dale wouldn't care if we laughed at his funeral, thank God, because we're all busting out now. Hell, he'd laugh too.

"Whitley," I put my hand on her shoulder, mostly to hold myself up through the laughter, "she doesn't slug people. Well, not often. It's a term," I catch my breath, "for a good batter, like softball."

"Ohhh," her cheeks flush and she rests one hand over her heart, "of course. Thank goodness."

Laney's grinning ear to ear and I really am glad to see it. It's such a sad day, and of all people, Whitley had found a way to brighten her mood. Hell, she brightened all our moods. Whenever I think of Dale, having to carry his casket, standing in the rain with Laney and her boyfriend…I'll smile at the end when I remember right now.

Or then again, maybe not. My back stiffens and the hairs on my neck stand up, sensing evil.

"Hey, Evan."

How tacky can you get, risking starting shit at a funeral? Whitley can sense my distress and looks up at me, worry in her eyes. Laney? Her grin has disappeared and I can see her teeth grinding from here. I give Dane a look, then dart my eyes to Laney, hoping he understands.

He must have, as one arm goes tightly around Laney's shoulders and he steps in closer to her. Laney won't disrespect Dale, or his family, by cleaning this bitch's clock at his funeral, but she *may* drag her off by her hair and do it someplace else.

"Kaitlyn," I bite out, not turning to face her.

Dane's eyes pop wide when I say her name. I'm guessing Laney told him because he stiffens and starts nudging Laney to leave. "Come on, baby, let's go."

Her whiny, sickening voice reaches out and stabs my ears. "Wait, I'm confused."

Laney's head spins around at her words, her eyes glowing. "Let me clear it up for you then. I'm still Laney, that's still Evan," she points, "that's Whitley, this is Dane, and you? You're still the backstabbing bitch from hell. All better?" She over-smiles facetiously.

"Pfft," she blows Laney off, coming to stand directly in front of me now. "Oh my God, did she dump you for him, Evan? I knew it, she never appreciated you." Her lecherous hand rubs up my arm, possibly burning the flesh from the bone. "Come back, Evan," she coos. "She's not—"

"Kaitlyn, don't," I interrupt her, not wanting a scene or to stomach hearing her voice.

"But, Evan, I'll love you, take care of you. In a way *she*," she turns and glares at Laney, then back, "never did. Don't you remember how I took care of you that night in your room?"

Fucking Kaitlyn, now she's trying to throw me under the bus. Her manipulation knows no bounds.

"It wasn't like that and you know it," I grind out. "It wasn't." I look at Laney, begging her with my eyes to believe me. It may not matter to her anymore, but it matters to me that she be sure I'm not a rat bastard.

Of course Laney would know better than that, instantly rolling her eyes and sending Kaitlyn a belittling sneer. "You're more delusional than I thought if you actually think I'd believe Evan would touch you with a ten foot pole. Even if he wasn't with me, he'd *never* be with *you*."

Still oblivious to the fact that no one here is buying her bullshit, oh, and that it's tasteless to start nonsensical, vicious drama *at a funeral*, Kaitlyn moves in closer to me. I abruptly step back, as though bitten, shuddering visibly. What happens next...well, I'm glad I stuck around.

"Why do we hate her?" Whitley asks me almost inaudibly out of the side of her mouth.

"She was Laney's best friend. She tricked her out of a scholarship at UGA; she wanted me," I hurry through the CliffsNotes in her ear.

When Laney gets mad, it's cute as hell, but you're kind of expecting it, right? Well, when Thumbelina goes off, it's a whole different kind of downright fantastic.

"Listen here you bushy-eyebrowed, needs-her-dead-ends-trimmed-severely *hoochie.*" Whitley cracks her knuckles, and hopefully only I catch her wince at it. "You're obviously as deranged as your hairdresser if you thought for one minute Evan would respond to deceit. And now, *you're* alone, and Dane and I are lucky enough to have them both in our lives. So once again, you really lose. Now, you've got five seconds to get the hell out of here or you're gonna have bigger problems than your ass in that outfit."

Dramatic pause for effect I guess?

"You want me to show you why they call *me* Slugger?" She wipes under her nose and growls. "And I don't play softball...feel me?"

Holy hard-on. *Sorry, Dale.*

I do a quick survey and cannot decide whose face is funniest. Laney's smirking, eating this up; if anything actually happens, there's not a doubt in my mind she'll jump in and put her money where Whitley's mouth is. Dane's jaw is unhinged and laying on the ground somewhere. And Kaitlyn is blood-red and fuming.

"Who the hell are you?" she snarls, hand on her hip, challenging Whitley.

"I'm lady enough not to show my ass at a funeral, but woman enough to kick yours if you don't back off my friends. Evan?" she glances at me, keeping her stance to Kaitlyn, "do you have anything to talk to this, this *person* about?"

I shake my head, trying so very hard not to laugh.

"Laney, do you?" she asks next.

"Nothing."

"And there you have it. You're of no use here, now go find your rock and crawl back under it. We're leaving," Whitley proclaims proudly.

We all robotically fall in step and follow behind our fearless leader, Whitley, but not before Laney gives me a wide-eyed smirk, like "well, look at this chic."

Oh, I am.

"Dale would have really liked you, Whitley," I hear Laney tell her, snickering, "and he'd have *loved* that! Very cool of you."

I just know Dale is looking down, laughing his ass off at the show we're giving him. I'm walking with Laney, her new boyfriend and the prissy little thing I'm trying desperately not to fall for, having just watched her bare her teeth against a girl twice her size to defend a girl who was tackling her not so long ago.

Quite a show.

Chapter 18

Man Hands
Evan

"Hey, roomie, glad you're back!"

"Hey, Zach, good to be back." I look around my new room, which is small, clean and of normal smell—*bonus*. "Did you unpack all my stuff for me?"

"Yeah right," he scoffs, "Avery did it for you. Don't worry," he waggles his eyebrows, "I thanked her already."

I collapse onto my bed, worn thin from the last two weeks. Spring Break, Dale, Whitley, tons of driving... I need to re-center badly.

"So..." Zach hesitates, "I was real sorry to hear about your loss. Are you okay? Laney okay?"

"Getting there; a little better every day. I just hope my buddy Parker and his mom are all right. I think maybe I'll go back and help them with their farm this summer."

He nods and starts lacing up his shoes. "Me and Ave are gonna go grab some dinner. You wanna go?"

"Nah, thanks, though. I just wanna shower and go to bed." I'm already half asleep just talking about it.

"All right," he slaps my leg, "I'll hang in her room 'til curfew then, let you get some rest. We'll have to work out a schedule one of these days, ya know. Socks on the door don't work; jackasses think it's funny to grab them off. My old roommate had the whitest ass you've ever seen."

"You don't have to worry about that with me," I groan.

"Oh yeah?" His brows shoot up mockingly. "Your ass is tan, huh?"

"Yeah, that's exactly what I meant." I laugh, more at my own sad state of affairs, of lack thereof, than the conversation. "Just let me know, though. I can make myself scarce."

"Evan, man, you gotta get back out there. This is *college*. You're young, wild, and free. You want me to hook you up?"

Going to regret this, no doubt.

Jumping in like a blind, lonely fool anyway.

"Actually," I sit up and let him see I'm serious, "I do. I kinda already decided I was gonna start dating, so if you have somebody cool in mind, I'm down."

"Atta boy," he offers his knuckles for a bump, "I'll see what I can do."

"Yup," I mutter, bumping him back weakly, "you do that."

———————⌇———————

Date #1—Friday night

Conspirator: Zach

Girl: Tiffany-blonde, Junior, Phi something something, in Zach's Anatomy class

Problem: Mannish

"Whitley?" I whisper, though I have no idea why. I'm pretty sure She-Man didn't follow me into the men's bathroom. Then again…

"Evan? Where are you? I can barely hear you," she whispers back, not realizing she's mimicking me.

"Listen, woman, I need your help."

"I thought you were on a date?"

"That's what I need your help with. What do you do when you're on a date that you really want to get out of…like five minutes ago."

"I have a friend call me and fake an emergency. But that's a girl trick, so she'll know what you're doing."

"All right, then what else ya got?"

"Hmmm," she mulls it over, "what do I get out of it?"

"Extortion?" I choke out, shocked. "Whitley, I'm appalled." I used appalled, a word pretty foreign to me, to cut at her root; she

131

appreciates Whitley language.

She giggles in my ear, getting way too much enjoyment out of this. "You have to tell me everything. Deal?"

"Yes, woman! Now help me!"

"Where are you?"

"The Red Door."

"Go back out there with her and act normal. God, you owe me."

I walk nervously back to the table, apprehensive of exactly what I've just put into play. "Sorry about that, there was a line," I mutter to my date.

There was a line? I suck at covert ops. If I manage to not blurt out a confession of "the plan" before Whitley gets here it'll be a miracle.

Her big, freakishly large man hand keeps inching closer and closer to mine on the table, so I shove my hands in my lap. I don't see an Adam's apple, but I'm still looking—it's gotta be there somewhere. Then, all at once, the heavens open and the angels scream.

"Evan Allen, how could you?"

Splash! Cold ice water to the face. What the hell?! I don't know that props were completely necessary, but who am I to complain? I pick up my napkin and wipe my face, eyes clearing to see Whitley standing over our table, glaring.

"Who is she?" she points at my date.

"Um—"

"Don't even try it!" she screeches. "You promised! No more cheating!"

Man, Bennett better look out, 'cause Whitley could easily steal her spot in the drama club. Look at those big, fake crocodile tears. Note to self—Whitley can cue waterworks on a dime.

She pulls out a chair and throws herself down, slamming her hands on top of the table. "Why, honey? Why? We just made love before you left! Aren't I enough?"

Everyone in this restaurant is staring at us now, and my date, well she's...she's leaving! But not before her water lands in my face. Small price to pay.

I finish wiping my face, again, and hesitantly peek over my napkin, scared this isn't over yet.

"She's gone," Whitley says, voice back to normal, tears gone as quick as they'd appeared.

"Damn, Whit, that was something," I say in shocked, but tickled, gratitude. "Thanks, though."

"You're welcome. Now what'd she order? I'm eating hers and you're still paying."

––––––––– ✎ –––––––––

Date #2—The next Friday night

Conspirator: Avery

Girl: Rae

Stats: After my last date, Avery assures me the name "Rae" was not because she was in any way now, or previously, a dude, and is in fact a very nice girl from one of her study groups.

Problems: I almost don't believe it myself.

Rae is pretty with a big smile and straight white teeth. Her hands are proportioned perfectly to her body and gender, which is also very attractive, more so than ever. We met up at the campus library, where she aides, and had a nice, easy conversation from there to my truck.

I'm actually having a pretty good time and even starting to relax while we wait for our food. Do I feel any five-alarm chemistry? No, but she's pleasant, and maybe I could see her again.

When our food arrives, I ask her if she wants to try some of my lasagna, which she eagerly does, then offers me some of her Alfredo. We don't feed each other or anything, just scoot our plates toward one another, but it's still nice.

I still can't believe I'm just starting to date. I'm almost twenty years old and never dated? Well, she lived three houses down…that's exactly how that happened. She didn't like to go to the theater, our town didn't have a bowling alley and…no other girl within miles compared to her. This is crazy; I'm grown and need to snap the hell out of all these feely schmeely BS thoughts, so I scoot my chair a little closer to Rae's, leaning in, smiling and laughing a bit more at things she says.

And then…she covers her mouth and tips her chair over in her jump and run to the bathroom, calling a barely audible "I'll be right back!"

Shit. I hope the shrimp wasn't bad. Do I go ahead and eat? Do I go check on her? I really have no idea what the right answer is, so I sit there until the waitress comes over to check on me. "My date's not feeling well. Can you bring the check?" I ask her.

"Certainly. I hope she feels better."

133

She's laying the tray with the slip on the table when Rae comes back and sits down, her eyes watery and face chalky.

"Are you okay?" I know she's not, I can smell the hint of vomit from here, but you're supposed to ask, right?

"Oh, I'll be fine now. Is that the check? We don't have to leave. I won't get sick again for a while."

She knows when she'll get sick? My money is on some weird make yourself throw up thing. Oh, and I also wish she'd quit talking, because her breath is not okay. There will be no goodnight kiss happening.

The waitress shoots me a questioning look and shuffles away as Rae merrily starts eating again.

"Do you think it was the food? Maybe you shouldn't eat any more of it," I suggest.

"The food's fine," she assures me, "finish yours. It's just morning sickness, except mine comes at night. It'll go away in a few more weeks."

Come again?

Oh, you have got to be fucking kidding me. This is the kind of shit that happens to Deuce Bigalow or victims on those punking shows, not real life schmucks like me. I'm tempted to look around for cameras.

"I'm sorry, what?" I choke out through a sweating throat.

"Don't worry," she grins and pats my hand, "me and the dad are broken up." She rolls her eyes. "We're so over."

"You're pregnant?" I'm not sure if I cough or laugh really.

"Yeah, Avery didn't tell you?"

That'd be a big hell no.

"No, no she didn't mention it."

"Huh, well I am, but that's not gonna stop me from finding Mr. Right."

No, really, camera guys, go ahead and jump out. Right now. Please.

———————— ✑ ————————

Date #3—Kiss my ass, not happening.

No way, no how. I could stand some real good company though.

Evan: Whatcha doing?

Whitley: Painting my toenails. You?

Evan: Nothing. Zach wants the room 2nite and I'm done

dating. **Wanna hang out?**

Whitley: Wish I could but I've actually got plans later. Raincheck?

Evan: Sure, I'll holler at you later. Have a fun night.

Whitley: U2, night.

Evan: night.

What's she doing later? Does she have a date? Nope—this is none of my business. I'm the one who declared we wouldn't go *there*. We're just friends. I have her rescuing me from dates...time to sleep in the bed I made.

Or the bed my mom made. I'm packed and on the road in 15 minutes, headed home for the weekend.

------------⤮------------

"Shit, man, stop talking or I'm gonna piss myself."

Parker's just cracking up over my dating stories. Hayden's snuggled up to his side, trying hard not to laugh with him and failing miserably.

"Who was the pretty blonde with you at the funeral? She looked nice, and not with child," she says, somehow with a straight face.

The diamond on her finger twinkles as she rubs her hand on Parker's thigh, always touching him in some way. He'd done it—he asked her to marry him, move home with him, and she said yes. She'll be finishing school online, helping him run the farm, and taking his name soon. I'd love to tell them again to slow down, that they're too young, but what the hell do I know? I think my glowing track record speaks for itself—I know jack shit.

"That was Whitley. She's a good friend, a sweet girl."

"Well, she's very pretty, and it was nice of her to come and support you." Hayden smiles, her eyes mischievous.

"Yeah, she's beautiful, and awesome, and..." I shut my mouth before I say too much, grabbing the remote to concentrate on the TV.

"Not Laney?" Parker asks.

"That's not even it. Laney's happy, and some days I don't even think about it. Can you believe that?" I ask him, my eyes big with my own shock. It's true. I never thought I'd see the day, but some days I don't think about Laney.

"Evan, you're so handsome. Sorry, honey," she kisses Parker's cheek and gives him a sheepish smile, "but you are. And kind. I don't understand the problem."

"Evan's a romantic," Parker jokes, "always has been. No hit it and quit it for that one." He tilts his bottle towards me. "He's a big softie. He wants to hear music and see stars when *she* walks in a room. Don't ya, Ev?"

"You mean like what happens to you when I walk in a room?" Hayden glares at him teasingly, her lips pursed, just daring him to deny it.

"Exactly like that," he growls, diving into her lips.

"Fuck off," I mumble, knowing he's right...and no longer paying attention to me.

Hayden wrestles him off her, catching her breath to turn to me. "Well, what do you hear when Whitley walks in a room?"

I laugh to myself just thinking about it. "Actually, I usually do hear music, because she's usually humming or singing to herself."

"Ahhh." Hayden's clearly a romantic as well.

As fun as this is, I'm no fool, I know how to get out of the hot seat *and* give Parker the proverbial finger. "So, Hayden, tell me about your wedding."

How ya like them apples, Park? I can just sit and nod, but Parker will have to interact while his starry-eyed girl rambles on and on.

Evan wins!!!

Finally.

Chapter 19

Third Base
Evan

Today is the first conference softball game for the Lady Eagles, hosted at home. I do love to watch some ball, but I probably wouldn't have gone, kinda awkward despite the rest of the "Crew" thinking we're all cool…but Laney had arranged it so Whitley will be singing the National Anthem.

The newfound *whatever* between Whitley and Laney mystifies me; if only it were that easy for me. Sure, I miss Laney, and care about her, and have even managed to be around her amicably a few times, but it still jabs me in the gut sometimes. It may always. But the whole group is going to this game and Whitley personally asked me to come watch her sing, so I'm going.

She sings beautifully, her voice, melodic and captivating, ringing out across the park. And I must say, to only myself, seeing her stand out on the mound in a ball cap, jersey, and little shorts…oh boy. My whole "date anyone besides her" plan seems like a real jackass one right about now.

"Pssst, Evan!" I hear from my left and look over to see a nervous Laney standing at the fence. She begs me over with a "hurry, come here" hand, so I make my way down the bleachers and over to her. "He's got me playing third, Evan. I don't play third. What's he thinking?" she asks, her voice panicked.

I chuckle at her, never understanding her lack of faith in herself;

she's an amazing ball player. Third isn't her most practiced point, but she can do it *if* she doesn't psych herself out.

"Laney, you could play third in your sleep. What are you so worried about?"

"This is college ball, Evan. I don't move fast enough for third. Why wouldn't he put me on first and Cassidy at three? Oh my God, Evan, I'm gonna make a fool of myself in the first game." She rests her head against the fence in premature defeat.

"Hey," I poke her in the forehead through the fence, "look at me."

She slowly lifts her head, eyes rimmed with doubt.

"Knock it off. You are a great baller, Laney. Get your ass out there and make it happen. I mean it."

She nods firmly, gritting her teeth, and heads for the dugout. I go back to my seat in the bleachers, Sawyer to my left and Whitley now settled in at my right. We're all kinda clumped in a group; Dane, Tate and Bennett right behind us and Zach on the other side of Sawyer. *One big, happy family.*

"Down and ready, three!"

I turn quickly—I know that voice. Laney's dad is here somewhere. I look around, but I can't see him.

"What was that about?" Dane's voice comes from behind me.

"Huh?" I turn around, not sure if he's talking to me…yeah right, of course he's talking to me.

"Laney; what'd she need? And why's she look like she's seen a ghost?"

"Oh," I shrug, "she's worried about playing third base. It's not her usual spot."

"Hmm…" is his only reply, so I turn back around.

Laney didn't get a single ball hit to her in the first, but she did lay a good tag on an out, putting the Eagles up to bat. She's fourth in the lineup—cleanup—smart coach. Smart pitcher, too, done her homework, 'cause she draws the swing and miss from Laney on a high, outside first pitch.

Seven pitches later and Laney's still battling, fouling them off like a champ. Whitley's nails are probably bleeding she's biting them so much and Bennett's in tears, clearly not used to watching softball. *Good God, it's gonna be a long season.*

I nudge my elbow backwards into Dane's leg and he leans down to me. "Yell at her to quit dropping her hands," I tell him. "Hurry." He stalls, so I elbow him again. "Now!"

"Quit dropping your hands!" He cups his hands around his mouth and yells, and I hold in a laugh. He has no idea what he just said or why.

I should have made him yell something stupid and look like a fool.

Not really.

I think.

The next pitch is a change, which falls short, and Laney's almost out of time. This at-bat has surely met its shelf life when the next one comes right down the middle, just a smidgen low. I take back what I said before. *Not smart, Pitch.*

"That's gone," I say to the group, almost subconsciously.

Crack!

I don't even bother watching it. I stand and cheer, grabbing Whitley's shirt so she doesn't fall down the bleachers in her bouncy celebration. Sawyer's got two fingers in his mouth, whistling, and I finally spot Jeff in the crowd, a proud smile plastered across his face. Laney just hit a two-run homer in her first college at-bat. No one, not even Kaitlyn, can ever take that from her, and my heart feels like it's about to burst with pride.

Laney just went yard. I couldn't be happier for her.

"Thanks, *coaches!*" she yells at Dane and me as she runs past us to home plate.

I don't turn around and look at Dane, but I do manage to hear him over the crowd as he leans in to thank me.

"That was so fun!" Whitley shrieks, wrapping her arms around me in a hug. "I hope she does that every time!"

"I don't know about that." I hug her back. "It wouldn't be as special if she did it all the time, right?"

She pulls back and scrunches up her nose. "No, it'd be cool every time."

"Yeah, I guess it would," I agree, taking her hand to sit her back down beside me. "Now watch the rest of the game, happy girl."

Avery strikes out two batters later, so our group goes from rambunctious and pumped up to solemn in a flash, but we do all laugh when Zach turns around and slaps Dane upside the leg.

"Where's all the tips for my girl, huh?"

It's the bottom of the fourth when time stops.

I see the hit, and where it's heading, my body bracing in tension until she plays it through. But instead, I see her misstep. She was nervous about playing third, psyched herself out and misjudged the bounce. The harsh smack echoes, sickeningly, and Laney drops like a rock, face forward in the dirt.

"Time!" The ump screams.

Barreling down the bleachers, I make it to the fence, searching frantically for a way in when a hand lands on my shoulder.

"Stay back, boy, let them check her out." Jeff. So calm, so collected. "She'll be fine, just a punk knot. It got a bounce first, took the heat off."

Then why's she lying face down in the dirt?

It's six hours, I swear it is, before she gets up and her coaches help her in to the dugout. Everyone claps and the players rise from their knees, resuming the game. Jeff and I stay put, right along the fence at the side of the dugout, waiting for answers. A few minutes later, she walks around the side to us and I can finally breathe, seeing her face, walking. I know she's going to be all right.

Dane has his arm around her shoulder, guiding her to us as she holds a huge bag of ice to her face, completely covering one eye. How the hell did he get to her? Past us?

"Hey," she grumbles, "just a shiner. Nose already stopped bleeding." She pulls down the bag of ice to show us and I hiss with my flinch. The inside of her eye is no longer white, but blood red, as in every blood vessel has popped. It doesn't look good at all, and I'm a little green around the gills thinking of how much pain she must be in, but her dad softly tisks beside me.

"That's gonna be a nice one, Slugger. Can you see all right?"

"Well, since the lid is hanging *over* my eye, it's a little tricky," she tries to smile, "but it didn't hurt my actual vision."

"Just misread the hop. All nervous, huh?" he asks with one know-it-all brow raised. He's probably about to tell her to rub some dirt on it and get back out there. "Gonna be scared to play there from now on?"

"No, sir," she answers quickly, her voice determined.

"Good girl. Probably won't ever happen again, so no need to shy away. Damn nice hit by the way." He pats her shoulder.

"Thanks, Daddy. You proud?"

"Damn proud, kiddo, damn proud. Who's the hardest hitting, toughest girl I know?"

"Me?"

"You." He nods. "I'm gonna head out, beat the rain home seeing as how you're done for the night." He kisses the top of her head. "Love you, girl. Call me tomorrow, let me know you're all right."

Dane watches the whole conversation with a silent, stunned expression. I can see how it'd appear her dad is a little blasé about the whole thing, but that's just the way he is; always has been.

"You sure you're okay?" I ask her, hands stuffed in my pockets. I'm not even sure why I'm still standing here; she's taken care of.

"I'm fine," she smiles at me, "thanks, Evan."

"What the fuck? She okay?" Sawyer says, too loudly, when I make it back to my seat.

Bennett and Whitley crowd in, faces anxious, wanting to hear my reply. Even Zach looks nauseous; yep—could've been your girl just as easily.

"She's fine, up walking and talking. She'll have one helluva black eye and probably a headache for a few days, but she's okay. Dane's down there with her. I'm surprised they let him in the dugout."

"Are you kidding?" Tate snorts. "He jumped that fence and pushed people out of his way; no one *let* him do anything. I'm surprised he hasn't landed Life Flight in the damn parking lot to whisk her to a specialist by now."

Bennett scowls his way and gives him an impish slap. "Hush! I thought it was sweet."

"There they are right there." Zach points, and we all look over to see Dane and Laney walking across the parking lot. "Where are they going?"

"I'm telling ya, he's taking her to the doctor," Tate chimes in again.

"He can't, the team trainer has to check her for a concussion first. He can't just sweep in and do it," I argue.

"Wanna bet?" Tate challenges me.

Oh, please. Mr. Rich and Fabulous may be able to do a lot of things, but he can't override the rules of collegiate sports.

"Looks like the softball team will be getting all new equipment,"

Sawyer smirks, "and ass cushions for these shitty bleachers, I hope."

There's no way I believe college coaches and Dane struck up a "dugout deal." This is ridiculous. But then again, he did just whisk her to his car; that cannot be denied.

Whatever. I'm sick of thinking about it. At least she's taken care of.

Chapter 20

Chosen One
Evan

There are different types of single. For example, some people are "Should Be Single," because, well, no one in their right mind would seriously date them. Not until they get their act together, anyway. Perfect examples of this category are Kaitlyn Michaels and Matt Davis. In fact, those two should probably just give up all hope now and go have evil babies together.

Sawyer is what I would call "Strut Your Single." He owns that shit and is happy about it. He would rather get in and get out, then spend the saved time with his friends. He's upfront about it and never gives the female false hope...he scratches the itch, then goes about things more important to him.

And then there's me. I fall into the "Quit Feeling Sorry for Yourself and Do Something about It Single." Yeah, no catchy title for mine, I'm as pathetic as the category.

Because I'm lying in my bed, lonely and staring at the ceiling, analyzing the categories of singledom, I know it's time to try again.

Date #3.5

Conspirator- Me, myself, and I

Girl- Amy

Stats- brunette, can be found at bar

Problems- None so far

Yes, I went back to the bar and found Amy, the girl Sawyer

threw in my lap the first night I hung with him. As horrific as dating has proven to be so far, I gotta branch out. I need more friends, preferably ones that do things besides hang out with Dane and Laney. I also need female companionship, other than the one I've sworn myself away from for reasons I refuse to justify in my head, again. I wish it was season so I could make friends with some guys on the team other than Zach. But with only open schedule weights and conditioning right now, it's just a "hey" or "what's up" passing my teammates in and out of the tunnel for now.

Which brings me back to my current outing with Amy. She's a pleaser. Everything I say, she agrees to, or she's done it, or she knows somebody who's done it. And who's she kidding? I am *not* that damn funny, yet she cracks up at my every other sentence.

She chooses the drive-in when I ask her where she'd like to go after dinner. *Grease* is playing. Fucking *Grease*. That movie is older than me, and that's what they're showing? I can't help it and I think of Whitley—she'd be giddy about a freaking musical at a drive-in. What is it about girls I know and movies with songs? You know how many songs there are in Disney movies? And we won't even revisit the Moulin whatever nightmare. And yet, here I sit, watching some beauty drop-out with pink hair and angels in curlers floating around.

I've taken nice guy and turned him into pussbag. My dick hates me—he told me so—and I'm all but ready for tampons and a training bra. Fuck this; I reach over and lay my hand on Amy's bare thigh, pulling for her to come a little closer. "You're awful far away," I say in a low voice.

She moves beside me, her thigh now pressed to mine, laying her head on my shoulder. Her brown hair falls against my cheek and smells like...smoke. Okay, moving on. Her arm snakes its way around my waist, one finger sliding under my shirt to tease along the waistband of my jeans. My grip tightens on her thigh, the crotch of my jeans growing uncomfortably tight. "What do you want?" she moves her mouth to my ear and pants.

"How about a kiss?"

"Mhmm..." She moves astride my lap like a ninja, bracing my hips on either side with her knees and *dives* into my mouth.

She tastes like smoke, too, and cinnamon. I hate both, but I go with it, returning each swipe of her tongue tease for tease. I grab her hips now, attempting to slow her gyrations just a bit; my windows aren't tinted. She locks her hand onto one of mine, moving it under her shirt, directing my hand to squeeze one of her breasts—fake. I can feel her nipple harden against my palm and she moans into my mouth, sending a fire through me, but only physically.

I should not be thinking about the other cars around us. I most definitely should not be thinking that "You're The One That I Want" is the most annoying song ever. And under no circumstances should I pull back and move her off my lap. Which is exactly what I do.

"We better go," I say, starting the truck, "don't want an audience."

"You're not shy, are you?" She's slid back over, her wandering hand making it very hard for me to drive. "You shouldn't be." She squeezes my dick. "Feels like something to be real proud of to me."

I refrain from saying "thank you," barely, but rather go with, "Ya think so, huh?"

"Uh huh." She tucks her head into me, licking up my throat and biting my earlobe. "I sure do. I wanna see if I'm right."

The snap of the button and rasp of my zipper coming down sound through the cab as if in stereo. My chest heaves up and down rapidly with my deep breaths, and I'm throbbing, so turned on I can only just keep the truck on the road. Maybe Sawyer's got the right idea. Maybe *this* is what I'm supposed to be doing.

I have no doubt Amy knows exactly what *she's* doing and could make me feel real good, but no matter what, I am who I am.

I veer off the road into the first empty lot I see, throwing the truck in park. "Amy," I grab her hand and pull it away, drawing it to my mouth and kissing her knuckles softly, "how about a second date?"

"W-what?"

Moving her hand back to her own leg, I rest it there and let go, then close up my pants. "Let's go out again, get to know each other. Sound good?" I ask her with a comforting smile.

Her eyes flash to mine and her smile brightens the dark cab. "That'd be great."

"Okay then, next Friday night?"

"Perfect."

———————— ✂ ————————

We've graduated to group messages, and boy oh boy, they've included me. And Whitley. I start humming the music from *The Brady Bunch* before I can stop myself. I should be using *The X Files* theme, though, 'cause it's just too hunky-dory to be real, right?

Laney to group: Crew hang at The K 2night at 8. C everyone there!

My phone's blowing up instantly with everyone's questions and replies. How the hell do you get yourself *out* of a group text?

Sawyer to group: Evan, you wanna ride with me?

Me to group: Not in. Have a date.

Sawyer, *still* **to the whole group: With who? Anyone I know?**

Zach to group: I'd say those odds r pretty good, unless he went 4 towns over.

Sawyer to group: Fuck you, it'd take at least 6 towns and u know it.

Laney to group: TMI Sawyer, yuck.

Bennett to group: RT Laney

Sawyer to group: WTF do TMI and RT mean? And WHO is your date with Evan?

Evan to group: Too Much Information and Retweet (even though we're not tweeting) and none of your business. How do I get myself out of this message? My phone sounds like Morse code going off.

Whitley to group: Why are you grumpy?

Sawyer to group: RT Whitley.

Insane…all of them. I turn off my phone and head out to pick up Amy. She looks great in tight, dark jeans, a black shirt that molds to her body and high, red heels. Her long, brown hair is down and curly. Amy's very hot, and I'm sure she still would be without such heavy make-up. Her eyelashes are so black and sticky looking that they kinda look like spiders coming at me. Other than that, though, not bad at all.

Tonight we eat at a pizza place Amy suggested and split a Meatlovers, except she picks off all the meat. "Why'd you agree to a Meatlovers?" I ask with a laugh. "We could've gotten something else, or half and half."

"It's fine," she concedes happily.

It's really not fine. You don't have to offer to put out on the first date and you don't have to pretend to like something you don't on the second. Whitley picks at her food all the time, which most guys think is annoying, but at least she owns it. She doesn't order to please me and then pick, she usually just dissects what she chose herself. But I digress…

"Amy," I take her hand in mine and rub my thumb in circles on her palm, "just be yourself, okay? That's who I want to know."

"Really?" Her voice is hopeful; she wants to believe I mean it. Wow, so I'm not the only one who thinks dating is a big, fat, scary ass mess where no one really knows what they're doing.

"Of course." I wink at her. "So, what would you *really* like to do after this?"

"Well…" she toys with her lip nervously, "there's something I'm really into, if you want to try it."

In the spirit of encouraging her to be herself, like I'd just preached to her, I agree, even though every instinct in my body bet the whole enchilada that I shouldn't have.

Amy's apartment is…interesting. I'm very happy to report that I'm not allergic to cats since I count five from where I'm standing, and I'm praying to God the glowing eyes underneath her TV stand belong to the sixth. And I'm also suddenly fond of the smell of smoke, seeing as how its stench is a welcome mask to the odor of cat piss.

"Make yourself comfortable," she coos, which must be a joke, "I'll go get my stuff."

There's no way in hell I'm gonna be comfortable until I'm home, but I try to navigate my way to the couch, in the dark. Amy is blatantly fond of red light bulbs instead of, you know, normal ones, and I can't see shit. Silly me, running out without my infrared night vision goggles and all.

"You ready?" She sits down beside me, a black bag in her lap.

"For?" My voice shakes, understandably.

"Well…" She starts pulling stuff out of the bag, arranging it on the coffee table in front of us. "This is what I'm really in to. So first," she turns to face me, "give me your palm."

I let her pick up my hand and she hunches over it, tracing the lines with one finger. How she can see anything is beyond me. I mean literally, not just the hocus pocus.

"Hmmm, very interesting. Okay, I need more. Here," she hands me a deck of oversized cards, "shuffle these three times then cut them twice with your left hand."

For shits and giggles, I shuffle and cut the cards as she instructed, then watch as she starts flipping them over and laying them on the coffee table in a big square.

"Oohhh," she groans, covering her mouth with one hand.

"What?"

She looks at me, worry lines creeping out from her spider eyes, then turns back to point at the cards. The middle one depicts some grim reaper looking dude, the one in the corner…I *think* it's a man head with a horse body. None of them look good; I must be doomed.

"Evan, what's your sign?"

"Right about now, I'm thinking Proceed with Caution."

I'm not kidding.

"No," she scoffs, "your astrological sign. Like Pisces, Aries."

"Oh, the Virgo one I think."

"Uh huh, just as I thought. Evan," she huffs, her shoulders dropping, "we can't see each other again, I'm sorry."

Well, of course we can't. Perfectly logical. And honestly, at the rate I've been going, I should have seen the creepy man-horse and the kiss of death coming, really.

I pretty much tune out after that. She may have said something about my house, which I don't have a house, or her moon, or barren harvesting…not even sure, but I'll recover.

"Sounds about right. I'll see ya." I stand and risk my way to the door, making sure not to "feel" my way, which would require touching things.

"Evan, wait!"

I turn back, ready for her to turn on the damn lights, change the litter boxes, and tell me she's kidding, but instead she sprinkles a circle of some white dust around me and wishes me luck with "my chosen one."

Chosen by who?

Nope, not gonna ask…keep walking, Evan.

Chapter 21

Crazy
Evan

"Dude, give it up, you're never gonna be as big as me." Sawyer grins and kisses his bicep.

"I'm pretty sure only the football team's allowed in here." I put down the weights and move to the leg machine. He's right, my arms will never be as big as his, even though I work out non-stop these days, but I know I've got him in leg strength, so I'm gonna work those while he's here; kinda an ego thing.

"Nobody else will be down here at ten o'clock on a Friday, Evan. They have lives. Pretty sure it's safe."

"I have a life."

"No man, you don't. Your first year of college is gonna be over before you know it and what do you have to show for it?"

"A 3.6?"

He whistles. "And what else?"

"A football jersey."

"You know what I mean. You don't go out, you don't hang with the Crew, and you even quit coming to the softball games. You don't date, no one ever sees you. What gives?"

"Nothing." I press out twenty-five reps before going on, trying to quell some of the aggression his accusatory words are building up in me. "I go home on the weekends to help Parker, class during the week, football stuff; just been busy."

"So how about tomorrow night? I got a double date lined up for us."

"No."

"Wait a second, hear me out."

"No."

"Come on, you'll have fun, I swear!"

"Sawyer," I stand and wipe my face with a towel, "I've decided there are no normal girls on this campus. I can't even imagine what would be wrong with the next one. I have had my fortune told by the crypt keeper, fed another man's fetus and I'm pretty sure I went out with a dude! I said no!"

"I'm sorry." He covers his face and turns his head, trying to hide his laughter.

"You done?"

"Sorry," he turns, under control now, "one more try, come on. You let Zach and Avery set you up, give me a chance. Listen, if there's anything super wrong with this girl, I'll let you kick my ass."

"Have you met the girl?"

He nods. "Many times."

My eyes narrow in suspicion. "Have you slept with her?"

"Not even close."

"Do you know anything you're not telling me? Like she's transsexual, pregnant, into voodoo, drinks blood, is married, has three nipples or *anything* else that *might* strike you as odd?"

"Nothing like that." He clutches his side as he loses the fight to keep a straight face. "Seriously though, totally normal. And hot."

"You had me at normal. I'm not kidding though, Sawyer, one weird thing and I'll stand up and walk out, then take you up on kicking your ass."

"Deal." He sticks out his hand for a shake. "Allister's at seven, cool?"

"I'm not picking her up?"

"Nah, they'll meet us there."

---⌘---

Date #4

Conspirator—Sawyer

Girl- Jenee

Stats- Sawyer and details? All he can positively attest to is that "she's normal" and he hasn't slept with her.

150

Problems- Nothing will phase me

"Why do you keep checking your phone for the time? Sawyer, I swear to God, if these are by the hour girls—"

"Relax, man, I don't have to pay for hookers. Neither do you, fool."

"So *are* they hookers?"

I think my paranoia is totally justified, considering.

"No, and shut up, mine just walked in." He stands and pushes his chair back, walking over to greet a voluptuous bottled-blonde. Everything about her and her cheetah print pants screams "Sawyer." He pulls out her chair, then something catches his eye briefly before he looks at me and smiles. "You're welcome. Turn around."

On pins and needles, I slowly stand and turn, ready to greet my next tragic date and grip the back of my chair to steady myself. My date is beautiful—long brown hair, dark, catlike eyes and a sexy but subtle outfit.

"Hi, I'm Evan." I offer my hand.

"Jenee," she *says*, just says. She doesn't giggle it, or say it with invitation dripping off it, and her handshake is just firm enough to let me know she's there.

I pull out her chair and awkwardly say, "You know Sawyer," because I don't know if he told me his date's name or not, and I absolutely don't want to chance a guess.

"Hey, J, this is Hailey," Sawyer introduces his date who either needs to sneeze or doesn't return Jenee's greeting very nicely. I don't try to guess that either, but when no sneeze comes, I think she might not like Sawyer knowing Jenee. *Have fun with that one, buddy!*

We settle in, just some light small talk and me arranging my silverware nervously, giving Jenee a smile every so often when good ol' Hailey goes and breaks awkward all out of its case by pouring herself into Sawyer's lap. This restaurant seems too nice for lap sitting; I mean, they provide high-backed, cushioned chairs, enough for everyone to have their own, but she doesn't seem to care. She *does* seem to think Sawyer needs his tonsils checked, which she is currently doing a very good job of…you know, in a restaurant.

"So…" I clear my throat loudly, trying to ignore the spectacle across from me. "Jenee, do you go to Southern?"

"I did." She tries to smile, her eyes flicking from me to *them* on their accord.

I understand, really. It's like a car wreck; you don't *like* looking at it, you know you're probably gonna see something gruesome, and yet…your eyes are drawn like bugs to a light.

"You go there, right?" she asks.

"Yeah, I transferred this semester from UGA."

"I heard that too. And you play football?"

I nod, taking a sip of my water as our waitress approaches.

"S-sir," she stammers, but a quick glance confirms she isn't speaking to me. "Sir," she insists, louder this time, tapping Sawyer on the shoulder.

Jenee and I sit silently, watching the whole tacky-but-hilarious scene unfold. Another sharp tap to the shoulder and Sawyer finally breaks free to acknowledge the waitress.

"Oh, hey." He throws her his best smile. "Take a seat, darlin'," he encourages Hailey, moving her to her own chair.

"What are you guys having?" he asks us, just as normal as can be.

"I'll have a glass of house red please," Jenee addresses the waitress politely.

I wait for Hailey to order her drink, but she's busy with a mirror and replacing the lip gloss she'd lost to Sawyer's face, so I go ahead. "I'll just have a Coke, please."

Once she collects the other drink orders, a beer and a Pink Squirrel, our waitress leaves.

Hailey is now sufficiently primped and ready to participate in conversation. "So, Jenny, how do you know Sawyer?"

Here we go.

"It's *Jenee*, and from work. You?"

"Me what?" Hailey pops her gum loudly.

I'm just shocked she came away with her gum.

"How do you know Sawyer?" Jenee's voice is polite, but screams "keep up."

"Here and there." She snickers, leaning over to bury her face in his neck, one hand disappearing under the tablecloth.

By the grace of God, our drinks arrive and we place our orders while Sawyer mauls the basket of bread just delivered. Jenee pushes back her chair, excusing herself to the ladies' room, so I stand to help her. As I do, I see her.

Across the restaurant, looking like a vision in a light pink (of course) top, her hair down around her shoulders, is Whitley. Sitting across from her, looking like a goon, is some preppy little worm in a suit. *A suit.*

"I'll be right back," Jenee says, jerking my attention back to her.

"R-right, okay," I stammer, consumed by my thoughts.

When Jenee has turned the corner, I look to Sawyer. "Hey, I see Whitley over there. I'm gonna go say hi real quick."

I'm off before he can give me shit about it, which he undoubtedly would. She looks up as I approach, quickly forcing her shocked face into a grin. "Evan, hi, what are you doing here?"

"Same as you," I shrug, "eating. I saw you, thought I'd come say hi."

"I'm glad you did. Evan, this is Thad Conner. Thad, Evan Allen," she introduces us.

Thad? That's not a real name.

He stands, placing his napkin that he had in his lap, need I say more, on the table. He offers me his hand with a "Thad Conner."

She just told me that, dumbass, I know your name.

"Evan Allen, still." I raise one brow as I squeeze the shit out of his hand. "Well," I focus on Whitley, "I better let you two get back to your date. See ya later, Whit."

She starts to say something but I walk away, not at all happy, and not at all sure that my face won't give away that fact if I stay any longer. Here I am, on a pretty decent date, mad that Whitley's on one too? Nothing like painting yourself into a corner…forcing yourself to date everyone but the girl who you don't like seeing date anyone but you. The whole "having your cake and eating it too" adage comes to mind, but that makes me think of cake; shortcake, in particular, with strawberries, that Whitley made me.

Not helping.

Jenee's already back in her seat when I arrive at our table, so I apologize, explaining I saw a friend and wanted to say a quick hello. I don't mention the friend is a tiny blonde who hums and digs worms and makes me cake and needs a real man who doesn't own a fucking tie to swoop her up…no, I just say friend. She dismisses it easily, not bothered, much to my relief.

For 2.3 seconds. Until Sawyer speaks.

He smirks. "Who's Whitley here with?"

153

"Her date," I grind out, offering Jenee an apologetic smile, ready to kill Sawyer for having the biggest damn mouth in Georgia. I grab a roll, amazed there's one left with "Mouth of the South" sitting across from me and all, and begin to butter it, welcoming anything else to concentrate on.

Music blares out of nowhere, a song I've never heard, thankfully, 'cause it's terrible, and Jenee scrambles to fish her phone from her purse. "Sorry, I have to take this," she barely offers before excusing herself again.

Offended? Not a bit…this looks like a big ol' opportunity to me. I whip out my own phone, firing off the first shot.

Evan: Do you need me to come rescue you? I owe you one.

Answer, come on, time's a wastin'.

Whitley: No, I'm fine. Are you on a date? Texting me in front of her would not be okay.

Evan: She had a phone call.

Shit. See what she did there? Got me to admit I'm on a date. Tricky female.

Evan: Thad is not a real name. I looked it up.

Whitley: Stop it.

Evan: You know what needs to stop? His ears growing. WAY too big for his beanie head.

I hear her laughter across the restaurant, like a siren's call. Above the noise, dishes clanging in the back, all else, I hear her laugh.

Evan: Funny AND true.

Whitley: Maybe a little.

"Here she comes, man, put that away. Work *with* me, dammit," Sawyer warns in a low voice.

I shove my phone in my pocket and stand just as Jenee approaches. I pull out her chair for her, leaning *way* back to catch a peek at Whitley, who's giving me a thumb's up. I chuckle; Whitley's being kind, approving of Jenee when it's *her* that's clearly the most radiant girl in the place.

"Everything all right?" I ask as I push her up to the table.

"Oh yes, fine. My roommate had a bad night, needed a little talking off the ledge. I'm sorry about that."

"No worries, that's nice she has you."

And I text bombed the lovely lass across the way the whole time you were gone.

"Thank God! My stomach was eating itself." Sawyer's boisterous announcement earns an eye roll from our waitress as she settles the stand and tray, serving our dinners.

Jenee and I barely speak through the meal, but talk about the other side of the pendulum…Hailey is feeding Sawyer off her fork and wiping his mouth after each bite. Oh, and let's not forget the kiss after every swipe of the napkin. It's so nauseating I can barely choke down a mouthful and Jenee is fidgeting so much she's either as uncomfortable as I am or she has worms.

"Sawyer!" I finally bark. "Enough! You know how to use a fork, I've seen you do it."

"You testy fucker, you need to get laid," he mocks me with a snarky wink. "You heard him, sweet thang, eat your own dinner and I'll eat mine," he directs his doting date.

"Thank you," Jenee says under her breath.

Hailey takes turns between pouting and glaring at me, Sawyer biting back a smirk at my obvious discomfort to her scrutiny. He and I are gonna have to have a talk soon about the difference between a little PDA and all out porno previews.

"I thought I'd come by and say goodnight." Whitley's voice comes from beside me and I look up to find her blue eyes zoned in on Jenee.

"Hey, Whit." Sawyer gets up and gives her a hug, eyeing Thad. "Sawyer Beckett, and you are?"

"Th-Thad Conner." I can see his hand shaking from here as he offers it.

Sawyer gives him a brisk, and I'm sure painful, shake and then introduces them both to our dates. I say nothing because I've already played nice with the fagbag one too many times; my angry glare only leaves him long enough to return to Whitley, hers still zoned in on my date.

"Do you two want to join us?" Jenee asks politely, almost as polished as Whitley would have done.

"Thank you, but I'm afraid we can't. I have a plane to catch." Thad straightens his tie as he speaks.

"That's right, well let's go then. Bye, Ev, Sawyer. Nice to meet you both." Whitley gives a small wave and turns to go with *him*.

"Bye, Whit," I respond, my aggravation evident.

My head turns of its own volition and watches her walk out, gray skirt swishing with each flick of her hips until she's completely gone

155

from view. *A plane to catch?* Is he some out of town secret? Someone she dated back home? How long was he here? Is he what she had planned when she couldn't hang with me the other night?

There it is—that familiar pain in my chest telling me I've blown it—again. If ever there was a guy better at complete lack of timing or finesse with making a big move at the exact moment she needs you to make it, I'd love to meet his ass and gladly hand over the title that hangs around my neck like a noose.

Fuck.

"Evan." I snap my head back to Jenee, who puts a hand on my arm and speaks. "Why is she not the one here with you tonight?"

Is there a right answer to this question? This feels suspiciously like a trick question that probably ends with another blast of cold water to my face. I'm being reeled in by the elusive female mind, begging me to trap myself right into a smacking or glass of ice cold water to the face.

But no, as I look for her tell, the twitch of an eye, flare of a nostril…I sense only empathy in Jenee's soft voice and gentle touch on my arm.

Still, I have to go on instinct.

"She's just a friend. I'm having a great time with you."

Not a total lie. As far as recent dates go, this girl wins hands down.

"Good answer," Sawyer says in a cough.

Jenee darts her eyes to him, warning him to butt out, then turns her warm, understanding brown eyes back to me. "Are you ready to get out of here?"

"Absolutely." I rise, helping her with her chair before pulling out my wallet. "Will you wait and pay, Saw?" I ask as I toss money down on the table.

"On it. You kids have fun now." He salutes us with a shit-eating grin.

"Nice to meet you, Hailey," I offer as sincerely as possible. Truth is, she'd offered little to the evening except exhibitionism.

"Bye," she giggles before smothering herself in Sawyer's neck, our exit obviously her green light to resume festivities.

I usher Jenee out with a hand to her back, and once outside realize we'd arrived in separate cars.

"Did you want to do something else, or—"

"Evan," she raises a hand to my cheek, "let's just have some fun, hmm? How about a drink, some dancing?"

"Sure, where'd you have in mind?"

I know of exactly two bars, and while my I.D. is pretty legit, how embarrassing would it be to get turned away in front of her?

Safe bet it is.

"Ya know what? I know just the place. Let's take my truck." With that, I nudge her and lead us to where I parked, helping her up into the beast. Her skirt tightens as she climbs in, offering a fantastic view that I genetically appreciate.

Once settled, her long legs cross at the ankle. "Thank you," she says smoothly, adjusting her skirt.

"Of course," I answer, shutting the door and moving quickly to climb in my side.

"You know The K?" I ask her, once in the truck.

"Yes," she snickers.

"Oh, ok. That good then?"

"Wonderful."

I'm missing something, I think. I'm not much of a talker, so the ride could be silent and it wouldn't bother me any, but Jenee is of a different opinion.

"Do you go to The K often, Evan?"

"I wouldn't say often, but when I do go out, it's usually there."

"So you don't go out much?"

"Not really. I like a cold beer as much as the next guy, but I'm not big on the club scene. You?"

"I love to go out, especially to dance. That's what I want to do one day, dance professionally, in a big city." Her voice lifts, like she's dreaming of just that while she says it. "I'm GM of a gym right now, but just to pay the bills."

Good for her. Everyone needs a dream, but as if I didn't know before, it's settled; Jenee and I will only ever be friends. You will never get me to live in a big, ritzy city, hobnobbing with the elite, clubbing for exposure with famous artists. No, sir.

I probably don't have to think so deep into first dates and could just go with the flow and have some casual fun, but casual and Evan Allen aren't familiar. Parker had nailed it on the head—I'm a romantic. Take it or leave it.

We're here, so I help her out of the truck and hold her arm as we walk in. Something about girls in stilt heels just screams "face plant" to me. The place is packed, loud beats vibrating the walls as hard as the bodies on the floor.

"You want a drink?" I try not to yell at her.

She bobs her head up and down. "Bay Breeze, extra pineapple please."

"You okay here or you wanna get a table first?" I again have to almost scream in her ear.

"I'm gonna dance. You grab a table and come find me, k?"

I nod, hating that plan. God knows we should stick together, but she's sober, and we're not cozy enough for me to be bossing her around... *No, I just can't do it.* I catch up to her, grabbing her elbow.

"Jenee, why don't you come with me to the bar, then we'll wander together?"

"Aren't you the sweetest thing?" She kisses my cheek and pats my chest. "I'll be fine, I promise."

"All right," I begrudgingly concede, walking away slowly, trying to keep her in my sights as long as possible, which isn't long once she moves herself into the middle of the pack on the dance floor.

The bar is packed. I've never seen it quite like this in here, and I'd bet money at least three fire codes are being broken right now. When I get close enough, the line barley creeping, I see Tate tending, sweat rolling down the sides of his face. And scrambling beside him, actually running into him and dropping stuff more than actually serving any drinks, is Zach. Ah, this is too good, I cross my arms and watch in amusement.

"What can I get—oh, Evan, thank Christ!" Zach is extremely happy to see me. "Text or call Sawyer *now*, and tell him to get his ass down here! DJ Funky something, local celeb I guess, came in and took the tables. Look at this fucking place!"

"You guys okay?" Dane walks in behind the bar, frantically searching Tate and Zach's reactions. "I'm closing the door, we're well at max."

"Good!" Tate yells over his shoulder at him. "Start paying people to go home! And where the hell is Sawyer?"

"I'll find Sawyer!" I assure them.

Dane's head jerks to me now. "Evan, hey, how are you? Yeah, if you could track down Sawyer, that'd be great. You guys good, Tate, or you need stocked?"

"I don't know what we need, haven't had time to look. How's Bennett? You'd better have somebody watching them!" He scowls, concentrating on drink slinging but clearly waiting for Dane's confirmation.

"I put Brock on them, they're fine. I'll check stock. Evan," I look up from my phone at Dane, "you got Sawyer? I need him down here ten minutes ago. Then can you go help watch the girls? Drinks on me, man, I'd appreciate your help."

No way am I drinking now. I have to herd in Sawyer and watch a bunch of girls we all care about in this crowd; I need my wits about me. "Yeah, I'm on both. Where are they?"

He points. "Table by the stabilizer pole. Look for Brock, big bald dude in a neon shirt, says 'Security' on the back."

I affirm with my head jerk, turning to fight the crowd. I hadn't forgotten Jenee's drink, I just don't care anymore. I know one of "the girls" is Laney, and I don't like this shit one bit. Surely she doesn't either, this place is a madhouse.

The big ass bald dude is not as easy to spot as one might think. Neon shirt, nope, not jumping out at me, either. Laney sitting at a table plugging her ears...bingo! I touch her arm and she jumps, her mouth open and eyes bulging for only a moment as she realizes it's me.

"Evan!" She leaps up to hug me, a stranglehold around my ribs.

Something rips me back, her falling away from me, and I flip around to see...a big ass bald dude.

"Can I help you?" he growls, lip snarled.

"Brock," Laney grips his arm, "he's fine. He's my friend. Let go!"

The big man, who would eat Sawyer's lunch like a snack pack, and that's saying something, releases his death grip with a skeptical glare. "Don't need to handle Mr. Kendrick's lady."

"Oh, Brock, stop! Go find the other three, I'm fine." Laney pushes him, not that it moves him, but bless her heart for trying. "Where's your date?" She turns and asks me, brows scrunched.

"How'd you know I had a date?"

"Whitley may have mentioned it." She shrugs.

What? Whitley called her? Or—No!

"Is Whitley *here*?" Just like that, my chest seizes and I see red. It's something completely different than what I felt when I knew I was searching for Laney in this mob, and I'll contemplate that later. Right now all I want to do is lay hands on Whitley.

"Yes, she's out there somewhere," she waves her hand toward the dance floor, "with Avery and Bennett. She's fine, Evan." She rolls her eyes at me, but then gives me a knowing smile just as fast.

Leave Laney alone and go find Whitley or stay here? Well, if this isn't the proverbial crossroads staring me in the face I don't know what is. My decision, already made, shocks and excites me in ways that give me hope and chest pains at the same time.

I think somewhere in my own deepest recesses, I knew already, but this makes it so…like the Psalms… I have truly turned the corner and emerged alive and well on the other side. It's like I had an epiphany—my number one priority has been realized and I feel alive.

Luckily, Brock hasn't strayed far or taken at least one corner of one eye off Laney, so I motion him over.

"Can you stay with her? I'll go find the others!" I yell ask him.

"Hmm," he grunts, moving closer to Laney.

"Don't move," I tell her before weaving my way into the mass.

Arms are waving, there's pushing, grinding, and people actually falling on the ground. I am never gonna find anyone in this nightmare, and honestly, I have a hint of vertigo setting in. Fuck this—I push, trying to make sure it's not into any ladies, my way to the DJ stand and climb it.

Holding on to the edge of the booth with one hand, I use the other to bang on the wood, getting Funky Fresh Jam's attention. "Gimme your mic!" I yell in his face.

"Shoot, get on," he dismisses me with a snort and brush of his hand.

"Dane, the owner, is my boy and he sent me. Now gimme the mic!" This time I've already grabbed the neck of the mic stand, curling it around to me. "Turn down the music!"

He complies, flipping some switches, and the crowd stops cold, boos starting to rise through the silence.

"Listen up!" I gulp, summoning the courage for this totally unlike me grandiose display. "Whitley Suzanne, raise your hand!"

That was okay right? I mean, I didn't want to announce her last name, but I also didn't want to summon any other Whitleys, so I went with her middle name. Surely there's not two Whitley Suzannes in the crowd.

My eyes run the crowd until finally, I see a little hand pop up, followed by a "Hi, Evan!" squeal from her.

"Hi, Whit." I laugh in the mic, relief starting to seep in and restore my blood pressure to normal. "Grab Avery and Bennett and meet at the table, woman. *Now*, please."

"Okay, Evan!" she yells back in all her preciousness. I can't see her, but I can hear her smile.

"And Jenee, wherever you are," her hand pops up from my right, "can you come here?"

The crowd remains still and silent, seeming content to watch my show, and I see them part for Jenee's.

"Very impressive," she says loudly, smiling up at me where I still hang, one armed, from the DJ booth.

I'm rather impressed myself.

"I need to take some friends home. This place is too crazy. You ready?"

"Come down, let these people dance and we'll decide."

Right, good plan.

"Thanks, man. Gimme a two minute head start before you start the music?" I beg him.

"Bet." He tries to high five me, realizing I'm using one hand to hold on and one to hold the mic, slapping the air instead with a laugh.

I hand him his mic and jump down, grabbing Jenee's hand to pull her with me through the growingly antsy sea of people. Whitley, Avery and Bennett are waiting at the table, as is Dane, his arm around Laney and a coy grin splitting his face.

"Nice work," he greets me.

"Sawyer make it in?" I hadn't had a chance to check my phone, so I have no idea if he'd gotten my messages and I'd accomplished that goal.

"Yeah, he just got here. He's behind the bar now, so I sent Brock to the door. Thanks for the help."

"Everyb—" The music starts up, so I try again, in a much louder voice. "Everybody, this is Jenee."

"Hi." She waves at them all then smiles at Dane. "Hey, Dane."

Dane's staring at the floor while Laney's staring at him, and I'm done caring, back to staring at Whitley, who's staring at Jenee.

"Um, okay, I'll go first." Bennett moves to the center of the group cheerily. "Jenee, I'm Bennett. My roommate is Laney," she points to Laney, "girlfriend of Dane, that you know...how?" She follows up with a smile as sweet as syrup.

"I work for him," is what I think she said, but we're yelling over bebop noise and a wailing mosh pit again, so I can't be sure.

"Oh, that's nice." Bennett's shoulders relax. "That makes perfect sense. So you may know my boyfriend, Tate, his brother."

"I do." Jenee lifts her hair with one hand and fans herself with the other. "So," she turns into me and almost yells, "I'm gonna stay. I have a huge group of friends here, I'll be fine. You go tend to your girl. It was a pleasure, Evan." She chastely kisses where my ear and face meet. "Nice to meet you all. Bye, Boss." And with that, she's sucked up into the dance vortex once again.

"Okay!" Bennett claps. "Avery, let's go sit at the bar with Tate. I'm sure that's where Zach is."

Dane grabs Laney's hand. "We're out."

"Bye, Evan, thank you!" Laney rolls her fingers and darts her eyes to Whitley then back to me, throwing me a wink of her own.

It reminds me, before the mayhem, that Laney and I were best friends; always in each other's corner. And she just said, "Go get her, Ev. Be happy," with a look. We were back.

Don't mind if I do, friend, don't mind if I do.

She won't hear me, a good seven feet between us, so I wait patiently until Whitley's big sapphires meet my radar on her, and point. Turning my finger over slowly and crooking it, I beckon her over, fighting any give on my face.

Chewing her bottom lip the whole way, she slinks over to me. "Hi, Evan, how are you?" Her words are breathy, tone hopeful.

"Not so great, pretty girl. You scared me, again. I don't like feeling that you're in danger and I can't stop it. Where's your date?"

She opens her mouth, but I place two of my fingers over it gently, no longing giving two shits where her date is. "You know what, hold that thought. Let's get out of here; my eardrums are bleeding."

No argument or agreement, no "let me say bye to..." No question in her eyes. Her tiny hand slips into mine and I squeeze, fighting our way to the door, her body tucked tightly, safely, against mine.

---------- ✍ ----------

"Where's your date?" I ask again. Okay, I do still give a shit and

162

nothing would make me happier than to hear she'd left him in there, alone, to leave with me.

"Nosey," she grumbles under her breath, looking out her window as we sit in my truck.

I haven't started it yet. I'm kind of just enjoying sitting here, knowing she's within arm's length and secure. There's nowhere else I need to be.

"I'm sorry, I didn't quite catch that," I tease, reaching over to tickle her side.

"Stop," she squirms and snickers, "I said you were nosey, *Nosey*. Where's *your* date?"

"You saw her walk away. She stayed there 'cause she knew I had other things to take care of." I wiggle my fingers, threatening to tickle her again. "Now spill, woman."

"Okay!" She scoots as close to her door as she can. "He wasn't my date, if you must know."

Oh, I must know.

"And?" I want her to keep talking.

"Thad works for my father. He was sent to discuss the changes my family will be facing. It seems my parents are liquidating certain things in preparation for an," she makes air quotes with her fingers, "'amicable division of assets.'"

"Your parents are getting divorced?"

"So it seems." Her face is sullen, eyes downcast.

"And they sent a suit to tell you?"

She nods, the movement causing a tear to fall from beneath the veil of her hair onto her leg.

I can't take seeing her so sad yet trying to be strong, stoic, hiding her pain from me. I slide across the seat in one motion, wrapping my arms around her. She curls into me and her body shakes as her sobs grow louder.

"Shhh, I got you," I whisper against her soft hair that tickles my lips. "You don't have to be the happy, strong one all the time, Whit. Let me have a turn to hold *you* up."

Her head lifts off my chest, nose pink and eyes shiny. "There's no way I'm as good at being your rock. Am I?"

I scoff. She has no idea. "All the damn time, woman."

She grins slightly. "Well, you bring out the best in me."

"Right back atcha, pretty girl." I wink down at her, earning me

163

another smile.

100% success rate—still undefeated with the wink.

"So, I guess that's what happened with your beach house? But splitting money doesn't mean you don't have any, so why foreclosure?"

What the fuck, Evan? Why are you asking shit, making her examine the details?

"Sorry, Whit, just thinking out loud, nevermind."

"It's okay," she says through sniffles. "I'm not involved, obviously, since my parents sent a messenger rather than talk to me themselves, but I know my father. My guess is, he let them '*take*,'" air quote fingers again, "the house so she doesn't get claim on it, but I'd bet anything he buys that cheaply priced, foreclosed property back under a business name."

Sneaky. And maybe illegal?

"Damn, that's some diabolical shit. What about your tuition?"

Again, Evan, stfu.

"That's fine, covered and paid. My house too, paid for and now in my name. "

"Well, there's something." I run my hand down the back of her head, embarrassed when I realize I've done it several times and probably more than necessary. "It'll all be all right, Whitley, you'll see. Parents split up, and it sucks, but you're grown, have your own life, and you're amazing all by yourself."

"Yeah?" She has no idea what it does to a man when a beautiful blonde peeks up, all doe-eyed and innocent, heart-shaped face pinked and lips parted, puffs of her breath hitting your neck.

"Yeah," I assure her, pulling my eyes from the glisten on her mouth and back to her eyes, "definitely. What can I do to make you feel better?"

Please don't let her say watch Moulin Rouge. I'd be down for another tattoo, but not that movie. It seriously sucks ass.

"You could kiss me," she says in a voice so quiet couldn't even be classified as a whisper.

And yet, I heard her in Dolby.

I *could* kiss her. And take care of her and hold her hand and take long walks. Give her a reason to sing and hum every day. I could quit fighting it, second guessing it, playing devil's advocate on why I don't or shouldn't feel what I've absolutely felt for a while.

That's what I could do.

I run both my hands up the sides of her face, moving back her hair to show me all of her ivory neck. "You sure are pretty, Whit."

I lay my lips on hers, unmoving, locking gazes. Her hands come up and lock around my wrists, tightening, holding me there. Whitley's lips move first, rubbing shyly side to side on mine.

"Kiss me, Evan," she breathes into me.

Tracing the seam with my tongue, I take my time learning her lips, her taste. She opens, letting me in. No begging, no me wanting her more than she wants me, just the two of us together, joining, *finally*. As our tongues meet, she whimpers, the sound crippling. Her hands move into my hair, tugging, hungry, truly wanting me closer. And in that instant, another crack heals and I feel closer to whole. Kissing her is electric, better than a game winning touchdown.

My fingertips trail down her neck, her shoulders, her sides, learning every dip, line, and curve that is Whitley. I end my gentle exploration with hands gripped around her tiny waist, hauling her whole body into mine. Releasing her sweet mouth, I nibble her jawline before feasting on her neck, her pulse drumming against my eager mouth.

"Ah, Whit," I growl, licking slowly up to her ear, "damn, you're sweet."

She grabs my cheeks and pulls my face to hers, eyes aflame. "You about done with the disaster dating thing?" Her chest heaves, her breaths coming heavy and hungry.

Oh how this little pixie makes me laugh. "Yes, ma'am. You forgive me?"

She twists her mouth, tapping her chin with a single finger. "I don't know. Seems like I should make you sweat it out since you made me so crazy."

"Only a crazy woman can love you like crazy."

"You better be ready to give as good as you get," she warns, nipping my mouth and bringing to life another part of me I thought for sure had died. The part that loves to cherish, the part that wants to be embraced, and the part that yearns, has always yearned, to have that embrace returned.

"I'm a thorough kind of guy, Ms. Thompson. I'll give you something to hum about every chance I get, you precious little thing." I tap her nose airily. "And no more dating for you, either."

"I told you, Thad wasn't a date." She wiggles, burrowing closer against me.

"Yeah, I know, but what about the other night when I asked you to hang out and you had plans? I assumed you had a date then."

"I didn't."

"Well then—"

"I sat at home, Evan. I wrote a paper, took a bath, and fell asleep watching a *Duck Dynasty* marathon."

I'm elated to hear she didn't have a date; I'd been trying to ignore the fact that it'd been eating away at me wondering what she'd done with who, since the minute she blew me off that night. But, now there are much more important matters at hand.

"*Duck Dynasty*! Why don't you ever force me to watch that instead of singing bullshit or whatever?" I slap her bottom. She squeals and jumps, landing her firmly in my lap.

"I didn't know you liked that show. There's a lot I have to learn."

"Whit," I sneak a kiss, "I'm from Georgia. I hunt and fish; *Duck Dynasty* is a pretty safe bet. In fact, anytime you have to choose between beards or singing, what do you think my answer would be?"

"Okay, okay," she giggles, "lesson learned."

"You guessed strawberry shortcake, my favorite dessert, but missed this? Crazy girl." I move for her mouth, already starving for another taste, but her body goes stiff as she gnaws her bottom lip, climbing out of my lap and scooting away.

"Hey," I reach out and rub her leg, "what just happened?"

She won't look at me, head turned to the window.

"Whit, talk to me, please."

Her head shakes. "I had almost forgotten, so it's not like I lied. I'm sorry."

What am I missing here? Did she steal the strawberry shortcake or something?

Her mutter is lined with worry. "I didn't guess about the shortcake. Or the fishing. Laney fed me some info a while back. I'm a big, fat fraud." Her fist goes to her mouth and she bites her knuckle. "I'm not in tune to you; I'm a cheater."

Do not laugh, Evan. The lady thinks it's serious, you take it seriously.

"Woman," I say, watching as she turns her head to me but her eyes dodge mine, "come here." I pat her spot in my lap.

166

She's unsure, thinking I'm mad, so I give her a smile and pat my lap again. Hesitantly, she crawls back in and I wink at her, letting her know I could care less. So she got the DL on me, so what. She cared enough to put her info into play...so I see no problem here.

"You worry too much, sweet girl. I love that you wanna know my secrets. I love that you wanna know me."

"Really? Okay. And just because she told me a few little tiny things doesn't mean our connection isn't real." The whole sentence came out in one rushed ramble with no pause for breathing. It was adorable.

"Really and agreed. Now relax." I kiss her forehead, still fighting the urge to snicker at her. "Ask me anything you want, anytime."

"Will you take me on a date?"

She needed no time to think about that one.

"You bet your sweet ass I will."

Chapter 22

Kiss Me
Evan

Date #1 (none of the rest count)

    Conspirator—Fate

    Girl—Whitley

    Stats—little blonde hummingbird, biggest blue eyes you've ever swam in, Junior

    Problems—nothing we can't solve together

"Hi." She opens the door, perky and smiling. Her eyes slowly survey me from head to toe, dressed in Timberlands, jeans and a long sleeved white Henley, and I hope she likes what she sees. "Sorry," she blushes and scoots out of the way for me to enter, "come in."

"Don't be sorry," I kiss her cheek, "I can wait all night. These are for you." I pull a bunch of daisies tied together with twine from behind my back. I hear her breath catch and trembling fingers take them from me. I figured your first real date called for a whole bunch of flowers, not one at a time like I usually hand her.

She's really nervous; thank goodness I'm not the only one.

"What were you so deep in thought about?" I ask her.

"What to wear." She glances down to her shorts and tee. "I've proven I'm an epic failure at dressing correctly for the occasion, so I was waiting for you. Where are we going and what should I wear?"

Oh, that smile of hers…did I mention it already?

"I'm not telling you, and wear whatever you want. But, you'd probably be fine in jeans."

"I can do that. Make yourself at home, it will only take me a minute."

"Do you want me to put those in water for you while I wait?" I glance to the flowers, still clutched to her chest.

"Sure, thank you." She hands them over slowly, seeming to not really want to part with them just yet. "There should be a vase in the cabinet above the fridge." She turns to go down the hall, but I catch her by pulling on the hem of her shirt, dragging her back to me.

"Don't be nervous, pretty girl. We've been on plenty of dates. We may not have called them that, but we always have a good time together," I breathe huskily in her ear and watch the goosebumps pop out over her bare shoulders and arms.

"I'm glad we're calling them dates now," she admits sweetly.

I run one knuckle down her neck. "Me too. Now gimme some sugar before you run off."

She kisses the tip of her finger then touches it to my lip. "That's all for now," she teases me.

"Go get ready. Quickly," I hiss, trying to swat her bottom and missing as she scampers away.

I found this spot on accident, just out driving by myself one day, thankful to find somewhere relatively close to school where I could hide way. But now, I don't want to keep it my secret; I want to share it with her. No more will it be the place I sit to stew on old memories, but the paradise where I make new ones.

"Stay put until I come get you, okay?"

"Okay." Whitley grins, giddy at the prospect of a surprise.

I chuckle to myself and shake my head as I climb out; she's so easy to please, so easy to make happy, but I plan to be the man who takes her from agreeable to delighted all the time.

The truck bounces a bit as I unload all the stuff out of the back of it, but she never turns around; I know she wants to prolong the surprise. I hate to think she holds on so tightly to times like these because she's not used to people doing them for her.

A few minutes later I have it all set up and open her door. "Whitely," I take her hand, "you can get out now."

She turns to face me, eyes squeezed closed. "I didn't peek, I promise. Should I keep them closed?"

"You are precious." I kiss the end of her nose. "Open your eyes, I don't want you to fall."

With a small pout, she opens her eyes and uses my hand and shoulder to climb out. It's once her feet are firmly planted that I move her hair and slide the one daisy I'd kept behind her ear. It pales beside her beauty. "Shame for the flower really; never had a chance." I wink and lead her by the hand through the dark to what I hope is a surprise of her dreams.

On the ground is a blanket surrounded by lit candles with a picnic set for two. Music plays softly from my phone hidden behind the picnic basket, and as my arms sneak around her waist from behind, I can feel her pounding heartbeat against my chest.

"Evan," she sighs, "it's beautiful."

"*You're* beautiful, Whitley Thompson, inside and out. And I need my ass kicked for taking so long to tell you." Brushing her hair back, I touch my lips to her ear. "I'd have taken you out somewhere, but I kinda wanted you all to myself. That all right?"

"More than okay." She turns, meeting my lips. "This is perfect," she murmurs against them.

I scoop her up and cradle her in my arms, carrying her to the blanket where I gently set her down. "As you can see," I attempt some sort of sexy accent, "we have champagne and cheeseburgers with," I reach into the basket to reveal the grand finale, "chocolate mousse for dessert."

Her beautiful giggle cuts through the night air, more brilliant than the stars above us. "May I propose a toast?" she asks, holding up her glass.

I grab my glass. "Ladies first."

"To finding your first choice," she delivers faintly.

"To overcats and admitting when you're wrong." I clink my glass to hers and wink.

We both take a sip, Whitley's eyes serious and locked on mine. "Wrong? About what?"

"A lot of things," I explain with a mocking laugh, "some good, some bad." I stand, offering my hand to her, which she quickly accepts. "Mostly worrying more about what I've always known instead of what I've always wanted."

What I've always wanted. Someone to meet me halfway, to be

the other half of my team. A bubble of our own that no one bursts through, where we're equally important to one another, we both know it, we both trust it, putting it before all else. When I lean in to kiss her, she's already up on her toes to grab it and give it back to me, with passion. When I walk in a room, she smiles like her day just got better, and my eyes seek and find her first in the crowd.

Honestly, I really don't ever compare the two, but I do realize something now. With Laney, I put her up on a pedestal, then spent all my time trying to get her to come down and see me. Whitley walked right up to me, out of anyone and everyone in the room, and asked me to sit beside her.

She's been right beside me, literally, ever since.

I feel her next to me now; lost in my thoughts, I pulled her body flush against mine, one hand curled around her waist…and there she stays, content and silent. "Dance with me, pretty girl," I croon, my voice low and sated in her ear.

"Mmm," she hums, slinking her arms around my neck, her little body fitting perfectly into every bend of mine.

Every spot we meet incinerates me, teases me. Her head lays against my chest as we sway so slowly we're almost not moving. "Kiss Me," by Ed Sheeran plays softly, my new favorite song. Goddamn it feels good. Right. This moment, probably made for girls to swoon about, rocks my soul. The deep, carnal beat of the song matches the one in my chest and the one in her throat where my thumb rubs lazy circles.

When the song ends, her head rises and she asks, cheeks flushed and eyes glazed. "Evan?"

"Huh?" I murmur into her hair, where my mouth has decided to rest.

"Just checking if you were still with me."

"Oh, I'm with you, Whit," I agree, now looking at her, "and you're with me. There's no reversing this spell."

Gradually, it kicks in, a glow moving across her face. "So no more dating?"

"No, there'll be lots and lots of dating."

She tenses in my arms. "Um…"

I don't drag it out too long. I didn't intend to tease her but know exactly what she *thought* I meant when she goes rigid. "Just me and you. Lots and lots of dating…each other."

"That was just mean," she grumbles, pulling out of my wrap on her and crossing her arms across her chest.

"I'm sorry," I say, knowing this is so not the time to laugh. "I didn't mean for it to sound like that."

"Hmpff." Her bottom lip pops out and she tries so hard to stay mad.

"Whit," I step to her and pull her closer, "forgive me." I nuzzle her neck, teasing her with my tongue. "Please."

"Convince me," she replies, then gives herself away with the moan.

"Yes, ma'am."

She can stay mad all night.

Chapter 23

Psychedelic
Laney

Freaking voicemail!

I haven't heard from Dane since he dropped me off last night around 11. His phone keeps going to voicemail and all my texts to him remain unread. So I sit here, forcing myself to finish up my Psych paper, which started out as your average pain in the ass homework assignment but has turned into quite the epiphany of self-reflection.

That's what alone time will get you.

The assignment was to write a ten page paper, double spaced, where you are both the Psychologist as well as the patient, and portray one session concerning one prime topic or "issue." Now if that doesn't sound like hella fun, I don't know what does. Yet here I sit, merely the medium, as the paper writes itself. It's suddenly one of my favorite assignments ever.

I was going to write about Evan and my feelings of guilt, heartache, some regrets, but the imaginary doctor started out asking "about me" (that seems like something the doctor would do first session, right?). After softball and Dane, I may have mentioned Disney movies, and then my family, or lack of…and voila! My paper, "Disney and Mommy Issues," is written. I'm thinking it's pretty brilliant.

Surely it hasn't escaped everyone's attention (but mine) that Disney doesn't do moms.

Bambi—mom killed in first ten minutes of movie.

Cinderella—mom dead, enter evil stepmother

Snow White—again with the evil stepmom

The Little Mermaid—no mom or stepmom

Finding Nemo—mom eaten in first *five* minutes of movie

Beauty and the Beast—you guessed it, just a dad

Sleeping Beauty—you see the mom for five seconds, long enough for her to let three fairies disappear with her newborn for 16 years

Aladdin—he's got no one, Jasmine's got just a dad

Peter Pan—no parent or bad parents? Who knows, but YO—there's a dude sneaking in your kid's window every night and flying away with your daughter!! Red flag!

I think I've made my point, and I fear I may be subconsciously drawn to Disney because I connect with the recurring absence of mother theme. Too much? Overdramatic? It's a *Psych* paper…I'm totally getting an A.

Am I playing it off like my mom thing doesn't bother me? Probably.

Am I now gonna actually mail her the letter I wrote her? Possibly.

The edge of the folder sticks out from the pile on my desk; I can clearly pick it out of the pile of clutter from here. All the information Dane gathered on her is in it, the answer to many unanswered questions just five feet away. Where she's been, where she's at, probably even an address. Does she love me? Okay, that answer probably isn't in there.

And why is it all of a sudden important to me to know?

Or has it always been important to me and I've just been kidding myself?

I should have never taken Psych.

If I lay across the bed and stretch this arm…a little further…got it! Page one, I already know all this; name, birthday, etc. Page two, yup, right there—address. She's only about two hours away.

Maybe I should take the chance. Maybe this is an opportunity to heal, unafraid of any backfire, any more hurt. Maybe it would help, or at least get rid of this nagging burn in my gut that surfaces out of nowhere every once in a while. Maybe I should send the letter. Maybe I should take a road trip.

Can you just show up for a visit at this type of place? I could call and ask. Yeah, I'll call and ask, and if they say I can't come, then that's my sign that this is in fact a terrible, Disney, Psych 101-induced bad, bad idea.

I clutch my phone, staring at it, willing Dane to call right now and talk me out of this. One more try; surely he'll answer this time and save me from doing something rash.

Voicemail again. So done.

Snatching up the paper and slicing one very painful paper cut into my finger, I dial the number. As it rings, that juicy, extra saliva in your mouth, tingly jaw, I'm about to puke feeling kicks in, but I bite it back. I'm a big girl now and I fight my demons like a big girl. By myself.

"Rosehill, can I help you?"

"Y-yes, I was wondering if I could just come visit my, uh, someone?"

"A patient here?"

No, the janitor; I really need to see him.

"Yes, a patient there."

"Are you a family member?"

"Um, yes, she's my..." I clear my throat, swallowing down the pool of nervous fluid in my mouth. "She's my mother."

"What's the patient's name?"

"Tricia. Trish. Tricia Walker." She probably thinks I'm guessing since I'm stammering like a skittish schoolgirl.

"And your name?"

"Laney. Laney Walker. I'm, well, I'm her daughter."

"I need to place you on hold for a moment, all right?"

"All right." Oh my God, is she going to ask my mother if she wants to see me? What if she says no? I am such an idiot, just laying myself out there for more fucking rejection. I should hang up. Shit! I gave her my name! *Breathe, in and out, breathe. She can't eat you through the phone.*

"Miss Walker?" the woman's voice comes back on the line, surprisingly stalling my panic attack.

"Yes?"

"I've put a call in to your mother's doctor as well as her guardian. As soon as I talk to them both, I can give you a call back. When were you wanting to visit?"

"I guess, I mean today is fine, if that's all right."

"I'll ask. What number can I call you back at?"

I give her my number and hang up, nervous she'll never call back, scared she'll call back and say no, terrified she'll call back and say yes.

I want to talk to Dane. Obviously I can't be left to my own devices—look at the catastrophic mess I stirred up. For years I've tucked it away, but left alone for one harmless Sunday morning and I'm planning reunion road trips and digging up bones with a big ass shovel.

And where the hell is he??? Lemme guess, he lost his phone and didn't memorize my number to call me from another one. Been there, done that; he better not even try and go there. He owns planes, he can get to a fucking phone. Or here's a thought…your brother dates my roommate—phone a friend! Use your 50/50!

Okay, so I'm losing it. Calling my other man.

"Hello?"

I feign cheerfulness. "Hi, Daddy."

"Slugger, how are you?"

"Fine, just thought I'd call and see how you were."

"I'm the same as when you called me yesterday," he goads, "what's new with you? I know your life has to be more exciting than mine."

"Nothing's new." *LIAR!* "Just missed you."

"Uh huh."

I know that tone…the jig is up.

"What's really going on, Laney? Out with it."

Deep   breath,   and   go, "IcalledtogovisitmymotherandnowI'mfreakingout."

"Did you go?"

"I just called a second ago. I wrote a paper, and Dane's busy, so I got crazy. Did you know Walt Disney's mother died of asphyxiation in the house he bought her?"

Perhaps I should be checked for PMDD. It's different than PMS, worse, in fact, and I'm almost positive the commercial I saw was scripted specifically to my current symptoms. Is the P before or after your time of the month? Either way, pretty sure I have it.

I take a minute and google it…that's how sure I am. *Jesus*, the list of side effects from suggested medication is longer than the symptoms! I think I saw everything from blurred vision to run out of gas in your car to give off a scent attractive to werewolves to ingrown nose hairs on there. *No, thank you*, I'll deal with this on my own…

"So, what'd they say?" His voice is as calm as ever, monotone and infuriating. Also, he seems to care nothing about the horrible news of Walt's mother, which is kinda harsh.

"They'll calling her doctor and her guardian and gonna call me back. She might not want to see me. And who is her guardian? Shouldn't that be, like, you?"

He may seem cool and collected, but once in a great while, like now, the slightest shift in his voice betrays him. "I have no idea who it is; I quit getting information or options years ago, Laney. Can't guard somebody who doesn't want me to. And she'll want to see you."

"You don't know that for sure, Daddy."

"It's the *only* thing I know for sure, kiddo," his voice doesn't exactly crack, but it's strained, "is that she's your mama, Laney. She loves you. Always did, always will."

My dad is a very "B comes after A" kind of guy, so he won't speak again until I do; it's simply my turn now in his eyes, but damn if I know what to say to that. We may just sit here in silent standoff for hours.

Finally, I croak out a "well—"

Must have been enough, 'cause he jumps in. "I'm proud of you, Laney. Real big thing you're doing. Praying it works out for you the way you want it to."

"Thanks, Daddy. Do you, uh, do you want to go with me?"

"Better not. I think this needs to be your thing. You understand?"

I nod even though he can't see it. "Yeah, I understand. Anyway, they may not call back or even let me come, so we'll see."

My phone beeps then and I'm not sure if I want it to be Dane or Rosehill more. "Daddy, I have a call. I'll let you know how it all goes."

"Love you, Slugger. Good luck."

I glance at the screen as I quickly flip the call over. It's not Dane. "Hello?"

"Hello, is this Laney?"

"It is." my answer anxious and wispy.

"Laney, this is Joan, calling you back from Rosehill."

"Yes."

"I spoke with both parties, and everyone is in agreement it would be fine if you came for a visit. You are over 18, correct?"

"Yes, ma'am."

"All right, then it is fine for you to come by yourself, which is the preferred plan as of right now. Your mother's guardian would also like to be present, so can you tell me what time you'll be here?"

"Um…" I look at the time on my phone; it's almost noon and I haven't showered. "Is around three o'clock all right?"

"Should be fine. I'll let her know and we'll see you then. Press the buzzer by the front doors and ask for Joan. I'll come up and see you back."

"All right, thank you."

I'm going to see my mother. In mere hours. What do I wear? Do I bring anything? I can look directions up on my phone. Do I have gas in my truck? I need a shower. I need to throw up. I need to calm the hell down.

Decided for me, I run to the bathroom, emptying all I had in my stomach and then some. When the dry heaves stop, I rise, brushing my teeth immediately. I use my left hand to hold the right one for the task, since just one alone isn't stable enough to do the job. Next I turn on the shower, going to grab my phone while the water heats up, trying Dane again. Even though I said I was going to.

All previous plans are obviously out the window; I can't even brush my own teeth functionally. I am officially a hot mess.

And his voicemail is now the most annoying fucking sound on the planet.

This time, I leave one in return.

"It's me. Not sure where you are, but when you get this, call me, please, kinda a big day here. I love you, Dane, I really hope everything's okay."

———— ⌇ ————

"Where we going?"

Oh, look, I invited Sawyer to go with me…except I didn't.

"Hello to you too, Sawyer." I laugh at the big teddy bear who just hopped in my truck out of nowhere. "*I* am going to see someone. Not sure where you think you're going."

"Someone who? Where? Where's Dane?" His eyes squint,

178

grumpy scowl aimed right at me.

"Someone personal, a couple hours away, and your guess is as good as mine. He hasn't answered his phone or texts all morning. Now jump out, stowaway, I gotta go."

"No can do, Gidge, no way you're going on a couple hour mystery trip alone. P.S. though, I'm excellent company. You just hit the fucking travel buddy jackpot. You need to recognize."

"You're pumping the gas every time."

"Done."

"And don't touch the music."

"Now hold on a damn minute," he growl-whines, "I said travel buddy as in buddy system, not dictatorship."

My lips purse as my eyes cut to him, my fingertips drumming the steering wheel. I'm actually very happy to have this silly man's company, he will no doubt lighten the stress of the trip, but no way am I showing my cards and listening to Metallica the whole way.

"How about every other song I get to pick?" How cute, Sawyer has a pweeeeaseeee face.

"How about you buckle your seatbelt and zip that lip right after you tuck the bottom one back in."

"Every two songs?"

"Sawyer!"

"Fine," he rips his seatbelt out a little too hard, "but no boy bands."

I'm already driving at this point, my Backstreet Boy playlist starting to shake the windows because I can. Sawyer tosses his head back against the seat with a dramatic groan, kicking his feet up on the dashboard. I know his big ass is uncomfortable right now, his knees scrunched up almost touching his chin, but I also know he's putting on a pout show that's awful important to him.

"So where are we going?" he frumpily asks.

I turn down his torture, aka the music. "I'll tell you, but unless I say different, it's between you and me. Okay?"

"Laney, you know the drill. If he asks, I won't lie to him."

"Well, he'd have to use a damn phone before he could ask, right? Maybe by the time he gets around to doing that, I'll have decided he can know."

"Did y'all have a fight?"

"Actually, no," I pause to slap the hand sneaking for the music,

179

"we didn't. So I don't know what's up."

"Shit, Laney, should we stop at the next store and check the back of milk cartons? I know my boy, and he wouldn't ever ignore you."

"He's probably just busy with work." I shrug my shoulders, not quite buying my own answer. It is odd, Dane usually texts me at least five times by this hour, and the mornings I don't wake up with him curled around me, I wake up to a "Good Morning" call or text.

"On a Sunday?"

"He gets calls on Sundays all the time."

"Why didn't you stay with him last night anyway?"

"I don't know." Hmmm now that he mentions it, why didn't Dane demand I stay with him on a Saturday night? I honestly hadn't even been thinking logistics when he dropped me off, but now that's it brought to my attention, something's not computing.

"I'm gonna text him just in case."

"Knock yourself out; he won't answer."

His big fingers are tapping away on his phone and I steal a quick glance and laugh; Sawyer's a one finger typing bandit. I turn the music back up, but he lunges for it desperately.

"No, no more, please! I'll be good, I swear," he begs. "Back to my original question, where are we going?"

I suck in as much air as my expanding lungs will hold, then let it out in a calming, smooth exhale. "We're going to see my mother. Well, *I'm* going to see my mother, you have to wait outside when we get there. Their rules, not mine."

"Whose rules?" He mouth twists in question.

His reaction confirms it for me; Dane hadn't told him my business, which I was pretty confident in, but it's nice to have my trust reinforced.

"My mother's not well. She left when I was very little and I never knew why, or where she'd gone."

I pause, waiting for him to say something, but he stays silent.

"Dane tracked her down, found out she has trouble." I refuse to say exactly what, 'cause honestly, I don't know enough to explain any questions he would have. "She lives in a special home where they can help her."

That's as much as he's getting, and I can't believe I told him that much. But Sawyer's all bark and no bite, one of the greatest guys I know, and I trust him.

"Do you go visit her often?"

"Never. This will be the first time I've seen her in almost a decade."

He lets out a long whistle, rubbing a hand over his almost shaved head. "Why today, now? Dane should be here with you for this, Gidge, not my insensitive ass."

Insensitive *my* ass. Who does he think he's kidding? If you somehow get Sawyer, I just realized I don't know his middle name, Beckett to take you into that caring, protective, hilarious, loyal bubble of his…you've struck gold. I'm very lucky to have him as a friend.

"One, we've already established why Dane's not with me. Two, I am perfectly capable of making rash, emotional decisions by myself. And three," I switch hands on the wheel to use my right for the jovial shoulder push I give him, "you're not nearly as insensitive as you give yourself credit for there, Biggun'. In fact, I'm grateful to know you, have you here."

Definite PMDD. I could write a tampon commercial write now.

"Plus, I'm fucking hot."

And Sawyer brings us right back on track.

"And that," I concede with an eye roll he can't see.

---------⌒˧⌒---------

When I arrive, Joan, who I spoke with on the phone, and a short, dark-haired woman with kind, smiling eyes named Tammy meet me at the door. Joan hands me a badge to clip on my shirt right before she runs a wand thingy over my body. While she does this, Tammy, apparently my mother's guardian and cousin, gushes on and on about the last time she saw me and how cute I was. She could have fallen out of a tree and landed on top of me and I wouldn't have known her.

"I need you to remove your keys, phone and any jewelry from your pockets and place them in here." She hands me a tray. "They'll be returned to you when you leave."

I don't say WTF out loud, but I know my face screams it.

"It's for safety reasons," Tammy says and pats my shoulder, "they have to make sure nothing's brought in that someone could use to hurt themselves."

How do you hurt yourself with a cell phone? No—I don't want to know.

"Your mom is having a really good day. She's so excited to see you." Tammy wraps me in an intrusive hug that for some reason, I allow. "I'm just so happy you came, Laney."

I'm silent, not even attempting to come up with something to say. You could hand me a dictionary and thesaurus right now and I still wouldn't be able to describe what I'm feeling. The culmination of every fear, insecurity and personal guard I've carried for years is coming to a head. By facing the woman waiting down the hall, I face the root of all it. If I face the problem head on, I know longer have it to hide behind...and that makes me feel completely and totally vulnerable.

Huh, I guess I can describe what I'm feeling after all.

I follow them down the hall, stepping over the lines where the tiles connect. You know the whole "step on a crack and you break your mother's back" thing? Yeah, that little ditty started playing in my head, and so naturally, I'm now taking big steps like a moron. Like a scared little girl.

She's sitting on the edge of her bed when we walk in, head down and staring at her hands in her lap, which is covered with a 70s puke green and orange quilt. Tammy announces our entry and her head lifts; now *her* I would know if she fell out of a tree on top of me. A few lines appear around her eyes, not as brown as mine but obviously where I get the green hue mine sometimes have. She's very thin and frail looking and there's hints of salt in her brown hair...but I'd know her anywhere.

I don't smile, nor does she. I don't move to her, she doesn't rise. Neither of us speak.

My eyes move around her room, which is bigger than I would have guessed and all hers as far as I can tell. The walls are a shrine to...me. There are pictures of me on every wall, mostly yearbook shots or newspaper softball articles that have been blown up and framed.

"Laney, would you like to have a seat?" Tammy asks politely.

I shake my head no, still taking in all the pictures, trying to dictate my scattered thoughts.

"Trish, why don't you show Laney your album?" she again persuades the start of a conversation; anything to break the ice.

"Do you want to see it?"

If every sense wasn't secretly, acutely trained on her right now, I wouldn't have heard her. Make no mistake—I may be staring at the walls, making no eye contact, but I feel it when she blinks.

"Sure," I reply, starting to think about maybe moving closer to her.

From under the quilt, she pulls out a large scrapbook; it was right under there, just waiting. "Laney won the Tennis Ball Throw in 6th grade at the Little Olympics. Second place in the 200 meter dash. Anchor on the Tug of War, they lost."

Of course we lost! Kaitlyn had the flu and I was the only girl on the team with any meat on her bones. Westwood's girls were corn-fed and smuggled in from the 10th grade, I'm sure of it!

Two different laughs, blending in harmony, startle me enough to turn and look. My mother's face looks young when she smiles, holding her side through the fit of giggles. Tammy is doing much the same.

Ohhh…apparently my rant about the steroid-laden cheaters was out loud.

I've also shuffled one inch closer to her, drawn to the melody of her amusement.

Gathering herself now, she turns the page. "Walker's walk-off made front page news in eighth grade. A two-run homer by Laney Walker won the game and sent the Bandits to regionals. Missed that one; too far and Tammy can't drive at night so well." Her fingertips trace the letters on the yellowing page. "Laney is a power hitter, batting .480 this year. Coach Walker, her father, expects big things for this girl."

Her speeches are jaunty, broken, and I think sometimes she's reading and sometimes recollecting out loud, or maybe repeating what she's been told…I can't quite figure it out.

One inch closer.

Page flip.

"'Logson lineup this year to dominate. Two freshmen on the team the ones to watch.'"

Okay, that one was definitely verbatim from the article.

On and on it goes until the side of my leg is now touching the edge of her bed, and somewhere in the middle of her monologue depicting my high school graduation, where I had no idea I was the 418th person to walk on the stage, I sit down beside her.

She shuts the book and looks at me, tears filling her eyes. "I'm sorry, Laney."

"For?"

"Trish—" Tammy tries to cut in but gets shushed with a brisk wave of my mother's hand.

"For being the way that I am, for having to go. But I'm never too far way. Did you get your flowers?"

One sentence, lots of information, and what flowers are we talking about? I got flowers several times. I thought I had an admirer, then a creepy stalker. Turns out I had a not-well-but-watching mom. I like the last choice best.

"Laney?" Tammy comes to sit on the other side of me, taking my hand. "I know this is a lot to take in, and it's important we go slow, talk about things over time, for your sake and your mom's, but please know one thing. Your mom has always loved you. She always kept up with your life and all your great accomplishments."

"I can tell her myself!" my mother snaps.

"Yes, of course you can," Tammy apologizes.

It feels like it might be my turn. "I didn't know it was you; I thought I had a stalker. You could have signed the cards. I didn't know what happened to you until this past Christmas. Dane told me."

"The young man I spoke to," Tammy supplies.

"I know that!" My mother's voice is still very agitated. "Is he your boyfriend?" she asks, her question to me suddenly gentle.

I face her, now misty-eyed myself. I'm about to discuss boys with my mother.

I'm about to discuss boys with my mother!!

Finally.

This is probably too soon and she hasn't earned it, except for the whole giving birth to me part, but God, do I feel like my heart is flying—I'm having a heart-to-heart with my mom! It's astonishing really, how much faster the heart forgives than the mind.

"Yes," I swallow hard, "Mom, Dane is my boyfriend."

Her smile warms her tired face and she shyly reaches a hand to my hair. "He's good to you?"

"Very," I squeak out and nod so much my head feels like it might fall off. I sigh. "You can't imagine." A tear traces its way down my cheek, maybe because I'm talking about Dane and feeling so disconnected from him today, or maybe it's because my mother is petting my hair.

"That's how it should be, angel, all your heart can hold. Laney is a good girl, never in trouble, good grades, loves her dad, so pretty and smart. Tammy says she dresses like a lady, goes home early. Laney is a daughter to be proud of." Her hand continues to stroke my hair but her eyes change, the dim light behind them now out.

What just happened? I feel like I lost her.

"I told Dad I found you. He didn't know where you were either. He's not mad though."

Great, now I have Tourette's.

I feel Tammy's hand come down on my shoulder so I turn, seeing her saddened smile. "I think maybe we're done for today, Laney."

"I'm sorry, it just popped out. I shouldn't—"

"Shhh, you're fine, child. Your mama didn't even hear that last part. Let's say goodbye and talk on the way out, okay?"

"Oh, okay." I stand, confused and disoriented.

My mother is laying back now, eyes open and on me. "Such a beautiful baby. You never cried, always just smiled and slobbered. Your first word was 'Dada.' They never say 'Mama' first," she comments, her laugh laced with exhaustion.

I don't want to leave. I want to stay and talk, ask questions, smell her, tell her all kinds of things, but she's done.

"Bye, Mom," I choke out, refusing to end my first visit crying. "See you." I reach out to her hand and squeeze.

She squeezes back.

"How'd it go?" Sawyer hustles up the walk to sling an arm around my shoulder.

"Good, I guess."

I have nothing to compare it to, but I assume it went pretty well.

"You're pale, Gidge. You okay? What happened?" His arm pulls me tighter to his side and he kisses the crown of my head. "I'll drive, come on, girl."

Sawyer helps me in the truck. All that I register is that he drives and there's no music. Outside of that, I'm in a daze. It's like that head in a bottle feeling, like when you have a really bad ear infection, and I can't quite shake myself out of it.

"Are you close with your mom?" I randomly spurt out, shattering the long silence we've been traveling in.

"Nope," he pops out effortlessly.

"Do you miss her?"

"Maybe I miss having *a mom*, but I'd rather go without than have her version."

"What's her version?"

I have no filter…must be delirious from the "ear infection."

"A cranked out, slap-happy whore."

Damn. He must be having pseudo-auditory problems as well. Aren't we just a truck full of eloquence?

"Sawyer…" I had every intention of chastising him, but it just came out sympathetic and weary. "I'm sorry I asked."

"No worries, Gidge. So sum up today's visit with yours for me."

"My mom's not unkind or *bad*, her mind just doesn't work like other people's minds do; she can't help it. She thought she was doing us a favor by leaving."

I realize, with those few words, that I've forgiven her. I saw it firsthand today; she didn't take off to travel or bag a different man and start a new family. She lives in her room, her world, thinking of me and trying to capture small pieces of what she had to let go so that I could have normalcy…whatever that means.

"What about your dad?" I ask him.

"No idea."

I could definitely have it worse. My dad is better than the best, and he never strapped me with an evil stepmother.

"Sawyer, I love you. Dane does, too. The whole Crew. You know you always have us, right?"

"Yeah, Gidge." He turns his head and flashes me a Sawyer smile full of deep blue eyes and dimples. "I know. Don't go feeling sorry for me over there. I'm all good."

It's the first lie Sawyer's ever told me, but I don't call him out on it. Instead I let it be, laying my head against my window, counting the rises and falls of my chest; I'm all talked out.

———— ✍ ————

"Laney?"

Go away, talky dream thing.

"Gidge, wake up."

My eyes open, Sawyer's face looming over mine while he shakes me awake.

"Huh?" is all I manage. I guess I fell deep asleep on the way home.

"Do you trust me, Laney?"

"Huh?"

"You're kinda a zombie when you wake up, aren't ya?"

I'm coherent enough to take in Sawyer's laughter at my disillusioned state. "Where are we?"

"Airport. Do you trust me?"

"Yes, Sawyer," I bark, not appreciating the onslaught of weird vibes and questions upon just waking. "Why are we at the airport and why do you need my trust?"

"Come on, I'll explain on the plane." He grabs my hand and helps me out of the truck.

Oh, ok, sure, let me just board a plane with you to God knows where immediately following the most emotionally-charged day of my life.

Is he high?

"Sawyer, stop! Explain now, you're freaking me the fuck out." I snatch my hand from his and dig in my heels.

"I'm not kidnapping ya!" He turns with a smug smirk that desperately needs wiped off his face. "Relax, I'm trying to help you, all of you. I swear, sometimes it really seems like you and Dane are one soul split in two bodies. You guys even unknowingly play your major drama cards on the same day. But then again, you tell each other nothing; not the big stuff anyway. You guys confuse the hell out of me."

He. Is. Exasperating.

"Can you try that again, in say, English?" My shoulders droop and I sigh loudly. "What are you *talking* about?"

"I found Dane. Should have clicked sooner, but, like I said, you guys both have major breakthroughs and shitstorms on the same damn day, so it didn't. Your boy's had a big day and he needs you. I'm taking you to him."

"Where is he?"

"Connecticut."

Just around the corner; sure, let's go. I wonder if my current friends know there are actually people in the world who have to wait for other people to pick up a phone or drive home because they don't have private planes on standby.

Seeing as how I am staring at a plane, stairs down and ready to whisk us to Dane's rescue, I guess not. "We're flying to Connecticut?"

"Yep."

"How'd you find him? That's his plane, isn't it?'

"Group effort and yes, one of them. I called Tate, Whitley, you name it, while you were visiting, and we finally fit the pieces together. Tate got us the flight and a car waiting on us, Whit tracked down the address where I'm sure we'll find him. Now all I need is you on the plane."

I slacken my stance, letting him pull me towards the awaiting plane now. He didn't say he talked to Dane, which tells me we're swooping in unannounced. If Whitley knew, and he's in Connecticut, this is something about his past; his life before Georgia.

Seems my love spent his day with his own ghosts.

"Okay, let's go." I square my shoulders and board, ready to go uncover another part of Dane.

Chapter 24

Haunted

Dane

Laney's got to be worried sick. I've ignored her calls and texts all day, like the coward I am, sitting here in my car hiding from everyone. I simply can't talk to her right now. I can't be who she thinks I am, her strong and capable man. Not today.

Samantha walks out the front door of the house I've been staring at for hours and I fold down lower in my seat, praying she doesn't see me. She hates me and I don't blame her. I have a new life in Georgia where an unbelievable girl loves me, my brother thrives, and I have all that money can buy while she's still here, dealing with the life I forced upon her.

So strong, resilient, loyal, loving—Samantha is an angel. Her brown hair is pulled back from her face, her beauty obvious even from here. She still looks as young and gorgeous, but her gait and carriage show she's tired, strained from years of carrying my burden.

She won't accept my help, my money, my calls; nothing. I've been buried along with everything else she can't think about; the hurt, anger, and betrayal is too much. I want to jump out, run across the street, and beg her to let me help her, but instead I watch from afar, the shrinking coward, as she struggles to unload the wheelchair from the back of her car.

Chapter 25

Positive
Laney

I gasp as the wheels touch down on the runway; it gets me every time. We've just landed in Connecticut after the shortest flight ever, giving me not nearly enough time to drag any helpful information out of Sawyer.

He believes what he's doing is right, of that I am 100% sure, but I can't help but be apprehensive. I'm not real big on walking into monumental situations blindly and uninvited, and Dane obviously doesn't want me to know, or need my help, seeing as how he didn't trust me with the details of whatever it is he's doing today. So yes, my mouth goes dry and my stomach rolls trying to guess what I'm about to find.

"Sawyer, are you sure about this?" I ask him for at least the tenth time.

"Do you love him, Laney? The stand by and support him through anything kind of love?"

I do, without a doubt I do. There are some things I wouldn't stay through, though. If I find him with another woman, I'm gone, but I know bone deep that's not what's going on with him today. Dane wouldn't do that, I know it just as I know I'm breathing right now. So whatever it is, yes, I'm beside him.

"Absolutely."

"Then yes, I'm sure. Now come on, let's go save your man."

Chapter 26

'Bout to Need Jesus
Dane

She reappears about thirty minutes later, Andy now in the wheelchair that she pushes to the car. Why won't she let me pay for a nurse to help with these kinds of things? Does Andy even know I've offered? He'd accept, want her to have some help.

One of the wheels gets caught on the edge of the walkway, and as if in slow motion, I watch the chair tilt, tipping to one side on two wheels, as Sam fights with all her might to keep it upright. Unwanted but needed, I fly out of my car and across the street. *Hold on five more seconds, Sam.* I make it just in time to grab a handle and turn all four wheels flat on the ground.

Six eyes, three heaving chests, one heartache.

None of us speak, flinch or move a single muscle for long minutes.

But, much like a woman, she can hold it no longer.

"Why the fuck are you here?" Sam hisses, hatred radiating from her every pore.

"Honey, don't," Andy lays a hand on her arm, "don't be someone you're not."

"You needed help. I didn't want him to fall." Even I wince at my poor choice of words, but Sam gasps, her head snapping back like someone just slapped her. "I mean, it looked like—"

"Shut up!" she screams at me. "You don't get to show up once a year and play hero! We don't need your help!"

"Sam, sweetie." Andy, helplessly watching from his chair, tries to calm her. "Please go inside, let Dane and I talk alone. I don't want you upset. Please," he begs.

"No, no," she shakes her head, "don't listen to him, Andy. *We* have nothing to say to him, it's you and me, babe. He'll trick you, *buy* you. I won't let him!" She's screeching now, barreling around his chair straight at me. "This is all your fault, you asshole!"

"Not another step or you're going down." Her voice is eerily calm, slicing through the tension with the precision of a deadly sharp knife. "You touch him, I touch you."

Sam stops mid-stomp, frozen by the other female voice cutting through the dusk. I turn around slowly, no sudden movements in front of the irate, protective girlfriend who has no idea where I've been all day or what she's just walked up on, but knows she'll protect me to the death regardless.

Love my badass girl so fucking much.

"Who the fuck are you? And why are you all even here?!" Samantha screams. "God, just leave us alone. Haven't you done enough?" She pokes her finger in my chest with each last word.

Laney's hand flies up and locks around Sam's wrist, wrenching and tossing it from my chest. Let the face-off begin. Laney's blonde ambition versus Sam's dark and dangerous...but both women I adore. Both strong, protective and scrupulous. I know my girl and I trust her ability to react appropriately, so I stay still. Andy, well, his jaw is in his lap, his eyes flying nervously back and forth between the two girls.

"I'm guessing there's a lot of past here, a lot I don't know, but whatever you need to say, you're gonna say without touching my man. Hear me, girlie? I'm not gonna say it again," Laney warns in a deathly calm voice.

"Dane, get out of here and take your psycho bitch with you! We don't need any more of your *help*."

"Oh, Lord." Sawyer steps from the shadows. "You need more than help, Sam, you 'bout to need Jesus." He turns to Laney. "Did she just call you what I think she called you?"

"She did," Laney nods, "but I'm willing to let it slide, long as she keeps her hands to herself." Laney smokes Sam with a deadly glare as she says it. "My daddy always said women who take that "man shouldn't hit a woman" rule as their free pass to put their hands on men expecting to get away with it are manipulative and for sure too weak to handle things if it backfires. So probably too weak to go around hitting anybody in the first place. What do you think, Sawyer?"

"I think your daddy is a wise man."

"Smartest man I know." Laney cocks one brow at Sam, asking silently if she's made her point.

Sam, wisely, remains silent, with her hands to her side, perfectly still.

"Good, now that we got that settled, why doesn't somebody tell me what's going on before things get out of hand again?"

"I agree with her," Andy pipes in, pointing to the love of my life. "Samantha, I adore you, sweetheart, but you need to go inside and calm down, lest Sawyer have to carry you in and *make* you calm down."

"Are you fucking kidding me, Andrew? This rich prick ruins your, *our*, fucking lives and you're threatening me?"

Her words pierce me, but they're all true. Just look what I've done to this wonderful people, my friends, my comrades. Samantha is tough but kind, hardworking and admirable, yet I've turned her into an angry, bitter screecher. And Andy, all-American guy, heading to college with his girl, the only apple of his parents' eyes, and I pulled him off the field and slammed him in a chair.

And Laney's hearing it all. Everything I never wanted her to know. The part of me that stayed in Connecticut when I came to Georgia…to find her.

She'll leave me now for sure, taking any hope of happiness with her.

"Sawyer," Andy beckons.

"On it, Chief," he mumbles, grabbing Sam around the torso, pinning her arms to her sides and moving her quickly to the house. "Good to see you, Andy, looking good, man!" he calls over his shoulder while hauling the livid Sam, kicking her heels into his shins furiously, inside.

"Laney." I turn to her, my eyes begging her not to leave me

forever, to forgive the man I once was. "Can you please give Andy and me some time alone? And *try* not to hate me before we've had a chance to talk, to let me explain."

She ignores me, offering Andy her hand and a sparkling smile. "Hi, I'm Laney. I'm not at all psycho, I swear. I hope you can understand why I couldn't let her continue like that."

"I do, I do," he laughs, shaking her hand with approval in his eyes. "Real pleasure to meet you, Laney. I can tell I like you already."

That's Andy for ya, ever the optimist, glass-looks-damn-near-full guy.

"Baby, please." I try once more to coerce her to go. I can't share my shame with her now, in front of Andy. I at least ask for privacy when she tells me she can't love a monster.

"Dane Kendrick," she bites out as she turns to me, cheeks flushed, lips straight and tense, eyes… Her eyes filled are with love, but I know that will change soon and the thought leaves me barren and hopeless.

Shit, what a mess! How had she even found me? How did she get here? We're in Connecticut, for fuck's sake! I swear to God, Sawyer and his do-gooder ass *could* find the needle in the haystack. While blindfolded. In the dark.

"You listening again now?" she asks, and I quickly nod, feeling like anything but the boss right now. "As I was saying, you've been missing all day. I've been to see my mother after years and years of nothing, I've seriously begun to question Mr. Disney's mindset, and I've been flown across the country in the blink of an eye by that Neanderthal in there and walked up to a woman trying to kick your ass. Do not say it again; I'm not leaving. I love you, therefore, you bossy, stubborn man, I. Am. With. You."

I should probably concentrate on the part about her mom, a huge revelation that I had left her alone for, but the last six words are all I hear, playing through my mind over and over like the perfect melody.

"Okay, baby." I sigh, turning to Andy. "She really isn't the boss all the time," I explain in an attempt at humor.

"Oh, I can see that," he goads, but his face quickly turns solemn. "How are you, Dane?"

"Better than I deserve." I feel stupid even asking, but it seems the natural thing to say next. "You?"

"I'm good. I know you don't believe that, and my girl's just as crazy protective as yours, so she makes it seem awful, but I really am good."

"Don't be too hard on Sam. She loves you, man."

"Best thing to ever happen to me. I *was* gonna let her kick your ass."

"Can't say I didn't have it coming; can't blame her. I know I shouldn't just show up, but today's the day—"

"I know what today is," he interrupts me.

I chance a look at Laney, wondering if Sawyer filled her in or if she's just standing there cluelessly supporting me in good faith, hand rubbing circles on my back.

Well, if she doesn't know, she's about to get an earful. There's certain things I'd come here to convey, whether she's listening or not.

"I...geez..." I struggle for the words. "I wanted to come and say I'm sorry. I'm so sorry, Andy, you have to know how much I mean that. I'd do anything to trade places with you. I wish you'd accept my help, let me take care of things for you, since you can't—"

"Can't what? Make love to my woman? Thanks," he jokes, his laugh forced and sarcastic, "but I don't want your help with that. Sorry," he apologizes to Laney with a blush.

"I was gonna say work," I mutter.

"What are you talking about? I work, six days a week, computer programming. Make damn good money at it too. Sam's just about to finish her LPN, which I helped her pay for, and we're buying this house." He points behind him. "I'm angry, but not at you, Dane. And some things challenge me, but I'm far from helpless." His voice is growing in volume and intensity. "My life's not bad, Dane. And what it is or it isn't," he pauses, making sure I hear him, "is *not* your fault."

"I tend to agree with Sam," I fire back, not about to let myself off the hook. I feel Laney's hand stop rubbing and tense on my back.

"Sam's angry, but not at you, really, just at life. She feels cheated; there are things I can't do for her or for myself."

I can't imagine not being able to make love to Laney. Worse yet, I can't imagine Laney having to remain faithful to me, not ever feeling the weight of the man who loves her on top of her body, breath and sweat mingling, cherishing her.

"I took that from you."

"You're not *that* powerful, Kendrick." His laugh is genuine now, but does nothing to ease my guilt. "I made my choice. You didn't hold a gun to my head. Now knock it the fuck off, enough's enough."

This man, broken but stronger than anyone I know, he's the epitome of life value. I don't deserve his forgiveness, but thank God I appear to have it.

"What can I do for you, Andy? Really, anything, just name it. Please tell me, it would mean the world to me to help you in any way I can."

"Jesus, but you're hardheaded. I'll tell ya what. I'll take your marker, and if I ever think of something, I'll let you know. Now let's go see if Sawyer's still alive."

———⌒∽⌒———

I should have known, between her and Sawyer, they'd find me, force my hand, and see me through. Those two together—hell on wheels.

Somehow, when we made it inside the house, Laney had found a moment to talk with Sam, calm her down and hear the story from someone affected more so than me. You can imagine all of our shock when the girls stayed in the kitchen for a while, alone, and we heard no signs of things breaking or fists flying. And I still haven't decided if I imagined it or not, but I *think* they may have hugged when we left.

There's just something about Laney; she draws them in like bees to honey.

When we got on the plane for home, Laney was full of questions and wouldn't let me hide any longer. The minute we were in the air, she was in my lap, which was a very clever way of holding me captive in one spot.

"So, Andy, a grown ass guy, decides to go skydiving with his best friend, you, and unfortunately—tragically—he pulls too late, hitting the ground with enough force that he's now paralyzed from the waist down. Am I right so far?

"Yes."

"I understand the anger; it's a shitty, unfair thing. But what I don't understand is, how is that *your* fault?"

"I talked him in to going, badgered him to death…may have even called him a pussy until he agreed." God but I did. "When my parents died, I was alone, young, suddenly very rich and mad at the damn world. I blew through 70k in mere months, Laney. Booze, rec drugs, cruises, women, parties; it was a total path of self-destructive, fuck the world bullshit. Andy was a good guy with whole world ahead of him, in love with Sam, young, free—my don't-give-a-shit daredevil ass landed him in a wheelchair for the rest of his goddamned life! Meanwhile, the guy who didn't value life walked away!"

"Did you hold a gun to his head and make him do it?"

"No." I frown at her question, knowing where she's going with this.

She simply kisses the frown line on my forehead. "Oh, so you pushed him out of the plane?"

"You know I didn't." I close my eyes, rubbing my nose behind her ear, burying my face in her silky, fragrant hair…where no one can find me.

"You see where I'm going with this, right?"

"I see where you're going, Laney!" Sawyer and his super hearing yell from the front of the plane. Not the very front, like cockpit, God help us, but he's at the front so we can have privacy in the back.

"It wasn't fair. My idea, my path, my wild life-loathing…his payment. I can't forgive myself and I was so afraid you'd see the damage I've done and leave me. I was a terrible person, but I swear, Laney, I will do nothing but keep you safe, always."

"Stop." She quiets me with two fingers on my lips. "Believe in me. Trust me to love you no matter what, like I trust you. I gave it all to you, everything I am and will be, leaving behind what I was. I'm asking you to do the same."

"You have no idea how much I love you, Laney." She lifts her fingers, my words now clear. "You are the best thing about me. The only thing in the whole world more beautiful than you is my love for you."

She melts in my arms, boneless, and her tiny hands begin to roam. I know she can feel what she's doing to me, which encourages her more, her ass swirling and bearing down as her fingers explore.

"Baby," I groan, jerking when her hand finds my bare stomach under my shirt. "We have to stop. I'm about to fill you up, gorgeous, gonna have to, and I really don't want Sawyer to watch."

Her giggle into my neck does *not* help matters. "We can be quiet." She feathers kisses along my pulse point now, testing my every resolve.

"I would never," nip on her earlobe, "*ever,* let another man take any part in your pleasure. "All mine," I growl in her ear, tonguing it like I want to her body.

"Then stop doing that." Her throaty plea almost changes my mind, *almost*.

"Want you so bad, baby, but not here, not now."

"Fine," she pouts, "Let's talk then," she moves back into her own seat, sparing us from voyeurism at its finest. She knew as well as I did that Sawyer would have run back here... His sixth sense would have picked up on the first button popping open.

"Tell me about visiting your mom, what brought that on?"

"It was good, cool. She switches from third to first person and past to present tense when she talks, but she loves me. She has a bunch of pictures of me everywhere and a pretty cool scrapbook."

"So you're glad you went?" I lift her hand, kissing every finger and then her palm, softly.

"I am." She nods resolutely. "I think I'll go back. If they'll let you, I'd like for you to come with me."

"They'll let me, and I'll be there." I wink, reassuring her she need not worry, I have ways and will be right by her side next time.

"I almost forgot," she crawls back in my lap, which tells me undoubtedly she wants something. It's pretty cute really, she has yet to figure out she need not persuade; she asks—it's hers. "You're paying for Samantha and Andy's in vitro when they're ready, okay? I really think that's the deeper reason for Sam's anger. She wants kids, and Andy can't, well, and—"

"Done, baby. Nothing would please me more. I will pay for them to have a whole damn bunch."

"I knew you would." She smirks, as pleased with herself as she is with me. "You're magnificent like that." Satisfied, she burrows into my chest, her arms around my waist. "Big day; tired," she says with a yawns.

"I got you, gorgeous," my lips find her hair, my hand her back, "get some sleep."

She sleeps against my chest, graceful, beautiful, and truly all mine. All this time I've lived with my guilt, hiding it from her, full of fear she'd find out and leave me. All that time wasted, shame I didn't have to bear alone; she supported and loved me through it, despite it. She has my back no matter what, and I know, more so than ever now, that she always will.

Landed, lighter than I've felt in years, I carry my sleeping girl from plane to car, car to bed.

Chapter 27

This Little Piggy…
Evan

"What song is that? I love it!"

"Yeah?" Yes, I may have snuck a ringtone for myself onto her phone, one of my "things" I'm willing to keep doing. Every guy has one—this is my special way of peeing on her leg.

"Oh my God! Yes, it's beautiful. I wanna look it up and hear the rest of it, what is it?"

"'Hey Pretty Girl' by Kip Moore."

"Ohhh," she coos, the sweet sound pleasing me to no end.

Yup, perfect ringtone. Gonna have to call her more instead of text to make sure she hears it and thinks of me…lots.

"What are you doing today?"

"I have Larks practice in a little while, but after that I'm free, why?"

"I was thinking of heading to see Parker later. I'm done with classes at one, and nothing tomorrow until weights at 11, so if you've got a block, I thought maybe you'd want to go with me?"

Parker needs to *meet* her. The introduction at the funeral had been short and probably didn't register with him or Angie. It's time to do it right. And if we happen to swing by and say hi to my parents, well, that's just because we're in town and it's convenient and all.

"You want me to go home with you?"

"Yeah, Whit, I do."

The pause is killing me; too much too soon? *Shit!* I could have sworn she's feeling me like I am her. About the same second my heart decides to drop to my stomach, her breathy voice comes back.

"That'd be wonderful, Evan. You just wanna pick me up at the Amp after your class?"

No, I wanna pick you up right this damn minute.

"I'll be there. You need me to load anything or grab your bag or whatever?'

"Are we spending the night?"

I hadn't planned that far ahead. We could spend the night at my parent's, where they'd make her sleep in a different room for sure, which is proper and exactly what I should be thinking...which isn't even close to what I'm thinking. Parker would more than let us stay there, but how tacky is that? *I know I'm in town, parents, but I'm gonna sleep at Jones' instead cause he doesn't cockblock.*

"Um, how about we pack for it and play it by ear?" Yes, this was the gentleman answer.

"K," she exhales.

I'm pretty sure she was holding her breath, waiting for my answer, but I have no idea what she wanted the answer to be. Glad I went neutral.

"I'll just bring my bag with me to practice then."

"All right, so I'll see ya at the Amp 'bout 1:15. Sound good?"

"Perfect."

───────── ✧ ─────────

We head to Parker's first, since I figure it's probably a good idea to *ease* her into meeting my hometown importants, aka let her get warmed up before taking her to my parents. My mom has a tendency to, well, mother.

Angie opens the door to us, looking more put together than the last time I saw her, but desolation is still lingering in her eyes that I think probably won't ever totally disappear. "Evan, come on in!" She props the door open with her back to grab me in a hug. "And who is this beautiful young lady?" she asks affectionately when she spots Whitley waiting timidly behind me.

"Angie Jones, this is Whitley Thompson, my girlfriend." I beam, grasping Whitley's hand and pulling her forward. "Whitley, this is Parker's mama, Angie."

"It's a pleasure," Whitley offers her dainty hand, "thank you for having us. This is for you." She presents Angie with a red box.

Where had that come from?

"Look at the manners on you!" Angie pats her cheek. "You make sure to rub off on my Parker. He's not near as sweet as Evan here." She laughs. "Y'all come in now. Parker and Hayden just went to check cattle, they should be back soon."

I step back and let Whitley go first, my hand at her back. We take a seat in the living room and Angie remembers the gift in her hand. "Now what in the world could this be, Miss Whitley? Bringing me a present," she says, then playfully tsks at her.

I'm anxious to see what it is too and can't possibly restrain my chuckle when Angie lifts the lid to reveal a large, wrapped circle of cheese, complete with crackers along the edges and a fancy little silver knife thing with a bow on it. "Well, my goodness!" Angie exclaims, as delighted as she is shocked, I'm sure. "Whitley, you shouldn't have, really."

"It was the least I could do, having us in your home, especially on short notice. I hope you enjoy it."

"Oh, Evan, honey," Angie smirks at me, "she's gonna whip you right into shape, isn't she? Unless, of course, you get her over to the country side first."

"I was thinking we'd meet somewhere in the middle." I wink at Whitley, thinking how precious she is.

Only Whitley brings a gourmet cheese circle to a farmer's wife on her first visit. And speaking of short notice—where the hell does Whitley spring these gifts from, one for any and every occasion? She must have a secret closet in her house filled with "just in case" presents.

"That's usually the best place." Angie smiles. "So Whitley, have you ever been on a farm?"

"No, ma'am."

"Evan! Go grab one of the four wheelers and show this girl around. Something tells me she'll love it."

"You wanna go check it out?" I ask her, hopeful brows raised.

She nods eagerly, eyes shining with excitement.

"Well, come on then." I give her my hand. "If Parker beats us back, tell him we won't be long."

"Will do. You kids have fun. Oh, and Evan?" she calls, and I turn back. "Show her Dale's favorite oak tree, why don't ya?"

With that comment, I know Whitley has a true fan in Angie.

Whitley skips beside me to the barn, so full of life, so accepting of new things. Her naïve innocence and carefree zest is contagious, spurring me to run up behind her and haul her up in my arms.

"You're awful excited," I comment, smiling down at her.

"I've kinda been floating since you called me your girlfriend. There's not much that wouldn't make me happy right now."

"You caught that, huh?"

"Uh huh." Her teeth grip her bottom lip with nervous excitement.

"You good with that?"

"Very." Now she adds the tip of her tongue, wetting said lip.

I bounce her up, catching her around the hips and she knows just what to do, wrapping her legs around my waist and arms around my neck with a squeal.

"You make me happy, Whit," I sigh, resting my forehead on hers, "more than I thought would be possible again. Better even."

It's true what they say—if you look for the really freaking amazing in people, that's what you'll find.

Found it.

Her lips crash to mine, ravenous and greedy...she did *not* learn how to kiss in her mother's refining classes. I try to keep up, lick for lick and nip for nip, simultaneously keeping my balance and tilting my hips back so I don't ~~poke~~ send the wrong message. Luckily, I could walk this barn in my sleep, so I'm able to navigate us, joined and hungry, to one of the bays, setting her down on top of the half door.

"Uh," she whines into my mouth, clenching onto me tighter.

"Let me, ahhh," okay just a little more, "get us out of here," one more taste, "killing me." Fuck it, so what if we get caught?

Sebastian must feel the electricity in the air, letting out a loud whinny.

"Ahh!" Whitley startles and shrieks, "what was that?"

"Oh, Whit," I snort, keeling over in painful laughter but keeping one hand on her so she doesn't fall. "It was a horse," still hee-hawing at her, I try to catch my breath, "down there." I point down the row. "Woman, you crack me up."

"Can we go see him?"

Suffice it to say our heated moment has passed, every part of me already craving the next one.

"Of course." I grip her hips and help her down, leading her to Sebastian's stall. "You ever ridden a horse?"

"When I was little, my mother tried to put me in some kind of lessons. But those horses were stuffy," she wrinkles her nose, "they didn't run or jump or anything; they just kinda walked around beside the teacher."

"Did you have to wear the little jacket and hat?" I tease her.

"Ugh, yes."

I was kidding; my bad.

"Well, Sebastian here loves to run and jump. I'll show you one day. And he's a sucker for pretty girls, aren't ya, boy?" I let him nuzzle my hand. "Look in the bucket over there. He's *really* a sucker for pretty girls who give him treats."

She reaches in the pail and scoops up a handful of honeyed oats, his favorite, extending out her arm as far away from her body as possible. I slide in behind her, pressing up against her. "He won't hurt you." I scoot us, as one, closer. "Flatten your hand. It's okay if some spills, he likes your hand flat."

"It tickles!" She giggles when Sebastian eats from her hand...I think. I have no idea what's happening really, having gotten lost in her silky blonde strands and the sweet smell of strawberries.

"Evan?"

I love strawberries.

"Evan?"

"Hmm?"

"He ate it all."

"Oh," I straighten, "right, okay. You ready to go see the farm then?"

"Yes!"

I place her to the side and back the four wheeler out, patting the spot between my legs for her to sit.

"Do I get to drive?" she asks hopefully, blue eyes as clear and bright as I've ever seen them.

I'm thinking country looks real good on her.

"We'll see." I wink, scooting flush against her once she's seated. "Hold on tight."

Now I admit, once again, I'm a bit of a romantic, but any tough guy who thinks he's not... I'm thinking he's never given a sexy girl her first farm tour. Every time she gasps, wiggling her little ass into my crotch while she points to some new sight excitedly, well, it does something to a man; I don't care who you are.

Sharing this with her all but takes away the trace of sadness in me when I get to thinking about Dale. He loved this place, his land and home, and made sure to make it all it could be for his family. I will always miss him, but I know he's watching (hopefully not the part in the barn earlier) and I know he would get a kick out of my girl here.

I show her the creek, the cows, all the chicken coops and the king of the farm, Mufasa, the Jones' prize Angus bull. Whitley doesn't much care for him and begs me to drive away quickly. Next stop--the pig pens. Now this… For this, she jumps off the four wheeler and splashes through the mud. It seems some babies have joined the farm and Whitley spots them right away.

One would think, upon first meeting Whitley, of which even I was guilty, that the only way to get this girl to "oooh" and "ahhhh" would be to take her to Tiffany's or maybe shoe shopping. But no, all it takes to elicit the sweetest sounds and smiles you've ever seen from Whitley Suzanne Thompson are muddy, squealing baby pigs.

When I heard Laney tell Dane she loved him, I thought *bullshit, not possible, too soon…* I'm not sure what it is I'm feeling right now, but I am sure that I understand Laney's predicament a tad better now. Maybe your true self only thrives in the accompaniment of the one made to bring it out in you.

Hmmm.

"Evan! Come over here and look at these precious little babies!"

I saunter over, *not* splashing mud everywhere. The vision of Whitley tugs at my heart. She seems blissfully unaware that she's covered, on her knees in a swamp of…well, pig shit, and that one big sow really wants her to unhand those babies. "Whit, we probably need to go. You're making their mama real uncomfortable, sugar. 'Bout time to meet Parker, too, *after* we get you cleaned up."

"What do they do with their pigs, Evan?"

They don't rub them against their cheeks and blow on their bellies, of that I'm sure. She's definitely not gonna like my answer.

"Well, they sell some," I rub the back of my neck nervously, "and they…um, some I guess probably serve as food."

The response you're expecting, girl goes crazeballs at the thought of her "precious babies" being eaten…that's exactly what

205

happened. There's a few tears, some wailing and stomping (all of which I find mesmerizingly hot) but mostly one pissed off, brooding female the whole ride back to the house. She doesn't smell great, either.

———— ✧ ————

"Feel better?" I ask Whitley as she joins us in the living room, looking perfect once again.

"Yes, much. Thank you, Angie, for letting me use the shower."

"You bet, honey. I put your clothes in the wash."

She comes and settles in beside me, smelling like Whit again, so I throw an arm around her and pull her into me side.

"So, Whitley, Evan tells me you have a bone to pick with me?"

Good idea, Parker, poke the sleeping bear with a stick.

Whitley had briefly met Parker and Hayden before heading up to shower, but had yet to unleash her wrath. I warned him though. "No," Whitley shakes her head, "I thought about it and I understand. I'm not an idiot, or a vegetarian," she bites her lip, eyes welling up, "but maybe, in this particular case, uh, well, I will buy the whole herd from you!"

Done for. Heart—tapping out.

Parker rolls off the couch, emitting hyena-like hysterical giggles, and Angie and Hayden both cover their mouths, trying not to join him.

I kiss her temple, absolutely enamored. "A herd is cows," I whisper in her ear. "It's a litter of pigs, but Whit, where are you gonna keep a bunch of pigs?" Now even I have to stifle a laugh; the thought of Whitley corralling a bunch of pigs just too tempting.

"Whitley, why don't you come help me?" Hayden stands. "Let's see what we can come up with for supper."

"I'll help too," Angie says as she rises. "You boys will be lucky to get fed, teasing sweet Whitley like that. Evan, why don't you invite your parents to come over and eat with us?"

Whitley's already smiling when I look at her and gives me a slight nod.

"Yes, ma'am," I reply. If Whit's comfortable with it, then it sounds great to me. I can't wait for summer and being home again sans driving back for training, helping Parker on the farm and…damn, I need to find out Whitley's plans.

I'm not going all summer without her.

Mom and Dad accept immediately, my mother practically leaping through the phone when I inform her she'll be meeting Whitley. I *may* have called home a few times and mentioned her. Tonight doesn't worry me a bit; my parents are the two most loving and accepting people on the planet, but there's no sense blindsiding anybody.

"You ladies need any help in here?" I ask them in the kitchen. It's good to see Angie smiling; I think having Hayden around will be very good for her. And wait until a baby comes—I know that's Parker's ASAP plan; she'll be over the moon.

"I think we've got it, don't we, girls?" Hayden wipes her hands on a towel and pours two glasses of tea, handing them to me. "You visit with Parker, Evan. He loves it when you're home."

"Whit, you good?"

She turns from the counter where she's busily cooking, giving me a shaky smile. "Are your parents joining us?"

"Yep, oughta be here any minute. My mama can't wait to meet you."

No one else would have caught it, but I do, her fleeting glance down at herself, followed by a lip bite and quick swipe smoothing her hair. "You're beautiful." I wink, watching her consideration, then acceptance, before my very eyes.

I hear the tires on the gravel outside and couple farm dogs barking. "That'll be them pulling up now. Come on, pretty girl." I hold out my hand, loving how she slips hers in mine without hesitation.

"I'll be right back," she tells the other ladies.

"No you won't," Angie points out with a smile, "you let us finish this. Charlotte's not gonna want to share you and we're not gonna make her."

"Oh, okay." Whitley questions me silently and I grin, knowing Angie's right.

"Come on." I kiss her nose briskly and pull her out.

"Will we see you at the house tonight?" My mom stops and asks at her door.

"I don't know." I look at Whitley, who looks at the ground. "We may stay here, or head back; we hadn't really thought about it."

My mom gets a knowing smirk on her face, shushing my dad as he hollers at her to "leave those kids alone and get in the truck, you busybody!"

"Whitley, it was so great to finally meet you; my boy talks about you all the time," she says, snagging Whit's little body up in a big hug. "He probably just doesn't want you to see his room. I swear, it *still* smells like gym socks. I don't think that smell will ever go away. Now, you call me the next time you have a performance, because I'm coming to watch. Oh, and make sure Evan brings you down for Mother's Day, unless you're going home, of course, cause we have a great big lunch with games, and—"

"Charlotte, I swear I'll leave you here! Take a breath, you're gonna scare the girl off!" my father yells again from the cab.

"Oh dear," a hand flies to her throat, "I haven't scared you off have I?" My mom's face is suddenly riddled with worry.

"Not at all." Whitley giggles and hugs her. "I think you're wonderful and I will definitely see you soon. Night, Mr. Allen!"

"Good night, Whitley, very nice to meet you, honey," my dad says, his voice going all soft—*sucker.*

When they finally pull away, I'm exhausted. I haven't spoken in probably fifteen minutes, just hanging back and taking it all in. Dinner with my closest friends and family, everyone immersed in love, laughter, good food and healing, Angie happy and smiling, my mother smothering the greatest girl in the world… Yeah, it's been a damn good, exhausting night.

Whitley, clearly not exhausted, jumps into my arms and I naturally, effortlessly, catch her. "I see why you're so great. Your parents are amazing!"

"Yeah, they are." I beam with pride. "But I'm not sure giving my mom your number was the best idea. She may drive you insane. She's always wanted a daughter."

Whitley bends back and I grab her waist tighter. "Spin me around," she says, her voice airy and fascinated as she spreads out her arms and looks up at the sky.

So I spin her, slowly at first, then faster with each of her delighted squeals. When we're both dizzy, I pull her up against my heaving chest, her cheeks flushed, hair wild and windblown. "Today has been the greatest day of my life," she exhales in the sexiest voice. "Thank you, Evan, for choosing me and giving me everything I ever wanted."

*Mine too, because of you, God you're amazing, never leave me...*all said back to her in tongues.

———————⟡———————

"Are you okay?" I'm not feeling my best either, on the road early after spending a night asleep in the hay, Whitley wrapped in my arms. That part was heavenly, but hay bales? Not the most comfortable bed and my body is stiff as hell this morning. But how do you say no when that's where you land, her lips not letting go... you just don't.

"Fine, why?"

"I thought I heard your stomach growling or *something.* You sick? You want me to stop and get you something to eat?"

"No, I'm fine. Just keep going. Maybe we should listen to some music?" She leans over to turn on the radio.

"I heard that Whitley! Are you in pain? Damn babe, I hear you whimpering too." Panicked, I immediately find a spot to pull over. "What's wrong, Whit, talk to me, where's it hurt?" I'm running my hands all over her, searching, when another noise comes and I'm close enough this time to know it didn't come from her. What the—

"Evan, I'm fine, really," she pleads, "let's just get back on the road and get home. And music! I am *really* in the mood for some loud jams to wake me up. I know, play my ringtone song for me!"

Who is she trying to play right now? Not this guy, and I'm so hoping I'm wrong right now.

As my head turns to look behind the seats, Whitley's hand flies up to turn that same head back to her. "Kiss me, Evan, right now," she demands, doing her best to sound sexy through her alarm.

Not falling for it, I lean up and over, lifting the blanket. And there, just as I realized moments ago there would be, is a baby piglet...staring up at me.

"Whitley Suzanne Thompson! You smuggled one of their pigs?"

"Smuggled is such a harsh word. I prefer acquired, and yes, I *acquired* this little piggy, who shall now be referred to as Tiny."

"Tiny for a couple months," I scoff, "then not so tiny. Whitley, you can't keep this thing. It's gonna get big. And messy."

"I already thought of that." She crosses her arms, chin rising in defiance. "When Tiny needs more room, I'll rent a no kill zone from Parker and go for visits."

That might actually work. Parker would never charge her, and if she asks, he'll house ~~her~~ his pig for her. And…what better way to spend her summer than back home with her pig, and me. I'm liking this ridiculous plan better and better every second.

It overwhelms me, that feeling inside that I can barely contain, screaming and making me want to scale buildings and fly. "Get over here," I growl and reach for her. "You're the cutest damn thing I've ever seen in my life. I just wanna eat you up."

"Mmm. I'm gonna hold you to that."

Chapter 28

Full Circle
Laney

Life is good.

The Lady Eagles are 28-12 and the team's free as birds Mother's Day Sunday, so it's time for me to go see my mom with Dane. Sam has started her pre-in vitro shots and my dad had a date with Rosemary, the receptionist at his work, last weekend!

And Evan, sweet and wonderful Evan, walks into Algebra every week with a smile on his face, a spring in his step, and a whistle on his lips. Seeing him happy sets my soul free and our friendship—I think it might just be okay.

First love? First love is so much about curiosity. I read that somewhere and agree. But what I've found, and what I think Evan may be discovering as well, is the only forever we were meant to be for each other is friends.

So when he asks me to take Whitley out for a girls' night so he can set up a surprise for her, I readily agree.

"I need a while, like four or five hours. You have curfew?"

"No, conference play is over; we're about done for the season. But five hours? What the heck are you setting up?"

"Everything she missed as a kid, so as much time as you can buy me would be great."

Look at Evan in his element—being a prince. It's such a good look for him.

"Sounds major—you need help?"

"I got Sawyer and Zach helping me."

"Well if I'll be out at girls' night, I'm sure Dane would be happy to help too. You want me to ask him?"

Me asking Dane to help Evan make magic for Whitley... I'd say we've just about come to the "growing up into bigger people" portion of the program. If there are 12 steps, we just scaled that shit like an anthill and built #13.

"Yeah, sure, that's be great." Evan's smile, and his eyes, tell me he just had the same "whoa" realization I did.

"I'll text him. Whitley's at six on Saturday good?"

"Make it like 6:30; pad your time to get her gone."

"Ev?"

He looks at me, raising his brows in question.

"I'm glad we're back."

"Me too, Laney." He winks, spreading his arms for me to walk into his hug.

Full circle.

Whitley, much like myself, is a lightweight. And the brighter color the drink, the quicker she seems to suck 'em down. With all our men off working on "Operation Whitley," we have Tate behind the bar, his eyes boring holes in us, and Brock breathing down our necks. But other than that, Whitley, Bennett, Avery, Kirby and I are on the loose...and it's not pretty.

Fun as hell. Hilarious. But not pretty.

"Let's dance!" Kirby pretends to ask us, slinking away, going trolling before anyone can ever answer.

I can't put my finger on it yet, but something has changed with our catcher and not in a good way. Avery follows after her, but I'm good right where I am, perched on my stool with my fruitalikey, aka I don't know what's it's called but it's good, in a glass.

"I'm gonna go kiss Tate," Bennett slurs, heading for her bartender.

"Thanks for inviting me, Laney. I'm having a great time," Whitley gushes, slurping her cup dry. "Excuse me just a minute, though," she pulls out her phone, "I have to check on Tiny. I don't know that Evan will keep a close enough eye on him."

"Who's Tiny?" I ask her.

"My pet pig. I rescued him from Parker's," she announces proudly while texting.

I spew my drink in shock. "Parker gave you a pig? And you're keeping it in your house? In town?"

"Stole, gave, whatever." She shrugs. "But yes to the rest."

"Damn, Whitley." I smile, fascinated really. "I never thought I'd say this, but I'm glad we became friends. You've got Evan home babysitting your stolen pig. You go, girl!" I offer her the high five she has certainly earned.

"Thanks!" She turns her cup upside down, then back over, as if she just can't fathom why it's empty.

"Um, Whit, do you want another drink?"

"Yes, do you?"

"Sure. Brock?!" I yell, the large man appearing instantly. "We need another drink. Would you prefer I go to the bar and get it or do you want to do it for us?"

Saves a lot of arguing if I give him choices.

"Stay. I'll get it."

"Dane's pretty protective of you, huh?" Whitley asks.

"Very," I nod, "but I like it. It makes me feel important and safe. Just wait, Evan will be the same way with you. He's a little sweeter about it, where Dane's all caveman, but same theory."

Brock sets our drinks in front of us. Added bonus of The K— we never wait for drinks. "Thanks, Brock," we chorus, which he acknowledges with a grunt, then moves back to assume the façade that he's giving me space.

"Ahhh!" Whitley presses her fingers into her forehead. "Brain freeze."

Not that I have a reason now to keep from it, but I can't help but like her. She's like Bennett once you get to know her—just happy to be here. "So how'd you like Parker?" I ask. "How'd his mom seem?"

"Parker's great and I love his fiancé, Hayden!"

Drink spewing again, this time accompanied with a fit of coughing. "Fiancé? Parker's engaged?"

"Ohhhh, I thought you knew! Oh, Laney, I'm sorry. I know he'd want to tell you himself and I spoiled it for both of you." She looks like she might actually cry.

And you know what endears me to her even further? Ten out of ten girls on the planet who are now involved with your ex, who know damn good and well that he still has more memories of you than them, would be insecure and spiteful, happy even that they just one-upped you by knowing a secret from "your" friends before you did. But Whitley? Nope, she's sincerely worried about me and Parker.

"Whitley, relax," I reach over and pat her hand, "I'm not upset at all. I'm just surprised. He'll tell me and I'll act shocked, okay?"

She nods, still looking unsure and apologetic.

"It's fine, I swear. So tell me about Hayden; I only met her briefly. She's nice?"

"She's so nice, and pretty, and she loves Parker so much. I think you'll really like her. She takes very good care of Parker and Angie and seems very down to Earth. She is definitely his gibbon!"

The girl has consumed her fair share of cocktails, and I know better, but I have to ask. "His what?"

"His gibbon," she chirps (which I now think of affectionately as her signature sound and not as the parakeet of older days), "like Phoebe and the lobsters."

Not surprisingly, as with most people on a drinking night…the more she talks, the *less* sense it makes. I roll my hand, enticing her to keep going. What can it hurt at this point?

"You know, the best *Friends* episode ever with Phoebe and her lobster thing?"

I have no idea, but nod and smile in the interest of time.

"Google says it's scientifically incorrect, that lobsters don't mate for life. Yes, I looked it up. But, it *does* give you a list of animals that *do*."

The polite thing to do here is ask for the list, right? Right. And honestly, I want to see if her drunk butt can pull it off. "So what animals made that list?"

Her fingers are already up, ready to count them off, and she couldn't be more pleased I asked.

"Lovebirds, gibbons, swans, black vultures—I know, but ugly things need love too—French angelfish, wolves, albatrosses," she smiles at me, "don't worry, I don't know what they are either. Termites," she shivers, "prairie voles, which I looked up and still don't know what they are exactly, and turtledoves."

"Wow, I'm impressed. That is a *whole lotta* information. How do you remember it?"

She shrugs like it's the most natural thing in the whole world that she has that list on standby. "I had to be on the lookout for my gibbon or my swan since National Geographic crushed me and said my lobster was never coming."

If this girl was any more perfect for Evan Allen, I'd fall right off my barstool. The hopeless romantic meets Mr. Tenderheart.

I miss Dane, really bad.

Laney: You guys about done? Need you.

"Hey, Whit, I'm about toast, gonna head out soon," I say, watching my phone like a hawk. "We should talk soon, though. Maybe we should throw Hayden a shower or something."

Parker's one of my oldest and dearest friends. Who he loves, I know I'll love, and something tells me Whitley could write a textbook on throwing a wedding shower.

Dane: Are you okay? On my way.

Laney: Fine, just miss you.

Dane: Give me 15 minutes. I'll make it up to you.

"That'd be wonderful! Oh my God, let's do it!" she gushes. "Hayden will love it and I have some great ideas! Oh, Laney, thank you!"

"Idea away, chick. Parties are soooo not my thing, but I'll help with everything else." Let the record show she has been warned— Laney only offered her strengths. "Dane's on his way, so I'm gonna go wait by the door. You staying or?"

"I'll wait with you and call Evan."

I catch Bennett's eye as we make our way to the door and wave goodbye, then freeze in place, seeing red. Whitley, looking at her phone and unprepared, slams into my back with an "umpff."

Seeing my demeanor, her eyes go wide. "What? What is it?"

Bennett caught it too and runs over, which actually means prances over as quick as she can on the toes of her killer heels. "Laney, what's wrong?"

"Tell me I'm seeing things." I point, feeling sick to my fucking stomach. Their eyes follow the end of my finger, searching, and two gasps echo each other when they find the object of my leer.

"What is she doing? Oh my God, Laney, what do we do?" Bennett's on the verge of tears on the spot, hating the pain of others.

"Did they break up?" Whitley's face is puzzled. "And doesn't she feel a breeze? I mean, leave something for the imagination, *please*."

215

"Baby," warm breath on my nape instantly soothes me, "I'd know this ass anywhere." I feel a hand squeezing the object of his recognition; I'd know his voice, his touch, anywhere. Part of me may have known the second he walked in. *Dane*.

"Did the other guys come with you?" I ask past the lump in my throat, distractingly excited for a moment.

"Zach and Evan did. Sawyer had a hookup waiting, why? Oh, Whitley," he says, "Evan asked me to send you out. He's parked right in front of the door waiting," he gets caught up in a chuckle, "he didn't think he should leave Tiny alone in the truck lest he face your wrath."

"Laney, do you want me to stay? What are we gonna do?" Whitley asks desperately.

"I don't know yet, but you go ahead, Evan's waiting. Have a good night, Whit. Dane, can you walk her out?" I hug her, knowing whatever Evan has in store for her will be amazing, even though my thoughts are clouded by the bitch across the room and her treachery.

Whitley breaks our hug with a bonus squeeze and whispered thanks. "No, Dane, stay. I'm fine, he's right outside the door."

"Night, Whitley," Bennett offers sadly and Dane looks back and forth between us all, confused and unsure if he's to stay or go with her.

"What just happened here? Laney," he turns me to face him, staring hard into my eyes while his are deciding between angry and scared, "talk to me, now."

I turn again, leaning back into his chest, needing the connection. I point again, and wait for it to click. "Fuckkk," he mutters.

Kinda what I was thinking.

"What do we do?" I ask him, praying that like always, he'll have the right answer.

"Are we sure it's her? She *is* a twin."

Oh, I didn't think of that! A spark of hope blossoms in my chest.

Bennett's already shaking her head back and forth. "Not unless they switched clothes in the bathroom for some reason. That's what Avery wore tonight."

"I'm not sure then, but I know what's *not* going to happen," he growls, closer to my ear, "you are not getting in her face or kicking her ass, 'cause I know you're dying to do just that. I say we stand here until Zach finds us and let him see for himself."

"You can check that box," Zach interrupts from behind us. "I see."

We all flip around at the sound of his voice, collectively flinching at the despair etched across his face.

"Don't listen to him, Zach, I will absolutely go kick her ass if you want me to."

He chokes out a chuckle. "I love you for offering, but no more things flying at your face for a while, huh? Let's just go. I've seen enough."

Oh, we've all seen enough. She's wearing red panties tonight, but I shouldn't know that…nor should half this bar.

"You sure, man? I could have the dude thrown out," Dane offers.

"Why would I have him thrown out? He doesn't know I exist, and he's not the one who owed me any loyalty. She is."

"And we're *positive* it's her?" Dane tries again, looking at me and Bennett. "It could very well be Kirby."

Zach just stands there, staring, so we let him. The second there's a break in the music, he screams, "Avery!"

The blonde pressed against the back wall, skirt hiked indecently and sucking the skin off some dude's neck, breaks and looks out of reflex.

"I'm positive," Zach mumbles.

Dane and I wave to Bennett and follow him out. I give Zach the front seat and keep them talking about the work they did at Whitley's the whole ride to drop him off. It sounds like a little wonderland what they've set up. Evan never ceases to amaze me with his grandiose acts of romance, but the desolate vibe in the car simply cannot be lifted.

I hug Zach when he exits, me climbing out to take the front seat, and whisper, "if you change your mind about the beat down, you just let me know. She fucking sucks and you're amazing. I'd consider it a personal favor if you let me make her hurt too."

"Love you, Laney." He kisses the top of my head, shoulders slumped as he walks away.

"How drunk was she?" Dane asks me when I'm settled and buckled.

"I don't know, they left the table to dance." I push the button to let the top down on the Camaro, by far my favorite of his cars. Right now I'm just craving the rush, the escapism of the warm night air blowing through my hair. "How drunk did she need to be? I don't think you can get drunk enough to cheat on your boyfriend, let alone be dry humped publicly."

"Glad you feel that way, baby, and totally agree." He takes my hand and kisses it. "Dumb question, forget I asked."

"Let's just drive for a while," I suggest, my voice lazy, "I love this car."

"I have something I want to show you; we'll drive there. I wanted to show you in the daylight, but this works too."

"K," I sigh, not caring at all. He can drive me anywhere and I'm good with it. "We need to find someone to set Zach up with, soon. I don't want him unhappy. You have any more hot girls like that Jenee that work for you? How about one of them?" If he thinks I missed the shift in his shoulders or the frown that flashed across his brow, he's wrong. "What?"

"Nothing, yeah, I'll think about it."

Nothing my ass.

"Nice try, Dane. What?"

"Baby, nothing," he replies, kissing my hand. "I love you and I love how you look out for your friends. I'll tell Sawyer to work on it."

"I knew it! You slept with her." I knew the minute I met her, and yes, I used the line of conversation to my advantage to confirm the suspicion that's been eating at me.

He doesn't say anything. Why would he? He can't deny it and he damn sure doesn't want to affirm it, but he doesn't have to.

"How long ago?"

"Before I knew you."

"Well obviously," I snarl, "how long before you knew me?"

"Laney, why are we talking about this? I don't ask you—"

"You don't? Really? I seem to recall reciting a play by play for you in the hot tub. Not that I had any actual sex buddies to tell you about. I can't even describe to you my joy at the thought of you being with her like you have me." I sniffle and wipe a fake tear. "And the fact that she works for you, is still in your life, just warms my fucking heart. Now, HOW. LONG?"

He stops the car and turns abruptly in his seat, trying to pull me in his lap, but I slap away his hands.

"Stop it!" I snap at him but he overpowers me and has me in his lap effortlessly despite my squirming and feeble attempts to escape, grabbing my chin and forcing me to look at him.

"This isn't about us and you know it. You're mad at Avery and sad for Zach and you're taking it out on me. Just because he couldn't trust her doesn't mean our relationship is doomed."

I'm not kidding anymore—how does he do that? In-fucking-furiating.

"I was never, ever, with her, or any other girl, like I am with you. Not even close. Yes, I fucked Jenee, maybe four times, the last time a couple months before I met you. She's attractive, she's discreet, and she was there. But I *never* made love to her, or anyone, and I will never be with another woman for the rest of my life."

I should be okay now, quit throwing a tantrum and realize he's right; I'm not mad at him tonight. I shouldn't care a bit about his past and should bask in the fact that I know he loves me and speaks the truth.

Coulda woulda shoulda.

"I am the luckiest man in the world that no one has ever loved you like I have, that I never have to think about that. When we're eighty, I will still be the only man who has ever been inside your sweet body, and I realize how amazing that is. And if I'd known you were on your way to me, I would have waited for you. If I could take it back, I would. But I can't, so you tell me something I *can* do to make it better."

Fire Jenee.

Just kidding.

Except not at all.

"How often do you interact with her? She works for you...do you see her every day?"

"I almost never see her. And as of right this minute, I will never see her again. I can fire her, transfer her, anything you want. Anything for you," he rubs the back of his hand down my cheek, "you know that. Just say the word."

"Was she the last one before me?"

"Yes."

This is where I resolve it in my mind and move on. Except the whole part about me not doing that.

"Was she good? Better than me?"

Oh shut up, you know damn good and well you'd be wondering

the same thing.

"She was exactly like any other person I was with; anatomically the same, pleasant and purpose-serving and cool about the situation. Jenee was actually the only one who meant it when she said she didn't need more, there was no stalking me or bugging me for more afterwards. But Laney, simply kissing you is better than sex with anyone else. So when I'm inside you, completely in love with you, nothing will ever fucking compare. My God, baby, you have to know I'd die if it was the only way to get to love you again, even just one more time."

He means it, and it works, unleashing in me the Laney who wants to own this man, wants him to own me. I glance around, no idea where we'd stopped, and see no one, no lights, just some dark street.

"Raise the top," I boss him, running my tongue along his neck.

I'm about to remind him what it feels like to be with me. And show him it doesn't always have to be sweet lovemaking either. I can be his love, delicate and gentle, or anything else he needs, but right now I'm about to alpha mama all over him.

I unbutton his shirt, kissing every glorious inch of his chest as it's exposed, his fingers digging into my hips with more and more urgency. A rumble starts growing in his throat and he pushes himself up into me as hard as I grind myself down onto him. Aroused and tingling from scalp to toes, I moan brazenly and feel a rush of heated moisture between my legs from our taunting game of up and down, push and pull, cat and mouse. Next is the button on his jeans, and when he tries to still my hand by covering it with his, I defiantly flick my wrist, and his hand, off mine.

"Yes," I bite out, deadly serious. I dare him, meeting the fire in his brown eyes with my own, to even think about stopping me again.

"Laney, we—" he starts, chest rising and falling with his invigorated breaths.

Using my knees, I raise myself off him, not-so-sexily working off my pants but leaving on my panties, then quickly tugging his pants and boxers to his hips. He raises himself, not really putting up the fight despite trying to stop me with his words.

"We are gonna do this, right here, right now." I nibble on his bottom lip and run my hands up his bare chest, circling my index fingers around his nipples and giving him my best "come fuck me" eyes.

"You sure, baby?" he moans, taking his hardness in hand and running the tip up and down the soaked crotch of my panties, teasing me, giving me the chance to change my mind…or to beg for it.

"God, yes," I'm lost, hands tugging at his hair, mouth moving rhythmless and crazed over his neck, trekking down slowly to his chest, now covered in a slight sheen of anticipation and fragrant of musky, virile man.

"Back pocket, wallet," he pants, "grab it for me. Hurry."

He tears my panties apart and off in one masterful move, tossing them on the dash and enflaming me with that conceited wink of his, using his nimble, seeking fingers to make it impossible for me to successfully retrieve anything from anywhere. Instead, I bow my back, head touching the steering wheel now.

"Grab my wallet, Laney, or my hand's gotta leave you."

The threat of losing his touch snaps me back into reality. As fast as possible, I reach around him and dig out the condom, but then realize he has yet again taken control…and I'm taking it back, showing him what his woman can do.

"Scoot the seat back; give me room to work," I demand.

He follows my direction, using the hand not currently driving me mad with its punishing in and out pursuit, all the while staring at me with a wild curiosity in his eyes. His tongue trails over his bottom lip in wicked invitation. I slink backwards, sliding to my knees on the floor board, my heels digging into my ass. Leaning forward between his legs, I grip under his thighs, just a hint of fingernails, and yank him forward, never breaking our connected stares.

"This time, *you're* gonna be a good boy." I lean in and give him a one long base-to-tip preview lick. "And you'll do exactly as I say."

The guttural noise that escapes him may be the sexiest thing I've ever heard. "For you," he throws back his head and groans, "anything."

"Put your hands behind your head," I trace one finger under his boys, back to front, "move them and I stop. Understand?"

"Mmm, for you," he hums, looking down, intent on catching every second of the show.

One finger becomes my whole hand, rolling his balls with enough roughness to satisfy him, to make sure he *knows* I've got him. Unable to help himself, he takes himself in one hand, rubbing up and down slowly, so as promised, I lean back, depriving him of all contact from me. My brows raise and I tilt my head to the side, waiting for him to move that hand or tell me we're done.

"You better get that sweet mouth on me soon or I'm taking back the reins," he warns, his voice low, throaty, and very menacing.

"Get that hand back up then."

With a sexy but warning pout, he inches his hand back behind his head in slow motion. The storm brewing in his eyes tells me my sexy as hell control freak is about to lose his ever-loving mind.

Feeling empowered, I pooch out my duck lips, kissing up one side of his dick and down the other, wet, sloppy kisses. "Now what?" I ask innocently, trying to let him have some facet of authority...but low and behold, I see one hand creeping back down from my periphery.

"Uh, uh, uh, Mr. Kendrick, no hands. *Tell me.*" I turn his sexy language on him.

"Suck all of me down, baby," he whines, shifting in his seat, just dying from this transfer of power. "Laney! Fuck!"

He moans then shouts as I take him in all at once, tightening my lips around him and hinting with my teeth on the upstroke. It stretches the corners of my mouth impossibly, leaving the faintest hint of saltiness at the back of my tongue and I suck with abandon, bobbing up and down like a dashboard doll, wanting *for once* to be the one setting the pace, driving *him* mad, making *him* shake uncontrollably and shriek *my* name.

I'm pulled off him, catching my bearings and breathing as he pants down into my face, an almost painful grip on my upper arms. *Oh yeah.* He's at that place he always takes *me* to...Fuck Me 'Fore I Die Town. Using my teeth to rip open the condom, I grin, reveling in this moment, and begin to roll it over him.

"You ready for me?" I blink flirtatiously, wondering if I can actually get fire to come out of his nose.

He laughs, deep and loud, almost evilly, and grabs under my arms, pulling me up on his lap at the speed of light.

"Spread those legs and straddle me." His voice leaves no room for argument. He has hit ground zero and my role as chief is over. My legs go apart and slide down on either side of his hips. "Soak my hand first," he demands, two fingers mercilessly gaining entrance as his thumb rubs circles right where it needs to. "You drive me crazy, baby, teasing me. Now be my good girl." He kisses me, biting and tugging my lip painfully, then apologizing with a smooth lick. "Move with it; fuck my hand just how you want," he croons as he ambidextrously uses his left hand to pull down my shirt and bra cup, sucking one painfully hard nipple into his mouth. "Give it to me, Laney. Come for your man." He bites down on the point and I explode, screaming his name through the shakes of my body and trembling of my thighs.

"Dane," I moan, coming down from the high only he can send me on, "so good. So good."

He pulls his fingers out, licking me deliberately off him. "Mmmmm baby," he rumbles, then grips that hand around his base, "take me there too, baby. Get on this," he demands, his voice low and gritty, "and slide down real slow."

Teasingly, euphorically, I take him in me, the physical connection shadowed only by the emotional one. It doesn't matter where we are, it always feels right. When my body is flush against his, I whimper as he growls, kneading the breast he'd bared manically.

"There's my girl." He thrusts up into me, emphasizing his murmured point. "Kiss me, hard."

Gladly, my lips fly to his, tasting his lust for me. A quake runs through him and I feel him throb inside me as he purrs in my mouth, "so close, with me, again baby." He uses his grip on my hips to show me what he wants. "Roll 'em down and hard, yeah, fuck yeah, like that."

Once again his thumb finds me as he warm mouth caresses my breasts. He knows exactly what I need. He's there; I can feel it and it sets me off, knowing what I can do to him. His name escapes me again, loud and long. "Love you baby, love you so much," he says sweetly as he kisses up my chest, my chin, ending mouth to mouth slow and sweet. My sweet, sensual caveman.

"Love you too." I lay my head against his chest, catching my breath.

He rubs up and down my back, kisses my head, every bit as good at afterplay. Finally, I move back to my seat, arranging myself as he, too, takes care of things. The windows are all fogged up, making me laugh, and I wipe out a circle.

"Where are we?" I ask, still not able to quite make it out.

"Come on!" He grabs the keys and opens his door. "I told you I wanted to take you somewhere."

He's waiting, hand out for me, when I put my shoes back on and open my door. "It's dark! What are we doing?" Outside of the car, it's easy to tell we're in the driveway of a house. "Dane, it's late, whose house is this?"

"Yours." He turns to me and smiles before inserting a key into the front door. "And it's not a house, it's a duplex." His hand finds the switches and two lights come on, illuminating both the porch and front room. "Go check out your new pad, Miss Walker," he says, kicking the front door shut behind him.

"Wh-what?"

"I bought this place for you. Next year, you don't have to live on campus; the athletic requirement lifts after your freshman year. This place is halfway between my house and school *and* has no 11pm curfew." He winks, stalking towards me. "So we can sleep together every night. It's a duplex, so if I have to be away on business, I know you're safe with Tate and Bennett living on the other side."

Duplex, to-ma-to...he bought me a *house*.

"Do Tate and Bennett know?"

"Not yet. If you hate it, we have to find another one. No sense getting them excited until my baby gives it her stamp of approval. So let me show you around." He laces his fingers through mine, beginning the tour after a chaste kiss to my fingers. "This is the living room, obviously, I thought we'd go pick out new carpet and paint this weekend."

I am still in shock, incapable of actual speech, letting him guide me as he sees fit. He bought me a house. *A house.*

"And this is the kitchen." He flips on a light.

The kitchen has empty, gaping holes where appliances should be. "You can pick out your fridge and stuff too. I'd like to see new countertops too," he knocks on it, "unless you like these." Offset is a kitchen area, the hanging light capturing my attention. "We can change that too; anything for you."

"I like it, it just needs raised up a bit."

"Done."

We move down the hall and he shows me the linen closet and guest bathroom, which I will gladly let him let me redecorate; it's hideous.

"There're two bedrooms, this is the spare one," he says as he ushers me in to the decent-sized room.

"Who will be my roommate?" I ask.

"You don't have to have one if you don't want. It's not like you have to make rent. We can make that room anything you want. Come on, let's see the master."

My room is huge, much bigger than any I've ever had, with a private bathroom (also needing severe redecoration), a walk-in closet, and the coolest bay window.

"I love it." I spin, wrapping my arms around his neck. "I can't believe you bought me a house. You're too good to be true." I kiss him deeply, trying to tell him all the big, fluffy words that mean I love you that I can't iterate.

"I can't wait to christen every inch of this place," he says, his wink on auto-pilot, "and hold you every single night. But for now, let's go to my house. At least until we get furniture here." He laughs.

"My dad will give me my bedroom furniture, but what am I gonna do about the other rooms?"

"You're going to fill them with stuff we pick out together. That way I'm there to ensure it's all sturdy enough." He answers my confused look by dipping me back, sucking right at the hollow dip in my throat. "Think about it, baby, you'll figure it out."

Chapter 29

Fortress

Evan

"So what'd you do all night?" Whitley whispers long after I thought she was asleep.

"I'll show you tomorrow when it's light out and you're sober. Go back to sleep."

"I'm sober now," she rolls towards me, "and I'm not tired. What was all that in the living room? I wanna go see."

I'd planned a big night, as much set up inside as out, but when I picked her up and found her drunk, I thought it'd be easier to just carry her in and tuck her in bed. How she'd remained floppy as a rag doll when I dressed her down to panties and a shirt for sleeping but somehow caught the production in the living room I'm not sure. I suspect I'd been duped and her snuggling up against me, bare legs thrown over me, was purposeful.

Not that I mind.

"You sure you don't want to just go back to sleep? You seemed pretty tipsy before."

"I'm fine now, promise. So will you show me?" She bounces, happy and perfectly coherent.

"Okay." I get up, taking her hand. I switch on her hall light as we pass so we'll have just enough ambience in the living room. I can't wait to see if she likes it. Everything I've done having a recurring theme—I want to give Whitley some childhood fun.

My childhood was great. Both my parents were involved; there were camping and fishing trips, sports, game nights, toys, backyard football, and sledding on the rare snow days we got. Basically, I got it all.

Whitley got next to nothing. Through comments she didn't even realize she'd made and the few stories she's shared, I learned a lot about her childhood. Whitley's her parents' starched and pressed trophy daughter, never allowed to let loose or get dirty.

Evan Allen's fixin' to show her the good stuff. You'll never be happy with where you end up if you weren't happy with where you've been. And I've seen enough glimpses into the real Whitley to know that the girl is dying to have fun, get filthy, and let her hair down…who better to do all that with than yours truly?

"Ready?" I lean my head around hers, making sure my hands completely cover her eyes.

"Yes!"

"Ta-da!" I remove my hands and watch as she takes in the scene before her, then tries to give me a counterfeit smile. "You don't like it?" I ask, disappointment setting in heartbreakingly fast.

"Oh, I'm sure I love it," she says politely, then nibbles her bottom lip, glancing over to me. "What is it?"

Poor, sheltered, ripped off Whitley. "It's a living room fort! Haven't you—" *No, you know she hasn't, fool!* "Come on!"

I drag her over and crawl into the makeshift fortress, which is constructed the good, old-fashioned way—every blanket and sheet I could find draped over and/or held up by every chair in the house and other tall, sturdy things. Every kid's favorite spot.

"Come in here with me!" I call out to her. "It's fun."

She probably thinks I've lost my ever-lovin' mind, but my powers only go so far. I can't make her a little kid again (never gonna happen) but I *can* bring the little kid to her.

Her sweet little face pops in through the opening. "This is awesome!" she says dreamily, crawling in further. "Wow, you thought of everything."

I'd stacked pillows and blankets inside, making the most comfortable bunker possible, and of course, stocked all the other necessities. "Here." I hand her one of the flashlights, flicking my own to life. "Stay here, I'll be right back." I run and turn out the hall light and hurry back inside with her, the flashlights now our only glow. "I have snacks, cards, and—"

"I think we should tell ghost stories!" she suggests with a giggle.

Oh yeah, she gets it, and she's having a blast. Sawyer had called me an array of names when he saw what I had in store; pussy, cheesy and cornball the ones I specifically remember, but Dane hadn't said a word, just shot me a knowing smile…'cause well, his girlfriend is Laney. Enough said.

Being best friends with Laney all those years, I know all about a girl's "inner child." Women try their whole lives to stay young; cosmetics, hair dye, tanning salons…plastic surgeons and Wonderbra companies have built empires around that fact. So any chance you have to make a woman feel young and whimsical, channeling her inner tea party and fairy…you do it. *Especially* if they never got to enjoy it in the first damn place.

"Excellent fort activity, Miss Thompson. Would you like to go first?"

"No, you go first." She lays down, her head in my lap. "I'm ready."

"This is called *Who Stole My Golden Arm*," I begin, laughing as a shiver runs through her body.

If you've never been woken up by a piglet rooting your face with its sloppy, wet nose, well, you're not living right, 'cause it is just great.

"Ugh," I groan, pushing the little pain in the ass away, "go see your mother."

"Come here, baby," she mumbles sleepily, pawing around to find him. "He's just jealous of how much I love you."

She may be right, but I'm too tired and stiff to think about it. I don't remember sleeping in a fort being this damn uncomfortable when I was a kid. Hay stacks, forts…one of these days I'm gonna hold Whitley all night long *in a bed*.

"You want coffee?" I roll over and face her. She looks adorable when she wakes up, messy hair and sleepy blue eyes peeking out at me from her blanket cocoon.

"I'll make it!" She smiles. "Will you take Tiny out? His leash is by the door."

Along with his monogrammed food and water bowl, his toy pile and his wagon. Yes, wagon.

Me and Ms. Thang are gonna go round and round when it

comes to our kids. My sons will not be pansies and my little girls will not be pageant brats.

Okay, so maybe my little blonde, blue-eyed princess would look cute waving to her daddy from the stage, all frills and bows…

The pig starts whining at me, climbing precariously close to my junk, breaking my trance. Was I just spacing out on mine and Whitley's babies? That's something I've *never* done before *ever*.

"All right, Wilbur, let's go out," I grumble, getting up.

"You'll confuse him if you call him other names!" she calls from the kitchen. My hummingbird has the ears of a werewolf.

"What are you gonna do when he has to go live on the farm?" I wrap my arms around her from behind, dropping a kiss on her cheek. "Will I get all that leftover attention?" My mouth seeks her neck now. "'Cause I'll take it."

"Maybe," she teases, and I could swear pushes her butt into me just a bit. "I'll make you pancakes while you take him out."

God, I hope there's no one outside, seeing me walking a damn pig on a leash. The things men do for their women.

"I'll clean up the living room when I get back in since you're cooking." I steal another taste of her neck.

"No, leave it, I wanna sleep there again tonight."

"Okay then," I chuckle at her, already feeling my back and legs stiffen up. "Come on, Porky."

I keep walking as she scowls at me behind my back. Yes, I'm sure.

---------✧---------

"There's more?" she asks, her voice chipper and anxious.

"Well, yeah, you didn't think it took me all that time just to set up the fort, did you?"

"I don't know," her shoulders pop up, "it *was* pretty fancy. Okay, okay, show me!"

I lower my hands, once again covering her eyes, and scoot back, leaning against the beam behind me. "Go crazy, woman."

It takes her a while, her face in delighted shock, awe, eyes bulging as she slowly and meticulously takes in every single thing. Her hands fly to her mouth, tears starting to roll down her cheeks as she gasps, then shakes her head, and gasps again. "W-where? H-how?" She stutters, then takes a deep breath. "You—how'd you?"

Now I move in, pulling her into my arms, kissing the top of her head as she moves into full-blown sobbing. "You like it?"

She nods, face buried in my shirt, and my heart bursts knowing I've shown her just a hint of what she means to me. I will never stop listening when she talks, never stop hearing what she's really trying to tell me, and for sure never get comfortable thinking I can't outdo my last big surprise.

"Come on, pretty girl, let's go have a closer look before everyone gets here." I lift her face with both hands and wipe her drenched cheeks. "Happy tears," I mumble, leaning over to kiss off what my fingers missed.

"Who's everyone?"

"The Crew." I grin. "The best part of all this? Having great friends to share it with. And don't worry, the mud puddle will dry up and grow back over when you're tired of it."

I'm not gonna lie, even with me, Zach, Sawyer and Dane working like dogs, this was quite the project. In the middle of the backyard, and the main event, is a super slide, complete with huge mud hole at the end, dug and filled by Sawyer. The trampoline in the corner, assembled by Zach and Dane, is covered in pre-filled Super Soakers.

Flowers of every color outline the entire perimeter of her backyard, planted by all four of us. We'd also laid a rock pathway from the patio, now adorned with white lights and tiki posts as well as a BBQ grill and chef station, all the way to the 13 gallon pool. I can see it's still not quite full, all the balls and blow up seahorses and whatnot bobbing at almost the halfway mark, but it will be soon enough. And at least it isn't filled with Jell-O like Sawyer suggested.

Yes, we'd gone crazy and her backyard now looks like Funapalooza threw up in it. It's maybe even a bit gaudy, and it'd put a huge dent in my savings, but I know it was worth it. Even now, her smile can't be wiped off and a tear sneaks out every few seconds.

I lead her to the far corner, where the big tree stands, to my favorite part. "Sit down and I'll push you." I kiss her softly, holding still the swing I'd hung from the tree for her.

"Evan, I can't believe you do all this for me." She sits in the swing, gripping the ropes. "This is the nicest thing anyone has ever done for me, ever. And, *ohhh*," her breath catches, exaggerated—she's spotted it. "Oh! Oh my God!" She stands, walking slowly to the tree. She traces it with one fingertip, finally looking back at me. "You carved our initials in the tree?"

"I did." I give her a wink and flirtatious grin, making my way to her.

"You are so," she turns in my arms, looking up at me, "kind and romantic and unbelievably sexy. Perfect."

She'd done such a fine job summing it up I don't think any more words are necessary. Putting my mouth to better use, I devour hers, reaching under her butt to lift her against me, then back her up against the tree.

"That too rough on your back, hummingbird?"

"No," she moans, "but don't you mean swan?" she pants, digging into my hair and driving me insane, "or angelfish?"

"Huh?" Actually, never mind, I can't take it another second. I have to see her, taste test a new part of her. I brace her harder against the tree with my hips and move a hand to her top, flicking open button after button until her pale pink bra comes into view. Whitley has an ample chest, and the skin falling out of the cups is too inviting, making it impossible to stop myself as I pull the lace down, freeing her breasts to bounce out before my eyes.

Damn, definitely more than a handful, with dusky pink nipples hard and begging. "You're gorgeous, Whit." I dip my head to try and smother myself, thinking it'd be a helluva way to go. "Tell me this is okay," I beg.

"It's so okay, oh my God, yes." Her head falls back, her chest pounding.

I know she can feel my body's response, and, caught in the haze of lust, I grind myself between her legs, our tortured moans synchronized.

"Hey hey hey!" Sawyer's voice reaches out through our daze and grabs my balls, twisting them mercilessly, as welcome as a prostate check from Captain Hook.

"Why does God hate me?" I whine into her soft, ivory flesh.

Her hands are working frantically to right her clothes and I painfully, begrudgingly, set her to her feet.

"Go let him in the gate; I'm gonna run in and freshen up," she says, rising on her tiptoes to brush her lips softly against mine. "Go on, grumpy, I promise to make it up to you later."

"Or you could wait right here and I'll go kill him real quick."

"Go on." She laughs and gives me a playful shove.

"Finally," Sawyer cocks off when I let him in, "what the fuck, you forget you invited us over?"

"Something like that," I grumble, taking stuff out of his arms. "What's all this?"

"Half the damn grocery store. Somehow I got nominated to go with Laney and Bennett's lists."

"It's good for ya. One of these days some girl's gonna snag ya and knock ya on your ass. This way, you'll be ready."

"You start drinking without me? No woman will ever tame me, or send me on fucking errands or tampon runs and bullshit. That chick doesn't exist. It's different doing it for Gidge, she's my buddy."

"Whatever, Casanova, help me get all this unpacked and put away. I don't want Whitley doing it on her big day."

"Doing what?" She breezes in the kitchen, stirring me up all over again, just when I finally had *things* under control. "Hey, Sawyer! My goodness," she looks around, "did you buy the whole store?"

"Hmpf," he pouts, "Laney and Bennett's doing; slave drivers."

"Ah..." She gives him a hug, or as close to a hug as she can, like Whitley's little arms will circle all the way around Sawyer. "How sweet of you to help out. Thank you so much." She pokes him in the belly. "I think you're wonderful."

"How wonderful?" He gives her his patented Sawyer leer and moves closer.

"Ow! What the hell?" He rubs the back of his head while Whitley bends to pick up the cantaloupe I just bounced off his noggin.

"Back away from the taken woman."

"The hot ones are dropping like flies, I tell ya. I'm gonna have to get new friends if I wanna get laid regularly."

"You get laid plenty, manwhore. And hello to the rest of you." Tate walks in through the patio door, setting down...more bags?

"Actually, I got shot down just last night. I put in a good two hours of 'conversation,'" Sawyer air quotes are quite humorous, "and kept her in drinks. When we finally got down to it, she played the 'I have my period' card. Can you believe that?"

"Maybe she really did, Sawyer. It does happen," Whitley pats his shoulder, "and heaven forbid you hold a conversation just because."

"Fuck that, I told her just because the Ferris wheel breaks they don't shut down the whole carnival, if you know what I mean."

Whitley looks baffled, turning to me, then Tate, meeting looks of equal confusion. "No, we don't know what you mean."

"Blowjob, hand job, something. Period only shuts down one ride, not the whole fair."

"Sawyer Landon, good God! Where do you get this stuff?" Whitley blushes enough for all of us. "Anyway," she scowls at him and turns to Tate, "where's Bennett?"

"She rode with Dane and Laney. They wanted to show her the new pad on the way."

"What new pad?"

"Dane bought a duplex about two miles from here. Laney's gonna live on one side and Bennett and I are gonna live in sin on the other. Cool, huh?"

"Who's gonna live with Laney?" Sawyer asks.

"No one, I guess," Tate shrugs.

"Bullshit. I will. If you're moving out and Evan's with Zach now, I can't be by myself."

"I live by myself," Whitley chimes in.

"That's right," Sawyer drawls, sidling up to her. "Want me to move in with you?"

Watermelon's probably too big, it might actually hurt him. Pineapple? Perfect. Wham!

"Mother of—" he yells. "Will you stop throwing shit at me?!"

"Stop hitting on my woman and I will!" I yell back, laughing.

Whitley crooks that finger at me, giving me a come hither look that pulses through me. I do her bidding in two steps, wrapping my arms around her waist, my nose headed straight to its home in her hair. "Yes?"

"Nothing," she coos, "you were just too far way."

I forgot how damn good it felt to have someone to give your lovin' to. And to have it given back, freely…even fucking better.

"Roomie!" Sawyer yells, making all of us turn to see the three stragglers walk in.

"Why is he calling you roomie?" Dane follows Sawyer's eyes to Laney and growls.

"Like I have a clue." She laughs. "Who knows why he does half the things he does? Sawyer," she says patronizingly, "can you please explain to my caveman here what you're talking about before you get me in trouble for something I, too, am clueless about?"

"Sure," he grins, "Dane, I'm moving in the duplex with Laney on her side."

"Wait," Laney holds up a hand, "before everyone goes crazy, where's Zach?"

Subtle subject change there, Walker.

I snort, unable to hold it in, because Zach's been standing behind them, outside the glass door, for a good five minutes. Smart man. I wouldn't walk in to that conversation either.

"What?" Laney looks at Whitley and me suspiciously, and Whit caves first, pointing. Laney turns and pops her hands on her hips. "What are you doing? Get in here."

"Do I have to?" he calls through the glass.

"No, we'll go out to him," Bennett says, "Tate can start the grill. I'm starving."

"Oh, okay," Whitley leaves my arms, "let me get stuff ready. Evan, can you get drinks on ice and maybe start some music, babe? I'll make burger patties and prep sides. Sawyer, if you'd cut up the big fruit, it won't fly at your head anymore."

"Stop right where you are, woman. *You* are not working. Go change into your backyard water and mud party apparel," I command, to which she quirks her brows and gives me a shocked but teasing smirk. "I mean it, Whit. We all got it, this is your day to have some fun."

She looks around the room, everyone taking the turn to nod or smile in affirmation.

"Really, Whit," Laney speaks up, "go get changed. We can handle it."

"All right then," she backs her way to the hall, "if you're sure."

———— ❦ ————

"Whitley, Tiny's hogging the mud hole again!" Zach's whiny yell comes from across the yard. "I'm just gonna slide into him if he doesn't move."

Slide away, man, 'cause that pig's not moving from the mud hole. That's Old McDonald 101.

"He'll move when he sees you coming!" Whitley hollers back from where she sits in my lap, slumped back and tuckered out from her day of water gun fights, mud sliding, jumping on the trampoline and playing half-full pool volleyball. "So Laney, tell me about your new place."

"*Our* new place," Sawyer corrects.

"Like hell." Dane glares at him.

I have to admit, today has been great. And The Crew? The Crew is one big family—functional, funny endearing, and truly accepting of one another. Everyone cares about the others and has each other's backs, and I'm really glad to be a part of it. I get to see Laney and spend time with my friends while holding the girl I'm so enamored with I can see nothing else. I can't believe it happened; it's so unbelievable. But it did. I'm honestly not a bit uncomfortable being around Dane and Laney now, and I'm pretty sure Laney feels the same way about Whit and I.

And Whitley is tickled pink, her words, to have Laney and Bennett as girlfriends. She's always talking about them, and even Hayden, and it makes me happy for her. Whitley's an incredible person and it's about time everyone else saw it too.

"Seriously?" Sawyer flips a beer tab at Dane. "You really don't trust me with her?"

"Don't answer that," Tate mumbles.

"No, fuck that. Answer me, Dane, do you not trust me with Laney?" Sawyer asks again, pointedly.

Wasn't I just reflecting on how amicable our group was? Musta jinxed it, 'cause this is hella awkward.

"Of course he does, Saw," Laney placates, "he's just kidding around."

"I want to hear him say that." Sawyer's teeth are clenched and a huge veins throbs in his neck.

"Yes, Sawyer, I trust you. And I definitely trust Laney," he ducks his head and kisses the side of her neck, "but it might be a little strange, having a man live with my girlfriend, that's all. Why don't I just buy the unit across the street for you?"

"Oh, Sawyer! You, Evan and Zach could share it!" Laney claps.

Claps. Laney Jo Walker does not clap unless she's celebrating athletic achievement.

Yep, she definitely feels as uncomfortable as I do.

"What am I doing?" Zach joins the group, wiping off the muddy hoof prints covering him.

"Dane doesn't trust me to share the duplex with Laney, so he's offered to buy another one for me, you and Evan to share." Sawyer is speaking to Zach, but never looks away from Dane.

"I just said I trust you, Sawyer. Why are you so hell bent on this?" Dane wipes a hand over his face in exasperation.

"Um, thanks," Zach rubs the back of his neck, "but I don't need Dane to buy me a place to live. I'm fine where I am."

"Same here," I cut in.

I'm come a long way with things, but I'm not living off Dane.

"Everybody shut the hell up!" Tate sets Bennett off his lap and stands. "Enough. My brother goes out of his way to buy us a place, and I don't think it's unreasonable for him to not want a guy to live with his girlfriend." He narrows his eyes at Sawyer. "And he's not trying to show off and buy Evan and Zach anything; that was Laney's idea. So everyone chill the fuck out."

I've never heard Tate say that much all at once and definitely not in that tone. Good for him.

"I'm out," Sawyer says abruptly and stands to go. "Thanks, Whit." He hugs her and slaps my shoulder, then walks to the gate.

"Sawyer, wait!" Laney yells and runs after him, and seconds later, Dane sighs loudly and follows her.

"What the hell is all that about?" Zach asks the remaining group, all dumbfounded.

Sawyer is never the one in a bad mood, as far from the source of drama as possible

"I'm thinking Sawyer's having some issues with change," Tate puts in. "Everyone's coupling off and moving out. Sawyer doesn't deal well with being left."

"How about if Evan moves in with me and Sawyer moves in with Zach?" Whitley says.

Zach's smirking, Bennett's grinning ear to ear and I'm, *oh shit*, I'm choking.

Tate starts beating me on the back, laughing. "I know, right? Kinda the same reaction I had about moving in with Ben."

"Oh, you did not!" She slaps at him. "You started packing that night, you liar."

I can't move in with Whitley. We've been dating what, a minute? I don't know anything about her— okay, so that's not exactly true, I know a ton about her, but I've never met her parents or shook her father's hand and promised to take care of his little girl. Which probably doesn't matter since her parents, by all lack of appearances or phone calls or acknowledgement in general, suck. But we might not be compatible around each other 24/7. Just because I miss her the millisecond we part doesn't mean moving in together is a smart move. What happens if things don't work out between us—then what? Oh yeah, I'll be in jail for murdering the other guy, so I'll be all set with a place to stay.

"Are you serious?" I ask her.

"Oh, hey, you're back. Get it all worked out in that head of yours?" she teases.

Busted.

"Yeah, I think so. We don't have to do anything 'til we get back after the summer, though. Only makes sense."

"Care to share with the class where *we're* going this summer?" she bats her eyelashes.

"You're coming home with me. I'm gonna work for Parker this summer, and you," I grip her hips tighter and pull her back against me, "are gonna keep me company, country girl."

"Yes, I am," she says proudly.

Huh, she must have heard a question in there somewhere.

"Hey, Sawyer!" I turn my head and yell, interrupting the ongoing debate the three of them are having. "Come 'ere!"

"What?" he grumbles when he gets to me.

"Why don't you come home with me and Whit for the summer? Parker's house is huge and he can use all the hired help on the farm he can get. You'll love it there, you'll make some money, and Parker's great."

"Um, hello?" Zach points to his chest. "Recently cheated on, nothing to do with himself guy standing right here."

"More the merrier, man," I chuckle. "And when summer's over, we'll regroup on where everybody's gonna live. Sound good?"

"Dane!" Sawyer busts out.

Lots of yelling going on today, and this backyard isn't that big. I think maybe everyone's a little on edge with the end of the school year and lots of big changes.

"I quit! Be back at the start of school!"

"Sounds good," Dane answers in a normal voice since he's now standing right beside us. "You go do your thing; duplex is waiting for ya when you get back. It'll be nice to know Laney's got you there when I can't be." He gives him a slap on the back. "And I'm sorry. I'd trust you with my life, which coincidentally, she is."

"I know, peckerhead," Sawyer wraps him up.

"We gonna sing Kumbaya now? You know it's bad when Sawyer sprouts a vagina. Come on, let's slide bitches!" Zach screams, running through the mud hole like a maniac.

Everyone joins in, whooping and hollering, dodging the squealing pig at their feet, but not Whitley. No, Whitley holds strong, here with me, resting her head back on my shoulder, sighing peacefully.

I couldn't agree more, pretty girl.

Chapter 30

Pillow Talk

Evan

"To us, the smartest fucking college students ever! May they *try* to invent the exam that stumps us!" Sawyer toasts.

The Crew members all hold up their glasses to his. "Cheers!"

"I can't believe this is our last Crew night until the fall," Laney says sadly. "I'm glad it's summer, but I'm gonna miss everybody."

"Laney, aren't you planning on coming home to see your dad some?" I ask.

"Of course."

"You and Dane swing by Parker's when you do. With me, Whit, Saw, and Zach there, it's a Crew night!" I explain.

"But what about Tate and Bennett?"

"Bring them along."

"It'll be fine, Laney," Bennett consoles her, "we'll try to make it a few times."

"See, now enough sad talk, baby, finish your goodbyes so I can get you home." Dane swats her butt. "What time are you guys leaving in the morning?" he asks me.

"Parker's supposed to be here with the trailer about ten," I say.

Tiny is no longer tiny and must be hauled to the farm in a trailer. Whitley had thrown a ringtail fit, cussing a blue streak at me for days until I finally called the ASPCA and had them tell her that it is, in fact, *not* cruel and unusual punishment but rather the safest plan for both pig and transporters.

You'll never convince Whitley, but pigs aren't nice animals, and the bigger they get, the meaner they get. I'm really hoping she's over it by the end of the summer and might settle for a cat.

"You guys need anything, just call." He reaches out to shake. "Sawyer and Whitley on a farm," he says with a laugh, "you're a brave man, Evan."

"Tell Parker we'll be down soon, and please swing by Dad's and make sure he's eating and has clean laundry, okay?" Laney worries her lip. "I'll be down after the charity clinic next week, I promise."

"I will, but he's fine. Now come 'ere." I pull her in for a big hug. "Don't worry so much, Copper. Everything's fine; we'll all see each other soon. Okay?"

"K, Tod," she mumbles, heading into Whitley's arms. "Have fun, Whit, and please call me, and—"

"Goodnight, everyone," Dane says for her as he carries her out the door thrown over his shoulder. "We'll see you in eight, long, excruciating days."

"Good idea. Come on, Ben," Tate yawns, "I'm tired, put your man to bed."

"Bye, guys." She hugs Whit and me, of course teary-eyed, because she's Bennett. "We'll visit as soon as we can. Tate's running the gym now, so we'll be a little busy."

"What?" Whitley asks.

"Oh yeah," Bennett lowers her voice, "you didn't hear?" "Ty's is now all Tate's, free and clear. Dane *finally* got him to take something to run and build from on his own. Didn't hurt," she smirks, "that Jenee's the GM there."

"Wh-whoa!" Whitley apparently catches on and giggles. "Everybody wins. Go Laney!"

"Exactly! Anyway, you guys be careful. Miss us!"

"We will!" Whitley shuts the door behind them. "You guys sleeping here to head out early or what?" she asks Sawyer and Zach, who I give a "no way" and throat slash to behind her back.

"Nah, I still gotta finish packing," Zach smoothly covers, "and I'll need a ride in the morning, so come on, Sawyer."

"I'll come get you, but I'm gonna crash here," he says.

Bastard.

"I'll go get the guest room ready then." Whitley heads down the hall.

"Dude, don't make her do that work just so you can yank Evan's chain," Zach chuckles. "Whit, don't bother, he's coming with me!" he yells down the hall.

"Who says I'm kidding?" He wags his eyebrows at me.

"You are such a prick," I shove him, "get the hell out."

"Oh yeah, boys, gonna be a fun summer!" Sawyer proclaims, rapping on the doorframe and chuckling at himself as they leave.

"What the—did they leave?" she says, drawing my eyes to her.

"Yep." I turn the deadbolt and switch off the main light. I reach behind my head and pull off my shirt, tossing it over the couch.

"Are you gonna take a shower before bed?"

"Nope."

I kick off my shoes then lean over and get the socks. I stalk her, my eyes telling her what's on my mind. Night after night I sleep beside her, holding her, doing nothing more than kissing and heavy petting, only a few times even under her shirt. Tonight, I'm hanging my gentleman hat by the door and hoping for more. I take her hand and pull her into the bedroom, shutting the door behind me. She watches my every move as I put my phone on her dock, starting my "Hummingbird" playlist, then turn back to her.

Her pupils are dilated and I watch her tongue skim across her lip; she feels the shift in the air, her nipples already hard against her shirt. Her chest rises and falls urgently. "I've never," she whispers.

"Me either." I hold her gaze.

"No?" She doesn't hide her surprise and maybe skepticism.

I shake my head no, unashamed.

"And you want me?" Her cheeks pink and she treats that lip to her tongue again.

This time I nod, moving closer to her. "I want you so bad, pretty girl. I want to love you," I wrap my arms around her waist, "I want to take care of you. I want to hold you. I want to be with you every chance I get." I capture her sigh in my mouth as I cover hers, moving my hands to her perky little ass and squeezing with a tortured groan. "You want me back?"

"Yes," she rasps out, sliding her hands down my back, around to my abs, which contract beneath her light touch, and finally to the button of my jeans. She guides each button free then yanks them down past my knees, where I finish kicking them off. Backing away but a step, her eyes rake over me, now before her in just my boxer briefs, up, down, then up again. "You are so hot," she moans, then slaps a hand over her mouth in embarrassment.

"Come 'ere." I hold my hand out and pull her flush against me. "Let me see you?" I ask, tipping up her face with one finger under her chin.

She nods, biting her lip, testing my patience.

"Arms up, gorgeous," I breathe against her neck, her pulse point, running my fingertips up her limbs as she raises them. I pull her shirt over her head, kissing her chest, neck, and collarbone as I reach behind and unclasp her bra.

Her arms come down and she lets it fall to the floor while her sultry eyes stay on mine, blue on blue, Whit on Evan. Just us.

"You steal my breath away, pretty girl. I can't stop looking at you." I move and sit on the edge of her bed, pulling her between my legs. My hands run along her sides as I suckle her soft, flat stomach. "So soft, so sexy."

My girl runs her fingers through my hair, whimpering as I kiss and lick every inch bared to me, taking my sweet time. Her body is more than beautiful, more than tiny and perfect; it's miraculous, entrancing. I can't decide if I want to see more yet. Have I done her heavy, rounded breasts justice? Does her navel know yet that I adore it? Her hips, her dips, is that hidden balloon, that balloon that *I* had put there, ready for me?

She thinks so, her fingers sneaking into her waistband and enticingly, agonizingly slow, pulling down her shorts. No panties. And no soft curls.

"Don't you move," I snarl manically. "Aw, babe," I rub my eyes, just making sure, "Whitley, you're gonna kill me." I use one finger to reach out and touch, outlining first my balloon, then her bareness, her beauty.

I've seen girls naked, I've messed around with a few more than Laney, but I have never even come close to the likes of a naked Whitley Suzanne Thompson. Laney's a gorgeous girl, her body a toned machine, and everything she showed me was respected and adored…and why I'm thinking about this right now I have no idea, but maybe it's because Whitley before me is short circuiting my brain.

She's so…delicate, so feminine, so not of this world. Seriously, her body is a temple; a smokin', tight, untouched, dainty, *bare* temple.

If I can only pick one body to look at the rest of my life, supermodels around the globe included, I pick the one standing right in front of me. She reaches up and lets her hair down, running her hands through it. I'm gonna come right here, I swear. She looks *that* good.

She climbs on my lap, straddling me, and pushes me back to lie flat on her bed. That strawberry scented hair of hers falls in my face as she lowers herself over me, kissing and running her tongue over my chest, my nipples, open mouth sucking ~~my~~ her tattoo. "I love your body, Evan." She blows along the places her mouth left damp, "and this," she runs a finger down the line of hair from my navel to where the head of my dick now sticks out of my briefs, "I love this." Scooting, she makes room to peel my underwear off, doing illegal things to both thighs on her way back up.

"In my pants, wallet," I pant, trying to calm myself as she hops off me to grab a condom or three. I've never wanted anyone more in my life, my head fells like it's about to explode and we've barely started. I don't want to quicknut and spoil our first time. Maybe I should say I have to go to the bathroom and knock one out first?

Or maybe I should share this, however it goes, with the woman who knows the *man* I am best. That's right; as a man, the person I am today, Whitley knows me best. And just like I know anything happening with her will be perfect and just as it should be, I know she'll feel the same.

Too late anyway, she's crawling back up me, my cock actually twitching up off my stomach on its own. And now we're draped together, nipple to nipple, stomachs quivering as one, and I can feel her moisture on me. There's one other thing I've never done, and she's the one. I flip her and chuckle when she squeals, then moan low and euphorically when my tongue, joined by one finger, first finds her.

Her nails dig into my scalp. "Evan, I—"

"You what?" I ask against her.

"I've never!" she wails. "Never—"

I guess we're gonna do a checklist as we go, which is fine by me. If you think it bothers me to get affirmation of everything that she's chosen to give to only me—it doesn't. The couple that learns together, stays together. *Catchy, I like it.*

Girls think guys want them to put out. They do, don't get me wrong, but a girl who gives it only to you? Yours. Only. Ever...you will never compete with that, no matter what tricks you have up your sleeve, easy girls. Doesn't matter who or what he is, the sole proprietorship thing is a universal turn-on.

"Me either, pretty girl. It's okay," I lay my left hand on her belly to ease her, "I got you, always got you." I wait, rubbing her stomach, kissing the inside of her thigh. "Okay?"

"Okay," she answers.

"Open up a little more, baby. That's it," I calm her as her knees fall further apart. When I feel her completely relax for me, I lay my mouth upon her once more.

Her hips bucking up wildly, almost startling me. "Ah, Evan!" she cries out. "I need."

I don't want to *hold down* her hips, but, well, I hold down her hips. "I know, baby, stay still for me and I'll give it you." I take one long, soothing lick. "Tell me, tongue or finger?"

I'm not too proud to stop and ask for directions. This sexy, thrashing dream come true is gonna come in my mouth, that's all there is to it. And once I learn what she likes, she'll never have to tell me again. I am a firm believer in dedication to practice, and pretty sure I'm already addicted to the taste of her.

"Both?" she asks in a shaky voice. "Finger in me…" she gasps as I slide one in, "a-and your tongue?"

Yes, ma'am.

I could do this all night. I've heard locker room talk, and I know there are some guys who hate this, refuse to do it—morons. I can't help thrusting against the mattress in rhythm to my feast of her; it's that damn enjoyable.

"Faster, and harder with your finger," check, "and right," she pulls my hair, forcing my head still as she shifts down, putting my mouth right where she wants it. "There! Right there, Ev, hard, on the very—ahhhhhh!" she screams.

Think I got it.

I dare not move my mouth to lap it up, but stay right where she put me, my chin drenched. My mouth just gave its first of many orgasms to this oral virgin. If possible, I just got harder, my ego bigger.

"You good?" I rumble, kissing up her sated body to her neck. I doubt she wants a kiss on the mouth right now so I stay with her neck.

"We're staying in the same room at Parker's right?'

"Yeah," I chuckle. Addicted little vixen. Whatever will I do with her?

"Just making sure. Really hoping you form habits easily."

"You're gonna have to learn to be quieter, though."

"Promise." She lifts her head and kisses me square on the mouth. Her tongue seeks mine first and she goes harder, taking control, as if the taste of herself turns her on. "Where's the—"

My hand pops up in a flash, condom in it.

She slinks down me, ripping open the package, then biting the end of her tongue in concentration as she carefully rolls it on me. It's the sexiest thing I've ever watched, even with my eyes rolled back in my head.

"Will you hold me afterwards?" she murmurs.

I lift my head slightly and look straight into her eyes, blue on blue, so she'll see how much I mean it. "All night, babe."

"So you'll be here in the morning when I wake up?" she pulls her bottom lip between her teeth.

"Yes. Whit, come here." I hold out my arms, asking her to let me hold her now. "We don't have to do this, pretty girl." I kiss the top of her head and cradle her to my chest as she absently traces my tattoo. "We can wait, and nothing will change, I promise. And if we don't wait, nothing will change, I promise that too."

"I don't want to be a tease, but I'm nervous. Sex changes people, and we're perfect. And boys brag to their friends and that will hurt me. And—"

"Shhh, everything's fine. Let me assure you now, when the time does comes, I won't brag to my friends." I can't help my small snort. "I think maybe you've watched too much *Greek*, Whit, and by the way I hate that show so I'm happy to help you over that. You just stick with *Duck Dynasty*; pay attention to how they treat their women. I will never disrespect you, and you're right, we are pretty prefect. So let's wait until the time is perfect too, okay?"

"You're sure?"

"Positive." I kiss the end of her nose as she peers up at me through worried eyes. "Even if I wasn't, wouldn't matter, you're the boss. Just like my mama and Dad; I may fight ya as we get older, but you're always gonna have the final word."

"And you're not mad?"

"Go to sleep, woman, we've got a big day ahead of us. You want the music on or off?"

"On," she answers sleepily.

———— ✎ ————

Surely it can't be morning already. The music is still playing and it feels like I just fell asleep with an aching, disappointed, not speaking to me dick. But in the dream I was having, my hummingbird's sweet pink mouth was wrapped around me, her fingers tickling below, and he was just about to forgive me. Yeah, it felt almost that good, like that—

"Whitley?"

"Mmmm?"

I lift the covers and look down. Not a dream. "Damn, babe," I rumble, "what got into you?"

I watch, enjoying the show, while she ignores me, hollowing her cheeks in utter bliss, twirling her tongue right under the rim before pulling off.

"I'm ready," she says in a deep, seductive voice as she rolls a new condom down me.

Like a moron, a brain dead glutton for punishment, I say, "Whit, I told you we could wait. What changed your mind?"

"You did. You talk in your sleep, did you know that?"

"No."

"You do. And if I ask you stuff, you answer." She prowls up my body, kissing a trail. "I trust you, and I want you too. Now," she adjusts, teasing her wetness along the length of me.

"Whitttt," I drawl out, crazed and feigning.

"I'm right here." She lifts and guides me to her, taking in just the tip. "Ahh!" she cries out.

I pull back and turn us so that she's on her back. "It'll hurt less this way, baby." I use my fingers to spread her moisture, then use another to stretch her while I suck a soft nipple slowly.

"Perfect song," she moans.

Only Whitley, I think with a grin, knowing she will probably hum this song every time we make love for the rest of our lives. Fine by me. I love her humming, her voice, this song...it's on my Hummingbird playlist after all.

When she's writhing, mumbling and begging incoherently, my fingers having about got her there, I slide in as slowly and gently as I

246

can. I'll never forget this moment as long as I live, the exact second I first joined with Whitley Suzanne Thompson, her back arching off the bed and her mouth dropping open, "Sideways" by Citizen Cope setting the perfect mood and saying the perfect words.

"All at once, babe, go," she tells me and winces, grabbing my ass and pulling me deeper.

I feel it, can actually feel it break, and she screams in sharp acuteness, killing me. "Shhh, I'm sorry, pretty girl, I'm so—"

"No, I'm okay, keep going." She sucks in a deep breath. "Slow," she murmurs, one tear dripping down her cheek.

I bow my head and lick the tear off, then kiss all over her face as I rock into her, closing my eyes and absorbing the madness of it all; my head's spinning, my heart beating frantically, sweat building on my back. Being inside her, it feels... There's nothing like it, nothing. "Whitley, I love you," I let my head fall back, "*love* you."

"I know, you told me." A sobbing moan breaks from her. "Me too, Ev, me too, so much." Her arms wrap around me, then her legs. "You feel so good, so close to me. Never stop." I feel her hand move down between us, and, oh, fuck me I'm done.

"'Bout to, ahhh, Whit, hurry!" I fight it, I fight it like hell, but the sight of her finger helping herself is my unraveling. It works its way up my legs, a bolt of electricity the likes of which I've couldn't have possibly imagined, until I'm erupting inside her and she's there with me, her muscles clenching over and over in rhythm to my thrusts.

It can't possibly be like this for everyone, with just anyone, every time...society would cease to function, the world meeting its demise as no one would do anything but this, all day, every day, twice, ten times, anywhere she says.

Taking another minute to come back to reality, my forearms shaking under my weight, I don't readily notice that Whitley is crying. *What the hell have I done?*

"Baby," I leave her body and roll to her side, "why are, oh God, did I hurt you?" I choke out, kissing her forehead, stroking her hair.

"No," she laughs, wiping her eyes, "happy tears."

"Yeah?"

"Yeah." She nods, wrapping a hand around my neck and pulling my face to hers. "I'm almost positive it's not supposed to be that perfect and special your first time." She giggles almost to herself. "Thank you for setting such a wonderful precedent."

"It was, wasn't it? I love you, Whitley, with all my heart, I do."

"I know you do." She rolls to me, snuggling into the crook of my arm.

I should probably clean up, but I don't have the heart to move her.

"You told me in your sleep," she admits. "That's how I knew for sure. You could dream of anything, anyone, but you dream of me."

"And I talk back?"

"Uh huh."

"Did you ask me embarrassing stuff, you little sneak?" I tickle her, basking in the sound of her laughter.

"Well, yeah," she squirms, "you'd do the same thing."

"So tell me our conversation." I use this break in intimacy to get up and amble into her bathroom to get cleaned up.

"You said 'I love you,' so I asked 'who do you love' and you said 'you.'"

I'm just right inside her adjoining bathroom, with the door open, so I can more than make out the happiness in her voice, which tells me that even in my sleep, I got it right.

"So I said 'what's my name' and you said 'pretty girl,'" she giggles, "which was very sweet, but I dug deeper, you understand. Anyway, I said 'noooo, what's my real name?' and you said 'my Whitley.'"

I stick my head around the corner and wink at her, never catching a cuter sight than her teeth tugging her bottom lip and eyes glistening.

"I am your Whitley," she whispers and smiles so sweetly.

"And then you ravaged me?" I joke, wanting her pretty eyes to clear up.

"Something like that." She shrugs. "What are you doing anyway? Get back in bed with me," she pats the spot beside her.

"Whit, baby, don't freak out, but you need to come in here." I turn and start the bath water, tossing in a washcloth for her. "Come on," I give her my hand, "I know it's late, but get in for me okay? You relax and soak, and I'll take care of stuff and come back and get you, and then I'll hold you all night."

"What," she rises, gauging my eyes then turning back to look at the bed, "oh," she blushes adorably. "How'd you—"

"There was blood on the condom, babe. No worries, I'll take

care of everything." I kiss her head. "Get in."

"Ev?" Her little voice stops me at the door. She's probably going to ask for some "period pills," which I'm already on top of.

"Yeah?"

"You're my angelfish."

"Still no idea what that means, babe," I chuckle, "but I'm glad. Now soak, woman."

Chapter 31

Fornication
Evan

"Evan Mitchell Allen, I know you're in here and I know you saw me pull up! Get out here and kiss your mother, boy!"

She's bluffing.

"One!"

Shit.

"Two!"

"All right," I come out from behind the hay bales, "I'm twenty years old, quit your countin'!"

"Why are you hiding from me?" She sticks out her cheek and taps it, so I kiss it. "And where is my darling Whitley? I found the cutest dress in town today," she lifts the bag in her hand, "I want her to try it on."

"I imagine she's in the house; I'm not sure. And I was hiding because I don't want another lecture about staying at the house again. Whitley's probably hiding from you too."

She gaps, holding her heart and giving me a look that shrinks me to nothing on the spot. "She wouldn't! Breaks my heart, my only son home, right up the road and too ashamed to stay under his own mama's roof. And turning Whitley against me! Well, I just can't imagine what I've ever done to deserve this from my only child."

Thank God I'm wearing my boots, cause she is laying it on thick.

"Mama, I'm not ashamed. I wanna sleep in a bed with Whit,

plain and simple. I can do that here."

"What does her mother say about that?"

"Her mother doesn't say much about anything. Her parents each call once a month, the exact same date and time every time; real personal, like an appointment," I scoff loudly, wishing they were here in front of my mom right now. She adores Whitley and I salivate just thinking how she'd tear into them. "And Whitley's almost twenty-two years old, Mom, she can sleep where she wants."

"Have you talked to your father about it?"

"Yes, he thinks you're crazy."

"Did he say that, that exact word—crazy?"

"Yes, more than once." I look around, not wanting to just outright laugh at her reddening cheeks.

"Evan, honey, she's such a nice young lady. I wouldn't want you to—"

"Mama."

"What?"

"I love her, and she loves me back. Not because I'm around, or like a buddy, she *loves me*." I smile. "Told me she's dying to fill up your house with spoiled little grandbabies."

"Evan Mitchell!" She tries to act scandalized, but I know she's holding babies in her mind's eye as we speak.

"I'm gonna marry her one day and she's gonna marry me right back. And we're gonna fornicate, often, until we're too old to do it without throwing a hip out. I'm careful, so is she, but if you want us there, then know I'm holding that girl in my arms all night, every night. Say yes or accept me staying here, please?" I give her the ol' Evan one sided grin, then really see if I can embarrass her. "I'd never let you hear us."

"I oughta tan your butt, Mr. Mouthy!" She grabs my arm and tries to spin me around, taking swings at my rear. "Talking like you were raised by wolves!"

"I was kidding!" I break away from her, laughing. "At least sorta. But I'm serious about the rest."

"You're such a fine young man, Evan. Come to your mama." She holds out her arms and I grab her up, swinging her around in a big hug before finally setting her down and kissing her kick. "I did such a good job on you."

"Yes, ma'am."

"Well, I suppose since her mother is," she lifts her hand and whispers behind it, which somehow makes her feel like she didn't really talk ugly about someone, "an idiot, then I need her at the house so I can mother her myself."

I force my face to remain serious. "She'll love that."

My days will never be boring, toying with the two crazy, amazing women in my life.

"Me too! I'll just go find her and tell her. Now I'll allow the sleeping together, but maybe you can trade off some nights, stay here when you need to—"

"Go, Mama."

"Okay, okay." She scurries away in search of Whitley.

"That was the funniest shit I've ever heard." Sawyer steps out of the shadows, laughing. "I can't wait to play this for Zach." He pushes play on his phone, the recording of my fornication talk with my mother burning holes in my ears.

"Why the hell am I friends with you? Seriously, I need my head examined."

"Shit, sounds like you're getting your head examined. Mine, on the other hand, is about to shrivel up and fall off from boredom. Where's all the hot country girls in cutoff shorts and bandana tops, hair in braids, rising up on their horses?"

"This isn't *Joe Dirt*, Sawyer."

"She didn't have braids, assmunch. Which is fine; the braids are totally optional."

"Go into town one night, there's a bar."

"Cool, tonight, pick me up at eight."

"I'm not taking you. I have a woman and free beer in the refrigerator."

"Dude, you can at least show me how to get there. Remember who helped you when you first got to Southern?"

Here we go.

"Take Zach. I'm positive he'll be able to make the two turns there are to get to Shotz. Now come on, let's go grab some lunch. We need to make a dent in that fence before dark."

Sawyer's dragging pouty ass behind me to the house, kicking up rocks with every step.

"Bye, Evan, Sawyer!" my mom calls as she gets into her car. "I'll see you boys tonight for dinner."

I turn around and give Sawyer a shit-eating grin. Mama just put the kibosh on his plans.

Whitley's arms come around my waist when I'm washing my hands and face at the kitchen sink. "Hey, babe," she greets me.

I turn around, loving the sight of her new sundress. My mom really does love me. "Hey, hummingbird, how's your day?" I steal a kiss.

"Good, we're eating at your parents' tonight. That's okay, right?"

"Fine with me." I glance at Sawyer and see poor guy's lip is on the floor. "Big boy's getting antsy though. We gotta find him some nightlife or something, soon."

"How's a bachelor party sound?"

"Whitley, you proposing?" I wink, copping a feel of her fine butt.

She swats my arm. "Parker's; things need moved up."

"Why is that? We've only been here a few weeks. Thought they weren't getting married 'til the fall?"

"You'll see." She smirks, raising up like only she does to kiss my lips. "Act surprised," she whispers.

"That shouldn't be hard, you haven't told me anything."

"Am I late?" Zach asks as the door slams behind him.

"Just in time," Angie smiles at him, "take these rolls and go sit at the big table. Evan, get that ball cap off, boy, and Whitley, sweetie, help me with the rest of this, please."

Parker, already seated at the head of the table in his daddy's old spot, looks proud as a peacock. He's tracking our moves, chomping at the bit for us all to get seated and settled. When Angie and Whit finally do just that, he takes Hayden's hand in his and clears his throat. "Hayden and I have some big news that we want to share with all of you, our family and loved ones, first."

Whitley is already bouncing in her chair. Clearly Hayden had told *her* first.

"Hayden is having my baby!" He beams, happier than I've ever seen him.

Well, that ol' dog. He gets a plan in his head and he goes after it all right.

I still worry they're too young, because I'm so old and wise and all, but ya know what? There's been enough sadness and loss in this family, this home, lately… Why not be happy about this new life, the blessing that it is?

Yup, that's my new plan.

Angie jumps from her seat, already crying, and lays kisses all over both of them, Whitley right behind her. Zach and Sawyer mumble a "congratulations," and I sit and watch for a minute. I wish Dale was here to watch his son get married, hold his first grandchild, and meet my sweetheart.

"Evan?"

"Sorry, what?" I look at Parker, grinning at me, waiting for my acceptance.

"Wedding's moved up; Hayden here doesn't want a bump in her dress, even though I said it'd be beautiful. So time to ask—would you be my best man?"

"Of course I will." I stand, as does he, and give him a man's hug. "Congrats, man, you'll be a great dad."

"Ya think?"

"Yeah, Parker, I think. Uncle Evan…" I muse, puffing out my chest. "That kid's gonna love me."

"Not more than their Nana," Angie pipes in, waterworks still going strong. "Now let's eat 'fore I flood the place."

"So when are we thinking for the wedding, and where?" Whitley is salivating, I can see it from here. My little event planner; so damn cute.

"I was thinking end of the month, maybe in the barn?" Hayden replies.

"Outside, in July, in *Georgia*?" Whitley asks. "Hayden, you might get sick in that heat in your condition."

"Whitley?" I try to interrupt.

"I'm just thinking of Hayden. I know what you're gonna say, I'm being bossy and trying to take over and it's not my wedding, but I just don't want poor Hayden—"

"Babe!" I cut her off.

"What?" she looks at me, already defeated.

"The horse barn is air conditioned."

She takes a minute, staying calm and maintaining her dignified face. "Nobody laugh," she points at Sawyer, "I mean it." We all focus on our plates stoically. "I think that's plenty of time, Hayden. I'll be happy to help with that," Whitley forces out, proper and ladylike.

"Thank you," Hayden barely gets out with a straight face. It really is easy to do if you don't have to look at her.

"You gonna help me plan a bachelor party, boys?" I ask Sawyer and Zach.

"Do you really even need me?" Zach grins. "Pretty sure Sawyer was born for that job."

"Is he allowed strippers?" Sawyer asks Hayden, literally willing her answer with his pitiful eyes.

"Of course, but no lap dance for him. He can't touch them and they can't touch him. I think that's reasonable, okay?" she zones in on Parker.

"My word, sweetheart," he swears with a nod.

"Plan away."

Sawyer gets the go ahead and almost falls back in his chair with his exuberant fist pump and "yesssss!"

Chapter 32

Slice of Heaven
Evan

"So what'd you ladies decide to do tonight?" I ask, unable to keep my hands off her. I'd much rather stay here with her tonight, maybe take a moonlight dip in the lake, but she tells me the best man must go to the bachelor party. We all know we're having the damn thing under traditional façade only so that Sawyer won't throw himself off a cliff, but Whitley's having no more argument from me.

"We're throwing Hayden a mobile bachelorette party. She can't drink with the little muffin baking, so we had to think of something fun and different. It's a scavenger hunt around town, and the other girls have to do shots at all the stops so Hayden can laugh at them. I'm driving."

"You sure you don't want me to go and drive so that you can play?"

"I'm sure." She pats my cheek. "You'll have a good time, just behave. Strip club," she mutters, shaking her head. "Don't even think about crawling in bed with me tonight if you have a speck of glitter on you or smell like cheap perfume."

"You know better than that, pretty girl. You're all I see. And it's not exactly a strip club, they don't have those here. It's a few girls Sawyer hired, dancing in our Podunk bar. Not the same thing, and only for Sawyer's, and maybe Zach's, benefit," I explain with a laugh.

"Well, don't keep Parker out all night; he has to get married tomorrow. If he rolls in hung-over and ruins my carefully orchestrated ceremony, I will personally blame you." She pokes at my chest.

Whitley had worked her tail off on this wedding. The horse barn has been converted into a cathedral that'd make the Pope weep. Chairs, tables, streamers, flowers, candles—you name it, she got it and draped it everywhere. Hayden's a good sport, too nauseas most of the time to care, and gave Whitley free reign. I shudder to think about the day I marry my girl. There's no telling what she, armed with my mother, will come up with.

"He won't," Parker says, walking in behind us. "I'm already ready to be home with my lil' mama. Before we head out, though, I wanted to catch you both. Hayden and I have a gift for ya."

"You didn't have to do that," Whitley starts, though her eyes get glassy.

"Sure we did. You're our best man and maid of honor, after all." He pulls *my* woman from me and to his side. "Hayden doesn't have anybody here, Whit, well, 'cept me and Mama, and you helping her these last few weeks, being such a good friend, and dating *my* best friend; well, I'd say you're the perfect little puzzle piece to it all."

I really should be the one hugging my now hysterically weeping girl, but no, Parker seems to be basking in it, his eyes getting teary now, too. He does realize the more he keeps saying things like to her, the worse it's gonna get, I hope.

"Come on," he chuckles, kissing her head.

Hayden's waiting outside for us, a beautiful glow to her as she rests one hand on her stomach and holds out the other to Parker. "Did you tell them?"

"And steal your thunder? Do I look stupid, sweetheart?"

"Then why is Whitley crying?" she asks, giving Whit a comforting smile.

"Evan told her she couldn't sing at the wedding."

"What?" Hayden screeches, turning a flesh scorching glare my way.

"I did no such thing," I quickly tell her, holding up both hands in mercy. "You're just running around getting everybody stirred up tonight, aren't ya?" I shove Parker in the back.

"Y'all get in," he stumbles and laughs, helping his bride into his truck.

"Park, where we going? The guys are waiting," I protest, already knowing I've lost and helping Whitley in.

"Let em' wait," I knew he was gonna say that, "this here's about us four, and all that matters."

Whitley casts a nervous, curious glimpse my way and shrugs, taking my hand in both of hers. The ride into the back of the Jones' land takes about ten minutes, but today closer to twenty as he dodges and slows for every dip or hole, eyeing his pregnant fiancé at every single one. She's around 15 weeks, last I heard, and not that I'm positive, or would *ever* ask lest Whitley'd slap me sideways, but she seems to be getting *big fast*. That baby will definitely be built like its daddy.

"Here we are," Parker announces, getting out and walking around to Hayden's side.

I've seen this exact piece of land more times than I'd even attempt to count, so I'm not sure what's he's showing us. Even Whitley's seen it at least fifty times, it's my favorite spot on this whole farm. There's a slight hill with a view of more wide open land to the east and north, the old hay barn to the south, and to the west…Amigo Creek.

That's what we'd named it, Laney, Parker and I—Three Amigo Creek. The town ledger says Mule Elk Creek, but we don't care; that's *our* creek, more than a mile of it running through the Jones' land. It's where I first went skinny dippin' with Parker and two females, neither of which was Laney. Laney was there when we hung the rope swing and Dale yelled at us that it wasn't deep enough and we'd break our necks and made us cut it down. She'd been to all of our campouts on its bank and popped the raft with us (again, not deep enough in some spots) and right over there…my tree stand still sits in the perfect deer hunting spot.

Yeah, *this* is what heaven looks like to me.

"You ready now?" Parker pushes on my shoulder, ornery smile in place.

"Huh?"

"Told ya." He smirks at Hayden.

"You sure did." She giggles and pats my shoulder. "Now I see what you mean."

What?" I ask, the plot still evading me.

"I told Hayden, don't matter how many times you stand in this exact spot, you always do the same thing. You leave the rest of us here and drift off, thinking about everything you love about this place. No one will ever appreciate my land, especially *this* land," he stomps his foot, stirring up dust, "more than you, Evan."

"There's just something about it, I guess." I half-smile sheepishly, not knowing how else to explain it really. "Feels like my happy place."

"That's why I'm giving it to you."

Somehow I hear Whitley's gasp, and hold her up, or use her for support, it could go either way. "W-what?" I mutter, dazed.

"Besides Hayden and my Mama, you're my best friend in the whole world. Laney," he chuckles, "Laney's gonna get taken care of, gonna go great places and see great things. I got real lucky, Evan. I didn't have to wait a lifetime to meet the best people I was ever gonna. I met them at birth, then grade school, and third day of college." He smiles adoringly at Hayden. "I won't ever need anyone else. I couldn't do any better, and I'd kinda like to keep ya close."

"Park, you can't just give me—"

"I can do whatever the hell I want. Already did, in fact." He pulls some rolled up papers out of his back pocket all businesslike. "This spot, and 80 acres all around it, are yours. We can build you and Whit a house, be lifelong fishing partners and sneak each other's kids shitloads of sugar." He has me in a bro hug before I can even respond. Or bawl like a little girl. "Love you, man."

"Park. Hayden." I look between them, unsure of what to say. I can't quite grasp what he just said. This land is *mine?* "I love you, too, but this is—" I start to say. "I mean, thank you."

"Oh my God. Evan. You guys," Whitley sobs.

This time I move quickly, my reflexes downright catlike, making sure I'm the one to comfort her, while Parker and Hayden slink away discreetly, giving us some privacy. "I'll only do this if you do it with me, hummingbird," I whisper in her ear. "When we're done with school, we can move here, build any kind of house you want. Could you be happy like that, Whit? Maybe teach at a school in town, then come home to me and raise cows, chickens…babies?"

Her pause makes me panic so I lean back to look at her, sweeping under her eyes with my fingers.

"Can we have pigs too?"

"Yes, love, we can have pigs."

"Then I am so in!" She jumps, wrapping her legs around me.

"We have three years until I'm done with school, babe, three years to plan and build your dream house." I place a kiss on the end of her button nose, then, to really seal the deal, I carry her with me to pick the wildflower I spot about ten steps away and hand it to her. "Try not to have it all planned out by the time I get home tonight, okay?"

"Will it always be this good, Evan? I love you so much, everything feels perfect; surely it can't stay like this forever."

"Nope, it'll get better."

Epilogue

Sawyer

Tate and Bennett, Dane and Laney, Evan and Whitley…Sawyer and Zach. Anyone else see the problem with this fucking picture?

Do I want a girlfriend, a relationship? *Hell no.* That's what I've always known to be true; the one constant I'm sure of.

But lately, something's eating at me and I can't shake it. It wakes me up at night. I shoot up in a cold sweat and look around the room…am I late for class? Did I hear my phone? Did I leave water running?

Nope, nothing, just some unseen force greater than myself rattling my nerves. Again.

Everyone is moving on and growing up around me. I'm stagnant, the same carousing, partying, unattached, extremely sexy guy I was when I got to Georgia.

Where's my too-good-to-be-true woman with Bennett's loving and kind sex appeal, Laney's sporty, witty smartass hotness and Whitley's caring, innocent and always happy gorgeousness? Oh fuck, I want all three rolled into one.

I could go for some real lovin', some day after day, but no one comes close to holding my attention longer than it takes to knot off the condom and pull my pants up. No, I get easy, clingy, uninteresting girls. Hell, since Whitley got initiated into The Crew, I don't even get the ones with the tiggest bitties anymore either.

And this bachelor party for Parker, who I've known maybe eight weeks—God, I'm jealous as hell of him. That Hayden of his fucking adores him, and she's even hotter knocked up than she was before. And she dotes on his ass in a very independent, non-blood sucking leech kinda way. Why can't I find a girl like that?

Obviously I've had too much tequila since I'm hosting my own little titbag party over here, feeling sorry for myself. Fuck this. I hold up two bills in my hand, I think they're twenties, and silver cowboy boots come over way too eagerly.

Challenge me, dammit! Engage more than my dick!

"What's this get me?" I slur, shoving the bills at her.

She kicks one ankle, then the other, getting my legs just as far apart as she wants them and climbs over them, onto my lap. "This," she croons and starts to grind. Her attempt to pet my chest all sexy-like is an epic fail, snagging one way too long silver nail on my nipple ring. She better not rip my fucking shirt—I love this shirt.

"How much to go in the back?" Two months on a farm is damn lonely.

She cuts quick, nervous glances around, then leans into my ear. "Not my usual club, so not in here," she whispers. "But for a hundred, I'll meet you outside after."

Just when I'm about to finalize the exact details, "Shook Me All Night Long," my favorite song ever, starts blaring. Now this dance I gotta see, moving Dracula Nails off my lap and outta my view to the stage, aka the flat area in this place.

Spank me and put me to bed…who the fuck is that?

"Zach?!"

"Zach?!" I yell louder.

"What?"

"Who. Is. That?" I point to the, um, we'll go with "dancer" for now.

"Cause I know her? I think they said Karma or something, but I doubt you'd find her in the phone book under that. Why?"

Look at him trying to be all smartass… Well, he fucked it up—who the hell uses a phone book?

"No reason." I bounce my shoulders in what I hope looks like casual nonchalance, never taking my eyes off her. That may blow my cover, but damn if I could look away even if I tried.

I'm thinking it's the beer, strike that, tequila goggles; has to be. I was just dogging every chick who came near me, ready to pay for a meaningless quickie, a scratch to an itch, and sheer perfection happens to strut in to my favorite song?

Yeah, and when I'm done here, I'm gonna ride home to the Playboy mansion on my flying fucking dragon that I bought with my lottery winnings.

This isn't real and up close she's probably a big mess with bad breath and a whiny voice…and herpes. Gotta be.

But here's what I do know, no guessing, no wishful thinking, no maybe to it—take it to the bank: her hair is so dark and shiny that you can damn near see reflections in it and it has purple streaks in it— hot as hell. AND, wait for it… IT. IS. IN. BRAIDS.

Usually two braids or ponytails are known as "handlebars" in my language, but on this girl, they're cute; cute, wet dream-inducing braids.

Her eyes are as dark as her hair and hold the fear and anxiety of a kitten stuck in a drainpipe when it's raining. I may never know where it came from, this instinct that up until this point I would have sworn on a stack of Bibles I didn't possess, but I swear I hear her mind screaming to mine, "you're big and strong! Protect me, Sawyer! Take care of me, hold me, make me unafraid!"

That body of hers is tiny. Not frail, just petite, and tan and muscular…and her own. She turns it to the side and away from the onlookers and keeps her hands over her barely covered breasts like the tease is part of the dance, but it's not. I'd bet you a nut this girl has never danced or stripped before in her life. And if she has, she should stop immediately, because she absolutely sucks at it.

Those come fuck me heels she's wearing? They're two sizes too big and she's never walked in them before. Also something she should stop doing immediately. If the teetering and wobbling didn't draw attention to her shapely legs, it'd just be sad, but the legs are worth the painful show. Oh and fuck me, she's *skipping* around in a circle, I hope she doesn't think *that's* a good cover for her lack of dance skills…*skipping*, for crying out loud.

And lastly, she loves this song. She's mouthing the words, keeping her eyes unfocused and on the back wall, dying for everything but the song itself to be over. And when it is, she runs like she's on fire for cover behind the curtain.

"Who was that?" I ask Dracula Nails, still standing beside me.

"New girl," she answers snidely. "First night, can't you tell?" She

263

laughs.

"Yeah, I can."

"So, I'll see you later?" She curls those inflated lips at me.

"Maybe, if I see ya I see ya." I get up, walking over to Dane. "Where'd you get these girls?"

"Hell if I know; Brock hooked it up."

"So the company, it's local to us, like in Statesboro?"

"I think so, why?"

"Find out for sure, I'm gonna hit the can. Be right back."

I really do need to take a leak, but somehow I veer off course, peering behind the curtain like the Great and Powerful Oz will be waiting to hand me the 411 on this girl. I don't see him, or *her*, only several other scantily clad women who only remind me how different she was. I want to bust in a demand they tell me her name and where she is, but I'm forced to duck out and shove the curtain back when their escort/bodyguard/whatever guy spots me.

No worries, Dane can find out for me, that man has scary ways of digging up the buried. I hurry back from the bathroom and catch him just as he's hanging up his phone. "Well?"

"Local company, kinda off the radar, Brock isn't sure they're on the Better Business Bureau, if you catch my drift."

"I don't."

He leans into me, talking low and discreet. "I know nothing, and I'm going to say this: walk out of here and never speak of it again. I may also fire Brock for being a dumbass. It's some on the side thing for one guy, mostly underage college girls needing money."

"Fuck," I mumble.

"Fuck is right. My name is never to be associated with this, ever. I had no idea and I'll kill Brock if he jeopardized any of us in any way. You hear me?"

"Wait, so college, as in our college?"

"Yes," he sighs, running his hand through his hair, mad as hell.

"My old job ready at The K?" Wait, better yet… "I'll replace Brock even."

"You always have a job with me, Sawyer, you know that. Just say the word."

"Word. I'm heading back early. Don't fire Brock until I say, okay? I need to talk to him first."

"You just fire him when you have what you need. My hands are washed of this whole thing. Now get the fuck out of here and pay for the party in cash. No paper, you hear me, Sawyer?"

"Got it. Go, man."

Look out, Skipper, Daddy's coming home.

Look for Entangled, Dane and Laney's Novella and Entice, Book 3, Sawyer's story! While you wait, connect with S.E. Hall and the boys and discover more about the Evolve Crew

Twitter: @emergeauthor
Facebook: https://www.facebook.com/S.E.HallAuthorEmerge
Emerge book trailer, by Lisa at Pixel
Pixie:http://www.youtube.com/watch?v=uWooZtXiQN8
Goodreads:http://www.goodreads.com/author/show/7087549.S_...

Dane facebook: https://www.facebook.com/DanefromEmerge
Evan facebook: https://www.facebook.com/pages/Evan-Mitchell-All...

Sawyer facebook: https://www.facebook.com/pages/Sawyer-Beckett/22...

Emerge playlist: http://www.pinterest.com/emergeauthor/emerge-pl...

Embrace playlist: http://www.pinterest.com/emergeauthor/embrace-p...

Other works by S.E. Hall- Emerge on Amazon

http://www.amazon.com/Emerge-Evolve-Series-eboo...
Amazon UK: http://www.amazon.co.uk/Emerge-Evolve-Series-eb...

!

Acknowledgements

If I named every single person who helped me through this process, said to them what's in my heart, my acknowledgments would be longer than my book...that's how blessed I am! So, I will try to keep it short and sweet, but sincerely hope that I do my job as a person to let you each know how much you mean to me.

When I wrote my debut novel, EMERGE, I never imagined the outpouring of love and support I would receive- it's been humbling, mind blowing and truly moving! Every one of you who took the time to read, review, promote and rate Emerge, THANK YOU. So many of you would stop by my page to tell me how the book touched your heart, the things in your life it reminded you of, the friends you recommended it to, the cool picture you found that was fitting, ask a question you had or just to say hi... I read them all and cried more times than I'm willing to admit.

In fact, I'm crying as I type this, lol.

My husband Jeff takes almost every burden off my shoulders. If he could figure out a way to bathe and eat for me, I think he would- that's honestly about all he has left that he doesn't do for me. He's the best thing that has, or will, ever happen to me. If I could marry anyone in the whole world tomorrow, I'd pick him again. I love you babe!

My girls- Lyndsey consistently makes me laugh and reminds me of how cool it is to be a young woman. How many people get a kid who's also one of their favorite people to be around? Brooklyn teaches me kindness, empathy and tenderness. I love you so much Brookie! Shelby Jo shows me every day with her independence and strength what it truly means to be a superstar, your own person, running your game no matter what reward or lack of waits at the finish line. And Brittany, she reads for me, gives me beautiful babies to spoil and consistently demonstrates the value of speaking your mind!

My family- again, one of those categories where you do NOT start singling people out and chance forgetting anyone. I will say, I have a pretty damn cool family. And by cool I mean crazy, loud, obnoxious, borderline psychotic and so much fun society can hardly stand it when we congregate in groups. But, they're all mine and I adore them, wouldn't trade you for anything!!!!! Cheers to floating tables!

The women in my family are strong, independent, brilliant, hardworking and funny as &*^% - I taught them everything they know. The men in my life are kind, gentle when needed and strong as hell the rest of the time. They are examples of where the bar should be set on fathers, husbands, uncles, cousins, godfathers, protectors and leaders.

Now that I said all that, I am gonna give a special shout out to my baby cousin Brandon…mostly because I'm so damn proud of him I can't see straight- my U.S. Navy stud, but also because he read all my work, over and over and over…and never once complained.

My homies- I have some ladies in my life who consistently restore my faith in humanity. The read my work, text me just because, make me baskets and buy me supplies, pimp me on whatever page I *happen* to point out and never refuse to been seen with me when I'm the only one wearing sweatpants and my hair in a bun, sans makeup or any apparent willingness to give a damn.

Angela Graham, my friend, my CP- if you could tone it down with the cross-country trips where there is no internet, that'd be great lmao, because you're the other half of my brain, my "detail" gal, my sounding board. If I hadn't met you, there'd be no Emerge or Embrace, you're simply that important. I love you girl.

Samantha Stettner- Little lady, you make my life easier and happier. You help me so much, always giving me pep talks and ideas right when I need them, taking care of everything for me….Basically, you are my right arm. I so wish you lived closer where I could sneak up on ya and wrap you in a hug!!!!!!

The **Dynamic Duo** of Toski Covey and Sommer Stein- for loving my work enough to take it under your wings and give it a fresh, amazing face!! The two of you are so wonderful, I can't thank you enough! I am but the humble recipient of your visions…I just sit back and prepared to be awed!

The Erins: Gotta Have Em'…..Erin Roth, my editor who has the eyes of an eagle and does the best job editing, even if she won't let me say "awnry" lol. And Erin Long, my formatter, who I swear hears my emails coming in, even if in the middle of the night, while I'm in full blown panic mode begging her to change something right that second. She's a speedy lil' lifesaver!

BLOGGERS- there is NO way I am naming you off individually. Knowing me, I'd forget one and it would keep me awake at night to have possibly hurt any feelings. Collectively- YOU ARE AMAZING!!!!!!! You change the lives of independent authors who had a story buzzing in their head, their heart, and took a chance on it- you take a chance of them, put your own jobs and families on hold for that spot of time to read their book and give back. SO many of you supported me, EMERGE, EMBRACE….and I'm proud to call many of you friends. Your ethics, integrity, selflessness, kindness and professionalism are recognized and appreciated!!!!

My AMAZABETAS, HALL'S HARLOTS STREET TEAM, DANE'S DOLLS and My "Crew"- you know who you are and I hope, what you mean to me!!! If you don't, I give you permission to kick my a** because I should be making you feel special every chance I get. You're always there when I need a quick fix, an idea, an opinion, a laugh, a cry…if I never wrote another book, I'd still need you in my life. See, this is the part where all your names are coming up and I have something special to say, but….my hands are shaking too bad to type at just the thought of forgetting someone, so I'll just say, I love you ALL!

A-Team….no words sweet, wonderful lady!

***I reserve the right to amend, make excuses for, beg forgiveness on or act clueless in general when it comes to this message *IF* I did forget anyone.

THANK YOU ALL!!!!!!!!!!
xoxo
S.E. Hall

Embrace Playlist

Endlessly—Green River Ordinance
I Never Told You—Colbie Caillat
The First Time Ever I Saw Your Face—Roberta Flack
Red Light Special—TLC
Wonderwall—Oasis
Let Me Clear My Throat—DJ Kool
Mama Said Knock You Out—LL Cool J
Umbrella—Rihanna
On The Road Again—Willie Nelson
Rockstar—Nickelback
Down On Me—Jeremiah & 50 Cent
Fishing In The Dark—The Nitty Gritty Dirt Band
My Guardian Angel—The Red Jumpsuit Apparatus
Kiss Me—Ed Sheeran
Hey Pretty Girl—Kip Moore
Sideways—Citizen Cope

While you wait, check out Book 2,

ℙRREPLACEABLE

by Angela Graham

Chapter 1

Sweet Dreams No More

In a haze of raw, undeniable passion, his strong hands gripped the backs of my thighs, torturously working their way to my ass, where his skillful fingers kneaded and teased me into surrendering to his every demand. His breath was thick and minty, with a hint of bourbon, and left me craving more. Goose bumps flared over my blazing skin. The weather outside was a numbing twenty degrees, yet I was heated from the inside out.

A giggle escaped my lips when he lifted me from the ground, my legs finding their way around his waist as his seductive growl kissed my soul. My hands were relentless, snaking under his shirt and over the toned muscles of his back. My eyelids fluttered wildly in a vain attempt to hold his gaze. The harder I fought to watch his every move, the deeper I lost myself in our moment of hunger.

Everything inside me screamed for more and I ached, truly pained with anticipation. Grinding myself against his hard body, I rolled my hips, demanding every part of him. The cool brick wall dug into my back, the thick coat I wore seconds earlier now lying abandoned on the blacktop beside us.

A lurid groan spilled from my swollen lips when his hands dug into my hair, his lips nibbling the corner of mine, the searing passion between us uncontrollable. Forsaking all logical thought, I submitted to his reckless frenzy, my lips quivering as his hand slid down the front of my dress. He tore it open in one swift move, leaving me bare and at his will.

"I need you, Cassandra."

Oh God, I needed him. I burned for his touch. It was the closest to serenity I'd ever felt, and I never wanted to lose it. His lips ravaged mine, taking my breath and eliciting panting when they began their descent down my jaw. His tongue ignited a trail straight to my breasts, which were on full display for his eyes only. The scruff of his jaw scratched across my skin, further awakening every hidden emotion and greedy desire I possessed.

The world around us ceased to exist. He and I were all that mattered—all I felt, saw, and needed. Lost in the strength of his grip and power of his lust, I remained at his mercy, fisting his short waves of hair as he dropped to his knee.

My head fell back, savoring his tongue working its magic down my stomach. A delicious purr spilled from my open mouth, expressing everything my brain couldn't process into words. I wanted more. I wanted it all, but in an instant, the rough, needy clutch of his fingers and moistness of his mouth were gone; the indescribable emotions he'd awoken in me were no more.

Dazed, I whipped my head back and forth, desperately searching the darkness that now engulfed me.

"Logan?"

Panic set in, filling my veins with fear-induced adrenaline. I reached down for the pieces of my tattered dress, the frosty air now stinging my clammy skin in his absence, only to find they were gone as well. There I stood, naked and vulnerable, alone in the night.

"Logan, please…don't leave me."

I stumbled forward, struggling to adjust my sight to see anything other than black. My hands smacked into another wall, and it hit me.

The alley. I was in the alley.

The air was pulled from my lungs, legs quaking as the harsh words he'd spoken replayed through me.

"I want to fuck you. Here and now. I'm tired of waiting."

"Logan!" My hands shielded my ears, shaking my head to make it go away. Make it stop. He wouldn't say that. Wouldn't treat me like another whore.

"Come back! Don't leave me." My words dripped into a slurred sob as tears sprung from my eyes, distorting my vision further.

Where was he? Why would he leave me like this? He wouldn't—not me. He cared about me. He had to be there…somewhere.

"Logan, please!" I cried out, a cracked whimper pouring from my soul as I fell to my knees, helpless, terrified, and completely alone. Something in my heaving chest broke.

My heart. It had to be.

With my hands covering my face, palms pooling with salty tears, my ears rang with a buzzing horn. I looked up, squinting into the distance.

There was a light ahead. Someone was coming back for me.

Logan.

It had to be Logan. None of it was real. He would never say those things. Never toss me aside.

The light drew closer, a blinding ray suddenly racing toward me.

I lifted my trembling hands over my eyes, tilting my

head, anxious to make out the approaching figure. It was so bright, too intense, and glaring into the wetness of my eyes. I couldn't see, couldn't understand, until the car horn blared through the air. Suddenly it was on me, crashing, barreling my body into nothing until all I felt was pain as the unknown consumed me.

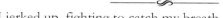

I jerked up, fighting to catch my breath.

The familiar dry air of the hospital room eased me back onto the thin pillows on the small bed. It was all a dream—a horrible nightmare I could never escape. Five long days trapped in tiny rooms, and every night I closed my eyes and found him waiting for me. Each kiss took away the painful memory of that night, slowly erasing it until I was lost in his arms in that dark alley. His touch and longing were all I felt, all I lived for there. But it wasn't real.

Made in the USA
San Bernardino, CA
24 February 2014